KISSING THE VISCOUNT

"The rules of society are not supposed to make sense, sweetness."

"Please do not call me that," she abruptly demanded.

"Why not?"

"Because it makes me wonder if you can actually recall my name."

His eyes briefly widened before a predatory smile curved his lips.

"Mercy. Sweet Mercy. As exquisite as a wood sprite," he husked, his head slowly beginning to lower. "I shall never forget your name."

She did not truly believe him, but it no longer mattered as his lips brushed over her own with a startling tenderness. She had expected the warmth of his lips and even the expertise as he stroked and teased at her mouth. But nothing could have warned her of the sharp pleasure that clenched her body. . . .

Books by Deborah Raleigh

SOME LIKE IT WICKED

SOME LIKE IT SINFUL

SOME LIKE IT BRAZEN

BEDDING THE BARON

SEDUCING THE VISCOUNT

Published by Kensington Publishing Corporation

Seducing
The Viscount

DEBORAH RALEIGH

ZEBRA BOOKS
Kensington Publishing Corp.
http://www.kensingtonbooks.com

ZEBRA BOOKS are published by

Kensington Publishing Corp.
850 Third Avenue
New York, NY 10022

All Kensington titles, imprints, and distributed lines are available at special quantity discounts for bulk purchases for sales promotion, premiums, fund-raising, educational, or institutional use.

Special book excerpts or customized printings can also be created to fit specific needs. For details, write or phone the office of the Kensington Special Sales Manager: Attn. Special Sales Department. Kensington Publishing Corp., 850 Third Avenue, New York, NY 10022. Phone: 1-800-221-2647.

Zebra and the Z logo Reg. U.S. Pat. & TM Off.

ISBN-13: 978-0-8217-8045-9
ISBN-10: 0-8217-8045-X

First Printing: March 2009
10 9 8 7 6 5 4 3 2 1

Printed in the United States of America

Prologue

The two gentlemen seated before the fire at the small coaching inn in the midst of Winchester appeared oblivious to the near riot they were causing among the guests and staff.

In truth, they *were* oblivious.

Raoul Charlebois with his white-gold hair and piercing blue eyes was accustomed to crowds gaping and fawning over his elegant beauty. As the most renowned actor in all of England, it would be more shocking if he could walk into a room without causing a stir.

Even Ian Breckford was familiar with such titillated interest.

Known throughout London as Casanova, he possessed a dark, sultry beauty that had captivated women from the moment he had left the cradle. He might not comprehend their fascination with his golden eyes framed by sinfully long lashes, or the thick ebony curls that tumbled carelessly about his lean, fiercely male countenance, but he was always swift to take advantage of their enthrallment.

The same way he was always swift to take advantage of

those gentlemen foolish enough to sit down opposite him at a card table or wager against him in the boxing ring.

He might have been born a bastard, but he had forged a position among society that even the most aristocratic gentlemen envied.

Now he lifted a glass of his favorite whiskey in a mocking toast.

"To Fredrick," he announced, a cynical smile playing about his full lips. "May his honeymoon be delectable enough to compensate for the years of being shackled in holy matrimony."

Raoul touched his glass to Ian's, his own expression one of satisfaction. Typical. Although Raoul had been fostered by Mr. Dunnington at the same time as Fredrick and Ian, he had swiftly taken on the role of older brother and devoted himself to bullying, encouraging, and at times comforting his young charges. Dunnington might have been the father they had so desperately needed, but it was Raoul who had rushed to Fredrick's rescue when the local ruffians attempted to rob him of his coins, and thumped Ian soundly when he caught him cheating at cards.

Now the ridiculously handsome man was nearly preening at the thought that Fredrick had managed to wed a woman he clearly adored.

"I do not believe he will object to being shackled to Portia. Indeed, he has never appeared more content with his lot in life."

Ian gave a sharp laugh. "Well, he always did have an appalling preference for the dull and tedious sort of existence. Why else would he tinker with those ridiculous gadgets of his? No doubt he shall feel quite at home as a respectable husband and heir apparent to Lord Graystone."

Raoul grimaced. "At least once he forgives his father for keeping his legitimacy a secret all these years."

"Ah, yes. The infamous secret." Ian tossed the whiskey down his throat as he recalled the moment the three of them had discovered that Dunnington had left them each a legacy of twenty thousand pounds on his death. Money that the tutor had extorted from their respective fathers to keep some deeply hidden secret . . . well, secret. Fredrick had traveled to Winchester to find the truth and learned he was not the bastard he had always been named, but instead Lord Graystone's legitimate heir. A discovery that was bound to change his life forever. "I suppose we knew when we heard of Dunnington's legacy that our dear papas must harbor something dark and wicked in their pasts. But to have allowed Fredrick to believe he was a bastard just to gain Wilhelmina Burke's dowry . . . well, that is one hell of a skeleton in the cupboard. It makes a wise man consider leaving his own skeletons alone."

Raoul shrugged, but his eyes were watchful as he studied Ian's tense features. "There are any number of bastards who would be delighted to discover they are true bloods."

"Devil a bit." Ian shuddered, quick to refill his glass with the whiskey from his flask. "I cannot think of anything more hideous."

"Why?" Raoul gave a lift of one pale, perfect brow. Everything about Raoul was perfect. "Your father is one of the wealthiest gentlemen in all of England. Not to mention he possesses a near-dozen homes and estates from here to Scotland. As his heir you would become one of the most respected and powerful men in the world."

Ian glanced toward a gaggle of maids who were currently giggling and batting their lashes in his direction. Not far behind them, two elegant women in the latest fashion were needlessly pacing near the door of the common room in an obvious attempt to gain his attention.

"I have no desire for power or respectability. God knows that I have devoted my life to avoiding either of those fine traits," he mocked even as his lips twisted with bitterness. "And I would rather be strung from the rafters than be beholden to the frigid Lord Norrington. I would not accept a groat from him, let alone his entire bloody fortune."

Without warning, Raoul set aside his glass and leaned forward. The brilliant blue eyes were filled with concern.

"Then return to London with me, Ian. There is nothing for you in Surrey but ancient secrets and wounds that have not healed. Both are best left alone."

Ian gritted his teeth. "Do you not think that I have packed my bags to return to London on a dozen occasions?"

"Then what has halted you?"

That was a question that had haunted Ian on far too many sleepless nights. Common sense warned him to avoid Surrey and his father, Viscount Norrington, like the plague. What good could come of uncovering some secret that no doubt had nothing to do with him?

Unfortunately, he never heeded common sense.

He was a creature of impulse and passion who possessed an uncanny instinct for finding trouble.

Realizing his friend was regarding him with an expression that warned he was about to whack Ian over the head and drag him back to London, Ian heaved a restless sigh. The older man had an unshakable belief that he always knew what was best for others.

"Fredrick had the right of it when he said that knowing my father is hiding some dark sin would be like a splinter in my flesh that is bound to fester. I have to know. I cannot explain why, but I have to know."

Raoul was not appeased. "And yet you have lingered here for near a month."

Ian gave a sharp bark of laughter. "You could not expect me to miss Fredrick's wedding?"

"No, I suppose not. But—"

"Just leave it be, Raoul," Ian growled, his expression warning he would endure no more. "I will travel to Surrey when I am ready."

Raoul studied him a long moment. "What are you looking for, *mon ami*?"

Ian turned his head to study the flames dancing in the fireplace, his heart oddly heavy.

"I suppose I will know when I finally find it."

Several hours later, Ian sat on the edge of the mattress and struggled to pull on his Hessians. It was a task that should not have posed a great deal of effort. He had deliberately requested that the boots be cut so that he could easily attend to them without the need for a valet. A gentleman who enjoyed spontaneous and frequent trysts had to consider such matters.

It was one of those tiny details that made the difference between a successful rake and a bumbling amateur.

Unfortunately, on this night his usual expertise was absent.

No doubt because he was gloriously, marvelously, and spectacularly drunk.

"Devil a bit," he muttered as he gave the demon-spawned boot a last jerk and nearly tumbled onto the rough-planked floor.

"Ian?"

The soft, sleepy voice came from behind him, and Ian glanced over his shoulder at the pretty maid curled beneath the thin cover.

They had retired to her cramped room above the tavern, leaving only a small fire burning in the grate to offer light. Now, with the shadows filling the room, Ian could make out little more than a round face with a cloud of brown hair that tumbled about her naked shoulders.

"Shh," he murmured softly. "'Tis late. Go back to sleep."

"What are ye doing?"

"I fear that I must be on my way."

"Now?" With a lazy smile, the maid tugged down the cover to reveal the lush bounty of her breasts. "We still have plenty of time before the sun comes up. Why don't ye lay back down and we'll have some fun?"

Ian's body stirred at the sight of her warm, luscious curves. Hell, what man would not be stirred? Stirred, stimulated, and stiffening by the moment.

And there were few things he would like better than to dive back beneath the covers and drown in her sweet heat.

It was only the thought of Raoul Charlebois that kept him from yanking off the damnable boots and tumbling back into the woman's waiting arms.

Although the older man had left for London after

their meal together, his smoldering concern lingered like a bad taste in Ian's mouth.

He had not come out and accused Ian of hiding in Winchester like a coward. No, the trained actor was far too subtle for that. But the unspoken words had hovered between them nonetheless.

Now Ian was faced with the unpleasant decision of whether to seek the truth of his own father or return to London and an existence that was becoming increasingly empty.

The feel of warm fingers stroking through the strands of his dark hair brought Ian out of his broodings with a small start.

Bloody hell. He should never have consumed so much whiskey. It was making him positively maudlin.

"A most tempting offer, sweetness," he murmured, turning to smile with open appreciation at the pretty maid. "You are as exquisite as a freshly bloomed rose. To pluck you is to know paradise."

The woman giggled at his flamboyant compliment "You always say the nicest things."

"I speak only the truth."

"Ha." She heaved a sigh, a hint of bewitchment in the wide eyes. "Ye must be Irish, speaking with that silver tongue. Stay, Ian Breckford. I promise to make it worth yer while."

"Any moment in your presence is beyond worth, beyond gold," he said as he leaned down and brushed his lips over her forehead. "Unfortunately, I have an appointment that will force me to awaken at some ungodly hour so I can continue my journey."

"I suppose yer off to London?" the maid pouted, tugging the blanket up to her chin. "I wish I was going. All them fine gents and ladies dashing from one fancy place to another. And them homes . . . la, so big and beautiful a girl could find her dreams in them."

Pulling back, Ian frowned at the petulant words. Rosemary was a common tavern wench who had clearly sold her innocence long ago, but he instinctively experienced the urge to protect her from her own foolishness.

He was a gentleman who thoroughly appreciated women. All women. And unlike most rakes, his admiration extended well beyond a quick tumble beneath the covers. How could you claim to love women and treat them with disdain the moment you had what you desired from them?

"No, sweetness, listen to a gentleman who is older and far more experienced than you. There are no dreams to found in London," he warned sternly. "I have seen too many young girls broken and left in the gutters. Remain here where you are loved and cared for."

"Here?" She cast a disdainful glance around the cramped room that held the chill and dampness of the late spring night. "'Tis nothing here for me."

He gave a shake of his head as he rose to his feet and reached for his coat.

"Do not be a fool, sweetness. You have family. And that is everything."

Chapter 1

The dreary spring weather that had draped Surrey in a relentless gray mist abruptly gave way to a watery sunlight that brought with it welcome warmth.

It also brought with it a flurry of spring cleaning that consumed Rosehill estate from attics to cellars.

With an enthusiasm that was near frightening in its intensity, the housekeeper herded the maids in a storm of scrubbing, polishing, and buffing that sent the residents of the elegant home fleeing for safety. Even the usually oblivious Mercy Simpson was forced from the shadows of the vast library to the surrounding countryside.

If she became lost in her studies as was her custom, there was a very good chance she might be tossed out with the rest of the rubbish.

Avoiding the formal gardens where Viscount Norrington and his sister, Miss Ella Breckford, had chosen to find peace, Mercy instead wandered for a time among the thick woods that surrounded the beautiful estate before coming to rest on a flat stone in the center of a small meadow.

With a faint smile, she studied the beauty spread before her.

Perhaps it was a blessing she had been forced to set aside her books and enjoy the lovely afternoon, she ruefully acknowledged. Too often she became so obsessed with the past that she forgot to appreciate the present.

At least that was the warning her parents delivered with monotonous regularity.

Her smile faded as she recalled the letter she had tucked into the pocket of her gown earlier in the day and promptly forgotten.

It was from her parents, of course. She had no other family or friends who would bother to write to her. Until she had come to Rosehill nearly a month ago, she had lived an isolated life in a small cottage near three hours away.

As the only child of two elderly parents, she had devoted her life to caring for their needs. She had never resented the responsibilities she shouldered or the endless duties that were expected of her. Not even when it meant she was rarely allowed the opportunity to leave the small cottage.

But since she had been at Rosehill . . . Well, she had to admit she thoroughly enjoyed her first taste of freedom.

For once she could concentrate solely on her overwhelming fascination with history. There were no chores to be tended to, no incessant bells to be answered, and no one to chide her for disappearing into her books for endless hours.

Although Miss Breckford had invited Mercy to Surrey to be her companion, she had swiftly made it obvious she had no genuine need for Mercy beyond assisting with her various charity events. The sweet-tempered woman with the twinkling brown eyes and ready smile possessed more spirit and vigor than most women half her age.

She had asked nothing of Mercy.

Nothing but her friendship.

It had been liberating for a young maiden who had always been expected to be at the beck and call of others.

Which no doubt explained why she was so reluctant to open the letter clutched in her fingers.

Over the past fortnight, her parents had become increasingly insistent in their demands that she return home. They claimed the nurse she had hired to care for them during her absence was incapable of keeping the house as clean as they preferred and that her father had taken a dislike to her cooking.

A part of her understood it was her duty to return and ease their discomfort. They were the only family she possessed. But another part, a part she was ashamed to acknowledge, urged her to remain just a few more days.

After all, once she returned home she would never have such an opportunity again. She would be forgotten in her small cottage as she aged into a lonely spinster.

Surely she deserved a few weeks just for herself?

She wrinkled her nose at her attempts to justify her selfish desires. Her father would tell her that it was the devil whispering in her ear. And he would be right.

"Dear God." The male voice floated on the air behind her, intruding into her dark musings. "Do not move."

Mercy instinctively stiffened in alarm. "What is it? A bee? A snake?"

"An angel."

She frowned at the unexpected retort. "What?"

"Ah no, I am mistaken." There was the sound of footsteps before a tall, stunningly beautiful man stepped into view. "It is a wood sprite come to welcome spring."

Just for a moment, Mercy was bewitched by the stranger. She had little experience with the opposite sex, but she did realize when she stumbled across a fine example of one. And this gentleman was . . . exquisite.

Even casually attired in a blue coat and buff breeches there was no mistaking he was built on the lines of a racehorse. He was all hard, corded muscles on a lean, elegant frame that moved with the grace of a trained warrior.

And his countenance complemented the fine, noble lines.

Her eyes skimmed over the finely sculpted features, the aquiline nose, the full curve of his lips, and the high arch of his dark brows. They lingered a moment on the astonishing golden eyes that were heavily lashed and filled with a wicked humor before moving to the thick, raven locks that tumbled carelessly about that magnificent male face.

Good . . . heavens.

This was the sort of gentleman her mother had always warned her about. The sort that possessed the beauty of an angel and the wiles of Lucifer. The sort that seduced naïve chits before tossing them aside without a care.

She should be terrified. Instead her heart was racing with an illicit excitement that she could feel to her very toes.

"Botheration." In an effort to hide her fierce reaction to his appearance, Mercy busied herself with knocking the clinging leaves from her muslin gown. "You nearly frightened me to death."

He offered a slow, lethal smile. "Forgive me, sweetness. I was caught off guard to stumble across such beauty in the midst of this godforsaken countryside."

Her own smile was wry, inwardly wondering if he offered such smooth compliments to every woman he encountered. She would bet her last quid he did. How else would he have become so very good at them?

"I doubt that God has forsaken such a lovely meadow. Indeed, it appears rather blessed."

"I stand corrected." His smile widened. "It most certainly has been blessed."

"Are you lost?"

"From the moment I caught sight of you perched upon that rock, my love."

"My name is Miss Simpson, not *sweetness* or *my love*, and if you are lost, then I suggest that you continue down the path to Rosehill," she informed him in her usual soft tones, glancing toward the horse he had left tethered to a nearby bush. "The groom would be happy to offer you directions."

He stilled, as if he were surprised that she had not yet melted into a puddle at his feet. Then, narrowing his brilliant golden eyes, he took a deliberate step closer, his expression that of a predator suddenly on the scent of his prey.

"I have no desire to seek anything from the cantankerous Delany, not even if he has managed to mellow in his old age," he drawled, his eyes running a restless path over her startled features. "I far prefer to linger in this meadow with you, Miss Simpson."

She took an instinctive step back. Not only because she was shocked by his familiarity with Rosehill, but because the warm, tantalizing scent of his skin seemed to tease at her senses in a sinful manner.

"You know Delany?"

"We have a passing acquaintance. I fear that he has never quite forgiven me for borrowing my father's prize horse and entering him in the local steeple-chase. Quite unfair of him since I did offer him half the prize money I won."

Her lips parted in shock. "You are Mr. Breckford," she breathed.

"My reputation precedes me, I see."

It certainly did. Although Lord Norrington never mentioned his bastard son, Ella Breckford could rarely allow a day to pass without some mention of her nephew. She spoke of his daring escapades, his success at the card table, the manner society fawned over him despite the fact he was illegitimate.

It was obvious she adored the rapscallion, although he rarely bothered to visit his family.

"You are not expected."

"I never am." He reached out to flick a careless finger down the line of her jaw. "The question, however, is how you would know whether I am expected or not. The last occasion I visited Rosehill it was decidedly lacking in wood sprites."

His light touch sent a strange sensation through the pit of her stomach. It was . . . well, it was something she had never felt before. She did know, however, that she liked it.

With an effort, she met his curious gaze. "I am Miss Breckford's companion."

"Aunt Ella has need for a companion?" Something that might have been concern darkened the golden eyes. "Is she ill?"

"She is in remarkable health, so far as I know."

"Then why the need for a companion?"

"She claimed that she desired a female to keep her company during the long winter months, but to be honest, I believe that she was simply being kind to me." An unwitting smile touched her lips as she thought of the older woman's endless generosity. "She knew how anxious I was to visit Rosehill."

"Anxious?" The concern faded as he studied her countenance. "Why the devil would a beautiful young woman wish to bury herself in that frigid mausoleum?"

"I happen to find Rosehill a fascinating estate, and I am much in your aunt's debt for extending her invitation."

His lips twitched at the unmistakable reprimand in her tone.

"Well, I must admit that it grows more fascinating by the moment. How did you come to know my aunt? I was under the belief that she rarely travels in society these days."

"We have corresponded for the past year. I wrote to her when I learned that your—" She broke off her words, not certain whether or not to refer to Lord Norrington as his father. Even in the short time she had been at the estate, she had sensed that the two gentlemen did not have a close or comfortable relationship. "That Lord Norrington possessed an extensive library. I hoped your aunt would be able to tell me if his collection included the history of the Byzantine era."

He once again appeared bemused by her response. "You are interested in the Byzantine era?"

"More precisely I am interested in Theodora, who was an empress during that era."

He gave a short, disbelieving laugh. "Do not tell me that you are a scholar?"

Her lips thinned. Delectable rake or not, no one was allowed to mock her work.

"I cannot claim to be a scholar, but if my research is successful I have hopes of writing a paper on the empress and having it published in one of the London journals. I have already written to several editors, and one has expressed an interest in my work. It is past time that the women who altered history are given credit for their contributions."

He held up his hands in a gesture of peace, but that smile continued to tease at his lips.

"I fully agree. Women have been the driving force of mankind since Helen launched a thousand ships. I was just startled such a young and lovely maiden would devote herself to studying the past when you could be enjoying the pleasures that society could offer."

"I have no place among society, Mr. Breckford," she said without apology. "My father is a retired vicar who has always lived a quiet life. And even if I did possess the opportunity to indulge in such a frivolous existence, I would have no interest. There are more important matters to keep me occupied."

"Ah." His smile abruptly widened. "Not a scholar, but a bluestocking."

She rolled her eyes at his typical response. Why did gentlemen presume that any woman who did not spend her days desperately attempting to attract the attention of some man or other must be a bluestocking?

Turning on her heel, Mercy began walking toward the distant estate. As much as she enjoyed bantering with the wicked gentleman, she would not waste her time with anyone who did not respect a woman for her mind.

"Actually, Mr. Breckford, I am simply a female with

enough intelligence to comprehend the difference between genuine gold and dross," she informed him over her shoulder.

His eyes widened before he was hurrying to catch up with her retreating form.

"Good Lord, have I just been hoisted upon my own petard?" he demanded.

"I certainly hope so."

"Where are you going?"

"Unlike you, sir, I do not live a life of leisure. I have duties awaiting me at Rosehill."

"And you are the sort of woman who must always have the last word?"

"Always." Reaching the gate to the meadow, she stepped through and firmly closed it before he could follow. "Good-bye, Mr. Breckford."

Not surprisingly, Ian's thoughts were consumed with Miss Simpson as he gathered his mount and continued down the path to Rosehill.

Actually, more than his thoughts were consumed, he acknowledged as he felt a familiar tightening of his groin.

The chit was a rare beauty with her satin curls the precise shade of sunlight and the dark, slightly slanted eyes that were as soft and beguiling as a midnight sky. Even her body was perfectly designed to tempt a poor gentleman with delicate curves and an air of fragility that stirred his most primal instincts to offer his protection.

And that voice . . .

It was the voice of an angel. Low and soft, it had brushed over him like the finest velvet.

The mere thought of listening to that melodic voice

whisper in his ear as he made slow, delicious love to her was enough to make Ian groan out loud.

Ah, yes. Before his stay at Rosehill was over, he intended to have a taste of the tantalizing wood sprite.

As if the thought of Rosehill suddenly conjured it into being, Ian rounded a sweeping curve to discover the manor house spread in all its glory across the parkland.

It was an enormous building, of course, but built along clean, crisp neoclassical lines that would be pleasing to the most fastidious eye. Covered in stone-colored tiles, it boasted four square turrets and a large portico as well as a stunning conservatory with a delicate glass rotunda that was Lord Norrington's pride and joy.

The surrounding parkland was dotted with formal gardens, hedge mazes, fishponds, deer parks, and a formal gazebo that overlooked the lake. In the far distance lay the rich fields and woodlands that had provided a steady source of income for the Norrington family for the past five hundred years.

Riding along the lane that was lined with rosebushes, he brought his horse to a halt in front of the double oak doors. A young stable boy that Ian did not recognize raced to take the reins while Ian leaped easily to the ground and paused to gather his composure.

No, not his composure—his courage, he ruefully admitted.

This opulent house filled with its acres of cold marble and lofted, gilded ceilings had always managed to make him feel small. Inconsequential.

Precisely as his father had always managed to make him feel.

On impulse, Ian turned from the looming portico and angled his way toward a side door. He disliked the pomp and ceremony that servants insisted were a part of a viscount's household. They were even more stiff-rumped than his father.

Quite an accomplishment.

For himself, he preferred a less formal entrance.

Slipping through the servants' door, Ian made his way through the silent, oppressive house.

Others might have been impressed by the sweeping halls with their mural ceilings and Van Dycks lining the satin-paneled walls. Certainly most would catch their breath at the magnificent black-and-white marble floors and Roman statues that filled the alcoves.

Ian, however, barely noted the exquisite beauty. Rosehill might be considered one of the finest estates in all of England, but he far preferred the shabby comfort of Dunnington's townhouse to such icy splendor. Or even the impersonal monotony of his rented rooms.

At least there he did not fear a mere sneeze might ruin a nearby masterpiece.

Making his way past the public rooms, Ian at last paused before the private back parlor that his aunt preferred for her tea.

He stepped over the threshold, a small smile curving his lips as his gaze skimmed over the fine Brussels tapestry that was framed on the walls and delicate porcelain that his aunt had collected over the years. Although less imposing than most of the house, it still held that unmistakable elegance that had made Rosehill famous throughout the world.

Not surprisingly, he discovered Miss Ella Breckford arranging a tea tray next to the bay window, humming softly as she cut slices of seed cake.

She had aged, he ruefully admitted. The puff of brown hair that she had dressed in pretty curls held far more gray than he remembered, and her round face held a few small wrinkles about her brown eyes. And if he was not mistaken, he would say that her curves had become somewhat plumper beneath the violet silk gown.

One thing that had not changed, however, was the vitality that crackled about her as she busied herself with her task. For all her sweet manners, his aunt could be a force of nature when she set her mind to it.

Quietly crossing the Persian carpet, Ian waited until he was standing directly behind his aunt before he spoke.

"Aunt Ella, when will you learn that you possess servants to take care of such tedious tasks?" he murmured softly.

"Ian?" Slowly turning, the woman clapped her hands to her face, her expression one of shocked pleasure. "Ian."

He chuckled. "It is I."

"What a wonderful surprise." Without warning, she threw herself into his arms, tears streaming down her cheeks. "What are you doing here? Has something happened?"

"Everything is well, my dear."

The older woman pulled back and gave a small sound as she noticed Ian's wrinkled lapels.

"Oh . . . forgive me, I have ruined your beautiful coat."

"It is no matter." Ian smiled fondly as warmth filled his heart. This woman's love was the only pleasant memory he had of his childhood. "I would ask how you do, but it is obvious you are extremely well."

Ella gave a flutter of her hands, a pleased color staining her cheeks. "I feel extremely well, but I fear that the mirror is not so kind."

"Nonsense." Capturing her fingers, he pulled them to his lips for a kiss. "Your beauty is the sort that will never fade."

"Ian." Ella pulled her hand free, lightly patting his cheek. "You were born with a silver tongue in your mouth."

"I seem to hear that with remarkable frequency," he murmured before his lips twisted in a wry smile. "Although I must confess that not all women share your appreciation for my supposedly silver tongue."

"I do not believe you," Ella denied with stout loyalty. "There is not a woman born who can resist your charm."

"You are wrong." He tugged off his gloves and tossed them absently on a nearby chair. "She has not only been born, but she is currently residing beneath your roof."

Ella tilted her head to one side. "Whatever do you mean?"

"I encountered Miss Simpson in the south meadow."

"Did you?"

"She was quite . . . remarkable."

"Yes, she is." His aunt regarded him with a peculiar expression. "Mercy has not only dedicated her life to caring for her aging parents, but she is an eager student of history. Having her here has been a genuine pleasure."

Mercy. He wisely hid a smile of satisfaction. The name somehow suited her. As did the knowledge that she would devote herself to her family and her ridiculous studies.

She was soft and utterly feminine, and yet possessed a steady, unshakable willpower that shimmered about her like the finest armor.

Devil take her, she had stood there in the meadow confronting a strange gentleman without the least hint of fear. She had even dared to chastise him as if he were no more than a harmless lad.

"That I do not doubt, but I am not quite certain why she is here." He met the brown gaze with a faint question. "There is not something I should know, is there?"

"Something you should know?"

He reached out to gently push a stray curl from her cheek. "I know you said earlier that you were well. . . ."

"Ian, I assure you that my invitation to Mercy was extended solely out of the desire to offer a sweet and generous young girl the opportunity to fulfill her dreams," she said firmly. "And, I suppose, I also wished for a bit of female companionship. As much as I love Norry, he does prefer locking himself in his conservatory to sharing tea with his tedious sister."

Ian gave a short, humorless laugh. He had spent the first seven years of his life in this icy tomb, each day struggling to discover some means of pleasing his father so that the stern, distant man would take notice of him. Hell, he would have been content if the bleeding sod had simply acknowledged his presence.

But day after passing day there had been barely a glance from Lord Norrington, let alone a pat on the head or a kind word.

He might as well have been invisible in his own home.

"Yes, Father has never bothered with such things as good manners or simple decency when there is a flower to occupy his attention," he drawled.

"Now, Ian, that is not entirely fair. Norry . . ." She deliberately paused. "*Your father* is like any other collector who becomes lost among his treasures."

Ian gave a shake of his head. "Do you know, Aunt

Ella, I believe Father could commit murder and you would find some means to excuse his behavior."

"As I would for you, Ian," she said as she reached up to pat his cheek.

Ian firmly thrust away the anger that always festered deep in his heart. His aunt had never been able to disguise her distress at the brittle tension that existed between him and Lord Norrington. She deserved better from him.

"Yes, I am certain you would," he said in lightly teasing tones. "Thank God that for all my sins, I have yet to actually make a habit of doing away with my fellow man."

"Of course you have not." Ella's sunny smile slowly returned. "Now, tell me what brings you to Surrey?"

"Can a gentleman not visit home without a reason?"

"Of course. You know I am always delighted to have you here." The brown eyes held a knowing expression. Ella Breckford could be incredibly tolerant of others, but that did not mean she was blind to their faults. "It is just that you are such a creature of London that I cannot imagine you being content with our quiet ways."

The image of wood sprites danced through his head. "Do not fear, dearest Aunt, I shall no doubt find some means of occupying myself."

"Hmm." A brief suspicion flittered over her countenance before she was waving a heavily bejeweled hand toward the nearby sofa. "Sit down and allow me to offer you tea."

Ian made no objection as he settled himself on the stiff cushions and allowed his aunt to fill a plate with a number of sandwiches and two slices of the seed cake. He was a man who thoroughly appreciated his appetite. All his appetites. "Will the lovely Miss Simpson not be joining us?"

Ella took a far smaller portion of the bounty for herself. "That depends."

"On what?"

"On whether or not you have managed to terrify the poor girl into hiding in her chambers."

"Poor girl?" Ian laughed as he polished off two of the sandwiches. "I was fortunate to survive the encounter. If anyone should be hiding in their chambers and licking their wounds, it is I."

His aunt smiled, as if pleased he had been neatly put into his place by the wench.

"Mercy is a strong-willed maiden, but she has little experience with gentlemen. Especially gentlemen such as you."

Ian assumed an expression of mock innocence. "And what is that supposed to mean? Gentlemen such as me?"

She shook a finger in his direction. "Although I am secluded here, I possess many acquaintances that are always eager to keep me informed of your exploits."

"Oh, I am quite sure they are." He gave a snort of disgust. "The old tabbies might grouse and complain about the wickedness of London society, but they are always the first to relish a tidbit of scandal."

Ella took a delicate sip of her tea. "If you do not wish to be the source of gossip, Ian, then you should not be constantly courting attention."

He opened his mouth to argue, only to give a sudden laugh. How could he possibly deny that he boldly forged his way through society, ruffling feathers and stepping upon toes whenever possible?

"Touché." He gave a dip of his head to acknowledge her direct strike. "And to ease your mind, I will promise not to force anything upon the lovely Miss

Simpson that she does not desire." He wagged his brows. "I will not, however, promise to resist if she should choose to force herself upon me."

Ella rolled her eyes. "I suppose that is the best I can hope for."

"It is, indeed." Popping the last of the cake into his mouth, Ian gracefully lifted himself to his feet. "If you will excuse me, I think I should seek a bath and change of clothes before dinner."

"Of course." Rising to her feet, Ella reached out to grasp his hands. "Oh Ian, I am so glad you are home."

Home . . .

Ian bent to kiss his aunt's cheek before she could see the bitter cynicism in his eyes.

He did not know where home might be, but it sure the hell was not at Rosehill.

Chapter 2

As was her habit, Mercy arrived in the front drawing room well before Lord Norrington and Ella descended from their chambers. She loved being alone in the blue and gold room with its rare Van Dyck paintings and delicate French furnishings. There was something very tranquil and ageless about the room. As if it had stood there unscathed for centuries and would remain for centuries more.

Not at all like her father's crumbling cottage, which was decaying a bit more with each passing year, she acknowledged ruefully. Soon they would be living among rubble and praying the roof did not tumble onto their heads.

Stepping into the room, Mercy had nearly crossed to the long bank of windows that overlooked the formal hedge maze when she realized that she was not alone. There was no actual sound or even movement; it was the prickling along her skin that warned that another was near.

No, not another, she silently corrected.

Ian.

She knew it in the very marrow of her bones.

The knowledge that she was so potently aware of a near stranger was more than a little unnerving, and it was only with an effort that she managed to slowly turn and regard his hard, fiercely male form in a distant corner.

Her breath caught in her throat as she was struck anew by his dark beauty. Good heavens, he looked like a figure from a Renaissance painting. A masterpiece.

A tiny shiver of excitement raced through her body as she studied the finely chiseled profile. She sensed that he was aware of her presence as intensely as she was aware of his, but he continued to study the large vase of roses as if she were invisible.

"They are lovely, are they not?" she said, smiling faintly at his deliberate ploy. He no doubt presumed that his pretense at ignoring her would pique her interest. Foolish when her interest was already dangerously captivated. "I believe Lord Norrington had them shipped from China."

He slowly straightened, his dark gaze running an intimate survey over her blue muslin gown that was modestly cut to reveal the barest hint of her small bosom. Only when Mercy was certain he had managed to memorize every line of her body did he lift his gaze to offer her that wicked, potent smile.

"I prefer the wild daisies that grow in the south meadow. They have a charming habit of luring wood sprites into their midst."

She gave a rueful shake of her head. "Good heavens, do you never halt?"

"Not until I am in my grave." He waved a slender hand toward the heavy sideboard. "Can I offer you a sherry?"

With an effort, she kept her own gaze from straying toward his hard, elegant body that was encased in a smooth champagne jacket and ivory satin waistcoat.

"Thank you, no."

"I assure you that I did not slip down here early so that I could poison my father's spirits." His smile twisted. "And even if I did, it would not be the sherry."

He did not need to say that it would have been his father's brandy. It was written in his mocking expression.

"I do not partake of any spirits."

"Of course." Folding his arms over his chest, Ian leaned against the satin-paneled wall. "I forgot you were the dutiful daughter of a vicar."

"I do not drink spirits because I do not care for the taste," she corrected.

The humor in his eyes deepened at the reprimand in her voice. "Ah. And do you also dislike the taste of tea?"

"I like tea very well."

"Then why, I wonder, did you so assiduously avoid sharing a pot with my aunt this afternoon?"

She smoothed her hands down her skirts, not about to reveal she had needed time to gather her thoughts. The man was smug enough without realizing he had managed to captivate yet another poor maiden with nothing more than a smile.

"I realized that Ella would be anxious to speak with you in private," she said calmly. "She adores you."

"I am fairly fond of her myself."

"Are you?" Mercy gave a lift of her brows. "You disguise it well."

There was a sharp pause before Ian tilted back his head to give a short laugh.

"The devil take you."

"What?"

He reached out to grasp her chin between his thumb and forefinger, gazing deep into her suddenly wide eyes.

"You have an uncanny ability to insult a poor bloke with the voice of an angel. I do not know whether to be annoyed or bewitched."

Her breath threatened to lodge in her throat as the heat of his touch speared directly to the pit of her stomach. He was so close. Close enough she could catch the scent of sandlewood warming on his skin. It wrapped about her with seductive force.

With a deliberate motion she took a step back. No woman could possibly think clearly when her heart was fluttering like a caged bird.

"I have come to care a great deal for Ella," she managed to retort, her voice surprisingly steady.

"And that gives you the right to chastise her beloved nephew?"

She shrugged. "Of course not. I am merely a guest in your home."

"But I notice that does not halt you."

Absently she reached out to stroke her finger over one of the vibrant rose blooms.

"I believe someone should inform you how your aunt longs to be a part of your life."

"She has just assured me that she has an entire legion of spies to keep her apprised of my every movement."

"That is not the same as having your company."

He muttered a low curse as his brows drew together in an annoyed frown. "Not that I need explain myself to you, Miss Simpson, but I do not like Rosehill."

She smiled wryly. "Yes, I had gathered as much."

"Then you should also gather that my father desires me here even less than I desire to be here."

There was no mistaking the edge in his voice. She was blatantly thrusting herself where she did not belong, but Mercy refused to back away. For all her tingling reaction to Ian Breckford, she had come to care too deeply for Ella not to at least attempt to make him realize just how selfishly he was behaving.

"I do not believe that."

"You should." With a jerky motion he pulled a small flask from beneath his jacket and took a deep drink. "It is the God's honest truth. I will even swear to it on the family Bible if you insist. A family Bible I might add that does not include my name."

His expression was hard as granite, but Mercy did not miss the flare of bitter pain in his eyes. Her heart threatened to melt at the realization that he truly suffered from the rift between he and his father.

Her expression softened as she reached out to lightly touch his arm. His muscles were rigid beneath her fingers, but he did not pull away.

"Fathers rarely find it comfortable to show affection toward their children," she said gently. "I believe it is because they always feel they need to be strong for their family. That does not mean, however, they do not love us."

His sardonic laugh rasped through the air. "You truly are naïve, are you not?"

She stiffened. "Now who is being insulting?"

Returning the flask to his jacket, Ian smoothly slid an arm about her waist, his expression shifting with a wicked intent.

"There is no insult in innocence," he murmured, his arm drawing her steadily toward his body. "Indeed, I find it quite enticing."

Mercy did not fight against his hold, not even when

she discovered herself pressed against the hard angles and planes of his male form. She had never been so close to a man, and the sensations streaking through her body were too potent to easily deny.

"I am beginning to suspect you find everything enticing."

The stunning gold eyes darkened, his large hand splayed at the curve of her back.

"Just *beginning* to suspect?"

She tilted back her head, not nearly as frightened as common sense told her she should be. Not even when she felt the surge of heat rush through her blood.

"Are you going to kiss me?"

He gave a choked sound. "Good Lord."

"What is the matter?"

"You are the most unpredictable female I have ever encountered." His gaze studied her upturned countenance as if she were some baffling mystery. "I never know what you might say next."

She breathed in deeply of sandlewood and pure male as he cupped her cheek in his hand, his thumb lightly stroking her heated cheek.

"I merely say what is upon my mind."

"Astonishing."

"I do not know why," she managed to mutter. "It has always seemed ridiculous to me that a maiden is expected to say one thing while she is feeling another."

"The rules of society are not supposed to make sense, sweetness."

"Please do not call me that," she abruptly demanded.

"Why not?"

"Because it makes me wonder if you can actually recall my name."

His eyes briefly widened before a predatory smile curved his lips.

"Mercy. Sweet Mercy. As exquisite as a wood sprite," he husked, his head slowly beginning to lower. "I shall never forget your name."

She did not truly believe him, but it no longer mattered as his lips brushed over her own with a startling tenderness. She had expected the warmth of his lips and even the expertise as he stroked and teased at her mouth. But nothing could have warned her of the sharp pleasure that clenched her body.

She felt as if her every nerve was suddenly tingling with a newfound awareness. As if something dormant within her, something that had been waiting all these years for Ian's touch, had been stirred to life.

Yes. This was what the poets spoke of. This was the magic that made perfectly intelligent women toss aside all sense for passion.

Instinctively she arched closer to the hard muscles of his body. He was so warm, so strong, so . . . male.

His fingers shifted to cup the back of her neck, keeping her head in place as he deepened his kiss. Mercy's head spun with pleasure, vibrantly aware of the stirring hardness of his groin as it pressed against her lower stomach.

It was the feel of his tongue parting her lips that at last shocked her back to reality. A reality that included the fact they were standing in the formal drawing room with the threat of Lord Norrington or Ella walking in at any moment.

Lifting her hands, she pressed against the broad width of his chest.

"Mr. Breckford."

His head shifted so that he could boldly nuzzle the fluttering pulse at the base of her throat.

"My name is Ian."

She swallowed a low groan before giving his chest another push. As much as she was enjoying (and she was enjoying) his delicious kisses, she was not so lost to reason as to risk being caught in such a compromising position.

Not only would her reputation be in tatters, but she might very well be sent back to her parents. And that she could not bear.

Not yet, at least.

"I did not give you leave to kiss me," she chided, well aware that her words were a tad ridiculous when her lips must be swollen and her cheeks flushed with lingering pleasure.

He chuckled softly. "I wished you to know that I can be as unpredictable as you."

Mercy lifted her brows. His words were even more ridiculous than hers.

"Actually, I would say that having you kiss me was very predictable."

His gaze slowly roamed down her body. "Because you are so irresistible?"

"Because, Ian Breckford, you are a rake, and for the moment, you are trapped in the country with only me to try to seduce."

For Ian, the dinner that followed was a mixture of fury and fascination.

Fury that his cold jackass of a father had not bothered even to acknowledge his presence as he had taken his seat at the impossibly long dinner table, and fascination with the tiny wood sprite seated across from him.

The fury he expected. When had there been an occasion that Lord Norrington had condescended to actually pretend he was anything but indifferent to his only child?

Against his will, Ian's gaze turned toward the man seated at the head of the table.

With his black hair perfectly crimped and styled to frame his thin face, Lord Norrington looked far younger than his fifty years. His body was lean beneath the tailored gray coat and black waistcoat while his face remained unlined. He could easily have passed for a gentleman half his age if it were not for the jaded glitter in his dark brown eyes. Those eyes revealed a man who had lived a life of disillusionment.

Which was ridiculous considering he had been handed every luxury in the world on a silver platter.

The fascination, however, was rather unexpected.

Readily he switched his attention toward the lovely Mercy Simpson.

He was accustomed to lusting after any pretty woman who entered a room. He was a man, for God's sake. And the fact that their kiss had shattered his staunch defenses to the point he had ached to back her against the wall and take her right there in the formal dining room was obviously because she was the most beautiful woman he had ever laid eyes upon.

His fascination had to be the knowledge that his entire body hummed with anticipation each time she opened those pretty lips that caught him off guard. There was something about that low, beguiling voice and the realization that he had no notion what words might come out of her mouth that held him almost spellbound.

She was completely unique.

A woman like no other.

He found his gaze lingering throughout the long dinner, barely aware of Ella's bright chatter or his father's occasional response. Instead he silently absorbed the sight and scent of Mercy as she delicately tasted the dishes set before her.

It was not until dinner came to an end and his father made a hurried retreat to his conservatory that Ian returned to his senses. Devil take him. He was not here to moon over some innocent chit.

A pity, but there it was.

There was only one person who knew the secret that Lord Norrington harbored. And that was Lord Norrington.

Escorting his aunt and Mercy to a small parlor, he kissed their hands and forced himself to make his way through the marble hallways until he at last reached the connecting passageway that led to the conservatory.

Reaching the glass doors, he found himself pausing.

As a child this room had been forbidden territory. His father had claimed that he was concerned that a young Ian might cause devastation among his precious blooms, but Ian knew even then that it was merely an excuse to escape his unwelcome presence.

So, of course, once his father had retreated to his bedchamber, he had nightly slipped from his bed to sneak into the sacred space.

Not only because he was just stubborn enough to prove (if only to himself) that there was no place he could not enter, but because he had some ridiculous notion that he might discover some key to his father's heart amidst the fragrant beauty.

Ridiculous, indeed.

Muttering a curse beneath his breath, Ian reached out and thrust the door open. The scent of rich, black earth and flowers in bloom hit him as he stepped inside and carefully made his way down the path. It was a scent that he detested, he acknowledged as he continued to the back of the glass-lined room, at last discovering his father carefully repotting a strange orange plant.

At his approach, the older man turned, his expression far from pleased.

Welcome home, Ian Breckford, he thought wryly.

"This is quite a collection," he murmured, well aware that his father would never speak first. He pointed toward the orange flower. "Very exotic."

With an awkward motion, Lord Norrington returned his attention to his plant.

"Lord Walford traveled to Africa last year and was kind enough to acquire several rare species for me. I am attempting to make them a sturdier plant to endure our English climate."

Ian hid his start of surprise. His father had not only spoken, but, wonder of wonders, it was not in a voice of dismissal.

Could the old man at last feel some guilt for treating his son as an unwanted bit of rubbish?

Whatever the cause, Ian knew that he could not waste the opportunity.

"Can you do that?" he demanded. "Actually alter them?"

"Perhaps someday."

Careful not to stray too close to Norrington, Ian moved to lean against the heavy wooden table, watching as his father deftly handled the fragile plant.

"How did you become interested in flowers?" he

asked, hoping if he could just get his father into a conversation, he might reveal something. Anything.

There was a long, awkward silence before Norrington at last cleared his throat.

"My mother. She loved to spend her days in the garden, and she taught me everything she knew." His profile tightened as he reached for a rag to roughly wipe his fingers. "My father disapproved, of course."

"Disapproved?" Ian studied the older man in confusion. "Why?"

"He thought his heir should be more interested in hunting and drinking with the other fribbles who lived in the neighborhood. It did not matter that my skills were increasing our crop yield and returning a profit he could never hope to achieve on his own." He gave a short, humorless laugh. "I was a disappointment, to say the least."

Ian felt a familiar sharp pang in the region of his heart. He knew all about being a disappointment. There was not a day of his childhood that he was not aware he was lacking what his father desired in a son.

Astonishingly, however, he realized there was something else in that pang. Something that might have been pity.

"Perhaps he resented your superiority as a farmer. Tending to your land is, after all, the most important part of being a nobleman, is it not?"

Norrington shrugged, using the rag in his hand to wipe the stray dirt off the table. The silence stretched. And just kept stretching.

For once, Ian resisted the urge to walk away in hurt disdain or fill the air with mindless chatter. He just leaned casually against the table and waited for whatever might come.

Chapter 3

At last it was the father who cleared his throat and turned to study the son.

"Is there a reason for your journey to Rosehill?"

Ian was prepared for the question. "Did you know that Dunnington recently passed?"

"No." Astonishment followed by . . . what? It was impossible to say. "No, I had not heard the news."

"I found London a depressing place with the old man gone."

"I see."

Ian smiled wryly. "Do not fear. I will not linger for long."

Stiffening, Norrington turned to fuss with the pots that were spread across the table.

"This will always be your home, Ian."

"Thank you." He didn't roll his eyes, but it was a near thing. "It is very peaceful here."

"Yes, it is. That is what I love most about this estate."

"But you do seek the entertainments in London on occasion, do you not?" Ian asked casually. "Peace is all well and good, but every gentleman is in need of a diversion now and then."

The wariness that suddenly wrapped about Norrington was near tangible. As if he had some reason he did not wish to discuss his trips to London.

Intriguing.

A gentleman could hide any number of sins in the crowded city.

Ian should know.

"I must meet with my man of business in the city at least once a month," his father at last muttered in low tones. "And, of course, my position in the House of Lords demands that I attend for the more important votes."

"I know that you rarely open the townhouse. Where do you stay?"

"I stay at a hotel or with friends who are kind enough to issue an invitation." The dark eyes stabbed him with a growing annoyance. "Why do you ask?"

Ian shrugged, his smile one of utter innocence. It was the smile he used when he was about to fleece his latest pigeon.

"I just think it odd that our paths have never crossed while you are there."

"Since we have little in common, I doubt that you would haunt the same establishments as myself."

"Oh, I do not know. My tastes tend to be wide and varied."

"Yes, so I have heard." Norrington returned his attention to the plant, his tone without censure. Of course, it was also without the least amount of interest. "It has Ella quite worried."

Ian's lips twisted. "But not you?"

"Whatever my concerns, I believe that a man should be allowed to choose his own path."

"Even if it leads him to hell?"

"If that is your desire."

Ian grimaced, his elegant fingers absently toying with a pile of recently trimmed blooms that had been left to wilt on the counter. His father was rather ruthless in his obsession with pruning, whether it was fading plants or unwelcome family members.

"I do not know if it is so much my desire as my curse," he muttered.

"Curse?" His father stiffened, almost as if he had a personal knowledge of curses, which was ridiculous. "Why would you say that?"

"I seem to possess a natural tendency to seek out trouble whenever possible. It is a pity I did not inherit your own delight in peace." Gathering the blooms, Ian absently scattered them over the floor, his gaze trained on the broken splashes of color against the paving stones. "Of course, when you were young, you no doubt sought your own share of trouble?"

"No. Not as a rule."

Of course he did not. Lord Norrington was nothing less than a paragon. Which begged the question of how he had ever managed to sire a son outside the holy bonds of matrimony.

"Surely there must have been some devilment?" Ian pressed. Dammit, Dunnington had managed to extort twenty thousand pounds from this man. There had to be some sin the prig was hiding. "We both know you were not a perfect gentleman at all times."

Norrington's hands stilled, his profile tight with some inner emotion.

"I have never claimed to be perfect," he rasped. "Indeed, I am far from it."

Ian narrowed his gaze. Christ, was that actual emotion beneath all that ice?

"And yet I have never heard a breath of scandal

attached to your name." Ian was careful to keep his tone casual. "Not even by those hideous tabbies that devote their lives to discovering the sins of others. Rather remarkable."

With an obvious effort, Lord Norrington wrapped his icy composure about himself like a cloak of protection.

"Really, Ian, it is rather unseemly to speak of such things."

Ian bit his inner lip, knowing better than to try and force his father to speak of anything he did not wish to. He had banged his head against that particular wall on too many occasions.

"As you wish." He lifted a nonchalant shoulder. "To be honest, I am simply interested in hearing of your life."

"Why?"

"You are my father. It seems strange that I know precious little about you."

"There is nothing you need know of me, Ian." Reaching for a damp cloth, Norrington carefully wiped the clinging soil from his hands, his movements as concise and contained as his manners. "If you wish heartfelt confessions, then seek out Ella. She would no doubt be eager to share any childhood memory you desire. Now if you will excuse me, I believe I shall seek my rooms."

Without so much as a glance in his son's direction, Lord Norrington turned and marched from the conservatory, his back so stiff it was a wonder it did not crack beneath the strain.

Abandoned yet again by the father who had devoted a lifetime to ignoring his only child, Ian sucked in a raw, painful breath.

"And they claim me the bastard," he muttered.

* * *

Despite the lateness of the hour, Mercy ignored the comforts of her bed and instead remained curled in a wing chair in the library with a large, leather-bound book spread open on her lap.

The room was her favorite. Although it claimed the same opulent elegance that Rosehill was famous for, with its lofty ceiling and bank of windows overlooking the rose gardens, there was a sense of warmth in the towering shelves crammed with Lord Norrington's astonishing collection of books and the sturdy English furnishings.

When Mercy had first arrived she had been speechless as she stepped into the room. Her mouth had actually watered as she stood in the center of the polished parquet floor and allowed her gaze to wander over the endless shelves. To a young maiden starved for the opportunity to widen her mind, it had seemed as if she had been offered a glimpse of paradise.

A paradise she was determined to savor until she was forced back to the dull reality of her future.

Lost in the past, Mercy had no notion of how fragile she appeared in the depths of the leather chair, or how the nearby fire flickered over the golden curls that had slipped from the once-tidy knot to brush her ivory cheeks and added a hint of translucency to her sensible muslin gown.

Not until there was a sharp intake of breath and she glanced up to discover Ian Breckford regarding her with a smoldering appreciation that sent a jolt of awareness down her spine.

"Ah, so wood sprites have infested even the library," he taunted, strolling forward with a predatory grace.

"Good heavens." Snapping the book shut, Mercy warily rose to her feet, her gaze trained on the advancing gentleman. He was still wearing the elegant attire he had chosen for dinner, but sometime during the evening he had loosened his cravat and opened the buttons of his linen shirt to reveal the strong column of his neck. With his raven hair tousled and his jaw darkened with a hint of whiskers, he appeared utterly earthy, utterly male, and utterly dangerous. Another thrill of awareness charged through her body, reminding Mercy that knowledge was not the only thing she was starved for. "Will you please halt your habit of sneaking up on me?"

"I was hardly sneaking." The golden gaze ran a lazy path down her body, lingering a deliberate moment on the modest cut of her bodice. "I believe an elephant could have stomped through the room without gaining your attention."

"Yes, well, I was reading a fascinating history on the plague that swept through the Byzantine empire while—"

"I will take your word that it is fascinating," he drawled.

She smiled wryly, more resigned than annoyed by his interruption. There were few who possessed her passion for the past.

"You have no interest in history?"

"I far prefer the present." He prowled forward, filling the room with a restless energy. "Especially when it includes a beautiful lady."

Barely aware that she was moving backward, Mercy came to her senses the same moment her back hit the book-lined shelves. Whatever was the matter with her? This gentleman might be a practiced rake, but he wasn't about to ravish her in his father's library.

Not unless she invited him to do so, the voice of the devil whispered in the back of her mind.

"Yes, I imagine you would," she managed to retort.

A wicked smile curved his lips. "You sound disapproving."

That was the problem, of course. Mercy was not at all certain that she disapproved of the heady sensations that were tingling through her body.

"Do I?"

His hands landed on the shelves on either side of her shoulders, his lean, muscled body trapping her in a cage of heat.

"If you must persist in thinking the worst of me, then perhaps I should take measures to live up to my reputation," he warned, his head angling down to brush his lips over the delicate skin of her temple.

"Mr. Breckford . . ."

"Ian."

"Ian." Her hands lifted to press against his chest. Not so much in protest as in an effort to catch her breath. That soft caress might be meaningless to Ian Breckford, but it shuddered through her body with shocking force. "You appeared troubled when you walked into the room. Is anything the matter?"

He pulled back to reveal a sardonic expression that was not entirely successful in disguising a deep, festering pain.

"I am always troubled after spending time in my father's company. He possesses an uncanny ability to rattle my nerves."

"I am sorry."

"Do not be. It is not your fault." His lips twisted. "Besides, it is nothing that a swig of whiskey will not cure. Well, perhaps more than a swig."

"It is very late to be partaking of strong spirits."

The smoldering heat returned to the golden eyes as he studied the soft curve of her lips. Certainly it is well past a proper maiden's bedtime. There are dangers to be found lingering in the shadows of a house."

"What sort of dangers?"

"Dangers such as this . . ." With a blatant sensuality, he leaned forward until his lips pressed to the pulse that pounded at the base her throat.

Mercy shivered, her hands instinctively lifting to grip the lapels of his jacket. There was the strangest humming racing through her body, making her knees weak and her lower stomach clench with a sharp excitement.

"Are you going to kiss me again?" she demanded dreamily, already imagining those warm lips exploring her mouth.

"I thought that was what I was doing." With a tantalizing nip, he pulled back, a bold challenge sparkling in the gold eyes. "Perhaps you would prefer that I try some other method?"

"Oh." Her heart missed a delicious beat. She had always thought of kissing as two sets of lips pressed together, just as he had done earlier. Certainly no one had ever whispered of any other possibility in her hearing. But there had been something wildly arousing in his lips teasing her throat and the brief flick of his tongue against her skin. Just how many other secrets were kept from stifled virgins? "Are there more than one?"

"Devil a bit." His short burst of laughter echoed through the vast room as he regarded her with amused disbelief. "You are either incredibly naïve or a fool."

Her lips thinned as realization struck. She truly was both naïve and a fool. His caresses had not sprung from a natural desire for her. They were nothing more than an effort to goad her.

He would not be the first gentleman to enjoy the game of Shock the Aging Spinster.

"Why?" Mercy arched a cold brow. "Because I am just a provincial bumpkin who is not sophisticated enough to comprehend the rules of such games?"

"Because you should be slapping my face."

"I may yet."

He stilled, studying her as if the answers to the universe might be etched upon her upturned countenance.

"Perhaps you truly are a wood sprite," he murmured. "I have never encountered another woman like you."

With a motion that was swift enough to catch Ian off guard, Mercy slipped beneath his arm and moved to stand beside the crackling fireplace. Slowly he turned to regard her with a steady, unnervingly watchful gaze. Rather like a predator considering whether to continue toying with his prey or pouncing for the kill.

"I presume that you came to the library in search of the whiskey you claimed to be in need of," she said, waving her hand toward the distant corner. "I believe Lord Norrington keeps it on the side table."

Rather to her disappointment, he did not pursue her, instead folding his arms across his chest and leaning casually against the shelves. Not that she was fooled for a moment by his seeming nonchalance. The very air prickled with his restless, tightly coiled energy.

"Actually, I appear to have lost my thirst."

"Indeed?"

"Nothing less than a miracle, I assure you," he drawled, his voice thick with self-mockery. "Perhaps it is because I am suddenly consumed with curiosity."

She shrugged. "This is certainly a suitable room to sate any curiosity."

"There is nothing of interest in the dreary tomes. Only you can . . . sate my need, Miss Simpson."

Sate. A renegade shudder shook her body. Heavens but he was an accomplished seducer. Even standing at a distance he managed to make her body feel as if it were tingling with glorious life.

The sensible part of her warned that she should flee to the safety of her bedchamber. Nothing good could come of playing such games with a practiced rake.

Another part, that secret feminine part she was forced to keep hidden, was reluctant to end the unexpected encounter.

"I presume we are still speaking of your curiosity?" she demanded before common sense could ruin the moment.

A wicked smile curved his lips. "What else?"

"What else, indeed." She rolled her eyes. "Very well, sir. What has stirred your curiosity?"

His head tilted, the movement oddly reminiscent of his aunt. "You seemed surprised that there could be more than one manner of kissing. Does that mean—"

She smiled as his words came to an awkward halt. Almost as if he could not comprehend a woman of her age being so painfully innocent.

"That I have never been kissed until you did so earlier today," she finished for him, unwittingly squaring her shoulders as she waited for his laughter. Who wouldn't be amused by a four-and-twenty-year-old woman who could not entice the slightest interest in men?

Instead, a frown touched his brow, an unexpected wariness darkening his whiskey gold eyes.

"Are the gentlemen in your village truly such dolts?"

She shrugged. "I suppose there are a few dolts as well as any number of fine gentlemen."

"No, I refuse to believe that there could be a one of them with any sense if they have failed to notice a wood sprite in their midst."

A silly warmth filled her heart at his hint of outrage. Whether it was genuine or not, it was still nice to think that someone had not readily placed her upon the shelf.

"I fear I am rather easy to ignore when I never attend the local functions and only travel to the nearby village to visit the butcher and greengrocer. The only occasion that I am in the company of gentlemen is during church, and most of them possess the manners to resist the temptation to seduce the vicar's daughter in such a holy setting.".

"Good . . . God."

Chapter 4

For once Ian Breckford found himself at a loss.

Oh, he understood his shock at her stark confession of never having been kissed. How the devil did any woman reach her age without having stolen into a dark garden with at least one eager gentleman? He even understood his continued erection despite the fact they stood a near acre apart. That soft, husky voice would make him randy if she were halfway across the world.

What he did not understand was the unnerving disappointment that clenched his heart.

Could it be that he still possessed enough of his tattered morals to resist despoiling such lovely innocence?

The devil take it, the chit was the most beautiful creature he had ever encountered. As exquisite as a Renaissance angel. And the mere thought of having her naked beneath him was enough to make his cock twitch with savage excitement. To actually think about forgoing the pleasure she could offer was a sin against nature.

Unfortunately, he could not shake a measure of queasiness at the idea of tarnishing such pure virtue.

When he had made his promise to his aunt not to

force Miss Simpson into an affair, it had been with the full belief that it would be an easy matter to seduce her into offering what he desired. A belief that had been confirmed during the brief moments he had leaned against her trembling body. Her desire had been potent enough to perfume the air.

The woman was ripe and longing to be plucked.

But by the gods, Miss Mercy Simpson was not just another female. She was intelligent and kind and prepared to sacrifice her entire life for those who depended upon her. She deserved more than a meaningless tumble by a jaded wreck of a man.

It would be like leading a lamb to slaughter.

Unaware of his tangled thoughts, Mercy shifted uneasily beneath his brooding gaze, her expression one of unwitting challenge.

"I do not need your pity, Mr.—" Her eyes flashed as he held up a warning hand. "Ian."

Strolling forward, Ian offered a short, mirthless laugh. "If I was pitying anyone, it is myself."

She blinked. "Why?"

"Because it is not often that I do not simply take what I desire and damn the consequences." He ran a longing gaze over her delicate form, excruciatingly aware of how the firelight outlined her soft curves beneath the thin muslin gown. If he did not get to his chambers so he could relieve his throbbing erection, he was going to burst. "In truth, I cannot remember the last occasion I have not done so."

A smile that could have launched those damnable ships curved her lips. Devil take her, for all her innocence she was clearly a born siren.

"And what is it that you desire?"

His breath hissed between his teeth as he made a determined path toward the door.

"You are not that naïve," he muttered.

"Are you leaving?"

"I am wise enough not to tempt fate, or my less-than-dependable sense of fair play." He wrenched open the door and paused without turning. One glance at that sweet, vulnerable face and he would be on her like a . . . he groaned in genuine agony. "Good night, sweet Mercy."

The night had been a restless one for Ian. Not an unusual event. Lately most of his nights had been plagued by nightmares.

Of course, until he had arrived at Rosehill his nightmares had not included elusive wood sprites who enticed him with their magical beauty and then danced out of reach when he attempted to grasp them.

It did not improve matters to awaken so hard and aching he was forced to relieve the pressure once again.

The sun had barely crested the horizon when he was out of bed and allowing one of the numerous male servants to assist him with his bath and shave. He expected his own valet to arrive later in the day, thank God. Reaver was accustomed to dashing about London and the surrounding countryside in a perpetual effort to keep pace with his restless employer.

Once attired in his black jacket and silver-striped waistcoat, Ian made his way through the hushed grandeur of the house to the back breakfast room.

As expected he discovered his aunt seated at a small table partaking of her morning meal. In some ways Ella was as predictable as her brother.

"Good morning, Aunt Ella."

"Ian?" The older woman regarded his entrance with genuine shock. "My gracious, either the accommodations at Rosehill have become shabby beyond repair or the earth is coming to an end. You never rise before noon."

Crossing the black-and-white tiled floor, Ian grasped his aunt's plump fingers and raised them to his lips.

"Only the pleasure of your companionship could possibly have lured me from the comforts of my bed at such an ungodly hour."

Ella clicked her tongue, but there was no mistaking the blush of pleasure that bloomed on her cheeks.

"Very pretty, but I am not quite so gullible as to believe such nonsense."

Straightening, Ian pressed a hand to his chest. "You wound me, my dearest."

"Rapscallion." Ella smiled fondly. "Will you join me?"

"But of course." Politely, Ian turned to the sideboard and studied the generous array of eggs, toast, kidneys, bacon, and his aunt's favorite scones. A smile touched his lips as he recalled the lean years he could barely afford a bowl of porridge while his father wasted enough to feed an entire village. It was a thought he was swift to banish. Nothing could be served by wounding his aunt's feelings. "Ah, nothing less than a feast," he murmured.

"If you do not recognize any of the dishes, please feel free to inquire," Ella teased.

Ian filled a plate and returned to take his place at the table. "It has not been that long since I enjoyed breakfast."

The older woman snorted. "I will eat my favorite bonnet if you have seen the sunrise in the past decade."

"Very well, your bonnet is no doubt saved from horrid mastication," he conceded with a grin.

There was silence as they both enjoyed the expertly prepared food, Ian draining two cups of coffee in the hopes it would rid him of the clinging lethargy.

At last Ella patted her lips with a linen napkin and regarded Ian with a curious gaze.

"Why are you here, Ian?"

Ian did not miss a beat as he carefully returned his cup to the Wedgwood saucer. "Have you not always insisted that this is my home?"

"It is, but you have determinedly refused to see it as such." Her head tilted. "Indeed, you have gone to great efforts to avoid Surrey. So you cannot blame me for being curious as to why you should suddenly arrive on our doorstep."

"Honestly, I am not entirely certain." That, in part, was true. If he possessed any sense at all, he would call for his horse and be back in London by this evening. "I only know that after Dunnington died, I . . ."

Ella's brown eyes softened in swift sympathy. "What?"

With an effort, Ian pressed back the raw pain, his hand unconsciously rubbing his chest above his aching heart. The devil take it, would there ever be a day when he could think of his old friend without the savage sense of loss?

"I felt a need to know more of my past."

Surprisingly, Ella's cheerful countenance was darkened by a hint of wariness.

"Your past?"

Ian stilled. Was it possible that his aunt knew of Lord Norrington's dark sin?

"That surely is not so strange." He leaned back in his chair, the very image of nonchalance. "I know nothing of my mother beyond the fact my father met her on his travels through the Continent and that she died during my childbirth."

Ella's gaze abruptly dropped to her empty plate. "Yes, well, I do not believe that Norry knew her for any length of time."

"He must have known her for at least nine months if he was at her side to bring me back to England with him."

"Actually, I believe he had traveled on to Venice when he heard of her death in Rome and returned to collect you from the orphanage."

It was certainly plausible, but for some reason Ian felt as if his aunt was hedging. What the devil could she possibly be hiding?

"So she had no family?"

"None that she claimed."

"Was she a common woman or a lady of society?"

"I . . ." Ella was forced to halt and clear her throat. "I believe she might have been a maid in the villa where he was staying. I am sorry I cannot tell you more."

Ian gave an unconscious shake of his head. It was not an uncommon story. Many gentlemen made a sport of seducing the local maids. Hell, he'd enjoyed his own share. Ella's discomfort was no doubt a mere reaction at the thought her perfect paragon of a brother sharing his seed with a common servant.

"It seems strange that my father would go to the effort to retrieve me and bring me to his home," he mused. "It surely would have been more in character to simply have offered a sum for my upbringing."

Ella lifted her head to regard him with a sad smile. "He is not as heartless as you would choose to believe, Ian. He is a good man."

"I must take your word for that."

"Ian—"

He interrupted the words he did not want to hear. "Are there any other bastards?"

"No." Ella's plump hands fluttered at the question. "No, of course not."

Ian shrugged. It had occurred to him that his father's sin might be foisting a brat upon some unsuspecting aristocrat. It was, after all, impossible for a gentleman to know for certain if a child was actually his own, and if his father had been conducting a discrete affair with some society tart, then he might be willing to pay Dunnington to hide the knowledge that he had left a cuckoo in the nest.

"I do not know why you would be shocked. It is not that uncommon for a gentleman to produce more than one by-blow." His lips twisted. "I merely wondered if I possessed any brother or sisters and why they were not brought to Rosehill."

"You are your father's only child," Ella said with a soft certainty.

Ian was struck by a sudden thought. "Yes. Odd, that."

"What is odd?"

"The old man is getting on in years. Surely he should be fretting over the need to pass his title to a legitimate heir."

Ella sucked in a sharp breath. "Really, Ian, this is hardly a proper conversation for the breakfast table."

"I would think it a conversation often shared around the breakfast tables of the aristocracy," he drawled. "That is the duty of a nobleman, is it not? To produce a herd of progeny?"

"I . . . I suppose it is."

"Then why has my father been so reluctant to fetch

himself a bride and litter the house with screaming brats?" he demanded. "Could it be that he has yet to discover a woman who can live up to his expectations of perfection?"

"Ian, as much as I love you, I cannot bear for you to speak so scathingly of your father." Without warning, Ella was on her feet and moving toward the nearby door. "If you will excuse me, I believe Mercy will be awaiting me in the parlor."

Ian watched her departure with a frown. It was rare for his aunt to lose her temper, and certainly he had never seen her actually storm from a room.

It was enough to make him wonder if she was truly angered by his less-than-flattering comments concerning his father or if there was something else.

Something she was hiding.

Mercy managed to ignore the pressing urgency to go in search of Ian Breckford until Ella had retired to her rooms to prepare for dinner.

It had been frighteningly difficult. More than once, she had discovered her thoughts turning to the wicked, fascinating gentleman when she was supposed to be addressing the invitations for Ella's charity luncheon. And even when she had been allowed her usual hours in the library to work on her studies, her gaze had annoyingly drifted toward the bank of windows, as if she feared she might miss the sight of Ian strolling through the gardens.

It was thoroughly aggravating.

And thoroughly unshakable.

At last she could resist the urge no longer, and, muttering beneath her breath, she left the sanctuary of the library. Moving down the corridor, she had reached the staircase when she noticed the tall, decidedly male form silently slip into the passageway that led to the conservatory.

For a heartbeat she paused. She might be innocent, but she knew quite well it was not proper to chase after a gentleman like a hound on the scent. Especially not a gentleman who was known throughout England as a prolific rake.

But then again, as Ella's companion, it was surely her duty to remind Ian Breckford that his poor aunt had been noticeably disappointed when he had failed to make an appearance for luncheon.

Not giving herself time to consider, she hurried down the steps and through the passageway.

It was the first time she had actually entered the massive iron and glass structure, and she was startled by the long bank of shelves that held pot after pot of fragrant flowers. Heavens. There had to be hundreds of plants stacked within the humid heat of the long room, and all of them putting out enough fragrance to choke an elephant. Mercy wrinkled her nose as she followed the paving stones toward the back of the building.

Rounding an elegant marble statue of Poscidon, complete with trident, Mercy's steps faltered as she caught sight of her prey standing next to the battered desk that was shoved near the workbench.

Even with his back turned to her it was obvious that he was rifling through the drawers, occasionally pausing to pull out a stack of papers before continuing with his search. Mercy frowned, but before she could speak, Ian was stiffening as if he sensed her presence.

She thought he slipped something beneath his

jacket before turning to flash her a smile that did not reach his whiskey gold eyes.

"Ah, a wood sprite has appeared among the flowers," he murmured. "You should wear bells, my sweet, if you intend to sneak about."

She ignored his taunt. "Are you searching for something?"

"I thought I might make off with the family jewels." He leaned against the desk, deliberately casual. "That is, if you do not mind?"

"Not especially." She drifted closer to the energy that shimmered about his elegant body, like an unwitting moth to a flame. "I believe Ella would be saddened more from your departure than the loss of any jewels."

He pressed a hand to his chest. "A killing blow. Not surprising. Intelligent women are always the most dangerous."

Mercy narrowed her gaze. "It does not take a great deal of intelligence to know that you are attempting to divert me."

His soft chuckle brushed over her in a tangible caress. "Sweet Mercy, you would not still be wearing that charming gown if I truly wished to distract you."

"Good heavens, do you flirt in your sleep?"

"I am not entirely certain." His gaze dipped to take in the simple lace that hid her bodice. "Perhaps you could research the matter tonight and inform me in the morning?"

Her heart fluttered with a dangerous excitement. What was it about this man that managed to stir sensations that she had never dreamed she possessed?

"I thought you were determined not to tempt fate?" she softly reminded him.

The aquiline nose flared, and his expression was suddenly wary, as if he sensed some approaching danger. Which was ridiculous. She was an awkward, pathetically innocent spinster.

Hardly a danger to any man.

"You make it all too easy to forget."

"Me?" She took another step closer, savoring the potent heat that was spreading through her body. "But I have done nothing."

"You have followed me here, have you not?" His eyes narrowed. "Or do you mean to convince me that your presence in the conservatory is a mere coincidence?"

"No, I followed you."

He appeared startled by her blunt honesty. "Why?"

"I am not entirely certain." She wrinkled her nose. "I told myself that I wished to chide you for ignoring your aunt when she is so desperate for your companionship. But I fear that may have been an excuse."

"An excuse for what?"

"I suppose I . . ." She squared her shoulders. In for a penny, in for a pound. "I wished to be in your company."

His breath hissed through his teeth in a small explosion of sound. "Mercy?"

"You are rather like an exotic, perhaps even dangerous, creature for a staid, aging spinster, you know," she admitted ruefully. "I have never encountered anyone quite like you."

"Christ." With a sharp movement he had pushed away from the desk and paced toward the statue, as if he might throw himself on the waiting trident. "Should I be offended or terrified?"

"I doubt anything or anyone could terrify you."

"You would be wrong," he muttered.

She frowned, not at all certain why his voice sounded

so harsh. Was he angered that she had followed him? Or angered that she had interrupted his furtive search through his father's desk?

For a moment she considered the very sensible notion of turning on her heel and leaving the gentleman to his strange antics. It was clear he was not overly pleased to have her company.

Then she gave a shake of her head. She had less than a handful of days before being carted back to her tedious life. She intended to enjoy every moment to the fullest.

And that included spending time with this gentleman who managed to make her feel so brilliantly alive.

"Tell me about your life in London."

He remained silent, his head bent as he studied the marble feet of Poseidon. She feared that he might simply ignore her before he heaved a deep sigh and slowly turned to face her.

"What do you wish to know?"

Everything.

She wisely kept the too-revealing word to herself.

"How do you spend your days?" she instead demanded.

His lips twisted in a sardonic smile. "I am a rake, my sweet. My days are spent abed recovering from a night of debauchery."

"Ah. And what does your . . . debauchery include?"

"Such things are hardly fit for virginal ears."

"Now you sound like my father."

"No doubt a wise man."

She folded her arms over her chest and regarded him with a challenging tilt of her chin.

"Perhaps, but if I am never to experience the wicked pleasures of London, then I should at least be allowed to know what I am missing. It is not really so much to ask, is it?"

His lips twitched, although he was careful to keep his expression bland.

"Very well, although I feel compelled to warn you that you will no doubt be disappointed."

"I think I should be allowed to decide for myself."

"As you wish." He shrugged. "My night of debauchery usually begins with a simple dinner with friends."

"At your club?"

"God, no." His crack of laughter echoed through the humid thickness of the air. "Bastards, no matter how wealthy, are not invited to join Gentlemen's Clubs."

Her cheeks flooded with color. It was difficult to recall this man was a bastard. Not when he marched through the world as if he were lord and master.

"Oh."

His expression softened, as if he regretted causing her sharp distress.

"No matter." His charming smile returned. "There are any number of pubs and coffee shops that serve a decent meal, most of them a great deal tastier than the boiled beefsteak to be found in the clubs."

Mercy returned his smile although she was not fooled for a moment. He was not entirely indifferent to the knowledge he was unwelcome among the exclusive clubs.

"Then what?"

"Then I make the difficult decision of which gambling establishment I shall honor with my rather illustrious presence."

"You gamble every night?"

"Most nights." He caught and held her gaze, as if attempting to convince her of the blackness staining his soul. "It is, after all, how I make my living. We are not all blessed with large allowances that allow us to flutter through society without concern. There are some of us who must earn our keep by whatever means necessary, even if that means fleecing the gullible."

She refused to be shocked. "I cannot imagine you ever fluttering. However, your aunt has spoken of several society events that you have attended, so you cannot spend all of your time at the tables."

He dismissed his rabid popularity among the London socialites with a wave of his slender hand.

"There have been a few hostesses who have been kind enough to send me invitations."

"More than a few, I think." She absently reached to brush her fingers over the petals of a creamy orchid. "Do you enjoy such parties?"

"They offer their share of entertainment."

"Dancing?"

"Seducing."

"Oh."

He regarded her from beneath hooded lids. "You did wish to know."

"Yes. Yes, I did." She licked her lips, hoping that Ian presumed the heat staining her cheeks was one of shock rather than arousal. Gads, but it was easy to imagine him prowling through the crowded ballrooms, his golden eyes smoldering with a predatory fire as he searched for the woman who could soothe his restless hunger. "What sort of ladies do you prefer?"

"Good God." His eyes widened, and a startled laugh was wrenched from his throat. "I fear I must draw the line at actually discussing my peccadilloes."

"Because I am a virgin?"

"Because I possess at least enough gentlemanly

traits never to bandy about my trysts with a lady. Such matters are private."

"How very noble of you."

"Not bloody likely," he muttered. "I can assure you that I do not have the remotest trace of nobility, despite my father's blue blood."

"I think in some ways you are a fraud, Ian Breckford," she said softly.

His expression abruptly hardened, as if she had touched an unwitting nerve, "I am a fraud in many ways, Mercy Simpson. Now, turnabout is fair play."

She blinked as he took an unexpected step forward, bringing him close enough that she could catch the tantalizing scent of sandalwood.

"What do you mean?"

"How do you spend your days in your quiet village?"

Her fingers tightened on the orchid, plucking one of the petals before she could halt the revealing reaction.

"You cannot be interested."

A raven brow flicked upward. "As you informed me earlier, I believe I should be allowed to decide."

Mercy grudgingly accepted that he did have a point. She had demanded that he ease her curiosity, and although it was far from sated, it was only right that she return the favor.

Still, she found her stomach twisting with dread. Speaking of her dull, tedious life in the village was a reminder that this time at Rosehill was no more than a brief dream that would all too soon come to an end.

"I awaken at dawn to feed the chickens and stir the fires. Then I return to the cottage to assist my parents in rising from their beds and preparing for the day." She kept her voice determinedly calm. "After that I cook breakfast and then spend the morning tending to the garden."

His brows snapped together. "You have no servants?"

"We have a maid that comes daily from the village to assist in the heavy cleaning and an old gardener who will occasionally stop by to help with odd jobs."

Expecting him to peer down his very handsome nose at her humble existence, Mercy was caught off guard when genuine fury darkened his eyes.

"So you are expected to take care of the cooking and gardening as well as tending to your parents?"

"I was born quite late in their lives, and they are now too old to assist in the chores. As their daughter, it is my duty to see to their welfare."

"You have no money to pay for servants?"

"My father has a stipend, and I was fortunate enough to receive a small legacy from my grandmother."

"Then why do you not have a proper staff?"

She shrugged. "My father is set in his ways and dislikes having others in the cottage. He claims they disturb his digestion."

"His digestion?"

"Yes."

"And he is more concerned with his digestion than the fact he treats his own daughter as a slave?"

Mercy stiffened. Her father was demanding and perhaps more obstinate than she would like, but he had always loved her. It was more than many daughters could claim.

"Hardly a slave."

"I would say precisely as a slave." He took another step forward, the heat of his body brushing her skin and making her shiver. "You said yourself that you are never allowed to enjoy the usual pursuits of young ladies and rarely even travel to the village."

"Yes, but—"

"Not to mention the fact that you have been denied the pleasures of friends and flirtations and the simple enjoyments all maidens deserve. The devil take it, you have been denied your very life. And all because your father is too selfish to think of anyone but himself."

She flinched at his harsh words, not at all certain why he was reacting with such vehemence. She was nothing more than a passing acquaintance, was she not? One that he seemed determined to keep at a distance.

"That is not true," she insisted. "My father loves me."

"Perhaps too much," he growled.

"I beg your pardon?"

"Have you considered that a portion of his determination to keep you secluded and overworked is because he fears you might someday discover there is a world beyond your isolated cottage, and that on that day you will leave him?"

Mercy took a sharp step backward, her heart clenching with a sudden fear. It was more than an unease at having a near stranger insult the man who had loved and cared for her for the past four and twenty years. It was the niggling horror that he might actually be right.

"Please." She wrapped her arms around her waist. "Stop."

"Mercy . . ."

She gave a desperate shake of her head. "No, it is bad enough that I must soon return home, without having you make it even worse."

Chapter 5

Ian sucked in a deep breath. He was not quite certain why the thought of some selfish old vicar crushing the life from this sweet, vulnerable woman made him long to track down the sod and wrap his fingers around his neck. Or why he wanted to grasp Mercy by the shoulders and shake some sense into her.

He only knew that the mere thought of this maiden being hurt stirred a dark, primitive need to protect her.

It was a new and decidedly disturbing sensation. One that, when combined with the pure lust that had flooded through him the moment he turned to see her regarding him with those midnight eyes, left him feeling . . . combustible.

"Forgive me." Even to his ears the words sounded stiff. "I did not mean to upset you."

Her brows drew together. "And how did you think that I would react to having you speak of my father in such a manner?"

Ah, direct and utter honesty. It was no wonder the innocent country miss managed to keep a hardened sophisticate off his guard.

He shrugged, deciding that she deserved honesty in return.

"I allowed my dislike for having love used as a weapon to overcome my discretion."

Her annoyance faded as she regarded him with a searching gaze. "You believe love can be used as a weapon?"

Christ, but she was an innocent if she did not yet realize the utter devastation that love could produce.

"You read of history, Mercy. Surely you of all people must appreciate that it is the most powerful weapon known to mankind," he drawled. "Can any saber or pistol ball equal the pain of unrequited love? Can any torture be as painful as a love that smothers a person until they lose themselves?" His lips twisted. "Or love that is withheld as punishment?"

"You are very cynical."

"Yes."

With a slow, deliberate step she moved forward, the fading light slanting through the glass ceiling to bathe her in a soft rosy glow.

He hissed as a savage need twisted his gut. He had never seen anything so exquisite. Surely not even a wood sprite could possess such magical beauty.

"That does not trouble you?" she demanded, that low voice spreading through his body and tightening his muscles along the way.

He should have left the moment she had interrupted his search of his father's desk. Had he not spent the entire day avoiding the temptation of her company? He might not comprehend why he reacted to the chit as if he were still a randy school lad, but he was intelligent enough to know it was imperative that he not test his dubious control by being alone with her.

Besides, he could hardly search for his father's secret if the damnable woman kept trailing behind him and popping up without warning, he acknowledged sourly.

Perhaps it would be best if he gave her a taste of just how dangerous this game she was playing could be.

Bypassing the opportunity to ponder the sheer stupidity of his plan, Ian reached out to grasp her upper arms, his gaze deliberately skimming down to study the soft swell of her breasts.

"It is who I am, and why tender young maidens should do their best to avoid me."

Rather than struggling, Mercy tilted back her head to regard him with her sweet, dewy innocence.

"And if they choose not to?"

With a growl, Ian had her pushed back against the nearby workbench. Damn the wench. Why would she not flee from him as every other proper maiden had the sense to do?

His hands shifted to lightly encircle her neck, his thumb absently testing the satin softness of her chin. His head lowered, his lips finding the small hollow behind her ear.

"Then they should not be surprised if they find themselves pinned against the wall with their skirts lifted," he muttered, his words deliberately crude.

Her hands lifted, but not to push him away. Instead, the aggravating minx actually arched her body closer, brushing against his throbbing erection and nearly sending him to his knees.

"Ian."

He gave her earlobe a punishing nip, but he could not keep his arms from wrapping about her, or his lips trailing down the enticing curve of her neck.

He had spent the entire damn night dreaming of having this woman tight against his body. Of spreading her legs and thrusting so deep inside her that she could feel him in her womb. Of filling her with his seed over and over and over. . . .

"Damn, you smell so sweet." He breathed in her light, vanilla scent, thankfully drowning the nauseating cloud of flowery perfume. During his childhood he had come to hate the heavy aromas that filled this room and drifted through the icy corridors of Rosehill. It was a constant reminder that his father preferred the companionship of these plants to his own son. "You should not have followed me."

Her head tilted back in invitation. "I wanted . . ."

"What? What did you want?" he prompted, his tongue tracing the line of her collarbone. "This?" His hands skimmed up the curve of her back as his hips compulsively rocked against the soft curve of her stomach. "Or this?" he demanded, nuzzling the frantic beat of her pulse at the base of her throat.

"Yes."

He nibbled his way back to her ear, swirling his tongue along the outer shell before following the path of her stubborn jaw. He knew where he was headed. Those damnable rosebud lips of hers had been haunting him from the moment he had caught sight of her in that meadow.

Still, he kept his pace excruciatingly slow, savoring each creamy inch of her cheek. There was something rather unnerving about being the only man to have kissed a particular maiden. He wanted to be . . . hell, he wanted to be unforgettable.

How embarrassing was that for a jaded man of the world?

At last reaching her lips, Ian nibbled at the corner of her mouth, fiercely pleased when she gave a low moan and her fingers clutched at his shoulders. He forgot that he was teaching her a lesson, that this was all to frighten her into avoiding him like the plague. He forgot that he had sworn not to debauch the virginal chit.

His every thought was consumed with the pleasure of drowning in the vanilla heat that she offered so sweetly.

Allowing his fingers to dance aimlessly over her shoulder blades, Ian outlined her trembling mouth with his tongue, patiently waiting for the sigh that parted her lips. Only then did he shift his head to capture her mouth in a soft, tender kiss.

For a breathless moment she stiffened, as if considering the wisdom of traveling this dangerous path. Ian was careful not to rush, his touch so light she would know that she could pull away at any moment.

She didn't.

Indeed, her arms abruptly encircled his neck, the movement arching her body against his clenched muscles and scalding him with her heat.

Holy hell. His body jerked as a biting urgency slammed into him, his hands splaying across her back as he deepened the kiss. The taste and scent of her was clouding his mind, making him think of meadows and fresh honey. It was a startlingly erotic image that made his previous seductions seem somehow cloying and unsavory.

Intoxicated far more than a rake should be, Ian urged her lips wider, dipping his tongue into the moist heat of her mouth. Her nails dug into his nape at the unexpected caress, but Ian was indifferent to the tiny prick of pain. Christ, it was nothing in comparison to the savage throb of his erection.

He swallowed her soft moan of pleasure, his hands shifting to slowly outline her slender waist before rising up and cupping the soft thrust of her breasts.

Against all reason he forced himself to pause and await her lead. If she had never been kissed, then it sure the hell reasoned that she had never enjoyed a man's hands on her breasts.

An aching beat passed, and then another. When it was obvious she was not on the point of slapping his face, he growled low in his throat and tugged at the buttons that held her bodice together. The thin muslin material readily gaped, revealing the sensible corset and shift beneath. A considerable barrier for most gentlemen. Thankfully, Ian was not most gentlemen, and with the skill only a true connoisseur of women could conjure, he had the corset loosened and the shift pulled down to reveal the bounty he was seeking.

Unable to resist temptation, Ian pulled back to gaze down at the snowy white mounds, his heart halting as the pale pink nipples hardened beneath his survey.

His hands actually trembled as he reverently palmed the soft weights, his thumb brushing over the tender peaks. They were more beautiful than in his dreams.

Ian was barely aware he was moving until his head had dipped downward and he had his lips wrapped around the bud of her nipple. He wanted to taste her in this exact manner when he spread her legs and penetrated her. There were few things he enjoyed more than suckling a woman as she screamed out her climax.

Well . . . perhaps having her suckle his . . .

The delicious image of Mercy's sunlight curls bouncing as she took him deep in her mouth was abruptly disturbed as her soft whimper echoed through the hushed air.

It was not a whimper of pain. Quite the opposite, in fact.

It was the sound a woman made when her passions were being stirred to the point of no return.

The devil take it.

It had been less than twenty-four hours since he had promised himself that he would not be the man to relieve this woman of her innocence. And yet, here he was, holding her half naked in his arms, a breath away from yanking up her skirts and doing precisely what he warned her he would do.

He was a fool.

Whether for presuming he could dare temptation without getting burned, or for denying himself what was so blatantly offered, was impossible to decide.

Lifting his head, he glared in frustration at her flushed features and dark, siren eyes.

"Do you have no sense of self-preservation?" he rasped.

"Why?" She blinked, her breath still coming in soft pants. "Do you intend to hurt me?"

His brows snapped together at the ludicrous question. "What I intend to do is to steal your virtue, which many women would consider worse than death."

She touched her tongue to her lips that were still swollen from his kisses. "You can hardly steal what I was freely giving."

A heat that could have rivaled the fires of hell seared through him, nearly undoing his brief moment of sanity.

"Damn you," he gritted, forcing himself to drop his hands and step back from her exquisite temptation.

"I will not have the sin of despoiling the daughter of a vicar on my soul."

With hands that were not quite steady she righted her rumpled shift and tugged at the stays of her corset. Ian felt a raw pang of disappointment to accept that the momentary encounter was at an end. He wanted to thump his head against the workbench, cursing his stupidity in allowing this chit to walk away unscathed. He would be suffering for days.

"So it is only the knowledge that my father is a vicar that halts you?" she demanded.

"Not entirely." With a muttered curse he brushed aside her fumbling attempts to button the tight bodice and efficiently slid the buttons through their matching eyes. "It may surprise you, but I have never made a habit of bedding virgins."

"Have you known any virgins?"

Dropping his hands as if they had been scalded, he regarded her with a dark frown.

"A few. All of them wise enough to slap my face when I became overly bold."

Despite the heat staining her cheeks, she met his frown with a challenging tilt of her chin.

"Why is it my duty to slap your face?" she demanded. "Why is it not your duty to avoid becoming overbold?"

"Because the penalty for my sins would be nothing more than a hotter place in hell, why you . . . you, sweet Mercy, would be the one to suffer for a brief moment of madness."

She appeared unimpressed by his argument. "That hardly seems fair."

"I did not make the rules, Miss Mercy Simpson, I merely play by them."

"I very much doubt you have ever played by the rules in your entire life, Mr. Ian Breckford."

Well, that was true enough. He had devoted a lifetime to flaunting authority and scandalizing the humorless prigs who sought to strangle him with their notions of right and wrong.

It was only Dunnington who had managed to reach deep beneath his defensive demeanor.

The wily old tutor had suspected Ian's talent for numbers at an early age and had used Ian's brash love for cards to teach him more than just gambling. Before Ian had ever realized what had happened, he was not only happily settled with Raoul and Fredrick beneath Dunnington's roof, but he was actually enjoying his lessons.

"There must be a first occasion for everything," he muttered.

Her smile was wry, clearly thinking of his refusal to be her first lover.

"Not for everything, it would seem."

With her dignity wrapped about her, Mercy turned and glided down the path to the house. Left on his own, Ian moved to slam his fist against the workbench.

Damn the aggravating wood sprite.

She was surely destined to lead him straight to hell.

Leaving her chambers well before dinner was to be announced, Ella Breckford headed down the marble corridor to the master bedroom.

She knew at this hour her brother would be seated by the fire in his private sitting room, sipping his favorite brandy and reading the evening papers. In some ways Norry was as predictable as the rising sun or changing seasons.

In other ways he could be an aloof stranger that not even his beloved sister could fathom.

With a light tap on the door, Ella pushed it open and peeked into the pretty lilac and ivory room that held her brother's framed etchings of his beloved flowers. Along one wall were shelves that held his private collection of first-edition books as well as several marble busts that immortalized the long line of Norrington men.

Her heart clenched at the familiar aquiline nose and high brow that had been passed down through the ages. The same nose and brow that marked both her brother and Ian as true Norringtons.

"Norry?" she said softly. "May I join you?"

Folding his paper and setting it aside, her brother readily rose to his feet.

"But of course." He touched his intricately tied cravat and smoothed his hands down his dark blue jacket as she crossed to stand before him. He was always exquisitely attired, regardless of whether he was attending a royal ball or dining alone in the country. "Is there something troubling you?"

"I . . ." She bit her words as her nerves tightened her throat. This had all seemed so much simpler when she had been alone in her chambers.

"My dear, you appear in need of a sherry." Moving toward the fireplace where a cheery blaze battled the spring chill, Norry poured her a generous portion of the delicate spirit and returned to press the glass into her hand. "Now tell me what is upon your mind."

Ella took a sip of the sherry, attempting to gather her fading courage.

"It is Ian," she at last said.

Norry's lips thinned, his expression guarded as he toyed with the signet ring on his little finger.

"I have already promised you that I would do my best to make peace with the boy, Ella. What more would you have from me?"

She swallowed a sigh. It was a pity that the two men were both so opposite. Unless one counted their stubborn belief that they were always right.

To make matters even worse, Ian had been naturally blessed with all the traits that had been admired by Norry's own father. He was an envied sportsman, a charming rake, a hardened gamester, and a favorite among society. All the things that Norry had lacked.

Perhaps it was inevitable that the older man would nurture a deep resentment.

"Yes, I recall your promise, and I believe you, Norry."

"Then what?"

Ella drained her glass and set it aside, her fingers absently toying with the ribbon at the waist of her green crepe de chine gown.

"He has begun to ask rather difficult questions."

Norry's wariness deepened. "What sort of questions?"

"Questions about his past." She arched her brow in a significant motion. "About you and his mother."

"And what did you tell him?"

"I merely repeated the story we have told for years."

"Then what is the problem?"

"I do not believe he was satisfied."

The dark eyes hardened. "A pity, of course, but there is nothing to be done. He will simply have to accept what you have offered."

She gently cleared her throat, as her fingers nearly ripped the ribbon to shreds. "Unless . . ."

"Unless what?"

"Unless we reveal the truth."

There was a thunderous silence as Norry regarded

her as if she had grown a second head. She was not surprised. She had known before she approached her brother that he would be far from happy with her desire to answer Ian's questions.

"Good God, Ella, have you taken leave of your senses?" he at last managed to rasp. "If the truth were to be known, I would be ruined, and you—"

"Ian could be trusted to keep our secrets," she interrupted, her tone urgent.

Rather than the anger that she had been expecting, Norry's thin features softened, and without warning he stepped forward to stroke her cheek with a gentle, sympathetic hand.

"No, Ella," he said, genuine regret in his voice. "You know as well as I that any confession would merely hurt Ian. He would naturally feel betrayed by the both of us, and his first thought would be to strike back at those who had lied to him. We cannot take such a risk."

The brief flare of hope that had burned in her heart began to fade, replaced by the familiar ache of regret she had carried for so long.

She had been foolish to believe that fate could be changed at this late date. And even more of a fool to believe that she could somehow make amends for the past.

Norry was right. To confess the truth now would only hurt Ian further. That was the last thing she desired.

She heaved a sorrowful sigh. "I hate to see him so hard and cynical."

With care not to muss her attire, Norry pulled her into his arms. "I promise I will do my best to heal the wounds that I unwittingly caused, Ella. But Ian can never, *ever* know the truth of his past."

Chapter 6

Rather than following his fleeing wood sprite to the house, Ian turned on his heel and made his way to the door that led to the inner courtyard. He was still fully aroused and in no condition to cross paths with his aunt. Hell, he was in no condition to cross anyone's path.

Besides, he had a task awaiting him that had been interrupted by Mercy's unexpected arrival in the conservatory.

Marching with a grim purpose toward the distant stables, Ian refused to recall the delectable if wrenchingly frustrating encounter. What was the purpose? Nothing could alter his brutal, near-consuming desire for the chit. Or the fact that she was the one woman he could not have.

With enough sense to choose the path that would take him to the gate rather than vaulting the low stone fence, Ian managed to contain his urge to snap and snarl before reaching the expansive stables that now contained only a handful of horses. He even had enough sense to halt in the tack room and grab a leather satchel.

Halting in the shadows he pulled a folded playbill

from beneath his jacket and studied the gaudy painting of two Greco-Roman wrestlers. He had never heard of the London theatre that was listed or the strange performances that were printed on the back. Certainly it was not a licensed theatre or the usual plays expected by London audiences.

It could be nothing, of course, but it had captured his attention hidden among the other magazines and letters that had been stuffed into his father's desk in the conservatory. And he had spent enough time in the more disreputable parts of London to know that such follies could be true dens of iniquity. Perhaps his father's deeply held secret was connected to such a place.

It was at least a place to begin.

Thank God, Mercy had not realized he was stealing the damnable thing when she had entered the conservatory and . . .

Oh, for Christ's sake.

Shoving the playbill into the satchel, Ian went in search of a servant. Maybe if he kept moving he could put the damn wench from his mind.

It took only a few moments before he managed to corner one of the grooms tending to his aunt's matching pair of grays.

"You there," he called softly. The fewer who knew of his visit to the stables, the better.

The thin, young man with a shock of red hair and a spotty face dropped the brush and stepped from the stall. His muddy brown eyes widened as he realized who had interrupted his duties.

Ian hid a wry smile. For all his father's less-than-admirable traits, there was no doubt he had ensured that his bastard son was treated with nothing but absolute respect by the staff. Ian could not remember a moment when his requests were not attended to with gratifying eagerness.

"Aye, sir?" the groom demanded, his gaze lingering for a wistful moment on Ian's elegantly tied cravat before returning to regard him with an expectant expression.

"I have a task for you."

There was no hesitation as the groom gave a nod of his head. Obviously the boy had been taught that Norrington's bastard son was to be obeyed without question.

"Very good. How may I be of service?"

Ian held out the leather pouch. "I wish you to take this satchel directly to Mr. Raoul Charlebois in Drury Lane."

The brown eyes widened in wonderment. "Raoul Charlebois, the actor?"

"Yes."

"Bloody hell."

Ian smiled. Even in the midst of the country, his friend managed to inspire a reverent awe.

"Do not allow anyone to open it." His narrowed gaze warned that this included the groom. "And for God's sake, do not lose it."

The servant appeared suitably offended as he reached to take the satchel. "Certainly not, sir."

"When you reach Mr. Charlebois, I want you to tell him it is from me and that I wish to know everything there is to know about what is inside." He held up a hand at his companion's puzzled expression. "He will understand, trust me. Can you remember all that?"

"I'm to deliver this here satchel to Mr. Charlebois in Drury Lane and tell him to find out whatever he can about the thing."

"Well done." Reaching beneath his jacket, Ian extracted a coin from his pocket and pressed it into the groom's hand. "If anyone is to ask, I sent you to London with a missive for my mistress."

The groom shrugged, clearly unperturbed by the request. "Aye."

"Make the journey as swiftly as possible and there will be another shilling for you."

A glint of anticipation brightened the brown eyes. "Aye, sir. Very generous."

Assured that the playbill would soon be in Raoul's hands, Ian turned and made his way out of the stables. If he were quick enough, he might have time to search his father's desk in the library before the older man came down for dinner.

A dangerous risk, but a better choice than returning to his rooms and having the opportunity to dwell on Miss Mercy Simpson and the unholy temptation she offered.

Choosing a side door, Ian swiftly made his way to the main house, knowing that the servants would be busy preparing for dinner. With any luck he would be able to reach the study without stumbling over half a dozen footmen and maids.

He did manage to climb the stairs and make his way down the corridor, but before he could actually reach the library the door to the study was pushed open and his father appeared.

"Ah, there you are, Ian."

Ian came to a smooth halt, confident that his flare of shock could not be read upon his carefully bland expression.

"Were you searching for me?"

There was an awkward pause before Norrington cleared his throat and waved a hand toward the study.

"I thought we might have a drink in my study before you change for dinner."

Ian would not have been more shocked if his father had sprouted wings and begun to fly about the house.

"Just . . . the two of us?"

"If that suits you."

Ian struggled to contain his disbelief. His father had never in his life issued an invitation to join him. Not even when he had been up to some mischief. It had always been enough for him to glare at his son with that cold disapproval.

So the question was, why now?

With a mental shrug, Ian forced his feet forward. Whatever the cause for the unexpected invitation, it was the perfect opportunity to learn more of his father.

"Yes." He managed a stiff smile. "Yes, of course."

"Good." Leading the way back into the private study, Norrington crossed directly toward the heavy sideboard. "I believe you possess a preference for whiskey?"

How the devil did he know that?

Ian hid his surprise and strolled toward the distant wall that held a number of framed charcoal sketches.

"Irish?"

"Of course."

Pouring them both a generous measure, Norrington crossed to Ian's side and pressed the glass into his hand.

"Thank you." Taking a sip, Ian nodded toward the pictures of various flowers. "Did you do these?"

"Yes."

Ian did not attempt to hide his admiration. He might not possess a great love for art, but he did know when he was gazing upon an accomplished work.

"They are very good. Did you ever consider studying art with a master?"

He sensed his father stiffen at his side. "It was a childhood dream of mine. However, my father considered artists unsavory characters and refused to allow me to train." His short laugh was painfully devoid of amusement. "Indeed, he tossed my etchings into the fire when he happened across them."

"Why? Many gentlemen of quality are devoted to art."

"He thought I should be practicing my fencing skills rather than sketching."

Ian tried not to imagine his father as a young boy watching his beloved etchings destroyed for no other purpose than sheer spite. Such a thought might make him consider the notion that his father had been trained by a brutal bully to hide his emotions behind a cold barrier of indifference.

"He sounds like a singularly unpleasant man," Ian muttered, wondering if his grandfather had also drowned kittens and taken potshots at poachers.

Norrington moved to stand before the fireplace, leaning his arm on the mantle as he peered at the cheerful blaze.

"Actually, most people found him quite charming," he said, his voice tight. "Unfortunately, we had little common ground to enjoy one another's companionship."

"Much like us, I suppose, eh, Father?"

The older man flinched. "Unfortunately, there is some truth in what you say. But perhaps we . . ."

"We?" Ian prompted.

With an obvious effort, Norrington turned his head to meet Ian's challenging gaze.

"Perhaps we can attempt to work through some of our differences."

Ian swallowed the whiskey in a startled gulp. Work

through their differences? The devil take it, had his father taken a blow to the head? Or had poor Ella at last nagged her brother into pretending a grudging interest in his son?

He could not believe that his father genuinely desired to heal the rift between them. Not after all these years.

"I must admit that this comes as rather a surprise," he said, careful not to reveal the bitterness that was a constant ache deep in his heart. If he hoped to learn anything, he had to at least pretend he was willing to forgive the past. "You certainly have never indicated that you desired a relationship with me before."

"We all grow older, Ian, and hopefully wiser. I do not wish for ill blood between us."

"I see. So now you wish to be a father to me?" he demanded, still certain this must be some evil plot.

"Yes."

"Rather late in the day, I fear." Moving toward the fireplace, Ian directed the conversation down a path that might offer valuable information. "I already had a father who I loved and respected. A gentleman who never judged or condemned me for my occasional misdeeds."

Norrington straightened, his expression unreadable. "I suppose you refer to Dunnington?"

"Yes." Ian dipped his head. "Giving me into his care was the kindest thing you ever did for me, although I do not suppose I thought so at the time. I recall clinging to Aunt Ella and bawling like a frightened child."

"You were young and quite attached to Ella. It is not surprising that you were afraid. Indeed, it should have been odd if you were not."

Ian caught his breath at his father's unexpectedly kind words. Over the years, Ian had recalled that tearful parting with a hint of embarrassment, convincing himself that his father must have been shamed by his tantrum. Instead, it seemed as if Norrington possessed genuine sympathy for the young lad who had been taken from the only home he had ever known.

"Thank you." Ian gave a slow shake of his head, forcing himself to recall his purpose in joining his father. "Do you know, I have often wondered how you discovered Dunnington. Raoul, Fredrick, and I were, after all, his first students. How did you know he intended to begin a school?"

There was no mistaking the sudden tension that gripped his father's lean body, or the wariness that hardened his expression.

Odd. It was hardly an unreasonable question.

"We . . . have mutual acquaintances," he at last confessed.

He was hiding something. Something to do with his connection with the old tutor.

"Dunnington was from Surrey?"

"No, we met in London."

"I would hardly have thought you would cross paths with a mere tutor," Ian drawled. "You certainly do not belong to the same clubs."

A log snapped in the fireplace at the same moment Norrington's glass slipped from his fingers to shatter against the Persian carpet.

For a moment Ian was uncertain which of them was more shocked by the older man's clumsiness. For God's sake, the nobleman was one of the most graceful men that Ian had ever encountered. Certainly he was never so gauche as to break his Waterford crystal.

So what the devil had caused the rare gaffe?

"No . . ." His father visibly gathered his shaken composure. "No, of course we do not. Foolish question."

Ian suspected it was more a disturbing than a foolish question. A pity he hadn't the least notion why it troubled his father.

"Forgive me, I did not mean to startle you," he murmured.

Norrington frowned, his fingers toying with the diamond stickpin that glittered in the folds of his snowy white cravat.

"You did not startle me. Nothing more than an unfortunate accident."

"As you say." Ian briefly glanced at the shards of crystal spread across the floor before lifting his head to meet his father's gaze. "You did not tell me which acquaintances that you have in common with Dunnington."

This time his father was prepared. "It was all a very long time ago, but I believe we met at the Botanical Society," he said smoothly.

"Really?" Ian did not believe him for a moment. "Dunnington had an interest in flowers?"

"Mr. Dunnington possessed an interest in everything, as I recall. He claimed a tutor needed to be capable of speaking to his students upon every subject."

Well, Ian could not argue with that. Dunnington had not only possessed the avid curiosity of all true scholars, but he was wise enough to realize that there were many different paths to learning.

"Yes." A surge of fond amusement briefly lightened his mood. "I do not believe he had ever touched a card in his life before taking me in as his student. After my arrival, he spent his nights teaching himself everything from faro to whist."

Something that might have been envy darkened his

father's eyes before it was firmly hidden beneath a perfunctory smile.

"I am happy that you had someone to nurture your dreams. That is important for a young boy." There was a brief pause, as if Norrington were struggling against a dark, unpleasant memory. "Far more important than most people understand."

Once again Ian was bothered by a twinge of unwelcome sympathy. Devil take it, Viscount Norrington was the last man who needed pity. Unless being rich, powerful, intelligent, handsome, and artistically talented had somehow become reasons for condolences.

"Well, I am uncertain if Dunnington intended for me to become a gamester," he muttered, shifting his feet with an uneasy suspicion the wounds he carried were nothing in comparison to those of his father.

"Perhaps not, but he did manage to teach you to be self-sufficient and capable of fending for yourself. An achievement that is not to be taken lightly."

Ian regarded his father with a growing bewilderment. "I thought you disapproved of my ramshackle lifestyle? You have often warned that the gambling and wenching would lead me to a bad end."

"It is hardly a lifestyle that leads to a long, healthy life, although my father would have been quite proud of you." A wry smile twisted the older man's lips. "You are far more his son than mine."

Ian gave a short laugh. "Somehow that does not seem a very high compliment. Indeed, I believe I am quite insulted."

"I am sorry, that was not my intent. We should all be allowed to live our lives as we see fit."

"As do you?" he prodded.

"Me?" There was a brief ripple of bitter amusement

before his expression became shuttered, effectively hiding his emotions from Ian's searching gaze. "No. There are some paths closed even to a viscount."

"I cannot imagine any path that would not be opened with enough wealth and power," Ian challenged.

From the depths of the house a gong echoed down the corridors. With obvious relief that the encounter was at an end, Norrington crossed toward the door.

"I will not detain you any longer, Ian. You must change for dinner."

"A moment, please," Ian demanded, taking a step forward.

Norrington came to a grudging halt, his hand on the doorknob as if needing the comfort of knowing he could bolt at a moment's notice.

"Yes?"

"I have one question," Ian confessed, swallowing his considerable pride. As much as he hated asking anything of this man, he had spent his entire life plagued by one question. This might very well be his one and only opportunity to discover the answer.

"And what is that?" Norrington demanded, his expression guarded.

"Was my mother merely a meaningless body in your bed, or did you care for her at all?"

There was a long, painful silence. Long enough that Ian steeled himself to be ignored. It would not be the first occasion his father had offered a cold rebuff.

Then, without warning, his father gave a slow nod of his head. "Actually, I loved her very much, Ian."

Ian released a breath he did not even know that he was holding. "Thank you," he whispered, his voice thick with a genuine gratitude. "It's stupid that it matters. . . ."

"But it does?"

"Yes. Yes, it does."

"Then know that she will always hold a place in my heart."

With his soft words delivered, Norrington slipped from the room and closed the door behind him.

Left on his own, Ian moved to pour himself another shot of whiskey.

During his journey to Surrey, his greatest fear had been expiring of boredom. There were few things more tedious than spending day after day in the country, especially when he was to be stuck in the marble mausoleum called Rosehill.

And not even the anticipation of uncovering his father's sins could offer more than a vague hope for entertainment.

Boredom . . .

His crack of laughter echoed through the silent room.

Chapter 7

Despite her best efforts, Mercy found herself lingering in the library long after she should have been in bed.

It was perfectly absurd.

Ian Breckford might have made an appearance at dinner and even have stayed long enough to play a game of chess with his aunt before bolting for the village pub, but as far as Mercy was concerned he might as well have been half a world away.

Never in her life had she ever been quite so thoroughly ignored. There had not been a word, or a touch, or even a glance the entire night. Which meant that it had to be intentional. No one could so assiduously avoid another without a great deal of effort.

Still, she found herself ridiculously hurt when she at last conceded defeat and climbed the stairs to her chambers.

Did the aggravating man fear she might force herself upon him at the dinner table? For heaven's sake, he had already made it obvious he did not consider her worthy to capture his jaded attentions. Did he have to rub her nose in his indifference?

Once in her rooms, she changed into the sensible night rail that was beginning to fray about the hem and brushed her hair into a tidy braid. Then, rather than climbing into her bed, she studied her reflection in the mirror.

In the flickering candlelight she could make out the pale oval of her face and the dark slant of her eyes. Nothing remarkable, of course. But surely not hideous, either.

So why was she continually overlooked, disregarded, or outright rejected by gentlemen?

What the devil was the matter with her?

Ignoring the knowledge that her father would be deeply disapproving of her display of vanity, Mercy continued to search her reflection for her fatal flaw, nearly missing the soft tap on her door as she remained lost in her broodings.

There was no mistaking, however, when the door was abruptly pushed open to reveal the gentleman currently plaguing her thoughts.

"Ian." She awkwardly surged to her feet, her gaze widening at the sight of his disheveled appearance.

Sometime during the evening he had lost his cravat as well as his elegant jacket and waistcoat. Now he was attired in nothing more than a thin linen shirt that revealed a disturbing amount of his wide, smooth chest and a pair of breeches that clung to the hard muscles of his thighs with an unnerving precision.

Her stomach clenched with a giddy awareness as she lifted her gaze to take in the tousled raven curls and the shadowed line of his jaw.

He looked raw and dangerous and utterly delectable.

"I saw the light beneath your door. . . ."

"For heaven's sake come in or out before anyone

notices you," she interrupted, annoyed by her ready reaction to his arrival. It seemed gruesomely unfair that she should burn with need when he was near, and yet he could remain indifferent.

Seemingly oblivious to the sharp edge in her voice, Ian entered the room and shut the door firmly behind him. Then, leaning against the wooden panes, he regarded her with an oddly muddled gaze.

"Sweet, sweet Mercy."

With a frown, Mercy moved forward, able to catch the scent of whiskey on his breath as she halted directly before him.

"You are foxed."

"No, I am not." He swayed, his hand grasping the doorknob to keep from pitching forward onto his nose. "I am three sheets to the wind, my dear. Quite different from being foxed."

"I suppose I must take your word for it. You are the expert, after all," she muttered, grasping his arm as he once again swayed. "Have a seat before you knock us both to the ground."

Without warning, he gave a sharp tug with his arm, knocking her off balance so she stumbled against him. Before she could recover, he had her pinned to his body, his arms wrapped about her waist in a ruthless grip.

"I do not want a seat. I want you beneath me on that bed as I part your legs and . . ." His eyes screwed shut, as if he were in actual pain. "Christ, you are driving me mad. I should have stayed at the pub. There were any number of women who were eager enough to ease my ache."

The momentary delight at being held so tightly in his arms was swiftly doused at his less-than-flattering words. Lifting her hands, she placed them flat against his chest and arched back to glare into his aggravatingly handsome face.

"No doubt," she hissed. "Why didn't you stay if they were so eager?"

"Because they were not you." His eyes snapped open, the whiskey gold gaze sliding over her flushed face before lowering to take in the thin night rail that did little to cover her slender curves. A sinful heat followed in the path of his gaze, searing over her skin and making her shudder with need. "It did not matter how beautiful or willing or skilled they might be, I remained as limp as an overcooked noodle." His expression was hard with self-derision. "It has to be you. Only you."

With a violence that shocked her to the very core, Mercy curled her hands into fists and smacked them against his chest. It was not that she could actually hurt the man. She did not doubt that her blows caused more pain to her hands than to his rock-hard chest. Still, it was utterly uncharacteristic of her to lash out like a common fishwife.

"You do not want me," she hissed. "You have made that clear enough for even a simpleton to comprehend."

"Not want you?" With a sharp laugh, he grasped her wrists, easily halting her foolish attack. Then, with a low groan, he bent his head to brush his lips over the pulse pounding at her temple. "There are moments when I fear that if I do not have you soon I will shatter into a thousand pieces."

She stilled, her body humming with excitement at his light caress. "Then why . . . ?"

His lips moved to explore the curve of her cheek, his hot breath sending a rash of prickles over her sensitive skin.

"I am not completely depraved, Miss Simpson, or at least I was not until stumbling over a delightful wood sprite who will not leave me in peace."

She wanted to be offended by his accusation. He made it seem as if he had no choice in forcing his way into her room and wrapping her in his arms as if he would never release her.

Unfortunately she could barely think beyond the sensation of his knowing lips as they nibbled a path to the corner of her mouth.

"You were the one to seek me out on this occasion," she rasped.

His hands splayed against the low curve of her back, squeezing her between his parted legs until she could feel the hard length of his erection pressed against her hip.

"Because it does not matter if I am in a pub a mile away or in London, I cannot get you out of my mind." With a groan, he plundered her mouth with a savage kiss, his tongue thrusting between her parted lips as if he were desperate for the taste of her. At last he eased the hard pressure to mutter his words of frustration. "Your scent . . . the feel of that satin skin . . . the taste of your lips . . ."

Mercy was forced to clutch at his shoulders as her knees went weak. She felt as if she had been tossed in the midst of a maelstrom that threatened to drown her in sensation.

"Ian," she breathed. "Wait."

"Wait?" He gave the lobe of her ear a sharp nip. "I have bloody well waited for hours. Hell, I am beginning to suspect that I have waited my entire life."

She struggled to think as his tongue traced the line of her throat. This was precisely what she had desired . . .

what she *still* desired . . . but it was all happening so swiftly she could barely keep up with the emotions battering through her.

"What do you want from me?"

He deliberately rocked his arousal against her, his mouth skimming down to the line of her bodice.

"You are not that naïve."

A soft groan was wrenched from her throat as his lips found the upper curve of her breast, seeming to savor the feel of her skin. Already her nipples were hard and aching for his touch. She had never dreamed that a man's lips on the sensitive buds could cause such exquisite pleasure.

"I do not consider it naïve to presume a gentleman who cannot so much as glance in my direction is indifferent to me."

He muttered a curse as he raised his hands to tug the narrow bands of her night rail off her shoulders, his eyes glowing with a ravaging heat as the material drifted down to pool at her feet.

"Only a gentleman desperate to be buried deep inside you would ever go to such an effort to avoid you, sweet Mercy," he rasped, his hands busily tugging her hair free of its braid. "If you knew how hard it has been to keep from ripping the clothes from your delectable body and having my way with you, you would be quaking in terror."

Mercy was quaking. But terror had nothing to do with her trembling.

No, it was the hand that he tangled in her tumbled curls as he sharply angled her head back to meet his demanding kiss, and the pained rasp of his breath.

Even in her innocence she realized that this was not the smooth seduction of a practiced rake. There was nothing polished in his desperate touch or the shudders that wracked his body.

The knowledge was far more erotic than any amount of skill, and, tossing aside her lingering hurt at his earlier rejection, Mercy wrapped her arms around his neck.

She was drowning in a delicious heat despite the chill that brushed over her bare skin. A heat and excitement that she could feel to the tips of her toes.

Ian growled deep in his throat, his tongue thrusting with a slow rhythm that mimicked the same thrust of his hips. Mercy felt an ache bloom deep in the pit of her stomach.

Instinctively she arched closer, the rasp of his clothing an unwelcome barrier to the hardness of his body. She needed . . . dear heavens, she needed something. Something only Ian Breckford could offer.

"Oh," she gasped as his lips wrenched from her mouth to dip downward and close about a throbbing nipple. "Oh . . . God."

"Not God, sweet Mercy," he muttered, abruptly whirling until she was pressed against the wall. "Not even close."

Mercy gazed down at the dark head, her breath lodged in her throat as he continued to suckle her with exquisite care. There was a restless urgency clenching her body that made her long to scream in frustration.

His warm lips felt so wondrous against her breasts, his tongue making her whimper in delight. This was the reason women tossed aside all sense and gentlemen sacrificed thrones.

"Ian."

"What, my sweet?" Lifting his head, he regarded her with a hungry gaze. "What would you have of me?"

She shook her head in a helpless motion. "I do not know."

For a long moment he studied her upturned face, as if he were memorizing each sweep and curve of her features.

"Will you trust me, Mercy?"

"I . . ." She licked her lips that were swollen and tender from his kisses. "Yes. Yes, I trust you."

His eyes flashed gold in the candlelight. "Then allow me to teach you of pleasure."

Without warning he was slowly lowering to his knees directly before her. Her eyes widened in shock as she realized his head was even with her most private parts. Even more shocking was the realization that his avid gaze was causing an embarrassing dampness between her legs.

"What are you doing?"

With a hint of reverence, Ian lifted his hands to slide them up her bare legs, his light touch sending jolts of electric excitement through her.

"You said you trusted me," he chided, his voice oddly raw.

Mercy's breath was trapped in her lungs as she struggled not to swoon.

"I do, but surely we should be on the bed—" Her words came to a startled squeak as his hands determinedly parted her legs at the same moment he leaned forward.

Her fingers clutched at his hair as she felt the stroke of his tongue and the rasp of his whiskers against the sensitive flesh of her inner thigh.

"No bed," he muttered as his tongue traced a pale blue vein.

Her heart came to a sharp halt as he neared her

tender slit. The last thing she desired was to distract him at such a critical moment, but then again, she was not entirely certain her shaky knees would hold her up much longer.

"Why?"

His grip tightened on her thighs, his head grudgingly tilting back to meet her bemused gaze.

"I have spent the night at the local pub trying to forget you, sweet Mercy," he rasped, a dark flush staining the narrow line of his cheekbones. "When I take your virginity it will not be when my mind is clouded with whiskey and my body so hard with need that I risk hurting you."

"Then what are you doing?" she whispered, her stomach clenching with dread. Oh Lordy, he could not be thinking of ending things at this late point. Could he? She would beat him with her slipper if he tried to bolt.

"I am attempting to please you," he said, his eyes dark with longing. "If only you would allow me."

"But—"

"Shh, Mercy, enough speaking." His mouth returned to tease at the inner skin of her thighs. "I will go mad if I do not taste of you."

He shifted higher, his hands steadily urging her legs to part. Mercy hissed, grasping his shoulders as her knees threatened to collapse. He was close to that aching void. So very, very close.

Mercy moaned as he teased and taunted, his breath brushing the vulnerable region and making her squirm with fiery excitement. Restlessly she explored the line of his shoulders with her hands, amazed by the hard muscles. He was so wonderfully, unmistakably, utterly male.

"Mercy," he rasped, his hot breath searing over her skin. "May I please you?"

Please her?

If he pleased her any more, she would surely expire upon the spot.

"Yes . . . yes."

The agreement had barely tumbled from her lips when his fingers at last parted her intimate folds, giving his tongue unfettered access to her tiny nub of pleasure. She nearly screamed in bliss as raw heat exploded in the pit of her stomach.

God almighty.

Her head banged into the wall as she was suddenly consumed with a tension that shimmered through her. Oh, he was wicked. *This* was wicked. Nothing could feel so damnably good and not be a sin.

As if sensing she was willing, even eager, to know more of the paradise he offered, Ian slid a slender finger into her damp heat.

She gasped, her eyes fluttering shut at the gentle invasion. With a slow thrust he pressed his finger deeper, using his tongue to suckle that pleasure point over and over.

Tension spiraled within her, clenching her stomach and halting her heart as his tongue stroked her with the same relentless pace that his finger slid in and out of her.

There was something approaching. A crucial, elusive goal that trembled just out of reach.

"Ian," she moaned, her body bowed and her teeth clenched.

"Shh, my sweet," he murmured, seeming to comprehend what she was pleading for as the swirl of his tongue quickened with a gentle insistence.

Lost in sensation, Mercy shoved her fingers in Ian's hair, riding on the crest between pleasure and pain.

Oh . . . yes. This was what she was striving for. This breathless moment out of time.

The very world halted. Then, with a last, lingering stroke of his tongue, she was catapulted through a shower of brilliant stars, a soft cry of pure bliss wrenched from her throat.

Glorious heaven above.

That was . . . brilliant.

Ian possessed enough scruples to realize that he should feel guilty as he scooped the trembling Mercy in his arms and carried her to the bed. Not only had he intruded into her room while his mind was clouded with whiskey, but it had been with the clear intention of easing at least a portion of his smoldering frustration.

His evening at the pub had not gone at all like he had hoped. Not only had the whiskey done nothing more than fog his wits, but the women had left him as cold as an Artic winter.

He had returned to Rosehill with one thought.

To hold Mercy in his arms as she experienced her first orgasm.

Oh yes, he should be wracked with guilt.

Unfortunately his scruples were no match for his smug satisfaction as he tucked her beneath the covers and studied her dazed expression.

She looked precisely as a woman well-satisfied should look, and he took full pride in knowing that he had been the one to provide that satisfaction.

It was almost worth the raging pain in his cock.

Settling on the mattress, Ian reached out to gently push a stray curl from her cheek.

"Are you well?"

"Better than well." She heaved a dreamy sigh. "I feel as if I am floating."

His erection gave a sharp jerk. In this moment he would give his entire legacy of twenty thousand pounds to crawl beneath that cover and join her. Not a small sacrifice considering he was a gentleman who had always been forced to count his shillings.

"You are so exquisite," he said, his voice husky as an unfamiliar tightness squeezed the air from his lungs.

With a content smile, Mercy pushed herself higher on the pillows, the blanket lowering to reveal the upper curves of her breasts. Ian gritted his teeth, resisting the urge to howl in frustrated need.

"I did not realize that . . ."

With an effort, Ian forced himself to concentrate on her soft, hesitant words.

"What?"

"That a gentleman could do such things to a woman."

He wanted to tell her that there were a dozen—no, a hundred—different things he could do to her. Instead, he gave a faint shrug.

"Yes, well, I doubt a vicar would share such knowledge with his daughter."

She snorted in disgust. "My father refuses to share *any* knowledge with his daughter. It is very frustrating."

He moaned in genuine pain. "Please, Mercy, if you have any pity at all, you will not mention the word frustrating."

"Why . . . ?" Her cheeks reddened with comprehension. "Oh. You did not . . ."

"No, I did not," he wryly agreed.

She worried her bottom lip as she regarded him with her dark, unnervingly steady gaze. Then, as if coming to a decision, she took a deep breath.

"Is there something that I can do to help?"

Ian flinched, his entire body clenching with a flare of raw, savage heat.

The thought of her delicate hands on his cock, gently squeezing and pumping him to release . . . Christ, it was enough to make him come without a single touch.

"You really are going to be the death of me," he groaned.

"Ian, I want to help." Her brow pleated, her tone earnest. "I want to learn how to please you as you pleased me. Surely there is nothing wrong in that?"

Ian abruptly realized that the fires of hell were not solely the domain of Beelzebub. They could also be conjured by a dewy-eyed wood sprite with the smile of an angel.

He trembled as he battled back the tidal wave of sheer, undiluted lust.

"There is everything wrong."

"Why?"

"Because young ladies do not—"

Without warning, Mercy was on her knees before him, astonishingly indifferent to the fact that the blanket had dropped down to reveal her bare body.

"Stop that," she commanded, her fingers pressing to his lips. "You sound like my parents, and I will not tolerate it from you."

Ian was caught between amusement at being chided as if he were a schoolboy and the searing desire that was threatening to consume him.

"No?"

"No." Placing her hands on his shoulders, Mercy slowly leaned forward to place her lips against his. "Tell me what to do."

"Mercy—"

"Tell me."

Later he would blame his lack of willpower on the whiskey he had consumed and the lateness of the hour. After all, a renowned rake could not admit to being completely undone by a fragile virgin with no more than an awkward kiss.

"God . . ." Shaking with the anguished need to have her closer, Ian wrenched his shirt over his head and tossed it onto the floor. Then, grasping her hands, he pressed them to his chest. "Touch me. Just touch me."

With tentative strokes she explored the taut muscles of his chest, her expression oddly enthralled, as if she were fascinated by the feel of his skin.

"Like this?" she demanded, taking a moment to toy with the hard pebbles of his nipples.

"Oh . . . yes," he groaned, knowing that he had never experienced anything quite so amazing as her hands on his body. "Perfect. So perfect."

He forgot to breathe as her exploration headed ever lower, the muscles of his stomach contracting with anticipation. The devil save him. Just a few more inches.

As if deliberately hoping to put him in an early grave, Mercy paused a wrenching moment at the waistband of his pants. Ian groaned, far past the point of being capable of denying the frantic desire clawing through him.

With a swift motion he was on the bed, matching her kneeling stance to be poised directly in front of her. Then, fumbling with the buttons, he managed to release the aching length of his erection.

There was another hesitation, and Ian braced himself for Mercy's shock. Why hadn't he considered her sensibilities? It had to be disturbing to be suddenly confronted by a fully aroused male.

For the first time in his life, Ian found himself

uncertain in bed with a woman. Even as an untried youth he seemed to possess an instinctive knowledge of how best to please a woman. Now he hesitated, not knowing whether to cover himself or . . .

The choice was taken out of his hands. Or rather, the choice was taken into her hands.

Reaching out with a mysterious smile, Mercy allowed her fingers to skim down the length of his throbbing cock. Her touch was a mere whisper, but Ian had to swallow a shout of pleasure.

How perfectly ironic.

He had bedded some of the most skilled courtesans in all of London, but he threatened to be unmanned by the untutored touch of a wood sprite.

Her smile widened with a wicked knowledge of her own power, and, curling her fingers around his length, she set about discovering the best means of making him groan in blissful agony.

With a Herculean effort he allowed her the opportunity to explore to her heart's content, his manful pride refusing to acknowledge that he was incapable of controlling his own body.

The effort, however, was no match for the building pressure.

His entire body was stiff with a sharp, ruthless pleasure that was like fire in his loins. The beckoning climax was close. Too close.

Tossing pride by the wayside, he muttered a curse and grasped her hand, curling her fingers tightly around his shaft. He leaned forward to capture her lips as he pumped himself to a frenzied climax.

The world exploded, and for a breathless second Ian simply savored the taste of her satin lips and the heart-stopping sensation of her fingers stroking him to paradise.

Somewhere in the back of his mind, Ian knew with a chilling certainty that he would never, ever forget this exquisite moment in time. That the taste and scent and feel of this woman would be forever branded in his mind.

But for now he merely allowed himself to enjoy the shudders of delight that quaked through his body.

Barely aware of his actions, Ian stretched out on the mattress and urged Mercy down beside him. Then, with a tug of the blanket, he had them cocooned in welcome warmth.

No doubt he should have gathered a wet towel and washed the evidence of his climax from her tender skin, but he found himself unable to resist the need to hold her tightly in his arms as his lips brushed over her soft curls. Soon enough he would be forced to return to his cold bed. For now he merely desired to relish the strange peace that flooded through him.

A peace that was as unfamiliar as it was unexpected.

Snuggled against his side with her head tucked in the hollow of his shoulder, Mercy at last tilted her face upward to meet his slumberous gaze.

"Ian?"

"Yes, sweet Mercy?" he murmured, breathing deeply of her vanilla scent.

"Did I do something wrong?"

He jerked in genuine surprise. "God almighty, you could not have done it more right. Why would you ask such a ridiculous question?"

"You are very quiet."

"Ah." A slow smile curved his lips. "I was pondering a most astonishing discovery that I have made."

Her fingers absently trailed over his chest, her touch stirring the usual sparks as well as a most unusual contentment. As a rule he did not like having women stroke and cling to him after sex. It made him feel . . . trapped.

Mercy's touch, however, made him tug her even closer.

"And what discovery is that?" she demanded.

"I have always wondered if wood sprites possessed magic, and now I know. They are quite capable of bewitchment."

She gave a disbelieving click of her tongue. "Obviously you are still bosky."

"No." His finger slipped beneath her chin, his gaze holding hers captive. "I do not claim to comprehend what spell you have cast over me, but it is most certainly a potent one." He grimaced at the memory of his hand holding her fingers as she stroked him to orgasm. "So potent I cannot even regret that I have tutored a young, innocent virgin in pleasuring a man. No doubt the fact has lowered me yet another rung on my ladder to hell."

Her eyes darkened as she lifted her head to glare at him in annoyance. "And what is to be my punishment?"

"What do you mean?" Ian cautiously demanded. He knew he had blundered; he just didn't know how the blazes it had happened.

"If you are to burn in hell for conceding to my demands, then I can only wonder what purgatory is awaiting me."

He gave a shake of his head. Her father had done enough to manipulate this poor woman with a sense of guilt. He would not add to her burden.

"You are an innocent. There can be no blame for your—"

"I think I can decide where to place the blame, Mr. Breckford," she interrupted.

He lifted his brow. "Can you, Miss Simpson?"

"Yes, I can, and I choose to accept full responsibility for what has occurred."

His lips twitched. Good God, she was magnificent. A true original.

"I . . . see."

"Do not be patronizing," she snapped. "There has never been anything in my life that is entirely mine. I have been told what to think, how to behave, how to employ my every waking moment. I have even been told what my future will hold." She deliberately paused. "At least give me this."

Ian was momentarily caught off guard by her vehemence. It seemed ridiculous that she would be so determined to take blame for being seduced by a practiced rake. She was, after all, a complete innocent. Or rather she *had* been a complete innocent.

Then, as he gazed deep into those dark, severe eyes, he realized that she was quite sincere.

She needed to feel as if she were in command.

That he could understand. Having been born a bastard meant that his life had too often been filled with uncertainty and fear for his future. From his earliest days he had struggled to find the means to bring a measure of security to his world.

He had found that in Dunnington.

This woman was still searching for a means to overcome the constant dread of being bullied or manipulated or browbeaten into submission.

Dropping a tender kiss on her lips, Ian pulled back to regard her with a wry amusement.

"In that case I give you full responsibility, my sweet.

Indeed, I am beginning to suspect that I have been shamelessly coerced. You are fortunate that I am far too weary to be properly outraged."

She rolled her eyes at his teasing. "I doubt that there is a person born who could ever coerce you." She held up her hand as he gave a wicked lift of his brows, his fingers deliberately brushing over her naked back. "At least not against your will."

"You would be wrong, my sweet."

Her disbelief was tangible in the air. "Really?"

"Really." A pang of loss tugged at his heart. "I assure you that my old tutor Dunnington managed to lure me into hours of study with no more than a cut of the cards."

"Cut of the cards?"

"When I awoke in the morning, he would bet me that he could draw the higher card from the deck. If he won, I had to spend the day at my books. If I won, I could spend the day at the racetrack." His lips twisted in a reminiscent smile. "Do you know, now that I think back, I am quite certain the old fox cheated me. There is no reasonable way he could have drawn the highest card nearly every day."

"He sounds like a very dedicated tutor," she said softly.

"He was much more than a tutor. He was a father to me and the other young boys who attended his school."

She studied his expression as if searching for some elusive understanding of his complex personality.

"Your aunt mentioned that you were close with two of the other students."

"Oh yes. Raoul and Fredrick are my brothers." His sardonic expression returned. "The only family I have left now that Dunnington has passed."

"That is not true, Ian," she protested, her slender

hand returning to his chest to press directly over his heart. "You have a father, and an aunt who loves you very much."

With a growl, Ian cupped the back of her head to return it to the hollow of his shoulder.

"No, I will not have this moment spoiled with thoughts of my father."

"But—

"Shh, Mercy." He kissed away her looming lecture. "Let me hold you in my arms as you fall asleep. I promise to be gone by morn."

Chapter 8

He was as good as his word.

When Mercy woke the following morning, it was to discover her bed empty and all signs of his brief visit removed. Even the mattress and pillows had been smoothed with a skill only a true rake could employ. She might have thought that she had dreamed the entire glorious event if not for the fact she was perfectly naked beneath the covers.

Not for the first time, Mercy was grateful she had been steadfast in her refusal to accept Ella's insistence that she be attended by a maid. There did not seem to be a convenient lie that would explain her current state of undress. At least none that would satisfy a gossipy servant.

Quickly washing and attiring herself in a gown of pale ivory with Brussels lace about the hem, Mercy tugged her hair into a tidy knot and regarded her reflection in the mirror.

To her critical eye it appeared her lips were a bit swollen from Ian's kisses and her cheeks flushed with a lingering pleasure, but she was confident that there was no blatant evidence of her night of wicked delight.

With a tiny smile, she at last turned to leave her rooms.

She knew that she should be wracked by guilt. She had been raised to believe a woman's virtue was her dearest possession and that it had to be guarded with grim diligence. And while her virginity remained intact, she most certainly had lost a portion of her innocence.

What Mercy felt, however, was nothing remotely akin to guilt.

Last night had been . . . magical.

She had always suspected that passion between a man and woman could be a beautiful, powerful experience. Why else would history be filled with stories of love that altered the world? But she had not realized the sheer joy of being held in a man's arms as if he would never release her.

It was the intimacy that she hungered for. The comforting touch and soft teasing that was as much a part of the lovemaking as the actual act.

Or at least, it had been with Ian Breckford.

Mercy was not so naïve as to believe that every gentleman was willing or even capable of initiating her into the delights of desire with such tender care. Which was no small part of why she desired him to be her first lover.

For all his wicked reputation, she had easily sensed that he was a man who could be trusted. Not only with her body, but with her honor as well. She did not fear for a moment her name would be bandied about like so much rubbish.

And, of course, it did not hurt that he was gorgeous, sexy, and more charming than any man had a right to be.

With steps light enough to make her feel as if she could float on air, Mercy headed directly to the small parlor at the back of the house. As much as she longed to trail behind Ian Breckford as if she were a silly school-girl, she would never intrude into his time with Ella. The older woman cherished every moment she could have with her nephew.

They were all too rare.

She was seated at the delicate rosewood desk rearranging the seating for an upcoming luncheon when Ella swept into the room, filling the room with her enthusiastic energy. Mercy rose to her feet, hiding a wry smile.

Ian Breckford might have inherited his dark beauty directly from his father, but his powerful resolve was a gift from his aunt.

"There you are, Mercy." The older woman regarded her with a hint of curiosity. "Why did you not join me for breakfast?"

"I did not wish to interrupt your time with Mr. Breckford. I know how special his companionship is to you."

Ella reached out to pat her hand, her smile wistful. "Very thoughtful, my dear, but unnecessary. Ian left at the crack of dawn for Guildford."

"Oh." Mercy struggled to disguise her flare of shock. Ian left Rosehill? Without even a word to her? "Does he have business there?"

Ella shrugged. "He did not say."

Strolling to the window, Mercy gazed blindly down at the sunken garden that was just coming into bloom. A part of her knew that it was none of her concern. Ian was a grown gentleman who was perfectly free to come and go as he pleased. Certainly he had no duty to answer to her.

But even as she lectured herself on her ridiculous disappointment, a part of her could not help but dread the thought she might never see him again.

"But he intends to return?" she demanded, unable to halt the question.

Ella moved to stand beside Mercy at the window. "Well, he did leave behind his luggage, although he has been known to disappear and send later for his belongings. In truth, I believe his poor valet, who only arrived yesterday afternoon, spends most of his time traveling from one destination to another in a ceaseless effort to catch up with his master."

"I see."

The older woman reached out to take Mercy's hand, forcing her to turn and meet her narrowed gaze.

"Mercy?"

"Yes?"

"I hope . . ." She paused as if carefully considering her words. "I do hope that you will not allow your head to be turned by Ian's practiced flirtations. As much as I love him, he is not at all the sort of gentleman to be in the company of a young lady." She grimaced. "He cannot seem to help himself from seducing every woman who crosses his path, and I would not wish to see you become one of his heartbroken conquests."

On this occasion Mercy managed to disguise her reaction. Perhaps because Ella's warning was so absurdly unnecessary.

"I may not be a sophisticated lady of London, Ella, but I am capable of recognizing a hardened libertine," she said dryly.

"The danger to us poor women is not in recognizing a libertine, but in the fatal belief that we are the one to mend his wicked ways." Ella's expression hardened with an uncharacteristic bitterness, her eyes holding a distant light. "We always think that we can bring a rake to heel."

Mercy frowned, quite certain that the older woman was no longer speaking of Ian.

"Ella?" she said softly.

"'Tis nothing." With an obvious effort, Ella dismissed her unpleasant memory. "I am just worried for you, my dear."

"Well, do not worry." Mercy patted Ella's plump hand and offered a reassuring smile. "Even if I were foolish enough to believe that I could somehow bring a man such as Ian to heel, it would all be for naught. I cannot even think of marriage."

Ella appeared genuinely surprised at her words. "Why ever not?"

"You know that my parents have need of me, Ella," she reminded the woman. "It was difficult for them to allow me even this brief stay at Rosehill."

"Well, yes, certainly they have come to depend upon you, but surely they must understand that some-day you will wed and have your own family."

Turning on her heel, Mercy paced to the center of the room, the restless ache that had been temporarily eased by Ian's seduction returning with a biting vengeance.

"Actually, they are not at all convinced that I must wed. Indeed, they are quite insistent that I remain a spinster."

"But, my dear, that is grossly unfair."

"It is not a matter of being fair. It is my duty to care for them as they cared for me."

Ella's lips thinned, as if she were battling back words that were not entirely proper for a respectable lady. Then, drawing in a deep breath, she crossed to stand directly before Mercy.

"Certainly we all feel a duty to our families, but

that does not mean we are expected to give up our own lives."

"Have you not remained unwed to stay with your brother and act as his hostess?" she countered.

Ella gave a firm shake of her head. "No. As much as I love Norry, I would never have given up my dream of a family to remain at Rosehill. Unfortunately . . ."

"What is it, Ella?"

An ancient, profound pain darkened her eyes. "Unfortunately, I never received an offer to wed."

"Oh." A pang of sympathy squeezed Mercy's heart. She sensed that while Ella might not have received a proposal, there had been a gentleman that she desired to offer her one. "I am so sorry."

"I have reconciled myself to my fate." A wistful smile curved her lips. "But that does not mean that you should, Mercy. You deserve to have a home and a family that loves you."

Mercy gritted her teeth against the surge of frustration. Did Ella think that she had no regrets? That she was pleased to rot into a forgotten spinster in a lonely cottage?

"I have a family."

"If they truly loved you, they would be anxious to see you settled with a gentleman who adores you and will devote his life to seeing to your care."

A startling image of Ian flashed through her mind before Mercy was firmly squashing it. For heaven's sake, what was the matter with her? Ian possessed no interest in a wife and children. And even if he could be persuaded to become a respectable gentleman (well, at least a less disrespectable gentleman), she would be the last woman he would desire for a wife.

Not when he could have his pick of beautiful and no doubt wealthy young women.

"Is such a creature to be found?" she demanded, hoping her cheeks were not as hot as they felt.

Ella smiled wryly. "I have heard rumors of such."

"Actually, it seems to me that most women are settled with a gentleman who devotes himself to his own care and expects everyone around him to cater to his needs."

Ella lifted her brows. "You are far too young for such cynicism, my dear."

"It is not so much cynicism as observation." Mercy shrugged. "A small village does not possess secrets, not even to those who are only casual visitors."

"No doubt there are any number of unhappy marriages, but I refuse to believe that they are all miserable," Ella said, the eternal optimist. "There must be those who live in wedded bliss."

"Perhaps a rare few," Mercy conceded, thinking of her own parents, who lived more as bickering siblings than as man and wife.

"I think with the right gentleman you could find such bliss, Mercy," Ella said, reaching to pat Mercy's cheek. "Your heart is kind and generous and loyal. Precisely what men desire in a wife."

Mercy resisted the urge to sigh. She was not nearly so convinced that a gentleman cared a wit about a woman's heart, but it did not matter if he did.

"Well, since the only gentlemen about are Lord Norrington and Mr. Breckford, it appears that any hope for an offer of marriage is doomed to go unfulfilled."

"Yes." Ella grimaced, thankfully diverted by Mercy's light teasing. "It is a pity about Ian. If only he were not such a determined rake and gamester, he would be perfect for you."

Mercy could not prevent her abrupt laugh. "I doubt he would share your opinion, Ella."

The older woman merely smiled. "Who is to say?"

Mercy bit back her instinctive denial. When the older woman had a notion set in her mind, she could be remarkably stubborn. Instead, she sought to take advantage of the discomforting conversation. After all, it was Ella who had introduced Ian as a subject.

"I understand that Mr. Breckford is not close to his father," she said, her voice carefully impassive. "Is there a particular reason for the estrangement?"

Ella paused, her fingers lifting to absently tug at the string of pearls about her neck.

"I fear that Norry never knew quite what to do with a boisterous young boy who was forever underfoot and in constant demand of his attention. It was easier for him to retreat to the peace of his conservatory than to try and find some means of communicating with the unruly scamp." She heaved a deep sigh. "And perhaps, I own some share of the blame."

"Now that I refuse to believe," Mercy protested. "I know how much you adore him."

"Yes, and it broke my heart to see him feeling shunned by his father." The older woman heaved a deep sigh. "So of course I spoiled him unbearably. He learned at a far too early age that he could manipulate women with a dimpled smile and a bit of charm. Perhaps if I had been—"

"Ella, you are being absurd," Mercy interrupted, her expression stern. "Mr. Breckford is obviously an intelligent, successful gentleman who is envied by all of society. What more would you have of him?"

"I would have him with a devoted wife and a dozen

children running about his house. Perhaps a silly wish for a man such as Ian."

Mercy discovered that she did not care for the image of Ian happily wed with a pack of children. Oh, it was not that she would ever wish him to be miserable or alone. It was just . . .

It was just that she was an utter fool, she severely chastised herself.

"If he is happy with his life, then surely that is all that matters."

"Yes, I suppose." Ella gave a disapproving click of her tongue. "That is, if he *is* happy."

The memory of Ian's very, very happy expression as she had squeezed her fingers around his manhood threatened to rise to mind. Swallowing a small squeak of alarm, Mercy cut off the thought before she could cause Ella even more suspicion.

"Would you like to see the seating arrangement for the Wounded Soldiers Charity Luncheon? I believe I have most of the guests settled, but I would like your opinion on Squire McKnight's wife. She is always so difficult to please."

As hoped, Ella was immediately distracted. There were few things that could get the older woman's blood to a fevered pitch more than the mention of her treacherous adversary. There was nothing quite so frightening as two rival hostesses in full-scale battle.

"Good Lord, the woman is a plague and a pestilence. If it were not for her very generous donation, I would seat her in the nearest privy." Hooking her arm through Mercy's, Ella tugged her toward the rosewood desk. "Come along, my dear, and let us see how we can manage to place the woman so she is not allowed to entirely ruin our meal with her evil tongue."

* * *

The bookstore was precisely the same as every other bookstore that Ian had ever entered (not that there had been many). The air was ripe with mildew and the scent of aged leather, while the endless stacks of books threatened to topple and crush the unwary. Even worse, there was a thick layer of shadows cloaking the long room that made a suspicious man wonder what was hiding among the dusty shelves.

On this afternoon, however, Ian had a pleasant purpose for his visit, and, ignoring his natural distaste for his surroundings, he concentrated on the wiry gentleman with a ferret countenance and threadbare coat. His brows lifted as his gaze lowered to the badly patched leather shoes. Obviously peddling books did not offer a particularly luxurious existence. A knowledge that Ian tucked away.

"The Byzantine Empire, you say?" the ferret-faced man demanded, dry-washing his hands as his gaze darted about the cramped shop.

"Yes, any books that you feel are written by a reputable scholar."

"I do have a few in the back," he said, his expression one of wary apology. "I fear that it is not a subject that is often requested."

A small smile touched Ian's mouth. Of course his wood sprite would choose an obscure empire to study. Her tiny rebellions were all that kept her magnificent spirit from being crushed.

His smile threatened to fade at the memory of her soft yet poignant confession of a future filled with nothing but cold duty. What sort of parents would make such a demand of their only child? And to do so in the name of love?

The devil take them, it was entirely their fault that Mercy had been driven into the arms of a renowned rake. If they had allowed her to have the normal flirtations of a young lady, she would no doubt be properly wed with a pack of children. Certainly she would not be so desperate for intimacy that she would put herself at such risk.

Not that he was blameless, he wryly acknowledged.

Despite his promise to ignore her blatant offers, he had given into lust readily enough. Why else had he gone to her chambers when he had been bosky and incapable of denying his need? Still, he found his guilty conscience was not enough to dim the fierce pleasure he had found in her arms.

Or the realization that he intended to be in her arms once again.

Suddenly aware that his thoughts had drifted, Ian cleared his throat and met the worried gaze of the bookseller.

"No, I suppose not."

Seeming to take heart in Ian's absent agreement, the man cleared his throat. "Now, the Roman Empire or even the Ottoman . . . well, they were great moments in history."

"Perhaps, but my interest lies in the Byzantine. Do you have anything?"

"Yes. Yes, of course." With a nervous step, the bookseller headed toward one of the distant shelves. "If you will just come this way?"

With a grimace at the dust that was bound to ruin the gloss on his boots, Ian obediently followed the man to the distant shelves, inwardly wondering how the devil anyone could make sense of the haphazard shelves and stacks of books that nearly consumed the narrow shop. The place would be a good deal improved by a tinder and spark as far as Ian was concerned.

Coming to the shelf against the back wall, the bookseller bent down to peer at titles that were nearly obscured by thick layers of grime.

"Is there a particular interest that you have in the Byzantines?" he demanded.

"Anything related will do, although I would be very pleased if you could dredge up anything regarding the Empress Theodora."

The man blinked in an owlish fashion. "You want to read of a woman?"

Ian peered down the long length of his nose. Of course he did not bloody well want to read of the woman, but Mercy did and he would not have her interest derided by anyone.

"Hardly an ordinary woman."

The man paled at Ian's soft, dangerous tone. "No. No, I suppose she was not."

"And really, what could be more fascinating than to research our fairer sex?" he pressed, not at all certain why he was bothered by this twit's badly hidden disdain for Empress Theodora and the Byzantine Empire. "Some would claim that a wise gentleman would make it his life's purpose."

"Oh . . . quite." The man swallowed and with hasty movements gathered three books from the shelf and straightened. "Here we are, then. Allow me to wrap them. They are rather dusty, and I would not have you ruin your attire."

Ian smiled sardonically as the man made a hasty dash toward the counter at the front of the store. The poor man seemed oddly terrified at having an actual customer within his walls. Or perhaps it was Ian who terrified him.

"Thank God," he muttered as he made his way at a much more dignified pace.

Wrapping the books in brown paper and tying it with string, the man handed the bundle to Ian and managed a tepid smile.

"Will there be anything else, sir?"

"Yes." Ian reached beneath his jacket for his leather purse. "Could you direct me to the Swan's Nest?"

"The Swan's Nest?"

Ian frowned at the man's startled expression. "I believe that was the name. There is such a pub, is there not?"

"Oh, certainly. 'Tis east of the big castle near the Wey River, but it is not at all the sort of place for a gentleman of quality." The bookseller shuddered with delicate horror. "Nothing but ruffians and gin swills gather there. You would be far more comfortable to find a nice tavern on Stag Hill."

Ian gave a sharp bark of laughter. "I appreciate your concern, but since I have always been more a ruffian than gentleman of quality I can only presume I shall feel quite at home at the Swan's Nest." Opening his small purse, he pulled out a handful of notes and tossed them onto the counter. "Here you are. I hope this will be enough to cover the cost of the books and the trouble of digging them from obscurity."

His companion momentarily struggled to breathe at the sight of Ian's generosity.

"Yes, sir," he rasped. "Very kind of you, I must say."

"If you hear of any other books to be found regarding the Byzantine Empire, I would appreciate you sending word to me."

"Yes. Yes, of course. It would be my pleasure."

Ian hid a smile. He was a true gambler, who never overbid his hand. With just a few pounds he had ensured that this poor bookseller would scour the shops from here to London in search of more books to please him. Meaning Ian had seen the last of musty shops.

"You can send your message to Rosehill Estate."

The owlish eyes widened. "Lord Norrington's home?"

"Yes, are you acquainted?"

"Oh my, no." The man was shocked by the mere suggestion. "At least not personally. It is only that I have heard that he possesses one of the finest libraries in all of Surrey. You are extraordinarily fortunate to have access to such bounty."

The memory of a lonely little boy sitting in the middle of that vast library hoping to catch a glimpse of a father who never appeared flashed through his mind before he could savagely thrust it aside.

"Oh yes, my fortune is quite extraordinary," he muttered, tucking the books beneath his arm. "If you will excuse me?"

"Good day to you, sir."

Chapter 9

Leaving the bookstore, Ian stashed his treasure in his saddlebag and urged his horse down High Street. It was not a difficult task to catch sight of the crumbling ruin of a castle on the hill south of him. Although it had once been a royal residence for Henry III, it was now little more than a shell that spoke of grander days.

Angling toward the river, he ignored the assessing stares from the local merchants and the ragged boys who followed him from the shadows of the narrow alleys. They would soon discover he was no addlepated dandy should any of them be foolish enough to attempt to cull him. He was as comfortable in the gutter as he was in the finest drawing rooms of Mayfair.

At last discovering the whitewashed pub tucked between a butcher shop and blacksmith, Ian rode through the stone arch that led to the inner courtyard and allowed one of the numerous young urchins to take the reins. Vaulting from the saddle, Ian paused long enough to whisper a word of warning into the lad's ear before striding across the cobblestones to the door of the pub.

He had no fear that his mount might mysteriously

disappear during his brief stay. Not when the boy was quite convinced that Ian would hunt him to the pits of hell if the animal were not treated as royalty.

Pushing open the heavy wooden door, Ian was prepared for the rank scent of stale ale and smoke. He didn't even flinch at the oppressive noise of the dozen roughly dressed men who filled the tables. It was all a great deal more familiar than his elegant, cold chambers at Rosehill.

With a firm step and hard gaze that warned he was not to be trifled with, he headed toward the windows that overlooked the road. His gaze scanned the tables until he caught sight of the silver-haired man with a pronounced stoop and weathered countenance.

Although it had been years since he had last seen Tolson, there was no mistaking the faded blue eyes that twinkled with kind amusement or the ears that stuck out like bat wings.

He had worked in the gardens of Rosehill for nearly forty years, first as an under-gardener and then head gardener before retiring to live with his oldest daughter in Guildford. If anyone were to know of his father's hidden sins, it was this man.

The question, of course, was whether or not he was willing to share those sins.

Tolson was one of the few people in the entire world that Viscount Norrington truly respected. The two had spent hours together as his father's vision for his extensive gardens was slowly realized. The old servant's loyalty was unquestionable.

Ian could only hope that the man could be lured into revealing some hint of past scandals.

Reaching the table, Ian took his seat and smiled as the older man inspected him with a fond gaze.

"Why, if it ain't little Ian, as I live and breathe," Tolson murmured, shoving aside his tankard of ale.

Ian gave a soft chuckle. "Not so little anymore, Tolson."

"Ach, well, I will always think of you as that scrawny brat who was up to some mischief or another."

Ian's smile widened. Unlike his father, this man had always encouraged Ian's reckless adventures, even going so far as to assist in hiding the evidence of his mishaps when necessary. Ian would never forget his kindness.

"I fear that I may have grown in stature, but my habit of finding trouble has not changed. I seem to manage it with remarkable ease."

Tolson waved a hand gnarled by years of hard work. "Only natural for a young man of high spirits. Never trusted those pious souls who are always spouting the evil of others." The man turned his head to spit on the floor. "More often than not they have done deeds that would turn your hair white."

"Somehow I doubt that my father would agree with you, old friend." Ian smoothly directed the conversation in the desired direction. "He would have far preferred a son with more piety and less of the devil in his soul."

The blue eyes softened with a ready sympathy. "Never you mind, son. Lord Norrington is a good man, but there are some that have no liking for children. 'Tis not their nature to be comfortable around young uns."

Ian struggled against his surge of frustration. Why the devil did everyone always rush to acquit his father of blame, as if he had no control over treating his only child like an unwelcome intruder into his home?

"Then it begs the question of why he would have brought me to Rosehill at all," he said, his voice bitter. "I am just a bastard. He could easily have dumped me in an orphanage, or, if he was squeamish of having Norrington blood mixed among the filth, he could have handed me over to one of his endless tenants. With the promise of a few quid, any of them would have been pleased to take me in."

The old gardener heaved a rueful sigh. "The master has always been very particular in his notion of duty. Especially when it comes to his family."

Duty. A word he was beginning to hate.

"Yes, that is true enough." With an effort, Ian gathered his composure. The devil take him. He was no longer a five-year-old to pout when his father forgot his birthday. "You knew him as a youth, did you not?"

"Oh aye." A reminiscent smile curved Tolson's lips. "He was no more than eight or nine when I became an under-gardener at Rosehill. Even then he knew the name of every flower that was planted and how they should be cared for." He chuckled at an ancient memory. "More than once I thought MacFinney, the old head gardener, would throttle the lad. He didn't like to have the boy know more of his job than he did."

Ian could just imagine. His father was as stubborn as a mule when it came to his flowers, and he never suffered fools gladly. Poor old MacFinney had no doubt felt besieged by a toddler.

"But you did not mind his companionship?" he teased, earning a wistful smile from the older man.

"Nay." Tolson scrubbed his fingers through his short gray hair. "He was a quiet and rather shy lad. And to be blunt, I felt sorry for him. He was terrified of his father, the previous viscount, poor little bloke. I can't say how often I found him hiding in the hedge maze to avoid being noticed. I didn't mind keeping me lips closed when there was a search made for the boy." He pointed a finger toward Ian. "Just as I kept me lips closed when you tossed a rock through the parlor window."

Ian gave a shout of laughter as he recalled the gardener's steadfast refusal to confess who had shattered the window.

"I will have you know that I did not toss that rock. I hit it with my cricket bat," he corrected with a pretense of wounded pride.

Tolson snorted. "Mayhaps, but the window was shattered just the same." Tilting his head to the side, the old man regarded Ian with a knowing gaze. "Why did you wish to meet with me, son? It can't be to recall long-gone days."

Ian arched a brow, caught off guard by the man's perception. Obviously age had not dimmed his shrewd mind.

"Could it not be that I wished to visit with one of the few people who made my life in Surrey bearable?" he demanded.

"Could be, but 'tis not." Folding his arms on the warped wooden table, Tolson leaned forward. "Tell me what you would have of me, Ian."

Ian gestured for the barkeep, ordering ale to give himself the opportunity to consider his answer. Awaiting the tankard, Ian at last drew in a deep breath.

"I recently lost a very dear friend, and I suppose it has made me reminiscent," he said slowly, his words not a precise lie. "I felt the need to return to Rosehill and heal some of the wounds of the past. Unfortunately, time has not eased the strain between myself and my father. I hoped if I knew more of what made him so . . . distant, I might be capable of bridging the gap between us."

Tolson clicked his tongue and reached to pat Ian's arm. His gentle soul could not abide the thought of anyone being unhappy. It was a weakness that Ian felt a surprising pang of guilt in exploiting.

"'Tis not your fault. As I said, his lordship was never intended for children."

"Because of his own father?" he demanded, refusing to waver despite his odd unease.

"In part, although he never expressed a desire to wed or produce offspring even as he grew into a man."

Ian shrugged. "Perhaps some maiden broke his heart and he still pines for her."

Tolson pondered the question a long moment. "If that is so, he kept the maiden a secret. It did not matter how many ladies the old viscount would invite to Rosehill, your father refused to dance attendance upon any of them." The old man grimaced. "Not that I entirely blame him. Can't be pleasant to be paraded before a crowd of mares like a stallion on the block."

"Or perhaps he simply preferred the sort of woman he could tumble and leave behind," Ian pointed out as he thought of his own mother. "He no doubt cut a swathe of destruction among the female servants."

"Nay." Tolson appeared genuinely shocked. "He was never like many nobs who thought any woman forced to become a servant was easy prey. The maids were always happy to serve at Rosehill."

"My mother is proof that he had interest, if only transitory, in at least some maids."

The blue eyes held something perilously close to pity. "It could be he cared for her, Ian," he said softly. "The heart can be a fickle thing."

Ian was suddenly struck by the memory of his father's tender expression as he confessed his love for Ian's mother. He had seemed so . . . sincere.

Christ. Could it be that the man had never wed

because he was still in love with the woman who had given birth to Ian?

With an unwitting shake of his head, Ian accepted that there was nothing more to be discovered with his current questioning. If his father's secret had something to do with a woman, it was so well-concealed not even his most loyal servant knew of it.

Obviously it was time to change tactics.

"As you say," he murmured. "What of his acquaintances? I assume that he must have possessed some friends as a youth?"

"Not many." Turning his head, Tolson regarded the pedestrians that cluttered the narrow street. For the moment, an inviting sunshine spilled over the town, encouraging the citizens to be about their business before the inevitable rain returned. "As I said, he was a solitary sort, preferring the gardens to the local gatherings. But there was one . . . Ach, what was his name?" Tolson wrinkled his brow as he struggled to shift through his memories. At last he gave a snap of his fingers and turned back to Ian. "Summerville, that was it."

The name meant nothing to Ian. "Is he a neighbor?"

"Nay, an old school chum who used to spend his school vacations at Rosehill." The old man chuckled. "Two peas in a pod, they were. Nigh on inseparable for years."

Ian choked back a disbelieving laugh. The mere thought of his father being a young boy with a devoted friend dashing about the frozen marble of Rosehill was as absurd as him picking up a shovel to make an honest living.

"I have never heard my father mention this Summerville," he murmured.

"Ah, well, your grandfather took a dislike to him.

Never understood it myself. Seemed like a decent enough young man, always polite and well-behaved, but the old man did take queer starts. One day he simply had the boy's bags packed and ordered him from Rose-hill." Tolson shook his head, a sadness rippling over his weathered features. "Of all the disappointments your father suffered, I believe that affected him the most deeply."

Well, this was a bit more promising. Did the two lads hock the family silver to pay their gambling debts? Had they used the picture gallery for target practice? Did they murder old MacFinney and bury his body in the rose garden?

Ian leaned forward, his eyes narrowed.

"And you have no notion of why he was banned? Did he lure my father into some mischief?"

"Not that was spoken of." The old man paused as the barkeep returned to slap two tankards of ale on the table. "So far as I know, his lordship simply took a dislike to the boy and ordered him from the estate."

Ian lifted the tankard, grimacing at the bitter drink that slid down his throat.

"My grandfather sounds like a rotter."

Toslon grimaced before he could disguise his reaction to the previous viscount.

"He did have a nasty temper and a habit of bullying those who sought to stand against him." He shuddered. "Not an easy man."

Ian battled that unwelcome sympathy for his father. Damn, he did not want to imagine Norrington as a frightened boy cowering in the garden to escape his father's wrath. He was here for a purpose. A purpose that was growing increasingly difficult to recall.

"Do you know where this Summerville lived?" he forced himself to demand.

Tolson took a swig from his tankard, obviously immune to the bitter dregs that soured Ian's stomach.

"From London, I believe." He wiped the foam from his lips with his threadbare sleeve. "His family had no lands, although I believe they were wealthy enough."

Ian frowned. "Were they Cits?"

"The word was not used in my hearing, but . . ."

"But it might have been something my grandfather discovered and held against this Summerville?"

"Aye." The gardener shrugged. "He was proud enough to be offended by those who smelled of the shop. It was all a very long time ago."

Ian heaved a sigh. It was becoming obvious that Tolson either had no notion of the scandal that had caused his father to pay Dunnington to keep silent or was refusing to confess the truth.

Either way, there was little point in beating a dead carcass.

"Yes, it was," he grudgingly conceded. "Let us turn our attention to the present. Tell me how you go on."

It was near an hour later before Ian could politely excuse himself and leave the pub.

Stupidly he found himself anxious to return to Rosehill as he gathered his horse and urged the restless mount into a steady trot. It was a sensation that was as astonishing as it was unexpected. Certainly he had never experienced it before.

Then again, Rosehill had never before been graced with a beautiful, magical wood sprite, a tiny voice whispered in the back of his mind.

He cursed his treacherous thoughts as his body instantly stiffened with need. The journey was bound to be long enough without adding in the discomfort of being fully erect as he bounced over the rutted paths.

Despite her best attempts, Mercy could not entirely shake her sense of lethargy throughout the long day.

It was absurd. Beyond ridiculous. And utterly annoying.

Why should the absence of a gentleman she had just met make the day seem a bit duller and her studies a bit less intriguing?

Good heavens, this time at Rosehill was a dream come true. It was her one and only opportunity to exploit her love for learning and perhaps, if she were very fortunate, even have her work published by a London journal.

Until Ian Breckford's arrival, her stay had been a source of endless pleasure. There had not been a moment she had not savored.

Now . . .

Damn. Now she wanted more.

Aggravated more by her treacherous emotions than by Ian's absence, Mercy forced herself to choose a gown in bright yellow muslin. It was plainly made with only a bit of lace about the hem and a satin ribbon threaded through the bodice, but it always managed to make her feel less drab.

She was just finishing tugging her hair into a simple bun atop her head when she heard the door to her room open and close. With a frown at the unexpected intrusion, she rose from the dressing table and turned to regard the tall, achingly handsome gentleman.

Her heart came to a complete, perfect halt as she caught sight of Ian's stunning beauty enhanced by the black jacket and silver waistcoat. Good . . . Lord. It should be a sin for a man to exude such wicked temptation. A poor maid simply had no chance.

She barely noticed the large package he dropped onto the bed as he prowled forward, his lithe body moving with a fluid ease. All she could think was that he had returned. He had not abandoned her after all.

Well, that was not *all* she could think of.

There was a most disturbing image of rushing forward to rip the clothes off that hard male body and running her hands over his smooth chest.

"Ian." She battled against the jolt of lust that nearly sent her to her knees. "I thought . . ."

He arched a dark brow as he halted directly before her. "Yes?"

She unwittingly licked her dry lips, her breath catching as his brooding gaze watched the telltale movement with a smoldering intensity.

"I thought perhaps you had decided to leave Rosehill."

"I did leave for a few hours." A sudden comprehension brought a faint frown to his brow. "You thought I might not return?"

Mercy attempted to steady her breath. Just having this man near was enough to set her every nerve on fire. It was . . . unsettling, to say the least.

"Ella did mention that you do on occasion slip away without warning."

For some reason her words seemed to annoy her companion. "And you thought that I would leave you without even saying a word."

She blinked at his flat, accusing tone. "It is not as if you owe me—"

Without warning, Mercy was hauled roughly against

Ian's hard body, his mouth claiming hers in a kiss of sheer possession.

Mercy's lashes floated downward as his tongue gently parted her lips to dip inside and stir her willing desire. He tasted of fresh air and heat and sheer male ambrosia. Melting pleasure pulsed through her blood, her body arching in silent encouragement as his hands stroked down her back to grasp her hips.

For timeless moments they remained lost in the wonder of the passionate kiss. Then, with obvious reluctance, Ian pulled back to regard her with a glittering gaze.

"Miss Mercy Simpson, I may be all kinds of a scoundrel, but I do not seduce innocents and then sneak away like a thief in the night," he said huskily.

A combination of joy and aggravation surged through her at his low confession. Joy that he would not leave her without at least a proper good-bye, and aggravation that he would not accept that she was a grown woman who was perfectly capable of taking responsibility for her own choices.

"You did not seduce me," she protested.

His lips curled in a wicked smile. "Very well. Then I do not sneak away after being thoroughly and wondrously compromised. Especially not when there might be the faintest chance that I might be compromised again. For that I would wait a very . . ." His head lowered to touch his lips to the pulse just below her ear. "Very . . ." His mouth nibbled a line down the curve of her throat. "Long time."

Mercy was forced to grasp his arms as her legs threatened to give way. She was vividly aware of the hard press of his body and the rising evidence of his arousal. Just as she was aware of the tempting bed only a few feet away.

She wanted him to throw her onto that mattress and cover her with his lean form. She wanted to drown in the feel of his hands stroking over her body. She wanted him to fill that empty ache that was blooming between her legs.

Ian groaned, his fingers digging into her hips as if he could actually sense her explosive reaction.

And perhaps he could, she fuzzily acknowledged. She felt as if she were going up in flames. It was a wonder the entire room was not scorched.

It was only when his mouth had stroked a searing path down her bodice to linger upon the slight swell of her breast that she realized they were rushing toward a perilous point of no return.

A thought that might send a tremor of exquisite excitement down her spine but was hardly feasible when dinner would be served within the quarter hour.

Forcing herself to press her hands against his chest, Mercy arched back to dislodge his distracting mouth.

"Ian, we are expected downstairs," she protested, her voice so thick she barely recognized it.

His lids were half lowered as he swept a slumberous gaze over her modest neckline.

"Do you suppose they would miss us?"

Her stomach clenched with a biting need. Now was not the time, but perhaps later . . .

Please, please let there be a later.

"Not me, but you would be conspicuously absent," she murmured. "There might even be a search launched."

"Highly doubtful. Still, I suppose I must be patient. Not one of my finer talents, I fear." With a deep sigh, Ian allowed his hands to drop and strolled toward the bed. Perching on the edge of the mattress next to the small package, he leaned back on his arms and regarded her with a gleaming gaze. "Are you not the least curious about what I have brought to you?"

Mercy blinked in genuine surprise. "It is for me?"

"Of course."

"What is it?"

"A gift."

She gave a slow shake of her head, bafflement warring with pleasure. "But why?"

The dark eyes narrowed in confusion. "Does there have to be a reason? Can it not simply be because I desired to please you?"

Realizing that her response was swiftly stealing Ian's pleasure, Mercy ruefully smiled and moved to stand beside the bed.

"I am sorry. It is just that I have never had anyone but my parents give me a gift."

His expression lightened. "Then perhaps you are unaware that when someone gives you a gift, you are supposed to open it," he teased.

With unsteady hands she reached out to tug off the string and pull the wrapper open. She was not certain what she expected. Some pretty trinket perhaps. What she discovered instead had her abruptly sitting on the edge of the bed as her hand reached out with reverent care.

"Oh . . ." She lifted one of the leather-bound books to discover it was a history of the wars of Justinian. The second concentrated upon the building of Constantinople, and the last . . . a personal account of Empress Theodora. "Oh."

"Take care, they are dusty," Ian warned.

They could have been covered in feathers and tar and

not taken away the smallest iota of Mercy's pleasure. Never in her entire life had she received such a priceless treasure.

"These are for me?" she breathed in wonderment. "To keep as my own?"

"For your very own." Ian brushed a tender finger over her cheek, his features oddly softened as he studied her flushed countenance. "The beginnings of any great library must start somewhere."

She gave a slow shake of her head, her heart squeezing with a near-painful emotion.

"I do not know what to say. They are perfect."

He smiled into her wide eyes. "Are you not going to examine them and assure yourself they are not the work of a worthless hack?"

"Oh, no. I want to save them for when I return home. I cannot tell you how much pleasure they will give to me." She paused as she realized he was regarding her with a strangely arrested expression. "What?"

"There are moments when your beauty astonishes me," he whispered.

Her breath caught and lodged in her throat. "I am not beautiful."

"You are without a doubt one of the loveliest women I have ever gazed upon," he countered, his eyes holding a hint of bemusement, as if he were as caught off guard by his peculiar mood as she was. "But I speak of a beauty beyond the physical. Your purity is . . . intoxicating to my black soul."

"Your soul is not black." On impulse she reached up to touch a raven curl that had fallen onto his brow, her senses savoring the thick, silky texture. "I think you could be a good man, Ian Breckford, if only you were not so determined to be bad."

His lips twisted. "Ah, but being bad is so much more fun, is it not, sweet Mercy?"

"Only when we do not hurt others," she said, a blush staining her cheeks.

"And that is where we are different, I fear."

"Not so different as you wish to believe," she persisted, holding his gaze as her fingers skimmed over his brow. "Perhaps someday you will discover the truth for yourself."

"Not bloody likely, my sweet, but if you wish to believe the best in me, then who am I to disabuse your fantasy?"

She clicked her tongue, knowing that beneath the hard surface this was a man of honor and compassion. A man who would understand that a stack of musty books would be a treasure beyond the finest diamond to a lonely spinster.

"You are too hard on yourself."

His sharp crack of laughter echoed through the room. "Good God, you are the first to ever make such an absurd claim. If you were to travel to London, I can assure you that the citizens would tell you that I am a wicked, self-indulgent bastard who cares only for my own pleasure."

"Because that is all you allow them to see."

There was a pause before his chest expanded as he sucked in a deep breath.

"And what of you, sweet Mercy? What do you see?"

The words seemed torn from his lips, and Mercy smiled gently, knowing that her answer mattered more than he would ever admit.

"A gentleman who pretends to care about nothing because he cares too deeply about everything," she said with soft honesty.

Abrubtly, he surged off the bed to stride toward the window. It was almost as if she had scraped a nerve too raw to bear.

"Well, that is truly the most convoluted sentence it has ever been my privilege to hear," he drawled in mocking tones.

Mercy refused to be put off by his defensive response. This man had been wounded on too many occasions to easily allow another close. Not even a woman who was no more than a passing diversion that would be forgotten the moment he returned to London.

"I may not possess the proper words, but I do possess the proper understanding," she said, rising to her feet to study the tense line of his shoulders. "I know what it is like to try and hide your feelings behind a mask. There are times when it is so smothering you just want to open the window and scream."

For a moment she thought she had pressed him too far. The lines of his profile were harsh, his hands gripping the frame of the window until his knuckles turned white. Then, without warning, the stiffness seemed to leave his lithe body, as if he had been pleasantly distracted by a new thought.

"Why do you remain?" he abruptly demanded.

Mercy frowned in confusion at the abrupt shift in conversation.

"I have told you why."

"What if there was another choice?" Slowly he turned to stab her with a glittering gaze. "What if your future was not set in stone?"

"What do you mean?"

"There is a world beyond Surrey, you know. You could come to London."

She stiffened in shock. "You must be jesting."

With a shrug, he moved forward, his gaze never wavering from her baffled expression.

"Why should I jest?"

"I do not have the funds or the means to travel to London, even if I were willing to leave my parents on their own, which I most certainly am not."

Halting directly before her, Ian gently outlined her lips with the tip of his finger.

"You would have nothing to fret about, sweet Mercy," he crooned. "I would see to whatever needs you might possess, including the hire of servants to care for your parents."

"You—" She broke off her words as a sharp, incredulous realization slammed into her. "Dear God, are you asking me to become your mistress?"

"You have revealed that you do not find my advances utterly repulsive, and we seem to enjoy one another's companionship outside the bed." He smiled, oblivious to the fury that was beginning to flow through her blood with a dangerous force. "It seems a logical decision."

Slapping away his hand, Mercy took a deliberate step backward.

"Logical?"

At last wariness touched his obscenely beautiful face. "Yes."

"Perhaps for you, but certainly not for me."

"Why ever not?"

His genuine puzzlement only fueled her temper.

Could he be so insufferably stupid that he would presume her a woman without morals just because she was willing to enjoy his touch? That she was willing to sell her virtue because she had found joy in sharing their passion?

Or was he simply so terrified of any genuine feelings

that he was determined to reduce their fragile relationship to a tawdry business deal?

Angling her chin to a militant angle, she gathered her dignity about her like a coat of armor.

"Because I do not trade my body for money, Mr. Breckford."

His brows snapped together, genuine outrage flashing through his eyes. "I asked you to become my mistress, not my whore."

"And precisely what is the difference, pray tell?" she snapped. "You implied you intended to pay my bills while sharing my bed. What is that but exchanging my body for money?"

His nose flared as he studied her with a rising annoyance. "So you would share my bed but not accept my protection?"

She was saved from a response as the echo of a distant bell filled the house. Spinning on her heel, she headed for the door, her body so tense that she feared she might shatter at the slightest touch.

Reaching for the knob, she was halted by Ian's soft, dangerous voice.

"Mercy . . . This conversation is not done."

She did not bother to turn. "Ian, if you have even the least regard for me, you will never, ever bring up this conversation again."

Chapter 10

Well, he managed to make a stunning ass of himself, Ian acknowledged as he sat across the table from a silently furious Mercy. What the devil had happened to the renowned Casanova, a gentleman toasted throughout London as having a magical ability to seduce even the most elusive of women?

Anyone could be excused for thinking he possessed all the skills of an overanxious greenhorn.

Of course, it was not entirely his fault. The wench managed to befuddle him in a manner that went against all reason. One moment she was a wide-eyed ingénue making him feel like a conquering hero as she sighed over the dusty books he had offered, and the next she was as wise as a sage as she touched his deepest vulnerabilities.

It was little wonder he had mucked up his offer of protection when his head had been spinning and his chest so tight he could barely breathe.

No, not just mucked it up, he silently corrected.

He had made a complete shambles of the entire affair.

Christ, he could not have offended the woman

more deeply if he had tossed a handful of coins in her face and told her to spread her legs.

Studying her grim features as she toyed with her lobster in butter sauce, Ian felt a stab of rueful regret.

A tiny voice in the back of his mind warned he should just cut his losses and move on. After all, he had not come to Rosehill in search of a mistress. Why should he? London was littered with females who were vastly more talented in pleasing a gentleman than a virginal spinster with a vicar for a father. Nothing good could come of panting after her like a dog in heat.

Unfortunately, it was a voice that Ian found all too easy to ignore.

Instead he allowed his aunt's bright chatter and his father's occasional grunts to wash over him as he brooded upon the best means of repairing the damage he had unwittingly caused.

A thing easier said than done.

Throughout the interminable dinner she refused to so much as glance in his direction. Ironic considering that only the previous evening he had done his best to ignore her.

Of course in his case it was sheer defense against her potent enchantment during his brief struggle with nobility, while she was in a full-fledged snit. A snit that was in no way diminished by the beef in burgundy sauce or exquisite raspberry tart.

At last Ella rose to her feet, motioning for Mercy to follow her from the room. Ian watched their retreat with a self-derisive flare of amusement.

He was a master in the game of seduction. His heated glance could gain the key to a seasoned widow's bedchamber, and a mere kiss on the fingers could cause a debutante to swoon. Hell, women had come to blows over who would be seated next to him at dinner.

Now he was being given the cut direct by a tiny slip of a woman who had never had so much as a *beau*. And instead of being outraged, he was . . .

The devil take it all, he was bewitched.

And more determined than ever to return her to his arms.

Rising to his feet, Ian watched Mercy's retreat, his gaze riveted to the soft sway of her hips. The mere sight was enough to make him as hard as granite.

On the point of following in the wake of the tempting minx, Ian was halted as his father cleared his throat and waved toward the hovering footman.

"A moment, Ian. I thought we would share a port before joining the ladies."

Ian blinked, barely capable of hiding his shock. His father had never requested they linger after dinner. Hell, the man was usually bolting for the nearest door before the last serving could cool on his plate.

Just for a moment he was gripped with a stark frustration. He needed to speak with Mercy. Now. The longer she allowed her resentment to smolder, the more difficult it would be to convince her that he had intended no insult.

It was the unwelcome voice of reason that halted his impetuous flight. Dammit. He had come to Surrey to discover the truth behind his legacy, not chase after Miss Mercy Simpson.

This was an opportunity he would be a fool to squander.

"Of course," he at last forced himself to mutter, taking his seat as the footman poured two glasses of the spirit.

There was a strained silence before his father cleared his throat. "Cigar?"

"No, I thank you." Ian sipped the port as he covertly studied his father's tense profile. Whatever the older man's reason for requesting Ian to linger, it was obvious he was now at a loss as to how to actually converse with his son. Ian would have to take command of the awkward situation. "I traveled to Guildford today," he said, taking the bull firmly by the horns.

"Did you?" Norrington managed a stiff smile. "A rather tedious journey for you, I should think. There is not much there to tempt a young gentleman."

"It cannot compare to London, of course, but I did manage to find a few shops of interest, and surprisingly I ran across an old friend."

"Really? That actor friend of yours?"

Ian gave a startled bark of laughter. "Thank God, no. Raoul Charlebois nearly created a riot when he attended Fredrick's wedding. I shudder to think what his appearance would do in a simple, bucolic town like Guildford. Certainly Surrey would never be the same."

The Viscount could not hide his displeasure. He was a gentleman who lived a life of strict propriety and possessed an abiding distaste for those who preferred a more flamboyant existence. Including his son.

As if sensing Ian's flare of weary pain, Norrington smoothed his expression to one of bland curiosity.

"Then who was your friend?"

Ian drained his port and forced his thoughts back to the matters at hand.

"Tolson."

"Tolson?" There was nothing but pleased surprise to be seen on his father's countenance. Certainly it did not appear that he feared the old servant would reveal any nefarious secret. "My gracious, I have not seen him since he went to live with his sister. How is he?"

"The same as ever." Ian smiled wryly. "I must admit that it was good to see him despite his insistence on reminding me of my various childhood mishaps. You would think that age would have dimmed at least a few of those memories."

A genuine smile curved Norrington's lips. "Tolson's talent with roses was only superceded by his talent for knowing when a young lad is up to some sort of mischief. Thankfully he rarely felt the need to share the knowledge of that mischief with anyone else."

"Thankfully, indeed," Ian agreed dryly. "I should not like to think of Aunt Ella's disappointment should she learn that I was not quite the angelic lad she has always supposed me to be."

Norrington arched a dark brow. "I believe, Ian, that your aunt was far more aware of your . . . mishaps than you realize. Including your habit of pinching her handkerchiefs to use as sails for your toy boats and the secret tunnel you dug beneath the kitchen gardens to the gazebo."

"Good God, I took such pride in that tunnel," Ian muttered, disgruntled to realize he was not nearly as clever as he had believed. "I was quite convinced that it was not only the finest tunnel in all of Surrey, but that it was so cleverly hidden that not even the most nefarious smuggler could stumble across it. Now I learn that it was never secret at all. I am uncertain that I shall ever recover."

Expecting the familiar lecture on his disregard for the rules, Ian was caught off guard when his father merely shrugged.

"Which is no doubt why Ella never told you that she knew of your underground lair."

"No doubt."

Norrington toyed with his port glass. "Although I must admit that I am not entirely clear on why a smuggler would be searching for a tunnel in our kitchen garden."

"It is where I hid my treasure."

"Treasure?"

"I believe my chest held a dead frog, a sea shell, a handful of dirty coins, and a fossil of some plant. For all I know it is still buried beneath the turnips."

"Thank God I have never cared for turnips." His father lifted his glass in a mock toast. "Please resist any urges that might come upon you to bury dead frogs beneath the carrots."

Ian choked in surprise. Was his father actually . . . teasing him? Christ, it made him seem almost human.

Which was a danger in itself.

Already he possessed an unwelcome sympathy for what his father had endured as a child, and even a grudging understanding of why the man found it so difficult to lower his guard, even to those who should be closest to him.

The very last thing he desired was to find him charming as well.

"I shall do my best." With a fierce determination, he steered the conversation back in the direction he desired. "Did you never have a secret tunnel?"

There was a pause before the older man grimaced. "Actually, I preferred to do my hiding in the hedge maze."

"Ah yes, Tolson mentioned your habit of sneaking into the maze. He said that you often enjoyed playing there with another lad. What was the name . . . ?" He pretended to consider a long moment. "Ah yes, Summerville."

Carefully monitoring his father's expression, he still nearly missed the brief shock that rippled over his countenance before it was smoothed away.

"Summerville?"

"He claimed the two of you were inseparable."

"Did he? How odd." Norrington took a rigidly controlled sip of his port. "I remember inviting a friend or two from school, but I cannot recall a Summerville. Of course, it was all a very long time ago."

"Yes, I suppose it was."

Without warning, his father surged to his feet, his smile strained as he offered Ian a small dip of his head.

"Forgive me. I must return to the conservatory. I received a shipment of orchids that must be transplanted without delay."

Ian watched his father's retreat with an odd lack of satisfaction. Dammit, he should be delighted. There was no doubt that the name Summerville had rattled his father. And his adamant refusal to even acknowledge a friendship only confirmed his suspicions.

It was not satisfaction he felt, however, as his father stiffly exited the room. Instead it was something perilously close to disappointment.

Almost as if he regretted disturbing the fleeting sense of companionship that had so briefly hovered between them.

The night air remained warm enough to leave open the French doors of the long parlor, allowing the welcome scent of spring flowers to waft through the room. Mercy discovered herself lingering near the door, her gaze trained on the dark garden beyond.

Lost in her thoughts she failed to notice when the

notes of the pianoforte fell silent. Not until Ella loudly
cleared her throat in an obvious attempt to wrench
Mercy out of her deep broodings.

"You seem very quiet this evening, my dear."

Turning from the door, Mercy grimaced at the realization that she had allowed her annoyance with Ian
Breckford to make her such a poor companion. Ella
deserved better.

"Forgive me, Ella. I fear my mind is elsewhere."

Ella rose from the pianoforte to cross the room.
She halted next to Mercy with a swish of heavy satin
and tangible concern.

"Some fascinating new discovery in your studies?"

Mercy struggled against the threatening blush. "No,
just woolgathering."

"Hmmm. You look pale. Are you certain that nothing is the matter?"

Sensing there was more to Ella's concern, Mercy
frowned.

"What could possibly be the matter?"

"I did note that the post brought you yet another missive from your parents." There was a deliberate pause.
"They must have a great deal to report to write so often."

"No, they live very quietly and there is very little to
report," Mercy denied. "At least nothing beyond the
usual complaints of the house being wretchedly dusty
and my father's dinners not at all to his taste. There is
also a vague hint that the nurse I hired might be pil-
fering strawberry jam from the pantry."

Ella blinked. "Why ever would she steal strawberry
jam?"

"That is not fully explained, although I suppose it is
to give me a distrust of the woman."

Ella pursed her lips. "Really, my dear, they are behaving rather like children."

"They miss me."

"Well, of course they do, but that is no excuse not to be pleased that you are being given the opportunity to enjoy your studies." Ella frowned. "I do hope you will not give in to their bullying."

"Hardly bullying," Mercy instinctively protested. "More of a . . . gentle persuasion."

"A gentle persuasion that is specifically designed to wrack you with guilt."

Mercy's heart clenched as she recalled Ian making the precise same argument. Then she cursed herself roundly for allowing the aggravating wretch back into her thoughts.

Not that she actually hoped to put him far from her mind. Not so long as she remained at Rosehill. How could she? There would not be a moment when she was not vividly aware that he could stroll into the room, his beautiful, whiskey gold eyes flashing with wicked temptation and his sandalwood scent teasing her senses.

Even now a part of her was tingling with tension, waiting for Ian to make his appearance in the parlor.

Which begged the question of whether it was time to consider returning home.

As depressing as her father's cottage might be, it at least did not possess an agonizingly handsome devil that could drive a sane woman to Bedlam.

"They have every right to expect their only child to assist in their care as they grow older," she said, her voice low to disguise her sinking sense of disappointment. "And in truth, it is time that I consider returning home."

Ella's eyes widened with sudden distress. "Oh, my dear, I do hope you will not abandon me before the charity luncheon. I would be lost without your assistance."

Mercy forced a weak smile. "Nonsense, you will do quite well without me, and since my parents are obviously unhappy with my absence, it does seem that my duty—"

"Am I intruding?"

Mercy stiffened at the dark male voice that cut through the air with a soft, lethal edge.

Slowly Mercy forced herself to turn, not at all surprised to discover Ian standing at the entrance of the parlor, his fiercely handsome features set in hard lines.

A nervous flutter attacked the pit of her stomach. She did not need to be a mind reader to realize he had overheard at least a portion of her conversation with Ella. And that he was not at all pleased.

"Oh, Ian, you must assist me in convincing Mercy that she cannot possibly leave Rosehill until the end of the month," Ella broke the tense silence. "I simply do not know what I would do without her assistance."

The gold eyes never wavered from Mercy's pale face as he prowled across the room to stand directly at her side.

"I should be happy to lend my support." Without warning, he reached to take her hand and placed it firmly on his arm. "Perhaps, Miss Simpson, you would care to join me on the terrace while I make my plea? It is too lovely an evening to remain indoors."

Despite her unease, Mercy could not ignore the potent jolt of awareness that shook through her body. The muscles of his arm were hard beneath her fingers, the heat of his body brushing intimately over her skin.

Blast the annoying man. She was supposed to be furious with him, not shivering with excitement because he was near.

"Since my visit is to be brief, I believe my time would be best served completing the menu for the charity luncheon," she said, cowardly hoping to avoid the inevitable confrontation.

"Nonsense." Ella waved a plump hand. "A brief stroll is just what you need, my dear."

Ian covered her fingers on his arm with his hand, his predatory smile sending a shiver down her spine.

"Come, Miss Simpson, or I shall fear that you have taken me in dislike." He squeezed her fingers. "You would not wish Aunt Ella to see us bickering like children, would you?"

The warning in his voice was unmistakable. He had something to say to her, and if she would not join him in the garden, then he would do so in front of his aunt. Even if it meant revealing her eager response to his kisses.

"Very well."

Ignoring her stiff anger, Ian flashed his aunt a charming smile before tugging Mercy through the open window and leading her down the steps to the sunken garden.

They strolled in silence until they reached one of the marble fountains. Coming to a halt, Ian released her hand and calmly lit a cheroot from a nearby torch.

"There, I did tell you that it was a lovely evening," he murmured.

Mercy licked her lips. She had expected Ian to explode the moment they were away from the mansion. His anger, after all, shimmered about him with a shocking force. Somehow his tightly coiled composure was even more unnerving.

"So you did."

There was another disturbing silence as he studied her defensive expression, his golden eyes narrowed.

"You know, Mercy, I would never have suspected beneath all that sweet innocence and determined bravado was the heart of a coward," he at last drawled.

Mercy jerked at the smooth insult. "I beg your pardon?"

"You are running away from me." Drawing deeply on the cheroot, he released a stream of smoke before tossing the thin cigar into a nearby rosebush. "The question is whether you are fleeing because I outraged you with my offer of becoming my mistress or because you are terrified you might agree."

Her heart lodged in her throat. No, she was not fleeing because she feared she might give in to his offensive proposal. She would never, ever trade her body for wealth.

Unfortunately, she was not entirely certain why she had been so suddenly struck by the urge to leave Rosehill.

It was almost as if her heart were whispering a warning that she did not yet fully comprehend.

Unsettled by the strange thought, Mercy sucked in a deep breath and squared her shoulders.

"Did it ever occur to you that my decision to return home might have nothing at all to do with you?" she demanded.

"Not for a single moment."

Her lips thinned at his absolute certainty. "I begin to understand your reputation for excessive arrogance, Mr. Breckford."

"Mercy, I am many things, but I am not stupid." Stepping forward, Ian brushed a finger down the line of her jaw. "Just a few hours ago you were distressed by the mere thought of returning to your parents' cottage, and now you are suddenly eager to leave Rosehill?"

His caress was feather light, but it sent a sheet of pure fire through her body. Even when she was angry with Ian, her body responded to his touch with a savage pleasure.

"I did not say that I was eager, merely that I feel it my duty." She stepped from his lingering finger. "No doubt you find it difficult to accept that there are those of us who take our responsibilities seriously."

"Obviously you do not take all of your responsibilities seriously."

"And what is that supposed to mean?"

"You are willing to abandon Ella just when she is most in need of your services, are you not?"

"That is absurd. I am not abandoning Ella."

"No?" He folded his arms over his chest. "Did you not promise to assist her with her charity luncheon?"

"The majority of the work is done—"

"A majority, but not all," he overrode her soft words. "Surely you owe the woman who offered you a home and extensive use of an extraordinary library the small courtesy of finishing what you have started."

It was a ploy, of course. He was playing upon her fondness for Ella to achieve his own ends. Unfortunately, she could not entirely dismiss her flare of guilt. Ella had offered her a home, access to one of the finest libraries in all of England, and her ready kindness. And all she had asked in return was Mercy's assistance with her luncheon.

Hardly an arduous request.

Still, she was not in the mood to be chided by a jaded rake who devoted most of his life to ignoring his poor family.

"And you claim that my parents use my emotions to manipulate me?" she gritted.

"I make no pretense of being an honorable gentleman. Besides, I have no intention of allowing you to disappoint Ella simply because you are in a miff."

She glared into his perfect countenance. Had there ever been a more aggravating, provoking, maddening wretch?

"I am not in a miff."

"A woman does not sulk through an entire dinner unless she is in a miff. If you wish to punish me, then do so, but do not make Ella suffer for my sins." He pretended to ponder some inner thought for a long moment. "Although, now that I think upon it, I must admit that it is grossly unfair for you to be upset at all."

"Unfair?" Her hands curled at her side. "You . . ."

"Yes?"

"You insulted me."

With a nonchalance that was exquisitely designed to set her teeth on edge, Ian leaned against the edge of the fountain, his expression mocking.

"By asking you to become my mistress?"

Her face flooded with color. "For goodness' sakes, keep your voice down."

"My sweet Mercy, if you will recall, I did my utmost to ignore the obvious attraction between us," he drawled. "Indeed, I behaved in a manner that could only be considered noble. It was you who pursued me in the hopes of forming an intimate connection." He leaned forward, his eyes glittering like molten gold in the torchlight. "I begin to believe that I should be the one offended to be teased with the promise of paradise only to be cruelly rejected."

The heat staining her cheeks deepened. He did have a point, damn him to hell. She had been the one to blatantly pursue him despite his obvious reluctance. In truth, she had done everything short of crawling into his bed to tantalize his interest.

Then again, her desire had been a natural response to a highly sensual man. He was the one who made it seem . . . sordid.

"An intimate connection is quite different from becoming a gentleman's mistress," she said, her voice pitched low.

"Is it?" Straightening, Ian regarded her with a hint of curiosity. "I must admit that the distinction eludes me at the moment. Perhaps you would care to explain the difference?"

"An intimate connection is the result of two individuals who are equally attracted to one another. A mistress . . ." Her words trailed away in a surge of discomfort. She could not believe she was discussing such intimate matters with a gentleman in the midst of a garden.

"Please continue, Mercy. I find myself fascinated."

She stiffened her spine at his sardonic amusement. He was being deliberately obtuse.

"As I told you in my bedchamber, a mistress implies that I am willing to trade my virtue for monetary gain."

"Ah, I recall now." The golden eyes flashed. "You are willing to allow me into your bed so long as you do not gain financially from the experience? Is that correct?"

Her chin tilted. "Not quite."

"No?"

"I am not at all certain I am willing to have you in my bed regardless of the circumstance." Proving that she could be as annoying as the man standing before her, Mercy performed a sweeping curtsy before heading back to the house. "Good night, Mr. Breckford."

Chapter 11

Ian awoke the next morning at yet another ungodly hour.

If he were an honorable man he would presume that it was a guilty conscience that had him out of bed and attired in a tobacco brown coat and buff breeches at the break of dawn. After all, he had not only seduced a complete innocent and then insulted her by requesting that she become his mistress, he had compounded his dastardly deeds by deliberately playing upon her tender heart to keep her from fleeing to the safety of her home.

Thankfully, he had never been burdened with anything so troublesome as a conscience, and instead of guilt it was determination that urged him from the comforts of his bed and had him ringing for his valet.

He intended to make certain that Mercy Simpson understood that she would be remaining at Rosehill. No matter what underhanded tricks were necessary to keep her close at hand.

They had unfinished business.

A business that had left him hard and aching throughout the long, long night.

Of course, he did have less enticing business to attend to as well, he reminded himself with a faint sigh. Waiting until his valet finished tying the complicated knot in his cravat, he rose to his feet and regarded the servant who had been with him for the past five years.

Not that Reaver was a typical servant.

The son of a dockworker, Reaver possessed his father's tall, brawny frame and barrel chest. His face was cut with square, clean lines and had no doubt been considered handsome before he had been slashed from his right ear to the edge of his mouth, leaving behind a gruesome scar that made grown men tremble. With his thick brown hair grown long enough to pull into a queue and his hard, black eyes, he appeared more a cutthroat than a valet.

Ian had encountered the man in one of the innumerable hells that he had frequented over the years. At the time, Reaver had been an employee of the owner, his intimidating demeanor and impressive bulk the only encouragement needed to ensure that all gambling debts were paid without a fuss.

On the night Ian had been in attendance, however, a wealthy young buck had brought with him several servants who took exception to Reaver's attempt to halt the cowardly fool from slipping out a side window.

Ian could not say why he interfered. It was not as if he had a great sympathy for his fellow man. Especially not those who frequented gambling hells. Nor did he particularly have a sense of duty to rescue those in need.

Perhaps it was merely a sense of fair play that had led him to step into the melee and even the odds.

Whatever the cause, Ian had discovered Reaver was a man of fierce loyalty, and once he had healed, he had arrived upon Ian's doorstep with an unwavering refusal to be turned away. In the end it had been easier to allow him to remain than to try and run him off.

Rather a stroke of fortune, Ian had to admit. Although Reaver was merely a passable valet, he possessed many other talents that had proven invaluable over the years. Not the least of which was standing behind Ian's chair as he gambled. It was nothing less than amazing at how few gentlemen were willing to attempt to cheat with Reaver's gimlet eye upon them.

And, of course, there was his willingness to perform whatever task, no matter how strange, without complaint.

That made him a servant beyond price.

Ian waited until the man had cleaned and tucked away the shaving kit (he made a habit of never discussing any subject while his companion held a sharp object near his throat) before revealing his decision.

"Reaver, I need you to return to London."

The large man folded his arms over his chest. "A collection?"

"Not on this occasion. It is more of a"—Ian smiled wryly—"Treasure hunt."

The man grunted, familiar enough with his unpredictable employer to reveal nothing more than a resigned curiosity.

"And what is this treasure?"

"A gentleman by the name of Summerville." Ian leaned against the highly polished armoire and straightened the cuff of his jacket. "I fear I do not know much more than that."

"Just Summerville?"

"Yes."

"He lives in London?"

Ian grimaced. "I believe so, although I am not entirely certain."

Reaver furrowed his heavy brow, his expression growing exasperated. Hardly surprising. He had just been given the task of searching for a very small needle in a very large haystack.

"Is he a nob?"

"It could be, although it is possible that he is the son of a wealthy merchant."

Reaver shoved his fingers through his hair. "That is not much to go on."

"Which is why I must send you, as much as I would prefer you to remain in Surrey. I cannot risk undue attention to my interest in Summerville." Ian smiled. "And besides, there is not a man in all of England you cannot track down, Reaver. You are like a damnable bloodhound when you are on the scent of prey."

Reaver grunted at the blatant challenge. "What do you want of him if he don't be owing you money?"

Ian pushed from the armoire to cross toward the window, peering absently toward the distant lake. Reaver was well aware of Ian's purpose in coming to Surrey, of course. There was simply no keeping secrets from the man.

"I believe he might have a connection to my father's past. It could very well be he possesses knowledge of the secret I am searching for."

"Ah." Comprehension flashed through the dark eyes. "Do you want me to haul him here once I've found him?"

"No. Just send word when you have tracked him down."

"There might be more than one, you know. How do I know which you are wanting?"

Ian shrugged, his gaze shifting to the stables. He

had already quizzed the upstairs maid to ensure that Mercy had not fled during the night, but he had no intention of lowering his guard. Not until he had the opportunity to demand her promise she would not leave.

"This particular Summerville will be of an age with my father and attended Eton as a lad. If I can discover more I will send word to you in London."

There was another grunt as Reaver considered his latest task, his expression revealing that he was not entirely happy to be sent back to London. The valet might grouse at the lack of entertainment to be found at Rosehill, but he was never happy to be parted from his employer. The ridiculous man had managed to convince himself that Ian was incapable of surviving without him.

"And who will be taking care of you?" he demanded.

Ian resisted the urge to roll his eyes. At least the man had not yet taken to holding his hand when they crossed the road.

"My father possesses a small army of servants. I am certain that at least one can be spared to stand in as my valet."

The dangerous features became downright frightening as Reaver scowled. "I do not mean someone to starch your cravats and brush your coat. Any fool could tend to those things. Who is to keep an eye upon your back?"

Ian deliberately glanced toward the window that revealed nothing more threatening than a distant cow.

"I should think that my back will be safe enough for the next few days. Rosehill has always been a frigid, unwelcoming sort of place, but it is rarely lethal."

"Oh aye. And when you grow bored and search out a game of chance?" Reaver growled.

Ian could not hold back his bark of laughter. "Perhaps you should pay better attention, my friend. The only games to be played in this neighborhood are charades and spillikin. Neither of which are renowned for leading to bloodshed."

"Bah. I know you better than you know yourself, Breckford. A fortnight ago you managed to turn a respectable vicarage into a den of iniquity."

"Ah, yes." Ian smiled as he recalled the unexpected windfall he had collected while waiting for Fredrick's wedding in Wessex. "I believe I won a beautiful pair of candlesticks that had once graced the altar of some poor church."

"And nearly had your throat slit by the desperate curate," Reaver was swift to remind him. "Do you believe that a half-witted farmer is any less inclined to commit murder after losing his fortune?"

Ian merely smiled. That restless itch that so often led him into the gaming hells or plunging into some reckless dare or another was oddly absent since he had stumbled across a beautiful wood sprite standing in the midst of a meadow.

"Do you know, Reaver, for the first time in a very long time, the last thing I fear is growing bored," he murmured, a tingle of anticipation inching down his spine. "Indeed, I haven't the least interest in searching out the local bumpkins to empty their pockets."

Reaver frowned. "Are you sickly?"

"More likely I have gone completely mad," Ian admitted without a hint of regret.

"I see."

"I am deeply relieved that one of us does."

Ignoring Ian's dry tone, Reaver shook his head in a gesture of profound disappointment.

"When a man loses interest in important matters,

it can only be because a woman is involved. Miss Simpson, eh?"

Ian did not bother to deny the truth. Why should he? He was not ashamed of his fascination for the golden-haired beauty.

"She has proven to be an unexpected distraction."

"A female is only a distraction if you allow her to be."

Ian regarded his companion with a flare of bemusement. He had known that Reaver preferred a quick tumble with a whore to stepping out with a respectable lass; still, there was an odd edge to his voice that hinted at darker emotions.

"How terribly pragmatic you are, Reaver. Have you never been struck by a passion so overwhelming that everything else fades in comparison?"

"Aye." Without warning, the man lifted a hand to touch the scar that disfigured his lower cheek. "And I carry the mark to prove it."

"A woman sliced your face?" Ian did not have to feign his surprise. He had never directly demanded an explanation for the long-healed wound, but he had never considered the possibility that the tale included a female. "Good God, for all these years I had presumed that you had been set upon by murderous footpads, or even taken prisoner by a crew of pirates and tortured for months on end. Now I discover you were bested by no more than an angry chit. I can not reveal the depths of my disappointment."

"I would trust a band of pirates to a wench," Reaver muttered, his voice bitter. "At least they are honest in their thieving."

Ian studied his companion a long moment. "So why would a woman desire to slash your face? Did she catch you in bed with another?"

Reaver stiffened. "I caught her pocketing my mother's pearl necklace. My father saved for ten bloody years to buy that bauble, and I wasn't about to allow the bitch to hock it for a few quid."

Ian grimaced. "A nasty bit of goods."

"A typical woman."

"No." Ian shook his head. It was not that he did not believe a woman could steal a family heirloom and then slice the face of a man attempting to halt her. Hell, he'd known a dozen women who would invite him to their beds even as their fingers were dipping into his pocket. A hard, ruthless life tended to breed hard, ruthless people. But he knew beyond a doubt that his sweet wood sprite was a woman of rare beauty, both inside and out. "Mercy Simpson is not like other females."

Reaver threw his hands in the air. "Bloody hell, those are the words of doom."

"Doom?"

"Whenever a man begins muttering those words, it means he is about to make an ass of himself." Reaver heaved a sigh of despair. "I never thought to hear them from your lips. A sad day, I must say."

Ian's lips twitched at the man's morose reaction. "Thankfully you will be in London, Reaver, so if I do happen to make an ass of myself you shall be spared the embarrassment of witnessing my downfall."

"Thank God."

Reaching beneath his jacket, Ian pulled out a leather bag and handed it to his servant.

"There should be enough money for your journey as well as any necessary inducement for those reluctant to share information."

Reaver scowled as he tucked the bag beneath his jacket. "I don't need coin to get information I desire."

"I am well aware of your talents, Reaver. However, on this occasion I would prefer you grease the wheels with money rather than your fists," Ian said, his expression firm.

"Why?"

"Because a discrete bribe causes far less notice than bloody carnage in the streets of London. I hope to avoid any unnecessary interest, if you will recall."

Reaver headed toward the door, his disappointment in being denied a good thrashing obvious in the resigned set of his shoulders.

"Waste of good blunt, if you ask me."

Ian rolled his eyes. "Thankfully, I am not asking you. Return here the moment you have information."

"Aye."

"And Reaver."

The man paused at the door, glancing impatiently over his shoulder. "What?"

"Take care." Ian's expression was somber. He would have his tongue cut out before admitting it, but he had grown annoyingly fond of the man. "I do not believe there is any danger, but I should not wish to have to train another valet. It is always such a tedious business."

Reaver's smile returned as he offered Ian a parting wink. "I'm not the one playing with fire, Breckford."

Waiting until the door had closed behind his valet, Ian sucked in a deep breath and smoothed his hands down his tailored jacket.

He should be laughing at the ridiculous warning. He was a master of playing with fire. God knew he had been doing it most of his life. He always knew exactly how far to press his luck without getting burned.

It was not amusement, however, that sent a small shiver down his spine.

No, that was pure, unmistakable foreboding.

With a shake of his head at his stupid imaginings, Ian forced himself to leave his rooms and make his way through the mansion. He had enough concerns to keep him occupied without brooding on vague imaginings.

He had nearly reached the back parlor when his steps slowed at the sound of his aunt's bright chatter and Mercy's low, husky laugh that tumbled through the air. It was not the women's obvious pleasure in one another's company that caught him off guard. He was well aware that they had become fast friends in their short time together. It was, after all, how he had managed to manipulate Mercy into remaining at Rosehill.

Instead, he was struck by the realization that the gold-veined marble suddenly did not seem quite so cold, nor the looming Grecian statues so intimidating. Even the rich velvet curtains glowed with a ruby warmth in the morning sunlight.

It was as if Mercy's presence at Rosehill was slowly melting the ice that had held the estate in its grip for so long.

Astonishing.

Continuing forward, Ian stepped into the charming breakfast room and regarded the two women seated at the table.

His aunt was as elegant as ever in her green and gold striped gown with her hair pulled into a simple knot at her nape. It was Mercy, though, that caught and held his attention.

His breath was wrenched from his lungs as he caught sight of her drenched in a golden ray of sunshine.

Christ, she truly was a wood sprite.

There could be no other explanation for her captivating beauty.

Certainly it could not be due to the simple blue gown

that would have been suitable for a nun, or the golden hair that was pulled into a tight braid. It was not even in the perfect features that glowed a warm ivory.

He had known far too many beautiful women to be so easily dazzled.

No, it could only be magic.

Abruptly aware that both women were regarding him with varying degrees of welcome, Ian performed a shallow bow.

"Good morning, ladies."

"Oh, Ian, what a lovely coincidence," Ella murmured, her eyes warming at his entrance. "I do hope you have no plans for the day?"

Ian slowly smiled, not at all put out by the knowledge his aunt was clearly determined to maneuver him into assisting with some tedious task or other. Instead, his gaze was trained on Mercy's wary expression.

"Not at all, Aunt Ella. I am at your complete disposal."

"Excellent." Ella clapped her hands together. "I have requested that Mercy search the attics for the trunk of good linen tablecloths and napkins that I had stored up there some years ago. They will need to be aired and pressed before the luncheon."

"The attics, eh?" Ian's smile widened. An entire morning alone with Mercy? Perfect.

Ella rose to her feet, seemingly oblivious to Mercy's stiff dismay.

"Unfortunately, I cannot recall precisely which trunk was used, so I fear it may be a tedious chore searching through the lot," the older woman murmured.

"How could any time spent in the company of Miss Simpson ever be considered tedious?" he questioned smoothly.

Ella smiled wryly. "Behave yourself, Ian, or you will be banished to mucking the stables."

"It would not be the first occasion." Ian placed his aunt's hand on his arm as he escorted her to the door. "I seem to recall spending a great number of afternoons with a pitchfork in hand."

"Much good it did," Mercy muttered from behind, her voice pitched so low that Ian suspected she had never intended for him to overhear.

Hiding his sudden smile, Ian paused at the door and regarded his aunt with a lift of his brow. "Where are you off to, my dear?"

"I must travel to the vicarage."

"At this hour?"

"Mrs. Delford has kindly offered to assist with the summer festival, and we must begin our planning." The older woman offered a vague smile, her thoughts already upon her next charity affair. "I shall see you both for luncheon."

Ian waited until his aunt had disappeared down the long corridor before turning to prop his shoulder against the door jam, his gaze running a hungry path over Mercy's pale face.

"I must say that I am rather relieved to discover you sitting here eating your breakfast, my sweet."

Rising to her feet, Mercy joined him at the door with a lift of her chin.

"I remained because of Ella, no other reason."

"Whatever the cause, it saved me the effort of devoting my morning to hauling you back to Rosehill."

She ignored the unmistakable warning in his words. Halting directly before the doorway, she regarded him with an air of impatience.

"If you will excuse me?"

"Where are you going?"

"To the attics."

Straightening, Ian held out his arm. "Very well, I will join you."

"There is no need." With swift steps, she had pushed past him and was headed toward the back of the house. "I am perfectly capable of searching through the trunks, and I am certain you must have better things to do."

With two long strides he was at her side, easily keeping pace with her brisk steps.

"I can think of at least one better thing to be doing, but I suspect that will have to wait until you are in a less"—he deliberately paused, waiting for the heat flood into her cheeks. He wasn't disappointed—"Combative frame of mind."

She frowned in disapproval. "Ian."

"Yes, my sweet?"

Meeting his wicked gaze, she gave a resigned roll of her eyes. "You truly are impossible."

"So I have been told."

They traveled toward the servants' staircase in silence, Ian content to savor the warm scent of vanilla that swirled through the air. Who knew just being near a woman could be so satisfying?

Christ, he was not even touching her.

Mounting the steep flight of steps until they at last reached the upper level of the mansion, Ian moved to step in front of Mercy before she could open the door.

"Perhaps you should allow me to go first and battle the cobwebs that have no doubt gathered."

Mercy paused, and then astonishingly she offered no more than a faint shrug.

"By all means."

"There is to be no argument?"

"I detest spiders."

"Wait here," he warned, tugging open the door and withdrawing his handkerchief to knock down the most tenacious webs. A Herculean task, he swiftly discovered, battling a path toward the landing. Once there, he grimaced. As a small lad he had often played among the various trunks and abandoned furniture that consumed a lion's share of the attics. He did not recall the dust being quite so thick, or the sloped ceiling quite so low. "Good God, I had forgotten how cramped it was up here. It all looked a great deal larger when I was a child," he muttered.

"Perhaps because you took up much less space in those days," Mercy pointed out, lingering at the bottom of the steps.

"Perhaps." Ian glanced over his shoulder. "I believe I have frightened off the most vicious of the spiders. There is nothing I can do, however, for the dust."

She climbed the stairs, indifferent to the dirt marring the hem of her skirt as she edged past his large form.

"I knew the rumors of your near mythical ability to satisfy a woman's deepest fantasy must be exaggerated," she taunted, her low, erotic voice sending a jolt of pure lust through his groin.

He was moving before he was even aware of his intentions, pressing her against the tall armoire that had been condemned to the attics at least a century before.

"Are you implying that you doubt my ability to please a lady?" he demanded, ignoring the cloud of dust that floated about them. Hell, the ceiling could tumble on his head and he would be impervious.

The only thing that mattered was the feel of her delicate shoulders beneath his fingers and the womanly heat that was searing through his clothing.

He had ached to touch her for hours.

Belatedly realizing the dangers of teasing him, Mercy sucked in a sharp breath.

"Ian."

Ian slowly smiled, his gaze running a hot path down the length of her stiff body.

"Perhaps you would care to make a little wager?"

"A wager?"

"I bet that if you allow me into your bed, I can satisfy each and every one of your fantasies."

"And what do I win if you fail?"

"I will scour every bookstore in London for books concerning the Byzantine era and personally deliver them to your doorstep."

"Hardly an arduous task."

He nearly choked on her ridiculous words. He was still recovering from his previous visit to the musty bookshop.

"Perhaps not for a scholar, but I can assure you that it would be nothing less than torture for a frivolous gentleman such as myself." He deliberately shifted so his body brushed against hers. A primitive flare of satisfaction raced through him at her unmistakable tremor. "So, do we have a wager?"

Her eyes briefly darkened with an uncontrollable awareness. Then, with a grim effort, she was pressing her hands against his chest in denial.

"Do not be absurd. I would never allow a man into my bed for a wager."

Ian refused to budge. His untimely proposal of making her his mistress had not destroyed her desire for him.

That was all he needed to know.

"So, you fear that I would win," he drawled, his words a direct challenge. "Very wise."

Chapter 12

Mercy was nearly consumed by the potent emotions that trembled through her body. Excitement, exasperation, and a small thread of unease.

It was not that she worried Ian would harm her. It was simply not in his nature. Unfortunately, the threat she sensed had nothing to do with such mundane danger.

Instead it had everything to do with the predatory male that branded her with his lightest touch.

When she had made the decision to remain at Rosehill, she had known it would be difficult. She might be infuriated with Ian, but it did nothing to lessen the fierce awareness that shimmered between them.

Foolishly, she had thought she could manage to avoid being alone with the man. So long as Ella was near, there was no concern that Mercy would give in to temptation. Not even Ian would attempt to seduce a woman beneath his aunt's nose.

Now she had to wonder if she had deliberately deceived herself.

Perhaps her aching need to remain at Rosehill was not entirely a reluctance to return home, or even guilt at abandoning Ella after the woman had been so kind to her. Perhaps she had secretly . . .

No, she would not allow herself to consider the disturbing notion.

Not when it was bound to reveal she had no option but to pack her bags and leave.

For once in her life, she wanted to turn a blind eye and simply hope for the best.

Stupid, of course, but soon enough she would be back to her dull, sensible self. All she asked was a few more days of freedom.

Meeting Ian's smoldering gaze, Mercy unconsciously squared her shoulders.

"It has nothing to do with fear of losing the bet," she lied without compunction. Hot pokers could not induce her to confess her absolute confidence he could satisfy her every fantasy. "I simply find the thought distasteful."

He brushed a hand up the bare curve of her neck. "For a woman who was so intent upon seducing me, sweet Mercy, you have a great number of conditions of how that seduction is to proceed. Are you always so demanding?"

Mercy quivered. Dear heavens, she was drowning in the scent and heat of his body. She pressed her hands flat against the armoire. It was that or throw her arms about his neck and beg for his kiss.

"I have demanded nothing of you."

"No, I would prefer that you had." His eyes darkened with a yearning he made no effort to disguise. "Instead, you have stirred my desire to a fever pitch and then refused to satisfy the need you have created. There are few things more cruel." His lips twisted. "Or more likely to send me stark, raving mad."

Mercy felt a small pang of guilt. There was no denying the fact she had done all in her power to lure this man into her bed.

Who knew a simple affair could become so bloody complicated?

"That was not my intent."

"Then what was your intent?"

She attempted to inch toward the side, her hand reaching for the small wooden knob on the armoire to offer her leverage. It was impossible to think clearly when her entire body was throbbing with frustrated desire.

"I do not wish to discuss this, Ian."

"But I do." His fingers lingered on the frantic pulse at the base of her throat, his head lowering to gently nibble at her bottom lip. "I am, after all, the one suffering."

Mercy could not hold back her low moan. His tongue lightly outlined her mouth, and her entire body tightened with anticipation. This man had tutored her in the delights of the flesh, and she was desperate to once again feel that glorious explosion of pleasure.

"Sweet Mercy," he muttered, abruptly kissing her with a fierce hunger that was echoed within her.

For a wondrous moment she savored the stark demand of his lips. There was nothing practiced or skillful about this kiss. This was not the famous Casanova seducing a woman.

It was a sheer, raw need that was far more thrilling than any amount of expertise.

At last it was the feel of his fingers gently cupping the aching weight of her breast that jerked her out of the blissful fog.

Her body had no confusion. It wanted Ian. It wanted

to melt onto the floor and allow him to fill the ache that tortured her.

Her mind, however, was not yet prepared to lower her guard.

She told herself that it was the memory of his offensive offer to make her his mistress. After all, no woman desired to be made to feel like a tart.

A tiny voice, however, whispered that she was not being entirely honest with herself.

"Ian . . ."

Her hand tightened on the knob of the armoire, causing the door to jerk open. A sudden avalanche of papers tumbled out of the dark depths, startling Ian enough to make him pull back in alarm. Mercy was swift to take advantage of his distraction, swiftly bending downward to begin gathering the scattered papers.

"Leave them," Ian growled as he knelt beside her, his expression tight with frustration.

She ignored his command, her eyes widening as she glanced at the thick parchment in her hands.

"Good heavens, how beautiful," she breathed.

Muttering a low curse, Ian snatched up one of the papers, his brows drawing together as he studied the charcoal sketching.

"The Coliseum . . ." He plucked another from the floor. "The Pantheon . . . These were done in Rome."

"Yes," Mercy agreed, holding up the sketch in her hand. "This one is of the Trevi Fountain."

He shrugged, his eyes still dark with suppressed desire. "My father must have sketched these during his Grand Tour."

"They may have been done during your father's Grand Tour, but they were sketched by your aunt."

Unexpectedly Ian stilled, as if disturbed by her offhand correction.

"What the devil do you mean?"

"They are signed and dated on the back." She held up her sketch to point out Ella's scrawled signature at the bottom corner. "See?"

"Impossible." Surging to his feet, Ian tossed aside the papers and paced toward the small window that offered the only light amid the gloom.

With a frown, Mercy slowly straightened. "Is something the matter?"

"Ella never mentioned that she had traveled the Continent with my father."

She studied the hard lines of his profile. "Does it matter?"

"It does if the dates are correct."

"Why?"

"She would have been with my father when he was in the process of seducing my mother." He slowly turned to meet her uncertain gaze. "Those sketches were completed just a few months before my birth."

"Oh." Mercy was still confused. She sensed Ian's coiled tension, but she was not certain of the cause. "And she never told you?"

Ian glared toward the scattered sketches. "Not only did she not tell me, but she more than implied that she knew nothing of my mother or my father's relationship with her."

"Perhaps your father kept it a secret," Mercy hesitantly suggested, uncertain of his strange mood. "After all, I doubt many gentlemen would be anxious to share the details of their intimate connections with their sister."

"Maybe not, but it could hardly remain a secret

once the poor woman died and left me in the care of my father." He gave a short, humorless bark of laughter. "Not even Lord Norrington would have been capable of hiding a newborn babe as he traveled across the Continent."

"No, I am certain that he must have revealed the truth once he claimed you as his child." She slowly shook her head as his gaze remained trained upon the sketches. "Ian?"

"Hmmm?"

"What is troubling you?"

He turned his head to meet her worried frown. Something flashed deep in his eyes before he was effectively hiding his emotions behind a smooth, unreadable expression.

"I am weary of my family's habit of shrouding even the simplest of occurrences in a cloak of mystery. Anyone would think they possessed something to hide."

She easily sensed that he was not telling her the full truth.

"You seem more angered than weary," she accused, unconsciously closing the space between them. "Could it be that your family is not the only ones with secrets?"

"I do not like the knowledge I have been lied to."

"Your aunt not revealing that she had traveled with your father is not precisely a lie. It is more a . . ." Mercy considered the appropriate word. "More an omission of facts."

He arched a dark brow. "A rather fine distinction for a vicar's daughter."

"It is very possible Ella merely presumed you would have no interest in her youthful travels." Mercy paused, her thoughts traveling back to Ella's lecture upon the dangers of rakes. There had been a haunting bitterness about the woman. "Or perhaps they are simply too painful for her to recall."

"Painful?"

"I have a distinct impression that your aunt suffered from a tragic disappointment in her life. It is quite possible she tumbled into love during her travels and after suffering through a broken heart packed away the memory of those days along with these mementoes." Mercy gave a lift of her hands. "They would only cause her pain to have them out again."

Ian stilled, his gaze suddenly shimmering with a heat that warned he was no longer consumed with the sketches or his aunt's travels to the Continent.

Before she could react, he had framed her face with his hands. "Good God, you are a romantic."

"What?"

"There can be no other explanation for such a ridiculous flight of fancy."

"And you are a cynic to immediately presume some nefarious plot against you," she swiftly countered.

"Obviously we are perfectly suited."

"Perfectly . . ." She shook her head in disbelief. "That is the most ridiculous notion I have ever heard. We have just established that we are utter opposites."

His thumbs toyed at the corners of her mouth. "Which makes for the most intriguing combination."

"You would think any combination that includes a female intriguing," she muttered.

"Well, it is certainly preferable to one that includes a male. Still, I am not without standards." He dipped his head, brushing her lips with a tender kiss. "Extraordinarily high standards."

Mercy shivered, her hands clutching at his arms as her knees went weak.

"Ian, we are supposed to be searching for the tablecloths."

He nipped at her bottom lip before trailing a path of blazing kisses down the length of her jaw.

"They will eventually be discovered."

"Not unless we search for them."

"We have plenty of time."

She splayed her hands across his chest, as always caught off guard by the ripple of muscle beneath her fingers. Ian was so slender it was easy to forget the strength in his lean body.

She could just imagine all that hard maleness covering her and . . . no, no, no. She forced her hands to press against his chest.

"Ian, stop this."

Ignoring her futile efforts, Ian buried his face in the curve of her neck.

"Christ, your scent is driving me mad."

He was being driven mad? Good Lord, his hands were creating a trail of destruction as they skimmed down her back and gripped her hips. With one yank, she was pressed intimately against his body.

She sucked in a sharp breath at the feel of his hard arousal pressed against her hip.

"No, Ian, I am still furious with you," she forced herself to mutter.

"Why?" Lifting his head, he stabbed her with his glittering gaze. "I am not asking you to become my mistress."

"That is not the point."

"Then what is?"

She had a point. Of course she had a point. It was just so damnably difficult to think when her heart was thundering and her lower body clenched with aching need.

"That you would presume I was the sort of female to agree to your proposal," she hastily accused as his head lowered to continue with his all-too-persuasive seduction.

His eyes narrowed, as if sensing there was more to her bout of nerves than mere outrage. Oddly, however, he did not press.

"I presumed nothing, my sweet Mercy," he denied. "My only thought when I requested you to become my mistress was that I desired you more than I have desired any other woman and that I wanted to ensure that I had you in my bed for longer than a handful of nights. That might very well prove that I am a selfish bastard, but it has no judgment on your character." He peered deep into her wide eyes. "I wanted you, and that's all I considered."

The indignation that she had nurtured began to falter beneath his simple words. He had been selfish, but not deliberately cruel. Much like any other man, no doubt.

Mercy, however, was more shaken by his precise words than by the overall content.

"Ian, do not say such things."

"Why not?"

"Because they are so obviously untrue," she said, her expression wounded.

His brows snapped together. "What the hell do you mean?"

She again shoved at his chest. With the same result. She would have more luck attempting to move the Great Wall of China.

"You do not desire me more than any other woman. It is absurd."

His scowl only deepened. "You presume to know what I feel?"

"I am a plain country miss who knows nothing of gentlemen. Hardly the sort to inspire passion in any man, let alone the renowned Casanova."

"Plain?" He gave a disbelieving shake of his head, his gaze searing over her pale face. "Christ, do you never glance into a mirror? You are . . . exquisite."

A blush stained her cheeks. "Hardly exquisite, but I spoke of my lack of worldly polish."

"Worldly polish?" He gave a snort of disgust. "Have you ever considered the notion that any gentleman would weary of the jaded sophistication to be found in London? I never realized just how intoxicating it could be to discover a woman who is capable of speaking what is on her mind." His hands tightened on her hips, the tiny pain sending a small thrill down her spine. "A woman who does not use artifice to attract the attention of a gentleman."

Her breath was squeezed from her lungs at his low, husky words. She was being ridiculous, of course. A seasoned rake always knew the perfect words to make a woman feel special. How else could they so easily lure her to his bed?

Still, she was an aging spinster who had never been courted or flattered or admired. She had never felt beautiful or desired by anyone.

How could she not feel at least some pleasure in his pretense of unwavering fascination?

"Ian . . ."

She was not entirely certain what she intended to say, but in the end it did not matter. His name had barely tumbled from her lips when there was the sound of approaching footsteps that halted at the bottom of the attic stairs.

"Miss Simpson." The maid's voice echoed eerily through the dusty gloom. "Miss Simpson, are ye up there?"

Mercy froze, her heart lodged in her throat. She had devoted a great deal of thought to being seduced by Ian Breckford, more thought than she cared to admit. But those daydreams had never included being caught in a dusty attic in his arms. She had no wish to become the latest fodder for gossip among the servants.

"Ian, you must release me," she hissed.

He lowered his head to whisper next to her ear, his sandalwood scent clouding her mind and making her knees weak.

"Ignore her," he whispered. "Eventually she will go away."

"More likely she will come up and discover us together," she warned. "You must let me go."

As if to make her point, the maid loudly cleared her throat. "Miss Simpson?"

With a glare at the man who refused to loosen his grip, Mercy concentrated on keeping her voice steady.

"Yes, Maggie, I am here. What do you need?"

"Ye have visitors."

"Visitors?" Mercy met Ian's narrowed gaze with a flare of confusion. "There must be some mistake."

"Nay, Miss." The maid sounded almost apologetic. "'Tis the Vicar and Mrs. Simpson."

"No . . ." Mercy grasped Ian's shoulders as a black tide of dismay swept through her. "Oh no."

Chapter 13

Half an hour later, Mercy was seated in a small back parlor as she poured tea for her elderly parents.

The two seated on the striped satin settee could not have been more different. Arthur Simpson had once been a tall, strapping man who had filled his small church with his booming voice. Age had stooped his shoulders and turned his muscle into a growing pouch around his waist, while his once-black hair was now a thin strand of silver over his balding head. Still, he managed to nearly overwhelm his tiny wisp of a wife, who perched in obvious discomfort at his side.

Lydia Simpson had once been a beauty with her fragile features and pale green eyes. Unfortunately her meek personality had never suited the role of a vicar's wife. She detested the endless rounds of visiting the poor and infirm. She had no talent for arranging charity festivals and was nothing less than terrified of the local gentry. She had long ago discovered her only means of peace was to hide behind the pretense of a delicate constitution.

They did have one thing in common, however. It

was the matching expression of peevish dissatisfaction with life.

Her father for his inability to claim success beyond a small church in the midst of Surrey, and her mother for being forced to forgo the large house and handsome allowance she had presumed would be hers by marrying a vicar.

For all their bitterness, however, they had loved her and provided her a comfortable home. It was far more than many young girls were given.

She attempted to keep that thought forefront in her mind as her father regarded her with a chiding frown.

"You appear flushed," he accused in his deep, rumbling voice. "Lydia, do you not think that Mercy is flushed?"

As always, Mercy's mother fell into ready agreement with her forceful partner.

"Oh, yes, quite flushed. Perhaps—"

"I hope you have not taken a nasty chill," Arthur Simpson continued, overriding his wife without compunction. "Not that it would be a surprise. A great drafty house such as this must be impossible to keep warm."

Mercy forced herself to continue pouring tea and arranging plates with the various cakes and sandwiches that the cook had prepared.

It was not as if she could argue. She *was* flushed. She could feel the heat that lingered in her cheeks. But when a woman was interrupted in midseduction by her parents, she was bound to be somewhat unnerved.

At the moment, however, she had more important matters to concentrate upon.

The most important of which was the reason for her parents' unexpected arrival. The journey was less than three hours, but the elderly Simpsons never traveled beyond their small village. Not for any reason.

"I have always found Rosehill to be quite comfortable, father," she murmured, handing him a cup of tea.

Arthur grunted, his gaze condemning as it flicked over the exquisite furnishings.

"Comfortable, eh?"

"Yes."

"Then why are you flushed?"

"If I am flushed, I suppose it is due to the fact that I was in the attics when you arrived and I had to hurry to change before greeting you." It was not entirely a lie, she silently reassured herself. She had rushed to change her gown. Of course, her detour had been more a need for a few moments to regain her composure than out of fear her dusty hem would offend her parents. Heaven knew she spent most of her days with dusty hems.

Predictably, her father's scowl only deepened. "Miss Breckford had you cleaning the attics? There, Lydia, I warned you that woman would invite our poor daughter to her home and then expect her to become some sort of unpaid servant. These rich people are all alike. Expect us to scrape and bow for a few crumbs from their table."

Mercy shoved a plate of cake into her father's hand. "Do not say such things, Father," she snapped, genuinely angered by his rude implications. "Miss Breckford has treated me as an honored guest. Indeed, she could not be more kind."

"Then why were you in the attics, might I ask?"

"Because I wished to help with the charity luncheon for wounded soldiers." She met his belligerent glare with a tilt of her chin. "Surely you would expect your daughter to lend a hand for such a worthy cause."

He appeared momentarily flummoxed by her unexpected defense of Ella Breckford. Not surprising. As a rule, Mercy found it much easier to simply ignore the older man's vigorous opinions. There never seemed much purpose in arguing when her father would as soon have his arm chopped off as admit that he might be mistaken.

On this occasion, however, she would not allow him to criticize a woman who had treated her as if she were her own daughter.

Impervious to the sudden tension in the air, Mercy's mother heaved a sudden sigh. Turning her head, Mercy watched as Lydia cast an envious gaze over the delicate satinwood furnishings and French Sevres china.

"This is a very grand home." There was another wistful sigh. "I suppose the viscount possesses a number of servants?"

"To be honest, I have long ago halted any attempt to keep track of them all," she admitted.

"Bah. A ridiculous waste of good money." Arthur gave a shake of his head. "Whatever could two people need with so many to wait upon them?"

"A good number of the servants are hired to keep the house in good order," Mercy pointed out, her voice thankfully calm. "This is more than just a home—It is a work of art with priceless treasures that need constant attention."

"You begin to sound like the nobility with all your fancy talk."

"Would you have these servants unemployed or working in the coal mines? At least here they are treated well and allowed to make a decent wage to support their families." Mercy forced herself to count to ten before handing a cup of tea to her mother. "Seed cake?"

As expected, Lydia remained lost in her covetous bemusement, absently nibbling at her cake.

"Yes, well, Miss Breckford obviously has a great deal of comfort in her fading years. Such a lovely home and servants to tend to her." Her lips thinned with sour regret. "We should all be so fortunate."

"She is indeed fortunate, but she is quite generous with both her wealth and her time." A fond smile curved Mercy's lips. "She devotes a vast amount of her days visiting the tenants and caring for others."

"Does she?" Lydia shuddered in horror. "If I were her, I would never leave this splendid house."

Arthur snorted. "Not every woman is a timid mouse like you, Lydia."

The older woman seemed to shrink beneath the disdainful tone. "Really, Arthur, you know my constitution is not at all strong."

"'Tis strong enough when you wish to visit the local dressmaker or circulating library."

"You have never understood what I suffer."

Mercy once again counted to ten, the beginnings of a headache beginning to form behind her eyes.

"You have yet to tell me why you are here."

Setting aside his empty cup and plate, Arthur regarded her with a stern expression.

"I should think that obvious enough." He narrowed his gaze. "We have come to take you home."

It was, of course, precisely what she had feared. There could be no other reason for her parents to put themselves to such an effort to travel to Rosehill. Still, to hear the words spoken with such blunt finality sent a jagged flare of panic through her heart.

Abruptly rising to her feet, Mercy pressed a hand to her heaving stomach. No, please no. She was not prepared to return to the isolated cottage.

Or the reality of her life there.

Not yet.

"Surely you received my letter telling you that I would be delayed until after the charity luncheon?" she demanded, restlessly pacing toward the window that offered a stunning view of the sunken garden. "I have promised Miss Breckford my assistance. After all her kindness, it would be extremely rude to leave her in the lurch."

Mercy did not need to turn to sense her father's annoyance. "She has a dozen servants to assist her."

She sucked in a deep breath, struggling to think clearly through her fog of desperation.

"None who are capable of writing out invitations or seeing to the unexpected troubles that are forever cropping up," she said, futilely hoping that reason could earn her a brief respite. "She has need of a secretary, not a maid."

"And what of our needs?" her father demanded. "Our house is in complete shambles without you. By God, I have not had a decent meal since you left."

"I am very sorry that my absence has been bothersome—"

"A great deal more than bothersome." The older man's voice boomed through the room. "I have not had a day of peace since you left, and your poor mother has taken to her bed to avoid the incessant chatter of that absurd woman you hired. We can endure no more."

Mercy briefly rested her forehead against the windowpane.

It would be so easy to concede defeat. To simply give in to the inevitable. After all, her parents would never have made such a long journey without the explicit intention of hauling her home.

In the end it was the memory of Ian's warning that her father would readily use love to keep her trapped in the small cottage that allowed her to grimly thrust aside her wave of despair.

"Mrs. Green came highly recommended," she said, forcing herself to turn and meet her parents' reproachful gaze.

Arthur leaned forward, his face ruddy. "No doubt from an employer who was anxious to be rid of her annoying companionship. Your mother is convinced that she is stealing from the pantry."

"If you wish to replace Mrs. Green with another nurse from the village, I am certain it can be arranged." She managed a stiff smile. "I know there are several very trustworthy widows who are always in need of additional income."

Her father pounded his fist on his knee. He was unaccustomed to having anyone stand against him. Certainly not his daughter, who had devoted a lifetime to giving sway.

"There is no need for a nurse. Not when we have a daughter who is perfectly capable of tending to our care."

Mercy wet her dry lips, trying to ignore the biting stab of guilt that clutched at her heart.

Perhaps her parents did use her emotions to manipulate her, but that did not lessen the knowledge that she had a duty to care for them. Or even her desire to do so. Her parents were the only family she possessed. She would never willingly turn her back on them.

Still, she had endless years lying ahead of her to devote to their care.

This time at Rosehill would be no more than a fleeting taste of freedom that would soon be gone.

She squared her shoulders. "I have told you that I cannot leave yet."

"Miss Breckford can very well do without you," her father growled.

"Perhaps she could, but I have not yet finished my research. There are still several books in Lord Norrington's library that I wish to study."

The older man's jaw tightened as he realized he could not bully Mercy into compliance. Slowly he leaned back against the satin settee, a sullen frown marring his brow.

"Well, I never thought to raise such a selfish daughter, did you, Lydia?"

"Oh, Arthur, I am certain that Mercy does not mean to be selfish," Lydia protested in fading tones. "It is just that she is enjoying her time among such unfamiliar luxury and has not had the opportunity to consider our own discomfort. Is that not so, my dear?"

The sweetly uttered reprimand was more cutting than any of Arthur's gruff scoldings.

Just as it was intended to be.

"It is not that I am unaware of your discomfort. You have, after all, reminded me of it in several letters. But you must know that I shall never again have access to such a vast library." A hint of pleading entered Mercy's voice. "Surely it is not asking so much to remain just a few more days."

"No." Arthur rose to his feet, his expression set in grim lines. "You have been gone long enough, Mercy. It is time for you to return home where you belong."

"But, Father—"

"I will have no arguments, young lady. You will pack your bags and prepare to leave within the hour."

"Actually, I fear that will be impossible, Mr. Simpson." A clear, resolute female voice came from the doorway. "I simply cannot do without Mercy."

* * *

The throbbing in Mercy's temple had bloomed into a raging headache over the next hour.

Granted she was deeply relieved by Ella's abrupt arrival. The older woman had taken swift command as she had swept into the parlor, a charming smile on her lips as she had ruthlessly overridden her parents' every protest.

If Mr. and Mrs. Simpson could not do without their daughter, then they would simply remain at Rosehill until Ella was prepared to allow her to leave.

That was the final word on the subject.

Of course, her father did not concede to the decree without a great deal of fuss. Anyone could be forgiven for believing he was making some terrible sacrifice to put aside his return to the damp cottage to remain among such luxury. Her mother, on the other hand, was swift to take full advantage of Viscount Norrington's generosity. With a fading voice, she had demanded a fire be lit in her chambers and a maid be on hand to assist with her bath, as well as her favorite tea be delivered to her chambers to ease her tender stomach.

Each complaint and command had been met with the kind yet unyielding force of Ella's personality, and at last Mercy had herded them up to their chambers. She had endured another lecture from her father on upsetting his peaceful existence and her mother's petulant refusal to be seen at dinner in her threadbare gown before she was at last allowed to escape.

The ache in her head had been well earned, she decided with a sigh, and no doubt would linger so long as her parents remained.

Returning to the parlor, Mercy discovered Ella

seated near the window, calmly sipping her tea. At
Mercy's entrance she set aside the cup and regarded the
younger woman with an expectant smile.

"Ah, Mercy, have you made your parents comfortable?"

Mercy grimaced as she crossed the room to lean
against the window frame. The warmth of the slanting
sun helped to ease a portion of her rigid tension.

"They are settled and already demanding that dinner
be delivered to their rooms since they have nothing appropriate to wear." She slanted Ella an apologetic gaze.
"I fear they will prove to be decidedly demanding houseguests."

Ella waved a dismissive hand. "So long as you are allowed to remain, they may be as demanding as they
desire."

Mercy rolled her eyes at the older woman's naïveté.
She had never been exposed to Arthur and Lydia
Simpson's grating personalities. There was a reason
that the local villagers avoided the small cottage.

"You have no notion of how difficult my parents can
be. You are bound to regret your generosity."

"Nonsense." Ella set aside her china cup, a stubborn expression settling on her face. "They can not
be any more difficult than my cousin Miranda and
her vast brood. Do you know that last Christmas she
arrived without warning and then proceeded to invite
nearly two dozen of her acquaintances to join her
here? Poor Norry was at last driven to London to find
a measure of peace at his club."

Mercy shuddered at the mere thought of Lord Norrington encountering her father.

"His lordship might very well decide to bolt once he
endures a few of my father's lectures. They are not
only long-winded, but they tend to condemn most of

mankind as evil, especially those with the poor taste to possess a bit of wealth." Mercy shook her head in regret. "A pity, really. I always suspected that his sermons might have been better attended if they had been somewhat more . . . tolerant."

"Do not worry about Norry, my dear." Rising to her feet, Ella reached out to pat Mercy's hand. "He is very good at keeping others at a distance. Sometimes too good, I fear."

Taking the older woman's hand in her own, Mercy gave the plump fingers a soft squeeze. She had never had anyone treat her with such an uncomplicated affection. There were no demands, no expectations. Just a simple pleasure in her companionship.

It was . . . refreshing.

"You are very kind to me, Ella," she said with a sigh. "I do not know how to thank you."

"For what?"

"If not for your timely arrival, I should be packing my bags to leave."

"Ah." A mysterious smile curved Ella's lips. "Actually, you must thank Ian for my fortunate return."

Mercy dropped the woman's hand in surprise. "What?"

"Ian arrived at the vicarage to claim that your parents had descended upon Rosehill and that unless I acted swiftly, you were about to be carted off."

Mercy's breath was suddenly elusive as she was struck by the image of Ian thundering toward the vicarage, wise enough to realize that only Ella could halt the tidal wave of doom.

Why had he gone to such an effort?

Was it only to keep his aunt from losing her

companion? Or had he possessed more selfish reasons for desiring Mercy to remain near?

Somehow the answer seemed vitally important.

"Oh," she breathed softly.

"He was very insistent that I not delay a moment," Ella pressed, a hint of speculation in her light brown eyes.

"I am certain that Mr. Breckford was merely concerned that you would be distressed by my departure."

"You are certain, eh?" Ella murmured.

"Of course."

Ella studied her deliberately guarded expression before giving a vague shrug. "Whatever the cause, I must admit that I was pleased he came to me so swiftly."

"As am I." Strolling into the room, Ian met Mercy's startled gaze with a smoldering intensity. "It would have been a shocking injustice to have Miss Simpson stolen away when she is needed at Rosehill."

Ian had intended to devote the next hour to searching his father's private parlor. He had witnessed the older man leaving in his carriage when he had returned from his mad gallop to the vicarage. It was the perfect opportunity to investigate his father's chambers.

Unfortunately, he had been unable to concentrate on the mysteries of the past when his future was being threatened by a pair of selfish country bumpkins who would hold their own daughter captive to ensure their comfort.

As he paced the room, he had told himself that the flare of panic that had driven him to the vicarage had been frustrated desire. Not only had Mercy's parents interrupted his determined seduction in the attic, but they threatened to steal her away before he could ease the ache that wracked him with a raw, merciless pain.

His thoughts, however, had not been centered upon his needs, but instead on the haunting memory of Mercy's stricken expression as he had spurred himself into action. In that precise moment he would have done whatever necessary to ease her distress.

At last he had been driven from his search to the small parlor. He had to be sure that Mercy remained at Rose-hill. He had to catch the scent of sweet vanilla and hear that soft, erotic voice brush over his skin.

Not halting until he stood at Mercy's side, he allowed himself to drink in her delicate beauty.

"Mr. Breckford," she breathed softly, her formality at utter odds with the awareness that flared through her spectacular eyes. "Ella informs me that I have you to thank for her return from the vicarage."

Ian silently cursed his aunt's presence. If Mercy desired to thank him, then he preferred it to be somewhat more . . . tangible.

Like throwing her arms around him and offering those sweet lips for his consumption.

Instead he was forced to offer a small dip of his head, his hands curling into fists to keep from reaching out and tugging her close.

"I presumed that you might need reinforcements." He briefly glanced about the room before returning his attention to Mercy. "Have your parents left so soon?"

"I fear not." Her expression hardened. "They intend to remain until I am prepared to return to Surrey."

He bit back a curse. Of course they had not left. From all that he had discovered, the elderly Simpsons were rather like barnacles that had attached themselves to their only child.

Nothing short of physical force would detach them.

"Ah," he muttered, obviously revealing his annoyance, as Ella gave a loud click of her tongue.

"And we shall treat them as welcome guests, will we not, Ian?"

Ian summoned a ready smile even as he inwardly rebelled at the capitulation. Everything within him demanded that he battle anything that would endanger Mercy's happiness. Including her overly demanding parents.

A pity that she had made it clear she would never accept a position in his life that would allow him the authority to rid her of such pests.

At least not overtly.

"If you insist, my dear."

"I do." Ella's eyes widened. "Oh, I must warn Cook that we will be needing trays. Excuse me."

The older woman scurried from the room, the stiff set of her spine warning that she was determined to be a proper hostess. Even if it killed her.

Alone with Mercy, he tucked a finger beneath her chin and tugged her face upward.

"You are pale." His brows drew together. "Did your parents upset you?"

She bit her bottom lip as if embarrassed by his question. And perhaps she was. Her love for her parents would make it difficult for her to admit she might be less than pleased by their arrival.

"I will not deny that I was disturbed by their insistence that I return home," she at last confessed. "I . . . I am not yet finished with my research. And of course I wish to assist Ella with the luncheon."

It was more her slight hesitation than her actual words that softened Ian's grim expression.

Even without having been present, Ian knew it had been a difficult task for Mercy to stand up to her parents' demands. She had been an obedient daughter for too long to easily stand her ground. It had to be a compelling motivation that allowed her to break a lifetime of compliance.

"Of course." He stroked the soft temptation of her cheek. "And there is no other reason you might wish to linger at Rosehill?"

Her eyes darkened in reaction to the rough edge of his voice. "Should there be?"

"I can think of one."

Despite her innocence, there was the age-old call of the siren in her coy expression.

"And what is that?"

His fingers slid down the length of her jaw, his thumb brushing the edge of her mouth.

"We have unfinished business, sweet Mercy."

Her breath was suddenly unsteady, her eyes wide with shimmering anticipation. Christ, she was so beautiful. So exquisitely enticing.

Not even a saint could be expected to resist such temptation.

And Ian was no damn saint.

"Is that why you went in search of Ella?" she demanded.

He hesitated. "In part."

Mercy stilled, regarding him with a questioning gaze. "And the other part?"

His lips twisted with a rueful humor. "I am attempting not to consider my motives too deeply. They would no doubt send me fleeing back to London."

"Ian?"

His chest tightened with a dangerous emotion. Something perilously close to longing.

"Never mind." He dropped his hand as if he had been singed, and in truth, it felt as if he had. He might not fully understand the sensations that blasted through him whenever this woman was near, but he knew they were the sort of thing a wise man avoided. Taking a step back, he cleared the odd lump that was stuck in his throat. "Will your parents prove to be a bother during their stay?"

She grimaced, readily allowing herself to be distracted.

"That is a certainty. My parents would not know how to exist unless they were being a bother to someone. I can only shudder at what your father will think of them."

Ian gave a short burst of laughter. "My father is very good at ignoring whatever displeases him. Trust me, I have ample evidence."

The edge in his voice was unmistakable, and Mercy slowly narrowed her gaze.

"Do you know, Ian, you have never fully explained your reasons for visiting Rosehill."

"And you, my wood sprite, never confessed why you truly desire to linger at Rosehill. I would say that we are even," he countered, flicking a finger over her cheek before forcing his feet toward the door. He had assured himself that Mercy was still safely settled at Rosehill. It was time to return his attention to searching his father's chambers before it was too late. "Until dinner, sweet Mercy."

Chapter 14

Although Ian's secretive search of his father's chambers managed to go undetected, his efforts had turned up nothing.

Which, in itself, seemed odd.

Who the devil did not have a few secrets tucked away?

Illicit love letters, smuggled brandy, bills from the local brothel . . .

He had not discovered so much as a hidden lock of hair.

It seemed more than a bit peculiar, but then he could not be certain that it was not his determination to discover some clue, no matter how vague, that made him leap to the conclusion there was something suspicious in the absolute lack of sinful evidence.

With a sigh, he returned to his chambers and changed for dinner. He had never assumed it would be easy to discover the truth of his father's secret sin. And he did have both Raoul and Reaver hunting down information.

For the moment he was at a stalemate.

Not nearly as disappointed in the realization he was

more or less stuck at Rosehill as he should be, Ian entered the library in search of Mercy. Even knowing being close to the bewitching minx would set his senses aflame and harden him to the point of pain, he could not resist the temptation to be in her company. She was rather like drinking too much champagne. A dizzying pleasure followed by hours of throbbing discomfort.

Ian adored champagne.

Entering the library, Ian paused at the door, his gaze sweeping over the elegant furnishings. He growled in frustration when he realized Mercy was not there. Instead, he found his father standing near the window with a pensive expression upon his countenance.

Norrington turned at his entrance, easily moving to pour Ian a shot of whiskey from the crystal decanter.

"Ian," he murmured, pressing the glass into his hand.

Ian sipped the amber spirit, relishing the smooth heat that slid down his throat.

"Good evening, Father."

Stepping back, Norrington linked his hands behind his back and regarded Ian with a wry expression.

"I have discovered we are to have houseguests."

"Unfortunately." Ian did not disguise his flare of annoyance. "Miss Simpson's parents have arrived and refuse to be dismissed. At least not without their daughter in tow."

Norrington lifted his brows in curiosity. "And this disturbs you?"

"It disturbs Ella, so, yes, it disturbs me," Ian smoothly countered. "My aunt takes great comfort in Miss Simpson's presence."

The viscount studied him a long moment, then, seemingly satisfied, shrugged. "Yes, she does. Of course, it would be difficult for anyone not to be pleased with her companionship. She is surprisingly peaceful for a young lady."

"Peaceful?" Ian was struck by his father's description. It was true that Mercy stirred a violent mixture of emotions within him, but underneath them all there was a strange sense of ease in her company. As if she could soothe the restless discontent that had plagued him for most of his life.

"Yes, peaceful," his father firmly retorted. "Unlike most females, she is not forever chattering or insisting that she be indulged in one social event or another. She seems quite content to spend her time in here with her studies or with your aunt planning her luncheon. Quite rare, if you ask me."

"Oh, yes, Miss Simpson is definitely a rare woman."

Norrington frowned, his suspicions once again aroused by Ian's soft agreement.

"Ian . . ."

Ian met Norrington's frown with a challenging gaze. "Yes, Father?"

The older man briefly struggled to choke back his words of warning. It was obvious he realized that chiding his bastard son from seducing a young lady was the height of hypocrisy, yet at the same time he wished to protect Mercy.

At last he heaved a resigned sigh. "I suppose you will do what you wish. You are rather too old to be taking advice."

"To be honest, I have never been good at taking advice, much to Dunnington's annoyance. A pity, really. My life should no doubt have been a good deal easier if I had heeded his words of warning."

Expecting his father to swiftly agree, Ian was startled when the older gentleman merely shrugged as he moved toward the heavy walnut desk.

"We all must discover our own mistakes." Perching on the edge of the desk, Norrington folded his arms over his chest. "Have you considered your future, Ian?"

Ian drained his whiskey as he warily regarded the man across the room. What the devil was this? A father and son chat?

Had hell frozen over?

"My future?"

"Do you have plans?"

"You must be jesting." Ian laughed at the mere notion. Unlike his friend Fredrick, he had no use for lists and schedules and daily routines. "I rarely plan from one minute to the next, let alone for some elusive future that I may or may not live to see."

"Then you should," his father retorted, his voice crisp but without the usual edge of censure. "Despite your obvious success at the tables, you will eventually weary of such an unpredictable occupation." He held up a slender hand as Ian parted his lips. "I know it is difficult to accept when you are young, but we all must age, and I can assure you that old men prefer the comfort of hearth and home to smoky gambling hells."

Actually, it was not difficult at all. Ian's return to Surrey had not been entirely inspired by his desire to discover his father's past. More than a small part of his flight from London had been his increasing boredom with his life.

Still, he was not yet prepared to admit, even to himself, that his life had lost any true enjoyment.

Such thoughts were dangerous.

With measured steps, he crossed to pour himself another whiskey.

"Surely you cannot expect me to become a respectable barrister or man of business at this late stage?" he demanded as he turned to meet his father's steady gaze. "Not only would I rather toss myself into the Thames, but there is not a person in all of London who would patronize my business." He tossed down his drink. "Christ, I would have them hauled away as a loon if they did. Who would ever trust a hardened gamester?"

Undisturbed by Ian's mocking words, Norrington reached to pull a stack of papers off his desk.

"There are other careers that you could consider."

Ian's laughter echoed through the vast room. "Ah, yes, the church would no doubt be eager to have me reform my evil ways, or perhaps I could buy a pretty uniform and march around Brighton with the other soldiers."

"I was actually thinking of something rather more suited to your particular skills."

His father thought he possessed skills? Well, hell. Who knew?

"And what skills would those be?"

"Your ability to calculate odds and confront risk with a level head." The older man shrugged. "There is also a measure of luck involved."

Ian narrowed his gaze, not entirely trusting his father's unexpected interest in his life.

"You do not intend for me to steal the Crown Jewels, do you?"

"The thought had not entered my mind, no," Norrington retorted dryly.

"I can imagine no professions other than those in the criminal world that would need such skills."

"There is one." His father held out the stack of papers,

waiting with a stoic patience for Ian to grudgingly cross
the floor to take them from him.

"What are these?"

"Information on my various investments."

Ian impatiently shifted through the various papers.
"A shipment of tobacco from the Americas . . . a brick
factory in Liverpool . . . a vineyard in France." He lifted
his head to stab his father with an impatient frown. "I
do not understand."

"It is quite simple. Although the bulk of my fortune
comes from the land rents and timber, I have discovered
that there is a great deal of money to be made if a gentleman is willing to gamble upon certain investments."

Against his will, Ian's attention was firmly captured.
"Gamble?"

Norrington was wise enough to reveal nothing more
than a cool acceptance of Ian's interest.

"There is always the risk of failure or even outright
deception." His thin countenance hardened. "There is
no lack of unscrupulous individuals who are willing to
lighten the pockets of the gullible or greedy. It takes an
enormous amount of research to ensure that a project
is legitimate, not to mention worthy of my funds. I must
calculate the rewards of my investment against the risk
and judge if it will turn more of a profit than any
number of other ventures I am offered. In other words,
I will bet upon what I believe to be my trump card."

Ian could not deny a flare of excitement. He had, of
course, known that many gentlemen discretely dab-
bled in various investments. Hell, Fredrick had made
a tidy fortune in his numerous inventions and patents.

Until this moment, however, it had always seemed a
dull affair, fit more for accountants than gamblers.

Now he realized that there was something rather . . .

enticing at the thought of placing his money upon a speculation that might end in failure or make him rich beyond all imagining.

"I'll be damned," he breathed.

His father pointed toward the papers. "As you can see, I have only a handful of investments at the moment. It is a time-consuming business that I can only indulge in when my responsibilities to my estates allow me." A faint smile curved his lips. "And to be perfectly honest, I do not possess the proper temperament to be truly successful."

It took less than a heartbeat for Ian to calculate the amount his father had invested and the current worth of the ventures. Such swift calculations, after all, were how he made his living.

"These appear successful enough."

Norrington shrugged. "They reap only small rewards because they are secure projects that have only a minimal amount of risk involved. To truly make a fortune, one must possess the nerve to lose it all. A gentleman who has the heart of a gambler and the soul of a mathematician." His dark gaze was pointed. "A gentleman like you, Ian."

Ian's odd sense of anticipation was abruptly shattered by the ugly reminder.

"A gentleman like me?" He tossed the papers back onto the polished desk. "You seem to forget, Father, I am no gentleman. I am a bastard."

Norrington regarded him with a cool, relentless expression. "I have not forgotten."

"Then you should realize that none of your prancing, blue-blooded friends would be overly anxious to have me as an investor."

"The world is changing, Ian, and those who are wise

understand that money, not bloodlines, is the currency of the future." There was a strangely awkward pause before his father cleared his throat. "Besides, I had thought we might consider a . . . partnership."

Ian regarded his father as if he had never seen him before. And indeed that was precisely how he felt.

The gentleman conversing with him as if they were two equals most certainly could not be the same man who had treated him with barely concealed contempt for the past twenty-nine years.

Folding his arms over his chest, Ian studied Norrington with unguarded suspicion.

"Perhaps I have been mistaken all these years, Father, but I possessed the distinct impression that you would not trust me to drop a quid in the offering box."

An indefinable emotion rippled over the nobleman's handsome countenance. "I cannot deny that I have allowed my distaste for your . . ."

Ian's lips twisted at his father's delicate struggle for the appropriate word.

"Gambling? Debauchery?" he helpfully supplied. "Straight path to hell?"

Typically, the man refused to rise to Ian's bait. "For your profligate lifestyle to influence my decisions regarding your support," he continued smoothly. "I always presumed that any allowance I might offer would be tossed away at the tables and whorehouses."

Ian shrugged. "A very wise presumption. That is precisely what I should do with it."

"No, Ian, I am discovering that your gambling is not the sickness that infects so many gentlemen of London." The older man offered a small smile. "It is merely a means to pass your days, is it not?"

"It also allows me to pay my rent. At least on occasion."

Norrington grimaced at Ian's pointed reminder. Unlike a legitimate son who could have expected a life of luxury as heir to the title, Ian had been forced to make his own way in the world.

"Over the years I told myself that you would eventually sow your wild oats and that once you were respectably settled in a career, I would see to a settlement that would ensure your future."

Ian snorted. "You mean once I became the dutiful son you always desired?"

"I realize now that I was no better than my father, Ian," his father said, genuine regret in his voice. "I wanted you to live the life that I thought best for you, not the one you preferred."

Ian tensed, his breath lodging in his lungs. Christ, what the devil was happening? His father was supposed to be the aloof, frigid stranger who had made him miserable as a child. A man with dark secrets that Ian was determined to uncover.

He was not supposed to become some repentant man who offered a future to Ian filled with possibilities.

Aware that Norrington was waiting for his reply, Ian was forced to clear his tight throat.

"I never expected anything from you, Father."

"But you had every right to. I claimed you as my son and then abandoned you when you had most need of me. For that I am sorry."

Spinning on his heel, Ian struggled against the painful emotions that flared through him.

He did not know how to react. How to bloody well feel.

He was quite simply stunned.

"If you are offering me money . . ."

"Actually, I am offering both of us the opportunity to make a great sum of money," Norrington overrode his stiff refusal. "If you will agree to my partnership."

For a long moment Ian regarded the tips to his boots, his mind as much in turmoil as his emotions. The cool logic of his brain warned him to tell his father to go to hell and be done with it. He had been disappointed too many times to easily trust. The less logical part of his brain, however, could not completely deny a pathetic need to prove he could be every bit as worthy of his father's respect as a legitimate son.

At last it was not his logic that made the decision. Hardly shocking. When did he ever allow logic to make his decisions? Instead it was his soul's craving for the promise of a new, exciting adventure.

His poor, tortured brain might not be capable of comprehending his father's suspicious transformation, but it did understand that he had endured a stomachful of dark, smoky card rooms and meaningless couplings with women he could barely recall the next morning.

Whether he was getting old, or merely bored, he was beginning to suspect that it was past time to retire his role as Casanova.

Why not discover if this investment scheme suited his taste? He slowly turned to face his father.

"What would it involve?" he demanded.

Norrington's lean features were unreadable. "I have the necessary wealth, but not the time to devote to discovering which investments might offer a lucrative reward for success. You could be an invaluable source of information."

"I know nothing of business."

"No, but you possess a rare talent for calculating odds.

You also are capable of mingling among the dockworkers to determine if a ship and its crew are as reliable as they promise," his father pointed out. "Or discovering if the gentlemen involved in the investments are addicted to gambling or other unsavory vices. Even those consortiums that are formed with the best intentions can be undone by a gentleman in sudden desperate need of funds."

Ian offered a thoughtful nod, realizing that he might indeed possess the sort of skills that would be useful. He possessed an uncanny sense for spotting a rook. Why would business be any different from cards?

"Yes, I can well imagine."

"And if you are truly interested, I would be happy to share what I have learned of business over the years. In time, you would be able to take over the majority of the work necessary."

"I—" Ian broke off his words, not yet prepared to accept the hovering anticipation. Not until he had the opportunity to sort through the barrage of unfamiliar sensations. "I will give it some thought."

As if prepared for Ian's wary suspicion, Lord Norrington offered a dip of his head.

"Of course."

Ian set aside his glass, in desperate need of fresh air to clear his scattered thoughts.

"If you will excuse me, I think I will take a turn through the garden before dinner."

Offering a bow, Ian turned and bolted through the door as if the devil was on his heels.

Ella slipped from the shadows of the marble statues that lined the hallways as Ian charged from the library and headed toward the staircase. From the poor boy's grim expression, it was impossible to determine if he were deep in thought or merely furious.

Unable to stand her agonizing curiosity another moment, Ella darted across the hall and entered the library to regard her brother with a concerned frown.

"Well, Norry? Did you speak with Ian?" she demanded.

Moving with that smooth elegance she had always admired, Norrington seated himself at his desk and leaned back in the leather chair.

"I promised that I would, Ella."

She barely resisted the urge to stomp her foot. Really, Norry could be the most aggravating creature.

"Do not keep me in suspense. What did he say?"

"He is considering my offer."

"Oh." Ella could not hide her disappointment.

She had been so certain that this was a perfect means of assisting Ian without his pride being injured.

Over the years, she had offered small gifts and tentative loans that had been sternly rejected. Ian would not consider taking his aunt's money. Not even if he were in desperate straits.

And of course, there was no means for Viscount Norrington to share any of his numerous estates with a mere bastard. The entail would never allow such a thing.

When Norry had mentioned his latest investment, Ella had hoped that this might be the means to allow Ian to discover a means to secure his future without the danger of the gambling hells.

And perhaps, just as importantly, a means to feel more a part of his family.

To have Ian working side by side with Norry . . . well,

it was a dream that Ella had always nurtured, even when Ian could barely force himself to visit Rosehill.

"He is intrigued," her brother soothed.

"Yes, but I had hoped—"

"I believe in the end he will agree to my scheme, Ella."

A portion of her tension eased. "Do you really, truly believe?"

He chuckled softly. "I really, truly believe."

"Thank you, Norry." Moving forward, Ella halted directly beside the desk. "I know that this will not be easy for you."

"That was my initial thought as well." Her brother glanced toward the stack of papers upon his desk. "Now, however, I find I am quite anticipating a partnership with Ian."

Ella blinked at the soft words. She better than anyone understood Norry's solitary nature and his dislike for having others intrude into his privacy.

"You are not simply attempting to make me feel better?" she demanded.

He templed his fingers beneath his chin, a thoughtful expression on his handsome countenance.

"Actually, I am not at all certain why I did not consider such an offer before this," he confessed. "Ian's connections with the less savory aspects of London society will offer an invaluable insight to those gentlemen who approach me with various opportunities. And, of course, once he has mastered the basic concepts of business, his sheer nerve will allow him to become a far more successful investor than myself." An unexpectedly proud smile curved his lips. "There are few gentlemen more suited for this particular career."

Ella was careful not to react to her brother's rare display of emotion. It would only discomfort him.

Instead, she heaved a small sigh, her thoughts turning to the young man who had forever altered the destiny of Rosehill. Whether he would ever know the truth or not.

"All I desire is for him to be happy."

Norry's lips twisted. "A rare gift."

"Rare indeed."

For nearly an hour after dinner, Mercy searched through the darkened gardens, and even the hedge maze, before the faint scent of cheroot smoke led her down a narrow path to the elaborate gazebo that overlooked the lake.

More than once she warned herself to turn back. She had no reasonable excuse to be chasing after Ian at such a late hour. Especially after he had gone to such an effort to be alone.

Stupidly, her compulsion to be near him would not be denied.

Throughout the evening, he had been distant—not angry, but more . . . distracted. As if he were contemplating some great puzzle. And then with a muttered apology he had slipped from the parlor into the garden.

She needed to assure herself that he had not disappeared into the gathering fog.

"Ian?"

There was the sound of a footfall, and a dark shadow abruptly appeared in the doorway of the gazebo.

"I am here."

She pressed a hand to her suddenly racing heart. In the glow of the torches set throughout the garden, his smoldering beauty seemed harder, more potent. Dangerous.

"Oh."

Leaning a shoulder against the doorjamb he regarded her with a brooding frown.

"It is late, Mercy. What the devil are you doing roaming the grounds?"

His overt lack of welcome should have sent her back to the comfort of her rooms. It was obvious that his strange mood had not improved.

Her feet, unfortunately, seemed to take on a mind of their own, and rather than retreating, she found herself climbing the shallow steps of the gazebo.

"I came in search of you."

His aquiline nose flared, as if drawing in her scent as she neared. "Why?"

Why? Well, that was the question, was it not?

Thankfully, she had no interest in pondering the compulsion that had led her on his trail. Not when she could pretend that it was nothing more than common human charity that had prompted her search.

"I was . . . concerned."

A dark, disbelieving brow arched at her explanation. "For me?"

"You were very quiet this evening. I thought perhaps something was troubling you."

His lips twisted, the golden eyes the color of aged whiskey in the flickering light.

"I suppose you could say that I have something upon my mind."

Halting close enough that she could catch the scent of sandalwood and clean male skin, Mercy studied his grim expression.

"Unpleasant things?"

"I have yet to decide." He cast a glittering gaze over her upturned face, his hand lifting as if to cup her cheek before abruptly pulling back. "You should return to the house. Your parents would not be pleased to discover you are alone in the dark with a bastard."

Her heart gave a sharp squeeze of disappointment at his withdrawal. Was it concern for her parents that halted his touch? Or was there something else?

"My parents are soundly asleep." She took another step forward, needing the heat of his body to ward off her sudden chill. "No one knows that I am out here."

She heard the sharp intake of his breath at her soft words, his lean body hardening with a sudden tension.

"A rather dangerous confession, my sweet."

Attempting to ignore the awareness shivering over her skin, Mercy concentrated on the memory of his coiled restlessness that had plagued him throughout the evening.

"Will you tell me what is troubling you?" she said, her voice as soft as the occasional wisps of fog.

He studied her in silence, as if debating the wisdom of ignoring her question. Then, turning to regard the ornamental lake, he heaved a faint sigh.

"My father has offered me a business proposition."

Mercy studied his rigid profile, wondering if she perhaps had misunderstood.

"And that does not please you?"

"It astonishes me." His harsh laugh echoed eerily through the still night. "Lord Norrington has publicly condemned me as a wastrel who would end his days in the gutter. You can imagine my surprise that he abruptly decides that I am just the sort of gentleman he desires as a partner in his various investments."

Her heart squeezed. Ian's tone was sardonic, but he

could not entirely hide his bitter cynicism. His father had always expected the worst in him, and that was precisely what Ian had offered.

Now he was clearly suspicious of his father's motives.

"Perhaps he realizes that he has misjudged you."

His expression revealed a hard disbelief. "Why now?"

"I beg your pardon?"

"Why would he suddenly decide that I am worthy of his trust?" He turned his head to stab her with a haunted gaze. "It is not as if I have changed my wicked ways."

Without thought, she reached to touch his arm, stepping so close that she could feel the hard thrust of his thighs. There was something so heartrendingly vulnerable deep in those eyes. A lingering wound she desperately wanted to heal.

"It could be your father who has changed," she murmured. "People do, you know."

The grim expression slowly eased as a prickle of awareness stirred the air between them.

"What of you, sweet Mercy?" he murmured, his voice husky as he trailed a finger down the curve of her throat. "Have you changed?"

She shivered, her heart racing with that delicious excitement she craved.

"Changed?"

"Have you brought an end to your desire to punish me?" His finger continued downward, tracing the line of her bodice. "Is that why you followed me?"

Chapter 15

Ian watched the emotions that flitted over Mercy's delicate features. Outrage, uncertainty, and at last . . . a startled acceptance.

She might not have considered her reasons for pursuing him through the dark. Certainly it had not been a logical decision to seek him out and seduce him.

He possessed high hopes, however, that a secret part of her was anxious to finish what they had started in the attics earlier in the day.

Mercy darted out her tongue to wet her lips, sending a shock of hunger through Ian.

He had sought out the gazebo to be alone with his thoughts. Even three hours after his father's unexpected proposition, he was grappling with the discomforting sensations that continued to plague him. Now any desire to be alone with his broodings was seared away by the soft scent of vanilla and satin skin beneath his searching finger.

"I—" She sucked in a shocked gasp as his finger dipped beneath the edge of her bodice. "I was not attempting to punish you."

"No?" He growled deep in his throat as his finger slid over the slope of her breast. That powerful ache in his loins was once again stirred to life, his erection pressing painfully against the flap of his breeches. "Then God forbid you ever do. I have suffered quite enough, I assure you."

Her lips parted in a soft sigh as his finger slipped beneath her corset to discover the hardened pebble of her nipple.

"Oh."

He wrapped a rough arm around her waist, hauling her close to his trembling body. Whatever his reasons for coming to the gazebo, he had only one thought upon his mind in this moment.

A most welcome distraction, he acknowledged, his head lowering to brush his lips over her temple.

"What of you, Mercy?" he breathed against the pulse that muttered wildly beneath her skin. "Have you suffered? Do you ache for my touch?"

Her lashes drifted downward as she clutched at his shoulders. "Ian."

"Tell me." He blazed a path of kisses over her cheek, pausing to nibble at the edge of her mouth. "Say the words."

She moaned softly. "What words?"

"That you want me."

"I . . ." With an obvious effort, she tilted back her head to regard him with a bemused gaze.

"The truth, my sweet," he commanded softly.

She shivered against his tense muscles, her eyes dark with a stark need that slammed into him with brutal force.

"Yes," she breathed. "Yes, I want you."

A consuming fire spread through his blood. Christ,

but she was a natural temptress. A woman seemingly born to lure him to madness.

"Thank God," he muttered.

"Of course, I am not at all certain it is wise."

He gave a short, humorless laugh. "I stopped being wise the moment I discovered a wood sprite luring me into a daisy-filled meadow."

A small, tantalizing smile curved her lips, her body deliberately arching to press her soft breasts against the hard planes of his chest.

"You must be easily lured, Mr. Breckford. I was doing nothing more than sitting on a rock."

He grunted, feeling as if he had just been kicked in the stomach. The devil take it, how had he come to such a pitiful state?

The woman had only to be near to cloud his mind and clench his body with a need that was positively indecent.

"Mercy, you are a very dangerous young woman."

She blinked, utterly unaware of the power she possessed over him. "Whatever do you mean?"

His sigh rasped through the night air. "I believe it would be easier to demonstrate, my sweet."

Not taking his gaze from her delicate features, Ian swept an arm beneath her knees, his other arm holding her back steady as he turned to enter the gazebo, kicking the door shut behind them.

At once the heated perfume of her skin reached out to wrap about him, and he choked back a groan. The maddening, wonderful minx had truly stolen his wits.

"Oh, how beautiful," she murmured, her gaze sweeping over the candlelit interior of the gazebo with its scenic wall panels and exquisite Italian furnishings.

"Oh, yes, astonishingly beautiful." His tone made

it clear he was not discussing the gazebo as he gently laid her upon the wide, cushioned bench. Reaching out, he brushed her cheek with light fingers. "You are a masterpiece of nature."

Her lips parted as she sucked in a sharp breath. "Ian."

Of its own accord, his hand lowered, drifting down the front of her bodice as he swiftly tugged loose the ribbons that held it in place.

"You are wearing too many clothes, my sweet."

He felt her tremble as she peered at him from beneath her tangle of lashes.

"Am I?"

His heart slammed against his chest as he tugged down the aggravating gown to reveal her slender body outlined by her tight corset and shift. She was sweet ivory skin drenched in vanilla. And he if he was not in her soon, he might very well explode.

"Mercy, if you knew what you do to me."

Without warning, she reached up to wrap her arms around his neck. "And what do you think you do to me? I never knew . . . I never understood the power of desire."

A tangible, branding awareness seared the air between them as their gazes locked and held. Her eyes were wide, darkened with need, and despite her innocence there was no fear to be found in the shimmering depths.

He was drowning.

And he did not give a damn.

"Neither did I," he muttered, lowering his head to sweep a soft kiss over her lips. "I thought I knew everything there was to know of women, but you have taught me that I was a fool."

His kiss deepened, urging her lips open to accept the thrust of his tongue.

For a heartbeat, Mercy was bewildered by his surge

of raw hunger, her fingers digging into the nape of his neck. Ian groaned, but before he could leash the savage need pounding through his body, she was tangling her tongue with his, meeting his every thrust with a ready enthusiasm.

Ian fell to his knees beside the bench, worshipping at the altar of the exquisite woman.

This was what men searched for their entire lives. It was what toppled kings, destroyed empires, and made reasonable men commit murder.

And if he had the least amount of wits, he would be fleeing as if the imps of hell were nipping at his heels.

Instead he impatiently tugged at the knots of her corset, vaguely realizing his hands were trembling as he pulled aside the stiff garment and peeled the thin shift from her slender body. Leaning back, he gazed down at her ivory perfection, his breath wrenched from his lungs in awestruck wonder.

Flushing beneath his heated gaze, Mercy shifted uneasily on the cushion. "Is something wrong, Ian?"

"God, no." He reverently cupped the soft mounds of her breasts. "You are perfect."

Too perfect, he inwardly groaned, lowering his head to capture a rosy nipple in his mouth.

She gave a keening cry as his tongue circled the hardened peak. The sound echoed deep within Ian, stirring a primitive, possessive part of him that he had never even realized existed.

This woman was *his*. The knowledge was as clear and unmistakable as the swift pounding of his heart.

His brief moment of stunning clarity was forgotten as his erection pressed against the button of his breeches. Later he could consider the strange sense of utter rightness that filled his heart. For now he simply desired to savor each touch, each caress.

Teasing the sensitive bud, Ian slid his hands beneath her back, arching her upward to meet his seeking lips.

Mercy moaned, her fingers plunging into his hair with a restless urgency, guiding his lips to her other breast. Turning his head, he suckled her with a dizzying pleasure.

He felt parched. As if it had been years, not a handful of days since he had held a woman in his arms.

Or perhaps it was simply the realization that he had not held the *right* woman in his arms.

With a swift motion he was off his knees and lying beside her on the narrow bench. Gathering her into his arms, he scattered heated kisses across her countenance.

"Is this what you truly want, Mercy?" he breathed. "There is no going back from this moment."

Her hands skimmed downward, awkwardly tugging free his cravat before working on the buttons of his waistcoat.

"This is what I want," she said with absolute certainty. "You are what I want."

Ian possessed a brief flare of guilt at the realization that this woman was offering a gift that should be treasured by a man far more worthy than himself, but as her fingers slipped beneath his shirt and over the rigid muscles of his chest, his thoughts were shattered by a lightning bolt of pleasure.

Christ, who cared why the woman would choose a debauched rake to be her first lover? It was far too late to halt the inevitable.

"Do not stop, my sweet," he moaned, his breath catching as her fingers found his sensitive nipples. "Dear God."

"I am not certain what to do," she whispered.

"Just keep touching me." His voice was a hoarse croak, his lips nuzzling down the curve of her throat. "I will take care of everything else."

She growled, her fingernails scraping lightly against his skin. "Why are you still attired?"

"I wanted to give you a last opportunity to change your mind." He nipped at her lower lip. "Now I realize it is already too late. I am lost."

"Ian," she muttered, her hands impatiently pulling his jacket. "I want to see you."

Oh . . . yes. God, yes.

Surging off the bench, Ian hurriedly yanked off his confining clothes, his hands shaking so badly that he tore the expensive linen of his shirt as he wrenched it over his head.

It was only when he was completely naked that he came to a halt, vividly aware of Mercy's darkened gaze sliding over his hard angles and planes before settling on the large erection he could not hide.

As if aware of his throbbing need, Mercy lifted herself onto her elbow and with a tentative hand reached out to lightly touch the tip of his cock.

Ian bit back a shout of bliss, savagely battling against his looming climax.

As if pleased by his response, Mercy allowed her magical fingers to skim down his throbbing shaft.

"Teach me what pleases you."

Unable to resist temptation, his hand curled about hers, pressing it against his erection.

Never had torture been quite so exquisite.

* * *

Mercy was fascinated by the sensation of his hard arousal beneath her fingers.

His skin was so soft, so warm. Like satin over steel.

Reaching the heavy sack at the base of his arousal, Mercy had barely started her exploration when he had clutched her wrist to firmly pull her hand away.

"No more, my sweet," he growled.

With a frown, she glanced up to discover his features set in grim lines, a dark stain of color crawling beneath his skin.

"Did I do something wrong?"

His sharp laugh echoed through the gazebo as he lowered himself onto the bench next to her.

"I have been unmanned by a virgin," he husked, his hands running a restless path of destruction over her shivering body. "I want you too much for such a delightful game."

Mercy was not certain what game he was speaking of, and as his head lowered to suckle her throbbing nipple she realized it did not matter. Not when her entire body was being stroked to a fever pitch by his tender touch.

She had not followed Ian for this purpose. Or at least, not consciously. Now that she was here, however, she realized that she had been aching for this since they were interrupted in the attic.

Whatever the warnings whispering through the back of her mind, she wanted this night. Just a few magical hours in the arms of a gentleman she desired beyond bearing.

Her parents' arrival had been a brutal reminder that time was slipping away. If she did not grasp this opportunity, she might never know the true meaning of being a woman.

Surely her vague worries could not compare to a lifetime of regret at denying herself her one chance at genuine passion?

Continuing to tease at her breast, Ian allowed his fingers to skim down the curve of her stomach, his touch sending a jolt of heat directly between her thighs.

Her low moan filled the gazebo, but Ian refused to be rushed. With a seeming fascination, he explored her body, gently parting her legs to dip his fingers between her inner thighs.

Mercy squeezed her eyes shut as she arched toward his touch. The storm was gathering within her, but she was not yet prepared to have it end so swiftly. She wanted . . . in truth, she did not know precisely what she wanted; she only knew that it included the heavy weight of Ian lying on top of her.

Lifting her hands to thrust them in the softness of his hair, Mercy tugged his head up to meet her frantic gaze.

"Please, Ian," she rasped.

His eyes were molten gold in the candlelight, smoldering with a raw desire that sent a shiver down her spine.

"I need you eager for me, my sweet," he muttered.

She frowned in puzzlement. Good heavens, if she was any more eager she would melt into a puddle at his feet. Parting her lips to assure him she was ready and willing for whatever was to come next, she gave a small scream when his finger slid into the damp heat between her thighs.

Digging her fingers into his shoulders, she arched upward. Around her the night air was filled with the scent of spring flowers and the rasp of Ian's heavy breath, but her world had narrowed to his expert caresses.

Nothing mattered but the sensation of his finger slowly slipping into her body, his thumb discovering the hidden nub of pleasure.

"Oh," she moaned. "Oh . . . heavens."

"Are you ready for me, Mercy?" he demanded as he stroked with a steady rhythm.

Mercy struggled to breathe as a relentless tension coiled in the pit of her stomach.

"Yes, yes."

"Tell me, Mercy. Tell me you want me," he commanded as her head twisted on the pillow.

"I want you," she moaned.

"Yes."

Continuing to stroke deep into her body, Ian carefully slipped in a second finger. Mercy gasped as she felt herself being stretched.

"Ian?"

He met her bemused gaze, his features tight with retrained need.

"Trust me, Mercy," he husked. "Can you do that?"

She gave a slow nod. It went against all logic, all common sense. But she did trust him.

As if her heart already understood far more than her mind.

"Come to me, Ian," she urged softly.

For a moment he stilled, his smoldering gaze drinking in her welcoming expression with a strange intensity.

"Christ, Mercy, what have you done to me?"

Before she could respond, he gave a low, wrenching groan and rolled on top of her willing body.

Mercy sighed in pure pleasure. Yes, this was what she needed. The solid weight pressing her into the cushions. His heated flesh melding with her own.

Following age-old instincts, she parted her legs to

allow his hips to cradle between her thighs. She shivered at the sensation of his hard arousal wedged against her damp heat, his chest brushing her sensitive nipples.

This is what she imagined in her deepest fantasies. The heat and scent and sheer intimacy of their bare skin rubbing together.

She hungrily explored the hard muscles of his back, savoring the feel of his male body. This night would have to last her an eternity, and she intended to enjoy every single moment.

On impulse she allowed her nails to scrape against his lower back, a smile curving her lips as gave a jerk and muttered a low curse.

It was incredibly satisfying to know she was not alone in this mindless need.

Resting on his elbows, Ian regarded her with a glittering gaze.

"I can wait no longer, my sweet."

She reached up to frame his face in her hands. "Neither can I."

An unexpectedly tender regret rippled over his face. "I have never been with a virgin, but I fear it might hurt."

"Ian, I want this," she swore. "I want you."

He groaned softly, lowering his head to scatter impatient kisses over her flushed countenance.

"Hold on tightly then," he murmured against her mouth. "There is no going back for either of us."

He claimed her lips in a possessive kiss as he poised his hips and settled the tip of his erection at her entrance. Mercy caught her breath, her arms wrapping about his neck as he began to merge their bodies.

She had known he was large, but knowing his girth and having it pressing into her with a relentless force

were two different things entirely. She was stretched to
the limit, so full that it was a breath from genuine pain.

"Ian?" she breathed.

His lips moved to close her eyes with light kisses.
"Just try to relax, my sweet, I promise all will be well."

Sucking in a deep breath, she concentrated on her
stiffening muscles, forcing them to ease as he shifted
deeper into her damp heat. He was trembling against
her, a thin sheen of sweat coating his body as he
reached the barrier of her innocence.

"Hold on tightly, Mercy," he commanded.

She tightened her arms about his neck, more frustrated than frightened by the momentous moment.

"Now."

The word had barely whispered through the air when
he murmured an apology and with one smooth thrust
buried himself deep inside her.

There was a flare of pain, enough to make her give
a small yelp, but there was also an astonishing sense of
completion as he buried his face in the curve of her
neck with a low, wrenching groan. For a moment she
stilled, simply absorbing the astonishing sensations.

"Mercy, are you hurt?" he rasped, his voice thick
with concern.

"I am . . . perfect," she murmured.

He gave a low moan of relief, his lips nibbling at the
curve of her throat to stir the smoldering embers of
her desire.

"Yes, you are," he whispered, shifting to capture her
lips in a kiss of sheer possession. "And you are mine."

Mercy might have been disturbed by his stark claim if
he had not chosen that moment to slowly rock his hips
forward, his sheathed erection creating a pleasurable

friction that swiftly had a sweet tension building deep inside her.

Mercy instinctively arched upward, meeting each thrust. She had never dreamed she could feel so intimately entwined with another. Not just physically, but in the passion that bound them together.

In this moment they were one.

Her fingers restlessly skimmed down his back, gripping his hips as he pulled to her very entrance before plunging back within. Her legs shifted wider, accommodating his quickening pace.

"This must be paradise," he muttered against her lips. "Never have I felt anything so sweet."

Mercy did not feel sweet. She felt deliciously wicked. A woman of passion and heat and life. Not an aging spinster at all.

Her nails dug into his skin. His every thrust was rubbing against her pleasure point, the tension within her reaching a critical peak.

"Ian, you must do something," she moaned.

He chuckled softly, pleased by her impatience. "I told you to trust me, Mercy," he murmured, his hands shifting beneath her hips to angle her upward.

With swift, relentless strokes he urged Mercy toward that perilous edge, his breath rasping through the air. Her eyes squeezed closed, her body clenched so tight that she was certain she would splinter into a thousand pieces. Then, just when she was certain she could bear no more, he gave one last surge, tumbling her into a maelstrom of exploding bliss.

He swallowed her scream of pleasure with a branding kiss, continuing to pump into her shuddering body until he abruptly wrenched himself from her womb to allow his seed to spill over her stomach in a flood of warmth.

Time seemed to come to a halt as they both floated in the golden aftermath, the silence that settled around the gazebo making it seem as if they were alone in the world.

At last Ian shifted to his side and pulled her into his arms. With a sigh, Mercy snuggled against his side, her mind clouded with wonderment.

She had known that Ian would be a skillful lover. He was, after all, the infamous Casanova. But she could never have suspected just how . . . moving the experience would be.

"Did I please you, sweet Mercy?" he whispered close to her ear.

She hid a sudden urge to smile. Good heavens, could Ian actually fear that his legendary reputation was in danger?

"I am more than pleased, Ian," she murmured softly, innately sensing that he was in no mood to be teased. "It was everything I dreamed it would be."

"No regrets?"

Her fingers skimmed across his chest, savoring the feel of his warm male skin.

"No, no regrets," she assured him, ignoring the tiny ache deep in her heart that warned she was not being entirely honest.

Chapter 16

Ian had never been a patient man. For the most part, he allowed instinct and raw impulse to guide him. An advantageous trait for a gambler, but decidedly uncomfortable for a stymied lover.

Pacing the balcony that offered a perfect view of the gardens below, Ian gnashed his teeth and glared at Mercy as she scurried from the house with a heavy tray that she set before her parents, who were settled beneath an ornamental tree.

During the past hour she had arranged and then rearranged her parents' chairs until they were satisfied that no stray sunlight might disturb them. She had fetched half a dozen cushions, her mother's needlepoint, her father's book, shawls, glasses, and endless handkerchiefs. Now she poured her father a large glass of the lemonade she had just brought from the kitchens.

The devil take it. He wanted to rush down there and shake some sense into the aggravating minx. Or better yet, to toss her childish, petulant, demanding parents into the nearest carriage and have them hauled back to their distant cottage.

Over the past two days he had not been allowed so much as a moment alone with Mercy. If she were not being pestered to death by her parents, then she was running some errand or another for his aunt. And while he had made a point of spending his nights in the gazebo with the hope that Mercy would eventually join him, it had proven to be a futile waste of time.

Was it any wonder that he was a tad grumpy to have been offered a taste of paradise only to have it snatched away?

A part of him, however, understood it was not just frustrated desire that was making his teeth clench and his chest so tight that he could barely breathe.

Oh no. The violent fury pounding through his blood was a direct result of watching the beautiful young maiden being treated with such selfish disregard.

By God, she should be drenched in luxury, not grubbing after her parents like an unwanted orphan. She should be surrounded by her beloved books and waited upon by a dozen servants. She should spend her night in the arms of a lover who would treat her with exquisite care. . . .

"Ian. Good heavens, I did not expect to find you here."

Ian muttered a low curse at the sound of Ella's voice floating from the French doors behind him. As much as he adored his aunt, he did not want to be interrupted in this moment. Not when he was busily convincing himself to charge into the garden and toss Mercy over his shoulder.

A beautiful fantasy that Ella was certain to nip in the bud.

Slowly turning, Ian watched as the older woman stepped onto the balcony.

"Where did you expect to find me?" He forced a stiff smile to his lips as he leaned against the stone balustrade.

"Norry mentioned at luncheon that you intended to spend the afternoon in the village," Ella murmured, moving forward.

"I have changed my mind."

"So I see." With a deliberate motion, Ella leaned over the railing to regard Mercy as she fussed over her father's cushions. "You appeared disturbed when I first arrived. Is there something wrong?"

Realizing that there was no means to hide the fact he had been spying upon Mercy like a loose screw, Ian allowed his smoldering anger to harden his expression.

"Yes, there bloody well is something wrong," he growled, jerking his head toward the small group below. "Why do you allow those intruders to treat Miss Simpson as a servant? She has been waiting upon them hand and foot for the past two days."

"It is a pity, but those intruders are her parents, Ian, and I have no right to interfere." Ella turned back to meet his accusing glare with a grimace. "As much as I might wish."

"They are not parents, they are a menace," he muttered.

"Perhaps, but what can I do?"

"You are the hostess of Rosehill. Send them packing."

"I could, but Mercy would no doubt feel obliged to leave with them." She paused, tilting her head to one side. "I do not believe that either of us is willing to lose her companionship yet, are we?"

Ian was not stupid. Well, not as a rule. He understood that Ella's seemingly simple question held a quagmire of implications that a wise man would avoid like the plague.

He was just too damned angry to care.

"No." His gaze narrowed. "I have no intention of losing Miss Simpson's companionship."

Ella wrinkled her nose as Mr. Simpson's voice boomed through the garden, sending his daughter scurrying to refill his glass.

"What Mercy truly needs is a champion," she said with a sigh.

"A what?"

"A knight in shining armor who will whisk her away from her personal dragons," the older woman clarified.

For a moment Ian was infuriated by the mere suggestion that some heroic, chivalrous knight might come charging to Mercy's rescue. He'd slay the bastard on the spot.

Then, realizing his aunt was regarding him with an expectant expression, Ian gave a short, disbelieving laugh.

"Christ, Ella, you cannot possibly believe that I could ever pose as St. George?"

"Why not?" She gave a wave of her plump hand. "I know you have come to care for Mercy."

"Whatever my feelings for Miss Simpson, I am no knight in shining armor." His lips twisted at the unwelcome knowledge of his sordid past. "An innocent would be better served to remain in the hands of her dragons than to be rescued by a man like me."

"Nonsense. You are not nearly so wicked as you would have others believe, Ian."

Ian rolled his eyes at his aunt's stout defense. The woman would claim the Marquis de Sade was merely misunderstood.

"You only say that because you want to see the best in everyone, my dear," he said dryly. "There are any number of people who would share with you the tales of my evil existence."

Something flickered over Ella's plump countenance before she was sternly giving a shake of her head.

"No, I have known truly wicked men, and you are not one of them," she said with utter confidence. "You have a good and generous heart, Ian."

Ian was briefly reminded of Mercy's suspicion that Ella had endured a disappointment in her youth. Perhaps it was not simply a matter of unrequited love. Perhaps it was something more sinister.

Certainly the gentlemen in his aunt's past must have been appalling if she considered Ian a worthy knight in shining armor.

"I am a hardened gamester and a debauched seducer who long ago traded my soul to the devil, Aunt Ella. Precisely the sort of gentleman most women are wise enough to avoid."

"You have no further need to gamble. Norry has told me you possess an uncanny talent for business. I have not seen him so excited about anything in years." She offered a sweet smile. "And, of course, every woman knows that a reformed rake makes the best husband."

"Husband?" Ian jerked as if he had been kicked in the stomach. "Have you taken leave of your senses?"

"Why not?"

There were a dozen reasons why not. A hundred. The fact that he could not seem to recall any one them as he gazed down at the delicate woman with her hair shimmering like the finest gold in the sunlight and her every movement as elegant as a wood sprite's meant nothing.

"I . . ."

"Well, Ian?" Ella prompted, a sly smile tugging at her lips.

His jaw clenched as a raw pain jolted through his heart. Dammit, what was the matter with his aunt? Not even her love for him could make her blind to his numerous faults.

"Not only would a woman have to be demented to desire me as a husband, but the last thing in the world I want is to be tied down to one woman." He hunched his shoulders. "I would be bored within a week."

"Not if she were the right woman," the older woman murmured softly.

"Enough, Ella." His voice was harsh with warning. "I will not discuss such foolishness."

"Then you will lose her, my dear. In a few days at most she will be forced to return to her home and beyond your reach." Ella reached up to lightly pat his cheek. "Consider that before it is too late."

Ella gave his cheek another pat before turning to leave the balcony. Ian watched her retreat with a deepening scowl.

Lose Mercy?

That was ridiculous.

To lose something you first had to claim it. And he would never be idiotic enough to think the woman could ever be more than just a passing fancy.

Would he?

That unexpected pain once again ravaged through his chest, making Ian grasp the stone railing. Damn. As much as he might want to deny the truth, there was a very large part of him that realized the inevitable.

He could not bear the thought of allowing Mercy to

simply disappear. Not from Rosehill, and most certainly not from his life.

Not yet.

Not until he understood the strange compulsion that held him in its grip. A compulsion that would drive him mad if she were to slip away.

Sucking in a deep breath, Ian was abruptly distracted from his disturbing thoughts by the sight of a lone rider entering the stable yard.

Reaver.

There could be no mistaking his massive size or the reaction of the servants who scurried out of his relentless path.

The question was what the devil he was doing back so soon.

Ignoring the fierce need to remain on the balcony and keep a watch upon Mercy, Ian forced his reluctant feet to carry him back into the parlor and toward the hallway. He was the one who had sent Reaver to London. It was not the servant's fault that his mind was too consumed with thoughts of Miss Mercy Simpson to recall his reason for coming to Rosehill.

Reaching his private chambers at the same moment as Reaver, Ian clapped his friend on the shoulder.

"I did not expect you back so swiftly."

The large man ran a weary hand through his hair. "I have the information you desire."

"Come, we will be more comfortable in my chambers."

"Aye." Reaver readily followed Ian into the elegant sitting room, dropping his large body onto a settee with a deep sigh. "I could use a drink."

Ian poured them both a large shot of his private whiskey, crossing the room to press one of the glasses into Reaver's hand.

"Here."

"Ah." Sipping the fine spirit, Reaver heaved a sigh of appreciation. "You shall be forced to pay for the hideous swill I was forced to endure on the road."

Ian chuckled. "I am under no illusion that it is my fine whiskey that holds your loyalty, Reaver, not my exceptional character."

"A man must have standards."

"Indeed." Leaning against the sideboard, Ian attempted to concentrate upon his companion. A task that would be a great deal easier if his bloody mind wasn't consumed with thoughts of Mercy. "So tell me, how did you manage to so swiftly track down your prey?"

"It wasn't particularly difficult." Reaver polished off his whiskey with a grimace. "This prey left a trail that even a lobcock could follow."

"He was in London?"

"Nay. From all I could gather, he left England near a decade ago and has never returned."

Ian folded his arms across his chest, only vaguely disappointed. Suddenly the past was not nearly so intriguing as the present.

Or the future.

"Do you know where he went?" he demanded, absently.

A slow smile curved the man's lips. "No, but I do know why he went."

Ian stiffened. "Scandal?"

"A rather nasty one."

Barely aware he was moving, Ian turned to replenish his glass, draining the whiskey with one long swallow.

Just a few days ago the news of a nasty scandal would have been precisely the information he desired. He was here, after all, to discover the reason his father had handed twenty thousand pounds to Mr. Dunnington. Now he could not deny a vague reluctance to pry into matters that were long forgotten.

"If he felt compelled to flee England, then I can only presume he was caught cheating at cards, or his debt was so great he could no longer avoid his creditors," he at last managed to mutter.

Reaver's smile widened. "Actually, it was an affair that was his undoing."

Ian did not have to feign his puzzlement. "You must be jesting. What gentleman has not indulged in an affair? Even if the woman were wed—"

"Man."

Ian blinked at the succinct word. "I beg your pardon?"

"The affair Summerville indulged in was with Lord Hinton," Reaver smoothly explained. "They were caught together by Lady Hinton, who was furious enough to reveal her husband's naughty little secret to anyone who would listen."

"Good God." Ian gave a slow nod of his head, considering the various implications of Reaver's information. It was common knowledge that many gentlemen of the *ton* possessed sexual fetishes. Some more exotic than others. It was expected, however, that those gentlemen would keep such fetishes discretely hidden behind closed doors. "I suppose that would cause a scandal."

"Precisely."

Ian paced the room, attempting to envision a young Summerville visiting Rosehill. It was not impossible he had given some hint to his unusual preferences.

"And it would certainly be a reason for my grandfather to forbid his presence at Rosehill if he somehow discovered Summerville's secret."

"Aye." Reaver rose to his feet with a shrug. "Such men will always be treated as lepers."

A faint smile curved Ian's lips at the man's stoic indifference. "You do not seem particularly shocked, Reaver."

The servant snorted. "Where I come from, there are few things I haven't seen. Some things no man should see."

Ian did not doubt that for a moment. A sexual preference for men could not compare with the evils to be discovered in the stews of London.

"Thank you for your efforts, my friend."

Heading toward the door, Reaver paused to glance over his shoulder. "Is that the information you desired?"

"I really have no notion," he confessed with blunt honesty. It might be a titillating scandal, but it had nothing to do with Viscount Norrington. Ian heaved an exasperated sigh. "In truth, I am not entirely certain what I am doing here. If I had the least amount of sense, I would pack my bags and return to London."

Reaver flashed a mocking smile. "Which, of course, means you intend to stay."

"Ah, you know me so well."

"Aye." Reaver deliberately narrowed his gaze. "Well enough to know you're courting trouble."

"When am I not?"

"There is trouble and then there is trouble."

Ian shrugged, well aware that his companion was referring to his uncharacteristic fascination with Mercy Simpson. Christ. He had conducted affairs with women beneath the noses of their fathers, their brothers, and even their husbands. Obviously, however, his skills at Casanova did not include concealing his bumbling attempts at seduction with a country miss.

"Very profound."

Reaver chuckled with undisguised enjoyment. "It's your neck in the noose, not mine."

The clock was striking nine bells when Mercy hurried into the upstairs salon that her parents had appropriated for their evening tea. After two days of endless waiting upon her parents, Mercy's feet were aching and her temper strained, but she forced herself to maintain her stiff smile as she stepped into the pretty pale green and ivory room with its delicate ornamentation and Satinwood classic furnishings.

Her smile was growing stiffer by the moment. Dear Lord, she would give anything to be in the peaceful solitude of Rosehill's beautiful library. Or better yet, in the shadowed gazebo with Ian's strong arms wrapped about her.

The past two nights had been nothing less than torment as she had lain alone in the dark. It was one thing to imagine the delights that could be found in the arms of an experienced rake and quite another to truly understand just what she was missing in her cold, spinster bed.

Unfortunately, she knew her parents too well.

They were annoyed by her refusal to simply return to their cottage and determined to punish her for her stubbornness.

If she were not close at hand to bear the brunt of their displeasure, then they would quite readily turn it upon anyone unfortunate enough to cross their path.

The servants . . . Ella . . . even Lord Norrington.

Mercy shuddered at the mere thought.

"Here is your tea, Father," she murmured, halting

at the door to study her parents, who had chosen to settle on a settee near the fire they had insisted be lit.

The older man closed his book with a snap. "'Tis late."

At his side, Mercy's mother heaved a small sigh as she patted his arm.

"Not so late, Arthur. I am certain that Mercy is doing her best."

"Hmmm." Arthur peered at the tray in Mercy's hand. "Where are my lemon tarts?"

Mercy grimly held onto her smile. "I believe that Cook has made a lovely plum cake."

"I told you quite plainly I wished lemon tarts with my tea."

"Perhaps tomorrow . . ."

"Really, Mercy, it is hardly an excessive request, is it?" Arthur complained, his cheeks reddening with his rising temper.

"No, of course not," Mercy murmured, anxious to divert her father before he could work himself into a full-blown tantrum. "I will bake a few tarts tomorrow—"

Her words were interrupted as a large male body brushed through the doorway, plucking the tea tray from her hands and roughly setting it onto a nearby table.

"Actually, you will do no such thing," Ian Breckford announced, turning to meet Mercy's startled gaze. "We possess an entire kitchen staff to tend to our cooking."

Mercy blinked, dumbfounded by Ian's unexpected appearance. For the past two days she had barely caught a glimpse of the wickedly handsome gentleman. Not that it mattered. Despite her efforts to keep a distance between them, he managed to haunt her every thought. There was not a moment of her day she did not recall the scent of his warm skin, the feel of his slender hands, the husky rasp of his voice.

Still, he had seemed content enough to remain at a discreet distance.

Perhaps even relieved.

Now she struggled to gather her rattled thoughts. "Good heavens, Ian, you nearly gave me heart failure. Whatever are you doing?"

In the firelight, his beautiful features were set in grim lines, his eyes smoldering with gold fire and his hair tousled as if he had run his fingers through the dark curls more than once.

Mercy shivered, feeling as if a caged panther had just been released into the room. The very air prickled with danger.

Stepping so that they were nose to nose, Ian glared into her baffled eyes.

"By some ludicrous twist of fate, it has fallen upon my shoulders to rescue you from your aggravating, pestilent, ill-mannered dragons," he growled, his voice oddly rough.

Dragons? Was the man tipsy?

"What?"

"You have carried your last tray and fetched your last shawl, my sweet. I will endure no more." Without waiting for Mercy to react to his abrupt attack, Ian turned to point an accusing finger at her father. "Since it has obviously escaped your notice, sir, I will warn you that your daughter is not a servant at Rosehill."

Arthur instinctively flinched as Ian's lethal power filled the room. Then, jutting his heavy jaw forward, he met Ian's glittering gaze with a stubborn expression.

Arthur Simpson did not admit he was wrong to any man, let alone a mere bastard.

"Of course Mercy is no servant. My daughter is a lady."

"Then treat her as one," Ian snapped. "If you desire fresh tea or lemon tarts or yet another damnable shawl, then you will ring for one of the maids. They are paid to see to your comfort."

Her father's countenance flushed with a dangerous color as he struggled to rise to his feet.

"Now you see here, Breckford, Mercy is quite happy to devote herself to her parents' needs." He waved a gnarled hand about the elegant room. "Perhaps among society it is accepted for children to consider only their own pleasures, but in most homes it is the Christian duty of the young to tend to their elderly."

Ian's laugh was deliberately grating. "I hardly believe it is the Christian duty of a beautiful maiden to be denied an opportunity for her own home and family so she can be at the constant beck and call of her parents."

Arthur scowled, refusing to acknowledge the truth of Ian's charge. "You know nothing of our family."

"I know that since you have arrived, Miss Simpson has not had a moment to enjoy her studies or to assist my aunt with her charity luncheon." Ian stepped forward and plucked the small bell from the table near her father. "Hell, she has not even been allowed to sit down and eat a proper dinner without having it interrupted by this infernal bell."

"No, Ian." Mercy gave a strangled gasp as Ian turned and tossed the bell directly into the fire.

Arthur sputtered in outrage. "How dare you?"

Ian growled as he took a threatening step toward the older gentleman. "Someone must halt your incessant bullying, and since Mercy is too tenderhearted to put her foot down, then I shall do it for her."

"By what right?" Arthur demanded.

"Ian . . ." Mercy rushed forward, sensing that the confrontation between the two men was more than a spat about a ridiculous bell.

"By the right of a gentleman who happens to care about your daughter's happiness." Without allowing his warning gaze to waver from Arthur Simpson's heavy countenance, Ian easily captured Mercy with one arm and hauled her close to his side. "Something you obviously have forgotten in your selfish desire to keep her your prisoner."

"Prisoner?" Arthur gave a blustering laugh. "That is absurd."

"Is it?" Ian trailed his fingers down her arm, his tender touch leaving a path of fire in its wake. "When was the last occasion that your daughter attended a local society event? Or enjoyed an afternoon of shopping with her friends? Or even spent a few moments flirting with a handsome young gentleman?"

Mercy's mouth went dry, her words of protest forgotten as an aching wave of need slammed into her.

Oh . . . heavens. This was a mistake. She could not possibly concentrate when she was drowning in the heat and scent of this man.

Unfortunately, her father had no such troubles. With a loud sniff, Arthur glared at Mercy, clearly expecting her to deny any wish for a life of her own.

"She has no interest in such things," he at last muttered when Mercy remained silent.

"Every young maiden has interest in such things," Ian countered, his voice thick with an aversion he did not attempt to hide. "You have simply denied Mercy the opportunity to indulge in harmless pleasures."

Pressing a hand to her heart, Lydia rose to her feet and regarded Ian with a wounded expression.

"We love our daughter, Mr. Breckford."

Ian was blatantly unmoved by her mother's gentle reprimand. Indeed, his expression only hardened.

"If you loved Mercy, Mrs. Simpson, you would devote your attention to her needs rather than your own self-ish comforts. You speak of duty, but you have utterly and completely failed your daughter."

Lydia sucked in a shocked breath. "Mercy, what is the meaning of this?"

Well, that was a bloody good question.

Although Mercy had suspected Ian would find her parents a source of irritation, she had presumed he would do as most people did and simply avoid them. She had never dreamed he would actually feel the need to confront them in this manner.

"Mr. Breckford has a rather unpredictable sense of humor." Threading her arm through his, Mercy sent him a warning glare. "If you will excuse us for a moment?"

Chapter 17

Mercy was not foolish enough to believe she could force Ian from the room. She would no doubt have better luck attempting to haul about a load of bricks.

Thankfully, the scoundrel made no effort to battle her persistent tugs on his arm, and with a mocking dip of his head toward her father, allowed himself to be pulled into the wide corridor.

Her flare of relief, however, was fleeting.

Pulling closed the door to the parlor, Mercy turned to confront Ian, only to find he had reversed her hold and she was now the one being towed down the corridor with a relentless force.

"Ian." She stumbled as he led her down the long flight of stairs and toward the side door that opened into the gardens. "Where are we going?"

He refused to answer her question, steering her with a grim purpose out of the house and onto the dark balcony. Then, as she parted her lips to share her thoughts on being yanked about like a hound on a leash, he pressed her into a shadowed alcove and claimed her mouth in a kiss of stark possession.

"Dammit, I can bear no more, Mercy," he muttered against her lips, his hands gripping her hips with rough urgency. "I do not give a bloody hell if they are your parents or not. I will not allow anyone to treat you like a common drudge."

Her hands lifted, intending to push him away before they fluttered and at last landed lightly against his chest.

Why pretend that she had not been aching for his touch, his kiss? Ian did not have to be Casanova to sense her body was melting with pleasure.

Of course, that did not mean she intended to concede total defeat.

Ian Breckford had a great deal of explaining to do.

"Ian, what on earth has gotten into you?"

"Beyond a violent need to have you in my bed?" he demanded, his lips skating down her jaw in a path of destruction.

Her heart jerked as she struggled to recall the reason she was alone in the dark garden with Ian.

"You cannot speak to my parents in such a manner."

"Actually, it appears that I can." Ian pulled back to regard her with a brooding gaze. "And I will continue to do so until they realize I will not endure watching you fetch and carry for them."

"How my parents treat me is none of your concern."

"Is that meant to be a jest?"

She licked her dry lips. There was a strange intensity smoldering about Ian that was more than a tad unnerving.

"Why would it be a jest? I am nothing more than your aunt's companion who will soon be gone. . . ."

His fingers tightened on her hips, his eyes glittering with gold fire.

"Damn you, Mercy, do not be a fool. You are a hell of

a lot more than just Ella's companion." He deliberately paused. "Or have you forgotten what occurred in that gazebo just two nights ago?"

Forgotten? The memory of being held in Ian's arms would be seared into her mind for all eternity.

"Of course I have not forgotten, but that does not change anything between us."

"On the contrary, it changes everything."

A burst of treacherous excitement exploded low in her stomach at his rough words. Was he implying that this fierce, near-overwhelming attraction between them was more than just a fleeting fascination? That it might be a deeper, more enduring connection?

Realizing the dangerous direction of her thoughts, Mercy sternly squashed the renegade flare of hope.

She had gone into this affair with no illusions. Indeed, she had deliberately chosen Ian Breckford because she had understood there would be no unpleasant complications, had she not?

Now was no time to begin courting disaster.

"This is absurd," she breathed. "For God's sake, you are the Casanova."

"Do not call me that ridiculous name," he snapped. "I am Ian Breckford, a man like any other."

"No." She gave a bewildered shake of her head. "Not like any other."

His lips twisted. "Should I be flattered or insulted?"

"You have had dozens of lovers. I cannot believe you felt the need to meddle in all their lives."

The golden eyes darkened as he lowered his head to bury his face in the curve of her neck.

"Only yours, sweet Mercy. Only yours."

Mercy shuddered at the sensation of his warm lips moving against her skin.

"Why?"

"Because I cannot halt myself." He growled low in his throat, as if not entirely pleased by the realization. "Christ, it does not matter how many times I tell myself you are just a passing amusement, I cannot get you out of my thoughts. You haunt my dreams. You are my first thought when I awaken, and my last before I go to bed."

Mercy gripped his coat as her knees threatened to buckle. "Ian?"

He scattered a trail of punishing kisses along the modest line of her bodice.

"I follow you about like a lovesick fool, consumed by the need to be near you."

"I . . ." Mercy moaned as his hands slipped upward, cupping the aching fullness of her breasts. "Wait, Ian, I cannot think when you are doing that."

He chuckled, his thumbs teasing the tips of her nipples. "If that is an argument to encourage me to halt, then you are far off the mark, my sweet. I do not want you thinking. I just want you to feel. To feel me."

She did feel him. Dear heavens, she was drowning in the searing awareness. The heat of his body. The tormenting pleasure of his touch. The frantic beat of his heart.

"I am trying to make a point."

"You can make all the points you desire later." He lifted his head to stab her with a glittering gaze. "Come with me."

"What?"

"I want to be with you, my sweet." His voice held a raw yearning that echoed deep within her. "I want to have you in my bed."

"We cannot risk being seen going to your chamber."

"Then come to the gazebo."

"But . . ." Mercy struggled to breathe. "My parents."

Holding her wide gaze, Ian lifted his hands to tenderly cradle her face.

"Sweet Mercy, your parents are not the only ones who have need of you." He shifted to press the hard thrust of his arousal against her stomach. "I ache for you."

She shuddered, her body clenching with a ruthless desire. For the past two days she had been the dutiful daughter, falling all too easily into her traditional role of pandering to her parents. She had denied her desire to concentrate on her studies or to simply enjoy a quiet tea with Ella. Even more unbearable, she had denied the sheer enjoyment of being with Ian.

In this moment, she was done with sacrifices.

"Yes."

He stilled as the word fell softly from her lips.

"Mercy?"

"Yes, I will join you in the gazebo."

"Thank God."

As if fearing she might change her mind, Ian swept her off her feet and cradled her against his chest as he charged through the rose-scented garden. Struggling to capture her breath, Mercy stared at Ian's dark features, a tiny thrill racing down her spine at the grim intensity of his expression.

There was nothing of the smooth, sophisticated Casanova in his urgent step or the beads of perspiration that dotted his forehead.

This was quite simply a man caught in the grip of an overwhelming desire.

As if to prove her point, Ian vaulted up the steps of the gazebo, kicking the door closed behind him as he carried her toward the cushioned bench. Claiming her lips in a demanding kiss, he set her on her feet and swiftly stripped her of her gown and corset.

Mercy welcomed his hungry onslaught, returning his kiss with the smoldering frustration that had plagued her for the past two days.

He tasted of whiskey and warm male desire. An erotic combination that made her head spin and her heart race.

It was only when her thin chemise was pooling at her feet and Ian was jerking off his jacket that Mercy reluctantly pulled back.

"Wait, Ian."

Ian groaned, leaning his forehead against hers as he struggled to control his fierce need.

"Forgive me, Mercy," he rasped. "I did not mean to frighten you."

"No, Ian, you could never frighten me."

Lifting his head, he regarded her with a wary gaze. "Then what is wrong?"

With a small smile, she reached up to unknot his cravat, tugging it free before attacking the buttons of his waistcoat.

"I believe this should be my honor," she murmured.

He chuckled, his fingers skimming lightly down the bare curve of her back. "By all means, my dear."

Mercy swiftly discovered that a gentleman's attire was considerably more complicated than she had ever dreamed possible, but with more than a few awkward stumbles and a good deal of giggling, she at last was able to strip away the last of his clothing and reveal his glorious form.

And it was glorious.

The world seemed to halt as Mercy lifted her hands to trace the smooth planes of his chest. Beneath her fingers she could feel his muscles flex at her touch, his breath hissing through his clenched teeth as his hands clutched at her hips.

"Mercy."

"Not yet," she muttered.

She allowed her fingers to skim lower, discovering the hard ridges of his stomach and the trail of dark hair that led to the thick jut of his erection. Just for a moment, she hesitated, unexpectedly embarrassed by her bold behavior.

"Please," Ian muttered, his voice a harsh rasp.

Gathering her courage, Mercy allowed her fingers to curl around the straining shaft, once again amazed how smoothly the skin moved over the hard muscles beneath. She stroked downward, reaching the soft sack before exploring back to the damp tip.

Ian's groans filled the gazebo as she stroked downward again, his lips capturing her mouth in a kiss of sheer desperation. Encouraged by his fierce response, Mercy continued her daring caresses, so lost in her heady sense of power that she was barely aware Ian was moving until she found herself flat on her back on the cushioned bench.

"The honor is now mine," he warned, poised above her with a predatory expression.

Mercy shivered, her hands clutching the cushions beneath her as he lowered his head and nibbled his way down the curve of her neck. Her body bowed in pleasure as he paused to tease the aching tips of her breasts, his tongue sending flames pouring through her blood. Gently he captured one beaded nipple between his teeth, chuckling softly as she cried out in delight.

"I did not know anything could feel so wondrous,"

she whispered, lifting her hands to shove her fingers in the thick satin of his hair.

"You are wondrous, Mercy Simpson." With slow, savoring kisses, Ian journeyed down the shallow curve of her stomach, smiling against her flesh as she wriggled beneath his teasing caresses. "There has never been another woman like you."

Mercy's hips lifted off the cushions as he stroked his mouth over her hip bone and down the sensitive skin of her inner thigh.

"Oh heavens." Her chest was so tight she could not breathe. "You must do something. I cannot bear much more."

"Be patient, my sweet tyrant." Ian relentlessly tugged her legs apart, slipping off the bench to kneel between her thighs.

Lifting on her elbows, Mercy regarded him with a smoldering gaze. "Ian?"

"I need to taste your sweetness."

"But . . ." Her protest died in her throat as he shifted and stroked his tongue through her damp curls.

She tumbled back onto the cushions, her eyes squeezing shut at the pure bliss that trembled through her body. Oh, this was decadent. Decadent and wicked and so utterly wonderful.

Moaning in pleasure, she allowed herself to be swept into the maelstrom of sensations. Over and over his tongue dipped into her gathering dampness, stroking with a steady rhythm until her soft pants filled the silence of the gazebo.

Then, gently, he sucked the tiny nub of pleasure into his mouth and Mercy screamed as the entire world exploded in a burst of shimmering stars.

Stunned by the sheer force of her release, Mercy was

barely aware of Ian sliding up her body and entering her in one smooth thrust. But as he captured her lips in a heated kiss, she instinctively wrapped her arms about his shoulders and arched her back to meet the fierce strokes of his invading erection.

"Mercy, my love, I need you," he husked against her lips, his entire body trembling as he jerkily surged in and out of her body. "Don't ever leave me."

Mercy barely registered his soft command, lost in the shimmering magic that was once again building in her lower body. With every thrust, he pressed deeper into her body, his fullness creating a friction that was rapidly urging her toward that breathless pinnacle.

"Yes, Ian . . . yes . . ." She urged him to a faster pace, raking her nails down his back as he bucked against her with a wild lack of control.

"Mine," he rasped as he pressed his lips to the hollow beneath her ear. "My sweet Mercy."

With one last surge he tumbled them both over the edge of reason, remaining buried deep inside her as he released the hot flood of his seed.

It was only the knowledge that he must be crushing the slender woman beneath him that gave Ian the strength to at last roll to the side and pull Mercy into his arms.

Christ, he felt . . . what?

Sated, of course. Utterly, blissfully sated.

And oddly peaceful. As if just having Mercy near was enough to soothe the restless beast that had plagued him for his entire life.

But beyond that, he felt a vague sense of dread that refused to be dismissed.

Pressing his lips into her vanilla-scented curls, Ian did not have to search far to discover the reason for the unease lodged deep in his heart. After years of taking precautions to avoid creating a child with his various lovers, he had just thrown all caution to the wind to release his seed deep in Mercy's body.

This woman was no longer a delightful distraction that he would soon put in his past.

In truth, the mere thought of losing her was enough to make his gut clench with something perilously close to panic.

The question was what he did now.

Although Mercy had been eager and willing to share her delightful body, she had never indicated she desired more than a brief affair. Quite the contrary. She had been one of the few females who had asked nothing of him.

There had been no pleas for his undivided attention, no demands for pretty baubles, no subtle hints of a more lasting connection.

Dammit. He was supposed to be an expert when it came to women, so why the hell did he suddenly feel like a bumbling novice?

Stirring at his side, Mercy heaved a faint sigh. "As much as I wish to remain here, I suppose we should return to the house."

His arms instinctively tightened, his lips nuzzling the soft skin of her temple.

"Not yet."

"Ian?"

"Mmm?"

"Is something the matter?"

"I just want to hold you in my arms."

Her fingers lightly brushed over his chest. "This is nice."

He shuddered beneath her touch, his body instantly hardening.

"A great deal more than nice. You fit perfectly against me," he husked. "As if you were made to be here."

"A good thing, considering this bench is rather narrow." Tilting back her head, Mercy offered a teasing smile. "I do not believe your ancestors intended it to be used for such a purpose."

Ian's heart came to a complete, perfect halt at the sight of her beautiful eyes dancing with amusement. Dear God, he would walk through the pits of hell for that smile.

"I would not be so certain." He brushed a kiss over her forehead. "Unlike my father, most of my ancestors were a lusty bunch. I should not be at all surprised to discover this gazebo had been built for the precise purpose of providing privacy for romantic trysts."

"Have you often used it for . . . trysts?"

Her tone was casual, but Ian felt a fierce flare of satisfaction. Mercy did not like the thought of him being with another woman.

"I cannot deny my past. Nor will I pretend that I did not find pleasure in the women I have known. They were each lovely and fascinating in their own way."

She stiffened at his blunt honesty. "I would rather not hear of your endless conquests, Ian."

"Allow me to finish, my love." Shifting onto his elbow, Ian caught and held her gaze. "As much as I enjoyed the brief liaisons, they never meant more than a delightful means to devote a few hours. And as much as I was attracted to my lovers, they did not truly stir my emotions. But you . . ."

Mercy's eyes widened, her hands lifting to press her fingers against his lips.

"No, Ian. Do not."

With a gentle insistence, Ian grasped her wrists and pulled her fingers from his mouth.

"I must. I do not know how or why, but you have become a necessary part of my life, Mercy. I cannot allow you to slip away."

Battling her way from his arms, Mercy stumbled off the bench and began tugging on her rumpled clothes.

"We have already discussed this, Ian. I will not be your mistress."

"Fine. Then be my wife."

A stunned silence filled the gazebo. For a long moment, Mercy stared at him as if he had taken leave of his senses.

And perhaps he had, Ian wryly acknowledged. Unfortunately, he did not give a tinker's damn at the moment.

At last Mercy sucked in a sharp breath and tugged her gown over her loosely knotted corset.

"That is not amusing."

Rising to his feet, Ian crossed to stand directly in front of her, gently knocking aside her trembling fingers to tie the ribbons on her bodice.

"It was not intended to be."

"You . . . you want to marry me?"

"That is the usual means of acquiring a wife."

She gave a slow shake of her head. "This is madness."

"Perhaps, but it is the most delightful sort of madness," he murmured, lowering his head to steal a gentle kiss.

Her hands fluttered against his chest before she was abruptly pushing him away, her eyes wide with a bewildered fear that tugged at his heart.

"Why?"

"I have just told you. I cannot imagine my life without you in it."

"No, I mean why me?"

His lips twisted. That was a question more suited to poets and philosophers, not hardened rakes.

"I could tell you that it is your unwavering loyalty or your generous heart or your inquisitive mind, but the truth of the matter is that I have no reasonable explanation for my belief you are the woman destined to be at my side." He brushed a finger down her pale cheek. "I only know that I have never been so certain of anything in my entire life."

"Ian."

Stepping closer, he grasped her shoulders in a tight grip. "Can you tell me that you do not feel it?"

"Feel what?"

"The power of the attraction that burns between us." Ian frowned, his lips thinning with a hint of frustration. "For God's sake, the very air nearly catches fire when we are in the same room."

"Of course I am attracted to you. You are . . ."

"What?"

She licked her lips. "A very desirable gentleman, as you very well know."

Ian's frustration became outright fury at her hesitant words. The devil take the woman. How dare she pretend she felt nothing for him? Even an untried schoolboy could have sensed her emotions in every soft caress, in every sweet response to his touch.

"And that is all?" he growled.

The pulse at the base of her throat beat at a frantic pace, revealing she was not nearly as composed as she would have him believe.

"There was never meant to be anything more. This was just supposed to be a harmless affair."

"A harmless affair."

Mercy flinched at his flat tone, clearly sensing the danger that prickled in the air.

"I only wanted to experience the passion that others take for granted," she said, her tone softly pleading. "I wanted to feel like a woman, not an aging spinster, if only for a little while."

"I see." His fingers tightened on her shoulders. "So I was just a convenient body to satisfy your curiosity."

"I—"

"Tell me, Mercy, would any man willing to climb between your legs have done?"

With a gasp, she wrenched from his biting hold, stepping back to regard him with a wounded expression.

"That is a horrid thing to say."

"Then do not try and tarnish what occurred between us," he snapped, pausing to gather his raw emotions. Damn. He had not intended to lose his temper. It was hardly the best means of convincing a jittering young maiden he was a gentleman she could trust with her heart and soul. Still, he would not tolerate having the exquisite bond between them dismissed as mere lust. "You would never have given your innocence to me if you did not possess feelings for me."

The emotions she tried so desperately to hide briefly flickered in the dark beauty of her eyes. Then, with an obvious effort, she was giving a sharp shake of her head.

"Do you presume that every woman who shares your bed must be in love with you?"

This time Ian refused to be provoked. "You are not other women, Miss Mercy Simpson," he said with gentle insistence. "You might have convinced yourself that it was no more than desire that led you into my arms, but your heart has always recognized the truth."

"Ian—"

The sound of a horse clattering into the nearby stable yard abruptly intruded into the gazebo, making them both stiffen in surprise.

Pressing a warning finger to her lips, Ian slipped toward the nearby window and peered into the darkness. From his vantage he could easily view the grooms scurrying from the stables and the tall, lean form of the gentleman who vaulted from the large stallion, the torchlight gleaming off the white gold curls peeking beneath his tall, beaver hat.

"What the devil is he doing here?"

Mercy moved to stand at his side, her vanilla scent filling his senses with that wondrous peace.

"Who is it?"

"Charlebois."

"Is he a friend of yours?"

Ian's lips twisted. "Not in this moment." Giving a reluctant shake of his head, Ian turned to meet her troubled gaze. As much as he longed to remain and force Mercy to admit that they were destined to be together, he knew better than most that the peace of Rosehill was about to be shattered. Raoul Charlebois' presence created a greater havoc than most royalty. There was not a person in all of England who did not recognize the actor and desire to have the privilege of claiming they had caught a glimpse of his famous beauty. "Forgive me, Mercy, but Charlebois is bound to be asking for me. You must return to the house before you are missed."

"Of course."

Clearly relieved by the timely interruption, Mercy

turned and hastily made her way toward the door, her hands fumbling as she reached for the latch.

"Mercy."

She paused, but refused to turn and face him.

"What?"

"This is no more than a temporary reprieve," he warned, his tone grim with determination. "We will finish this discussion, and in the end, you will be my wife."

Chapter 18

Later Mercy would have no memory of her flight from the gazebo to her private chambers. Thank heaven some inner sense of self-possession urged her to choose the back entrance to slip through silent passages rather than dashing headlong into the path of Ella, or worse, her parents.

Once in her bedchamber, she used the familiar task of changing into her night rail and brushing her hair into a simple braid to try and sort out her stunned thoughts.

Not that it did a great deal of good, she wryly acknowledged, pacing the beautiful Persian carpet with a restless step.

Marriage.

To Ian Breckford.

It was . . .

She choked back a laugh as she realized she had no words to describe the disbelief that held her captive. She would have expected the earth to open up and swallow her before she would ever have expected the renowned Casanova to propose.

Beneath her astonishment, however, there was another emotion.

A dangerous, bittersweet longing that refused to be dismissed, even after she told herself that Ian would come to his senses and realize that the very last thing he desired was a drab spinster as his wife.

She was still in the midst of her pacing when the door to her chamber was thrust open. Mercy's heart fluttered with renegade excitement before plunging in resignation as her mother stepped over the threshold.

Attired in a brocade robe that seemed far too heavy for her fragile frame, the older woman regarded her daughter with a fretful expression that always boded ill. In her own way, Lydia Simpson could be as ruthless as her husband.

"Mercy, am I intruding?"

Mercy bit back her instinctive words. Her mother's arrival *was* an intrusion. She had too much upon her mind to attend to the lecture that was no doubt in the offing.

Unfortunately, her sense of duty was too deeply ingrained to be easily dismissed. As much as she might long to demand a few moments of blessed peace, she could not force the words past her lips.

"I thought you would be in bed," she instead murmured.

The older woman sniffed, her expression wounded. "You could not possibly expect me to sleep after being attacked by that horrid man. I am not at all certain I shall ever be capable of closing my eyes so long as we are beneath this roof. Who knows what such a dangerous creature is capable of?"

Mercy's already raw emotions flared at the whining edge in her mother's voice.

"Oh, for goodness' sakes, you cannot possibly suppose that Ian . . . Mr. Breckford would actually harm you."

"Did you not see how angry he was?"

"That is only because he desires to protect me."

"Protect you from your own parents?" There was another sniff. "Absurd."

Mercy's heart twisted with an indefinable emotion. Ian's protective instincts did not seem absurd. They seemed . . . strangely wonderful.

No one had ever thought she needed to be defended.

"He believes that you and Father take advantage of my willingness to be of service to you," she said softly.

"I see."

Mercy was instantly wary at her mother's narrowed gaze. There was something calculating in her expression.

"If that is all—"

"You know, your father warned that allowing you to travel to this place would ruin your sweet nature, but I never dreamed that you would devote yourself to complaining of your family to complete strangers," her mother overrode the polite dismissal.

Mercy swallowed a sigh. "That is not true, Mother. I would never complain of you to anyone, certainly not Mr. Breckford."

"Then why did he presume to chastise us as if we are children?"

"He has become a friend."

"More than a friend, I think." Lydia's lips thinned, her expression hard with disapproval. "I am not blind, Mercy. I have seen how Mr. Breckford stares at you. He possesses dishonorable intentions toward you, and he knows that so long as you are under the care of your parents he cannot have his evil way with you. He is attempting to lure you away from those who truly care for you, my dear. Do not be fooled by his deceit."

Mercy choked back a near-hysterical laugh. What would her mother say if she knew that poor Ian was the victim and Mercy had been the one to have her evil way? Not that it had felt evil. In truth, it had been the most wondrous experience of her life.

Realizing that her mother was studying the sudden color that flooded her cheeks, Mercy cleared the lump from her throat.

"You are mistaken, Mother. Mr. Breckford's intentions are not dishonorable in the least. Quite the opposite."

"What do you mean?"

"He asked me to marry him."

"Marry?" Lydia abruptly sank onto the edge of a silk striped chair. "I do not believe it."

"You can be no more astonished than I."

"But this must be some sort of trick." Lydia slowly shook her head. "I have heard of those gentlemen who would pretend to wed an innocent maid only to steal her virtue."

Mercy stiffened. "Nonsense."

"Really, Mercy, you are being a fool." Lydia folded her hands in her lap, her expression one of profound pity. "Mr. Breckford might be a bastard, but he is publicly claimed by the Viscount Norrington as his son and welcomed among the highest of society. Why would he choose a penniless daughter of a vicar as his wife?"

Mercy forced herself to count to ten, uncertain if she should be more insulted by the implication that such a gentleman could possibly desire her as a wife, or the assumption that Ian was such a cad he would fake a wedding to steal a woman's virtue.

"Did you ever consider the notion that he might love me, Mother?"

The mere notion was dismissed with a wave of Lydia's hand. "Mark my words, my dear, this is some devious trap."

"That is enough." Mercy planted her hands on her hips. "Ian would never stoop to such treachery. He would never *need* to stoop to treachery. He has only to walk into a room for every woman to be tossing themselves at his feet. Besides, Ella would never allow him to deceive me in such a fashion."

Grudgingly accepting that Mercy was not to be convinced that Ian was luring her to her doom, Lydia licked her lips.

"Are you . . ."

"What?"

"Are you considering his proposal?"

Mercy abruptly turned to pace toward the bay window. When Ian had blurted out his astonishing desire to have her as his wife, she had been too stunned to think clearly. In truth, she had been terrified that he would realize just what he had said and instantly regret his impulsive proposal.

After all, her mother had not been entirely wrong. Mercy was a country mouse with no claim to wealth or connections. Ian could do a great deal better in choosing a wife.

There was a part of her, however, that longed to believe that he was sincere. To believe he truly loved her.

"I am not entirely certain," she at last whispered.

"Do you love him?"

"Yes." The word came without hesitation. She turned to face her mother. "Yes, I love him."

With a rustle of brocade, Lydia was on her feet, her eyes stricken.

"Oh, my dear, I have tried so hard to protect you from this."

"Protect me? From what?"

"Disappointment."

"I do not understand."

Moving forward, Lydia gripped Mercy's hand. "My dear, I know that you are not entirely satisfied with our quiet life, which is why I convinced your father to allow you to visit Rosehill. But I assure you that whatever your discontent, it would be nothing compared to placing your future in the hands of a gentleman who will have the authority to treat you in any manner he desires."

There was no mistaking the harsh sincerity in her mother's voice. Lydia Simpson truly believed that Mercy was in some mysterious danger.

"I do not believe for a moment that Ian would ever be cruel to me. He would never harm any woman."

Lydia shuddered. "A man need not beat you to be cruel. In truth, there are times when a blow would be preferable to . . ."

"Mother?"

Dropping Mercy's hand, Lydia took a step back. "You are not blind, Mercy. You comprehend that marriage is not what the poets describe. Indeed, I deeply regret not listening to my own mother, who warned me against accepting your father's proposal."

Mercy's stomach twisted with sick dread. "It could not always have been an unhappy union. You must have loved one another in the beginning."

"Oh, I had my head filled with a lot of foolish romance, but it did not take long for me to realize my mistake." Lydia moved to the door, halting to cast Mercy a warning glance. "Just as you will eventually realize that this man will only bring you heartbreak and disappointment. I only hope you do so before it is too late."

Having delivered her poisonous warning, Lydia swept from the room, leaving behind a troubled Mercy. Although not troubled in the way that Lydia had desired.

Mercy had, of course, known her parents' marriage was not a happy one. They hardly made a secret of the fact. Actually, they did their best to ensure that everyone around them shared in that misery.

But in the moment her mother had been warning her against the fatal mistake of marriage, Mercy had been struck by a revelation.

She at last understood the reason she had remained trapped in her parents' small cottage. It was not just her sense of duty. Or even the obligation as an only child.

Those were certainly handy excuses to hide from the world, but beneath her pretense of self-sacrifice, she was nothing more than a shameful coward.

A part of her, a deep, hidden part of her, had been terrified of marriage. She had assumed that every marriage ended in spiteful bitterness. Why would she not? Living such an isolated life meant that she had only her parents' marriage to judge the institution. Perhaps it was not so surprising she would have unconsciously taken steps to ensure she was never in the position to endure such disappointment.

It was only with Ian that she had lowered her guard,

and then merely because she had been certain that he was as opposed to marriage as she was.

Mercy pressed her fingers to her lips as a hysterical urge to laugh threatened. How vastly ironic that a virgin searching for a fleeting affair should encounter the one rake in all of England who was prepared to offer her marriage.

Cutting through the garden, Ian managed to join Raoul Charlebois as he entered Rosehill. Unfortunately, it was not in time to prevent the rumors of the famous actor's arrival to spread like wildfire through the household, and as Ian joined his friend in the marble foyer, there were near half a dozen maids peering over the banister.

A wry smile curved his lips. Despite his blistering need to return to Mercy and his growing discomfort at the thought of spying upon his own father, Ian could not help but appreciate the collective sigh as Raoul shed his coat to reveal his tightly tailored attire and tossed aside his tall beaver hat to better display the white gold hair and cobalt eyes.

Waving away the approaching butler, Ian halted directly before his friend.

"This is an unexpected surprise, Raoul."

"Ah, Ian." A pale brow arched as Raoul caught sight of Ian's tousled appearance. A man could not tumble his future wife in the gazebo without a few rumples and creases. "Did I disturb you from your bed?"

"Rosehill does tend to keep country hours."

"Hmmm. So I see."

"I am relieved that one of us does," Ian said dryly, his

gaze flicking toward the wild-eyed maids. "Perhaps we should speak in my chambers. I should hate for the family treasures to be destroyed in the impending riot."

With a shrug, Raoul fell into step beside Ian as he climbed the staircase. "I hardly ever cause a riot these days, old friend."

"Perhaps you should inform my father's maids," Ian muttered, wincing at the shrill giggles that followed in their wake. "Good God."

Indifferent as always to feminine admiration, Raoul allowed his steps to slow as Ian led him down the mistral's gallery, his gaze lingering on the vaulted ceiling painted with playful cupids darting among the clouds and the delicate stained-glass windows that lined the long corridor.

"Exquisite." Raoul paused at a gilt table that held a rare porcelain vase. "Your father is a fortunate man."

Ian grimaced. "Actually, my father is a very lonely man. It is something that I never realized until now."

Raoul sliced a questioning gaze in his direction. "Then your stay here at Rosehill has not been the trial that you dreaded?"

"Not entirely, no." Ian continued down the corridor, not yet prepared to reveal his father's business proposition.

"Are you having second thoughts, Ian?" Raoul fell into step beside him. "It is not too late to put the past behind you."

A chill inched down Ian's spine. "Did you manage to discover the source of the playbill?"

"Yes."

"I am beginning to suspect that you discovered more than just a theatre."

"As I said, Ian, it is not too late. We can have a drink, you can tell me of your latest conquest, and I will return to London."

The chill hit his stomach. There was something in Raoul's rough voice that warned he was not going to like what he had discovered.

Perhaps it would not be such a terrible thing to leave well enough alone. For the moment, he and his father shared a temporary truce that he would never have dreamed possible. And then there was Mercy. Did he really want to muck through the past when the future beckoned with such amazing promise?

"I will not deny it is a tempting notion."

"Then let it be. You will be happier for it."

Halting at the door to his chambers, Ian heaved a sigh. When in his damnable life had he ever been capable of leaving well enough alone?

"And do you intend to let it be, my friend?" he demanded. "Will you allow the truth to remain buried in the past?"

Raoul muttered a curse. "I will if I have any common sense."

"And when have we ever been burdened with something so beneficial as common sense?"

"True enough."

Ian entered his room, crossing the floor to rap on the connecting door.

"Reaver."

Within a beat, the terrifying valet stepped into the room, his hard gaze flicking over Raoul before returning to Ian.

"Aye?"

"Step into the hall and make certain we are not

interrupted." Waiting until the servant had exited the room and closed the door behind his bulk, Ian turned toward his companion. "Now, tell me what you have discovered."

"Wait." Raoul moved to the sideboard, pouring two shots of whiskey before crossing back to Ian and thrusting the glass in his hand. "We both shall have need."

Ian tossed the fiery liquid down his throat, not surprised when it did nothing to ease the cold ball lodged in the pit of his stomach.

"You are beginning to frighten me, Charlebois. Did my father commit murder?"

"Not to my knowledge."

"I suppose that is a relief. I should hate to think there was a body buried beneath the prized rosebushes."

"Really?" Raoul sipped the whiskey, his expression wry as he perched on the edge of the sideboard. "I have always thought that most rose gardens could be vastly improved by a body or two."

"Any bodies in particular?"

"My father comes to mind."

"Understandable." Ian set aside his empty glass. "There have been moments when I thought patricide should not only be legal, but encouraged."

"I sense that this would not be one of those moments."

Ian met Raoul's searching glance with a determined expression. "We shall see once you have halted your attempts to distract me and reveal what the devil you managed to discover."

"*Mon Dieu.*" Pushing from the sideboard, Raoul paced toward the carved marble chimneypiece, his gaze seemingly captured by the Gainsborough framed above the

mantle. Not that Ian was fooled. He knew his friend well
enough to know when he was deliberately hiding something. "I tracked the theatre to an obscure building near
Fleet Street. A near-damn-well-impossible task I must tell
you since no one in the theatre world would claim
knowledge of the place, let alone offer an address. I at
last was forced to seek my information among the stews."

"Ah . . ." Ian was more relieved than shocked. "A
bawd house."

"Actually, at first glance one would presume that it
is just another of the gentlemen's clubs that litter
London." Raoul grudgingly turned to face Ian. "I rode
past the damn building a dozen times before I accepted
it was the proper location. Of course, discretion would
be of utmost necessity for such an establishment."

Ian clenched his hands. He had faced utter ruin at
the card tables. He had risked life and limb for one
foolish wager after another. Christ, he had just asked
the one woman in all the world certain to drive him
to Bedlam to be his wife. And he had done so without
blinking an eye.

So why the devil did his palms choose to sweat and
his heart thunder at this precise moment?

"I am quite prepared to pummel the truth out of
you, *mon ami*. Get to the bloody point."

Raoul arched a brow at the sharp command. "Perhaps you have forgotten I am an actor, Breckford. If
you wish to threaten me, I will quite happily ensure
my stunning revelations take as long as a Shake-
spearean tragedy to be revealed."

Ian resisted the urge to beat the truth from his companion. He understood that Raoul was not attempting to torture him. Instead, the older man was

hoping that he would change his mind before the truth was revealed.

"Then get on with it . . . please."

Raoul sighed, shoving a hand through his hair. "As I said, the building appears unremarkable—until one attempts to enter the blasted place. It would be easier to waltz through the front doors of Carlton House than to step foot past the iron gates of the Adonis Club."

"Adonis Club?"

Raoul lifted a slender hand. "I am getting to that. First I was telling you of the imposing barricades and vicious guards I was forced to battle my way past."

Despite his dark premonition, Ian could not halt his grudging smile. Throughout his difficult childhood, Raoul could always be depended upon to tease him out of his black moods. It was a gift that Ian would never forget.

"Somehow I doubt they halted you."

"Certainly not. It would take more than a few thick-skulled barbarians to best Raoul Charlebois."

"Without question. So how did you get past them?"

"I arrived the next morning and knocked the coalman over the head so I could steal his cart and enter the club unnoted."

Ian choked on his shock. "Good God."

Raoul waved a dismissive hand. "Be at ease. I left the man enough money to compensate for the loss of his cart as well as the bump to his head. I do not doubt he devoted the day to toasting his good fortune in the nearest pub."

"My distress was at the thought that anyone could be stupid enough to mistake you for a common coalmonger," Ian corrected.

"Once again I remind you that I am an actor." Raoul gave a lift of his glass before polishing off the last of the whiskey. "I have not always played the role of kings."

"So I assume you managed to penetrate the fortress?"

"I did."

Ian counted to ten. "And?"

"And I discovered that the cook was a good deal more pleasant than those brutish guards."

"There has not been a woman born who is not a good deal more pleasant when you are near," Ian pointed out dryly. "It is one of the great mysteries of the world."

An unexpected frown marred Raoul's perfect features. "In truth, it was not nearly so easy as I presumed it would be. I comfort myself with the thought that the club must make a practice of only hiring those who can be trusted to remain discreet. Otherwise I must accept that my charms are not what they once were."

Ian was genuinely amused by his friend's pique. "We must all grow older, Charlebois. Of course, some of us are older than others."

The blue eyes flashed with amusement. "You love to travel a dangerous path, my friend."

"What other paths are there to travel?"

Raoul's amusement faded to a strangely wistful expression. "I do not know, but I believe I should like to discover them."

"Yes," Ian agreed softly, the image of Mercy's delicate features and comforting arms sending a warm flare of delicious heat through his body. With a pang of regret, he forced his thoughts back to the matters at hand. The sooner he was done with this damnable business, the sooner he could be with Mercy. "Tell me what you managed to charm from the cook."

Raoul paused. Then, muttering a curse, he squared his shoulders. "She admitted that the establishment is a private club and there is a small theatre in the cellars that caters to a select handful of gentlemen."

"Why the devil would they have the theatre in the cellars?"

"No doubt because the audience who attends such plays would be tossed into Newgate Prison if they were discovered."

"Treason?" Ian breathed, shaking his head. "No, that I will not believe."

"Not treason. The actors and those who come to watch them are all men who possess a specific taste."

"Which tells me precisely nothing," Ian growled. "What specific taste do you speak of?"

"For . . . one another."

Ian was genuinely puzzled. "What the devil do you mean?"

"It is a Molly house, my friend."

Molly house? Christ.

"That is absurd." Ian abruptly paced to the window, gripping the window frame until his knuckles turned white. That sick feeling in the pit of his stomach was expanding until it filled his entire body. "Why would my father have a playbill from such an establishment?"

"Because he is a member of the Adonis Club, and, from the quarterly accounts that I managed to catch a glimpse of in the private office, he has stayed there at least one or two nights a month over the past year."

Ian leaned his head against the windowpane, painfully allowing the clues to fall into place. His father's connection to Summerville, who had obviously shared his taste for men. His refusal to wed. His solitary shield that kept others at a distance.

Still, there was one glaring flaw in the logical explanation.

"You are certain?"

"I am sorry, Ian." Raoul moved to place a comforting hand on his shoulder. "I knew that the truth would distress you. It cannot be easy to discover your father harbors such tendencies. I should have followed my instincts and remained in London."

"I am more baffled than distressed." Sucking in a raw breath, Ian forced himself to turn and meet his friend's worried gaze. "How the hell does a viscount who possesses a preference for his fellow man father a bastard?"

"There are many such gentlemen who successfully hide their true nature." Raoul grimaced. "In truth, most of the members of the Adonis Club are married and managed to produce the proper heirs."

Ian was not particularly shocked. A man could not be a rake and a libertine without knowing that the parlors of Mayfair were littered with gentlemen who harbored any number of sexual appetites.

"Always presuming those heirs are truly their offspring," he absently muttered. "Women are exceedingly practical when necessary."

"My point is that these gentlemen are willing to put aside their natural tendencies for the sake of appearance."

Ian shook his head, unconvinced.

"But my father did not wed and produce the expected heirs to disguise his secret," he pointed out. "Instead, he supposedly had a clandestine tryst with a common maid, and it was only because my mother was inconsiderate enough to die and leave me an orphan that my father even bothered to claim me as his own."

Raoul took a step back, his brow furrowed. "Damn, you are right. A bastard son might assist in maintaining the image of virile manhood, but he would have been far better served to have wed and produced a legitimate child."

"Unless . . ."

"What?"

"Unless he is the sort who cannot bear the mere thought of being with a woman."

Raoul snorted. "Obviously he can do some bearing. At least enough to produce you."

Ian paced back across the carpet, sorting through the chaos in his mind. He reached the Flemish ebony cabinet at the same moment he reached the only logical conclusion.

"Not if he did not actually produce me." Rubbing the aching muscles of his neck, Ian turned. "He was traveling through Rome, after all, when he claimed to have filled the mysterious maid with his seed. Perhaps he plucked me out of a gutter with the hope that a bastard would be enough to still any suspicions of his lingering bachelorhood."

There was a shocked silence. Then Raoul's laughter echoed through the room.

"*Mon Dieu.*"

"What is so damned amusing?"

"Have you ever glanced in the mirror?" Raoul demanded. "Whatever the circumstances of your birth, there is no doubt that you have Breckford blood flowing through your veins. Just take a walk through the portrait gallery if you do not believe me."

Ian stilled. As much as he hated to admit it, his chortling friend was right.

"I suppose my lineage is rather difficult to deny."

"Does your father have any close relatives? Uncles? Cousins?"

"No, there is only Ella . . ." The entire world tilted as Ian was smacked with the horrifying possibility. "Holy hell."

"What is it? You look positively ill." Raoul moved forward in obvious concern, but he was a step too late. Even as he reached out, Ian was yanking the door open and heading down the hallway. "Dammit, Ian."

Chapter 19

It was only when Ella opened the door attired in her velvet robe that Ian realized just how late the hour was. Not that the knowledge would have halted his mad flight. He was here for one purpose, and one purpose only.

He wanted his aunt, the one person in his miserable life he had ever trusted, to assure him that she had not deliberately betrayed him.

"Ian." Blinking in surprise, Ella studied his pale face. "Good heavens, what are you doing here?"

"Am I disturbing you?"

"Not at all." Ella stepped back. "Please join me. Shall I ring for tea?"

Stepping into the sitting room that was filled with French mahogany furnishings and bright buttercup wall panels, Ian ignored the pain that stabbed into his heart.

This room had always been his sanctuary. The one place he could enter and know that he was welcome.

Christ, what if it was all a lie?

"No, I thank you."

"I fear I do not keep any strong spirits in my chambers. When one reaches my age, warm milk is all you are allowed before retiring." Ella moved to take a seat by the fireplace, folding her hands in her lap. "A pity, since I have always enjoyed a nice sherry after dinner."

Ian remained standing in the middle of the floor, his nerves coiled so tightly he could barely breathe.

"Is that a habit you acquired during your travels through Europe?"

Ella froze, whether from shock that Ian had learned of her trip to the Continent or because of his clipped tone was impossible to know.

"No, it was a ritual that has always been in place at Rosehill," she slowly admitted.

"But you did travel to Europe, did you not?"

"Years ago." Ella toyed with the ribbon that tied her robe. A sure sign of unease despite her carefully guarded expression. "It was quite the fashion for young ladies to take the Grand Tour in those days. So unfortunate that the war brought an end to such a pleasant treat."

Ian's jaw knotted, his blood running cold. "It seems odd that you never mentioned your journey."

"What interest would a young man have in my ancient travels?"

"Actually, I should have been very interested, considering you were traveling in the company of my father and must have at least taken notice of my mother, even if she was beneath you socially."

The ribbon abruptly ripped from the robe. "It was all a very long time ago."

"I know precisely how long ago it was," Ian rasped. Christ, Ella was hiding something. He knew it as surely as he knew it was going to alter his life forever.

With a wary frown, Ella pressed herself upright. "You are in a very strange mood this evening."

"Maybe it has something to do with the information Raoul Charlebois brought me."

"Oh yes, my maid informed me we are to have an additional guest," Ella breathed, a hint of relief flashing through her eyes. "I have ordered the Orchid Rooms to be prepared, but perhaps I should—"

"Do not bother. He will not be remaining," Ian interrupted, the mixture of pain and disbelief brewing deep inside him making his tone sharp.

"Surely he cannot intend to return to London at this hour?"

"It is not that great a distance, and he will have a performance tomorrow evening to prepare for. Something that seems to take an appalling amount of time."

Ella made a grim path toward the door. "Then at least we must ensure that he has a warm meal before he leaves."

With smooth steps, Ian was blocking her retreat. "Are you not interested in what information Raoul brought for me?"

Forced to a reluctant halt, the older woman nervously pushed back a silver curl that had escaped her braid.

"Should I be?"

Ian swallowed his wild burst of laughter. Ella's strange behavior warned him that he was charging down a path of disaster. Nothing unusual in that. He often awoke in the morning regretting his empty pockets or the homicidal husband scouring London for him.

But this . . .

This could destroy him.

So why the devil could he not halt this reckless plunge to disaster?

"I most certainly found it astonishing," he muttered, unable to listen to the warnings whispering in the back of his mind. "It has to do with a playbill that I found in the conservatory."

Ella managed a chiding frown. "Good heavens, Ian, were you searching through your father's private papers?"

"As a matter of fact, I was."

"Why would you do such a disgraceful thing?"

"Because I desired answers, and I am well-enough acquainted with my supposed family to realize that the only means of acquiring the truth was to seek it out for myself."

Sucking in a sharp breath, Ella turned to pace back to the fireplace, dropping onto the edge of the chair as if her knees had given way.

"You are not only babbling in the most incomprehensible manner, but you have most rudely abused your father's hospitality." Her rings flashed in the firelight as Ella found another ribbon to tug. "I had hoped that I raised you with better manners."

"If you will recall, it was Dunnington who had the honor, or perhaps dishonor, of raising me, and while he did attempt to impart a modicum of good manners, he was far more interested in ensuring I understood the importance of honesty."

She nervously wet her dry lips. "Dunnington was certainly a fine gentleman."

"You may not be so pleased with my old tutor when you discover he is the reason that I returned to Rosehill." A cold smile touched his lips. "You see, when Dunnington died he left me a legacy of twenty thousand pounds, along with a cryptic message that the money had been extorted from my father. I wanted to know what sin would be worth such an outrageous sum. It was not until Raoul arrived this evening, however, that I realized that

Lord Norrington was not the only member of my family
to harbor secrets."

"Stop this, Ian. It can serve no purpose."

"I thought that the truth was supposed to set you
free," Ian mocked.

Ella's eyes darkened with pain. "What do you want
of me?"

Clasping his hands behind his back, Ian ignored
the answering pain in his own heart.

"I want to know how a gentleman who possesses no
desire for women could possibly have fathered a bastard son."

"How did you—"

"The playbill is from a theatre at the Adonis Club
that caters to a very specific clientele," Ian overrode
Ella's shocked words. "A club where your brother happens to be a member."

"Yes well, many gentlemen belong to such clubs."

"Do not force me to embarrass the both of us by discussing the particulars of the Adonis. It is enough to
say that the viscount's membership there means he
could not be my father, and since there is no denying that I am of genuine Breckford blood, that leaves
only you as the donor of that blood, dearest *Aunt*."

Ella's stark pallor was replaced by a surge of crimson heat as she shakily rose to her feet, one hand out-
stretched in pleading.

"Please, Ian."

"Please, what?" he rasped. "Continue to believe the
lies I have been told my entire life?"

"They were for your own good."

That was the last thing Ian wanted to hear. Ella of
all people understood the anguish of his childhood.

Hell, she had been the one to comfort him when his supposed father had rejected him time after time.

His hands clenched, the sickening sense of disappointment flooding through his body.

"It was for my own good to believe that a man who treated me with barely concealed contempt was my father? It was for my own good that I believed I was not only a bastard but utterly unworthy of love?"

"I have always loved you, Ian."

"If you loved me, you would have told me the truth."

She bit her bottom lip, her hand dropping as Ian's fury pulsed through the room.

"You know that it was not nearly so simple, Ian. The truth never is."

"You are my mother."

There was a pause at the blunt question. Then Ella offered a small dip of her head.

"Yes."

Ian flinched, feeling the blow to his very soul. "And my father?"

"A handsome, wretchedly poor nobleman whom I fell in love with during my first Season." Ella pressed her hands together, an edge of bitterness in her voice. "I was naïve enough to believe his intentions were honorable, and perhaps they were in the beginning. He might have wed me if my father had not threatened to disinherit me." She gave a shake of her head, perhaps hoping to dismiss the bleak memories. "In any event, once he realized I might lose my dowry, he could not jilt me swiftly enough."

Ian briefly wavered beneath a jolt of pity for the young girl who had not only suffered a broken heart but had been left to confront the results of her affair alone.

"You did not tell him you were breeding?"

"By the time I realized the truth of my condition, he was already wed to an heiress by special license."

"His name."

"Lord Mayfield." The older woman's expression hardened. "He broke his neck during a fox hunt not long after I gave birth to you."

Ian was not particularly shocked to discover that he was created by a scoundrel who could abandon a young maiden he'd seduced without a second thought. It made far more sense than having a paragon as a father.

"So it is true that bad blood will show," he muttered dryly. "He never knew he had a son?"

"No."

Ian sucked in a deep breath, thrusting away the unsettling combination of pity for Ella and loathing for the father he had never met.

There were still answers he desired. Answers he *needed.*

"So how did you convince the viscount to go along with your mad scheme to travel to the Continent and pass me off as his bastard child?"

Pulling a dainty handkerchief from her sleeve, Ella dabbed at her eyes, the strain of the past few minutes clearly taking their toll.

"Actually, it was his notion to bring you to Rosehill."

Ian's fury returned with a scorching blast. "You must be jesting. Lord Norrington never wanted me. Christ, he can barely tolerate having me beneath his roof."

"That is not true, Ian. Norry—"

"Just tell me what happened."

Ella looked as if she wished to continue the argument, but a glance at Ian's relentless expression was enough to make her concede defeat with a heavy sigh.

"When I discovered that I was with child, I was numb

with horror. You do not recall my father, since he died while you were still a baby, but he was a loud, overbearing man who frankly terrified me."

"He seemed to evoke that emotion in many people."

"I knew beyond a doubt that if he discovered my secret he would have me thrown from the house without so much as a quid." Ella shuddered. "My father was a prolific sinner, but he possessed no sympathy for the weaknesses of others."

"A genuine bastard, then."

"Unfortunately, I had nowhere to turn but to Norry."

Suddenly restless, Ian paced across the carpet to the delicate rosewood writing desk. Among the clutter of parchment and quills was a charming collection of Venetian vases that no doubt had come from Ella's travels. Why the devil had he never noticed them before?

"I understand leaving the country to have the child. What I don't comprehend is why you did not foster me off to some family in Rome. It is what most women would have done."

"That was what I intended. I even had a family chosen who was anxious to take you into their home. But once I held you in my arms, I could not endure leaving you behind. It was like cutting out my own heart." Ella was forced to halt and clear her throat. "That was when Norry suggested that we take you back to Rosehill in the guise of his bastard son."

"And his only motive was to please you?"

"Does it matter?"

"It does if the reason you have lied to me all these years was to maintain Lord Norrington's image of bloody perfection."

There was a heavy footstep, then the sound of a familiar male voice that had Ian spinning in surprise.

"That is enough, Ian," Norrington commanded, still attired in the pale gray jacket and black breeches he'd chosen for dinner. "If you wish to be angry with someone, then it should be me."

Ian folded his arms across his chest, refusing to be intimidated. Those days were gone forever.

"Trust me, I possess enough anger for the both of you." He met the older man's wary gaze. "Did you use me to hide your . . . unusual preferences?"

Ian had to give the viscount credit. He did not so much as flinch at the bald question.

"It is true that I hoped that bringing you to Rosehill would divert my father's suspicions, but once he died I made no effort to thrust you into the attention of society."

"But you did not bother to deny the assumption that you fathered me."

The handsome features tightened. "No, I did not deny the assumption."

Ian slowly shook his head. "You know, I might have been able to forgive you lying to the rest of the world if you had told me the truth."

"Do not blame, Ella. I was the one who insisted that we maintain the charade. Can you even imagine the damage that would be done to us if the truth were ever revealed?"

"So you did not trust me?"

"It was not a simple matter of trust," Norrington stated. "Obviously when you were a child you could not be burdened with the responsibilities of such a secret. And as you matured, I feared that your desire to punish me for my lack of fatherly affection would lead to disaster. I . . ." The older man squared his shoulders. "I realize now that it would have been best to have taken you into our confidence years ago."

Ian pressed his fists to his throbbing head. He was not an idiot. Well, at least not most of the time. He perfectly understood the reasoning behind his mother's deception. He even appreciated the fact that she had chosen to return him to England just so he would be near.

That did not, however, excuse her endless lies.

How many years had she stood silent and witnessed his pathetic, desperate attempts to earn the respect of the man he thought was his father? How often had she traveled to London to visit him with some blithe excuse of why the viscount could not bother to spend a damned hour with him?

"Christ, I have to get out of here," he muttered, heading for the door.

Ella hurried in his wake. "Where are you going?"

"Anywhere but here."

"Ian . . ." Waiting until Ian grudgingly turned, Ella held out a pleading hand. "Please do not do anything foolish."

"If your concern is for whether or not I intend to reveal your secrets, you need not worry. I have no more desire for the nasty scandal than you."

Ella swallowed a soft sob, her expression unbearably sad. "That is not it at all. I am concerned for you. I wish you would not leave while you are so upset. If you would just allow me to explain. . . ."

"I think there have been enough explanations." Ian's voice sliced through the beseeching words. "I was the sacrifice needed to wash away your sins. What else is there to say?"

Astonishingly, Norrington moved to place a tender

arm around his sister's shoulders. "Let him go, Ella. He is not yet willing to discuss this in a reasonable manner."

Ian narrowed his gaze. "I do have one last question."

The viscount met his condemning gaze with a tilt of his chin. "What is that?"

"How did Dunnington discover your secret?"

"I should have thought that obvious."

"Indulge me."

A wry smile curved the older man's lips. "He was once a member of the Adonis Club."

Chapter 20

Despite the late hour, Mercy made no effort to climb beneath the sheets that had already been turned down for the night.

All in all, it had been an eventful day. Eventful enough that the mere thought of sleep was absurd. Instead, she returned to the restless pacing that her mother had interrupted.

Not that her circular path from the window to the cherry-wood armoire assisted in clearing her tangled thoughts, she wryly acknowledged.

She was no closer to comprehending Ian's stunning proposal. Whether it was a bit of temporary madness or a genuine desire to spend the rest of his life with her.

Or even her own feelings.

Was she prepared to take the leap of faith to become Ian's wife? Could she overcome her fear of binding herself irrevocably to another? Or would she be forever condemned to hide from the promise of love?

She was still wrestling with her uncooperative thoughts when there was a sharp rap on the door.

With a jerk at the unexpected interruption, Mercy

moved to discover Ian standing in the hallway. Her eyes narrowed. Not in shock at his brash intrusion—Ian Breckford had no concern for those pesky rules that prevented most gentlemen from intruding into a proper maiden's bedchamber—but instead at the sight of his disheveled appearance.

Good Lord, his hair stood on end, his cravat was untied and hanging down his unbuttoned jacket, and even in the fading firelight she could determine that he was shockingly pale. He looked like a man who had just walked through a battlefield and was still not certain if he had made it safely to the other side.

"Ian."

He regarded her with haunted eyes that made her heart stutter to a halt.

"Forgive me. I know it is late."

"That does not matter." Grasping his arm, she pulled him into the room and shut the door. In this moment she did not give a fig for propriety. "What is wrong?"

Leaning against the polished panels of the door, Ian twisted his lips in a wry smile.

"Am I so easy to read?"

"In this moment, yes. Tell me what has happened."

There was a long pause, as if Ian were lost in his dark broodings. Then he gave a sharp shake of his head.

"What has happened, my sweet Mercy, is that I have just discovered my entire life is a lie."

Mercy had braced herself to discover that Ian's friend had brought some tragic news from London. Perhaps the injury of a friend, or the theft of his belongings. Now she struggled to make sense of his ominous announcement.

"What do you mean?"

His bark of laughter was edged with raw, aching pain.

"My father at last confessed that he is not my father at all."

"I . . . do not understand."

"Lord Norrington might have claimed me as his son, but it was Ella who gave birth to me."

"Oh." Blank astonishment momentarily seized Mercy, making it impossible to think clearly. Then, ever so slowly, a dozen small hints and clues coalesced into a blinding flash of awareness. "Oh."

Ian stiffened as he watched the various emotions flit over her face.

"You do not seem nearly as astonished as you should be."

"Actually, it explains a great deal."

Anger flashed in the whiskey eyes. "You suspected?"

"No, no. Of course not." She reached out to touch his arm. "I have only wondered why Ella was so terribly protective of you. And why she treasured each tiny bit gossip that she could find of you in the paper. It always seemed somewhat excessive for a mere aunt. Now it all makes sense."

Ian pushed from the wall, stalking to glare into the smoldering embers of the fire.

"I am happy it makes sense to one of us."

Mercy studied his tense body and the stark lines of his profile. His fury was palpable, filling the air with a prickling heat, but it was the deep, biting betrayal in his eyes that squeezed her heart and lodged her breath in her throat.

No matter how he might stomp and storm about, he was fiercely wounded by Ella's lies.

Mercy stepped forward, seized by the need to ease

his pain, to somehow soften the shocking blow he had suffered. As ridiculous as it might be, she wanted her arrogant, swaggering, insufferable rake returned.

"I know this must be difficult, but you have to know that Ella loves you beyond measure," she said softly. "There is nothing she would not sacrifice for you."

His hands gripped the mantel until Mercy feared the marble might crumble to dust.

"Except the truth," he rasped.

"I am certain she must have had her reasons."

"It does not matter." Without warning, he glanced over his shoulder to pin her with a fierce gaze. "I am leaving Rosehill."

"Leaving?" Mercy's heart came to a suffocating halt. "When?"

"Now."

She pressed her hand to her chest, which had become unbearably tight.

"Where are you going?"

"That depends upon you."

Startled out of the dark tide of disappointment, Mercy blinked in confusion.

"Me?"

Ian turned, folding his arms over his chest as he regarded her with a guarded expression.

"I could return to my cold, lonely rooms in London, or . . ."

"Or what?"

"Or we could leave together and travel to Scotland."

"Why ever would you wish to visit Scotland?"

His grim features eased at her genuine confusion. "You know, Mercy, there are times when I forget just how innocent you are." He lowered his arms, taking a step closer. "I desire for the both of us to visit Gretna Green. We could be wed in a matter of days."

Mercy's mouth fell open, snapped shut, then fell open again as she reeled beneath an avalanche of sensations. Shock, giddy excitement, and sheer terror.

Gads, how was she supposed to think clearly when Ian kept blindsiding her with one astonishing pronouncement after another?

"Wed?"

His eyes narrowed. "In the event you have forgotten, I did offer a proposal earlier this evening."

"Of course I have not forgotten. But . . ." She shook her head. No. She could not make such a decision while her mind was trapped in a fog of bewilderment. No matter how her heart might urge her to leap blindly and damn the consequences. "You expect me to slip away in the midst of the night to elope with you?"

He shrugged. "Most elopements take place in the midst of the night. I believe that is supposed to be a part of the romance."

"I would hardly consider a hasty wedding over the anvil as romantic."

"Fine." With two long strides he was standing before her, grasping her hands in a near-painful grip. "Then we can travel to London and have a proper marriage. I doubt Westminster Abbey would throw open its doors to me, but there must be some church that would allow a bastard across their threshold. I do not care how we are wed, sweet Mercy, whether it is in Scotland or in London with trumpets blaring, just as long as you are my wife."

She trembled, her mouth dry and her heart refusing to beat. In this moment, Ian truly desired her as his wife. It was etched in the lines of his sinfully handsome face and smoldered in the depths of his whiskey eyes. If only she could be certain that his desire would not whither into the bitter regret of her parents.

"Ian, wait." She touched his cheek, willing him to understand her hesitation. "I cannot leave with you."

His fingers tightened, as if he were absorbing a painful blow. Then, with a twisted smile, he dropped her hands as if they were tainted.

"Of course you cannot." He hid his disappointment behind a mocking smile. "Is it because I am a bastard or a sinner?"

"Do not say such things, not even in jest."

His smile faded at her vehement tone. "Then why will you not be my wife? I know that you care for me."

"Yes, I care for you," she admitted softly. "I love you."

"God . . ." Ian seemed briefly lost for words. Stupid man. He could surely not be surprised he had stolen her heart? He had, after all, made a career of stealing hearts since he'd left the cradle. "Mercy."

She held up a warning hand as he looked prepared to toss her over his shoulder and head for the nearest vicar.

"But that does not mean I am yet prepared to be married. We are still near strangers in many ways."

A wicked smile curved his lips as he rapidly regained his composure. "Hardly strangers, my sweet. Shall I tell you the precise sound you make when I—"

"Ian."

The smile remained, but Mercy did not miss the frustration that flashed through his eyes.

"If you love me, then what else matters? We have years to discover whether you snore or are impossibly grumpy in the mornings or intend to fill our home with endless stacks of dusty books as you write your soon-to-be published articles."

"I am being serious, Ian."

"So am I, Mercy." He trailed his fingers down her cheek. "I may not know your favorite food or the name of your favorite doll when you were five or even if your toes are ticklish, but I do know that you have a warm and generous heart, that you are loyal to a fault, and that just having you near makes my world a more wonderful place to be."

Mercy barely made it to the nearest chair as her knees melted and she collapsed onto the padded cushion.

"Oh," she whispered, her thoughts stolen along with her breath. It was the nicest, most wonderful thing anyone had ever said to her. "Oh."

Kneeling before her, Ian gripped the arms of the chair, regarding her with fierce need.

"Say you will be my wife. Come with me, Mercy, and I promise I will take care of you for the rest of your life."

Take care of you . . .

Did he know just how seductive those words were to a woman who had spent her entire life tending to the needs of others? Just how often she had dreamed of having someone in her life she could lean on, depend upon?

God above, she wanted to say yes. The word trembled on the edge of her lips as her volatile emotions churned through her body and threatened to overcome her common sense.

A pity that her ingrained sense of duty would not allow her to toss caution to the wind and simply follow her heart.

"I cannot just abandon my duties, Ian," she whispered, her throat so tight she could barely force out the words. "Even if I do become your wife, I must ensure that my parents are settled back in their cottage with at least a housekeeper to assist them."

"And once you are back in your cottage, do you truly believe that they will ever allow you to leave?"

"It will be my choice."

Ian surged to his feet, his jaw knotted with disappointment. "Christ, they have hounded, bullied, and manipulated you for years. Why would you suddenly be capable of defying them?"

Mercy pushed herself upright, reaching out to lay a hand on his forearm.

"Because I now understand I cannot forever avoid my life," she admitted with a sad smile. "I have realized that I hide behind my responsibilities as if they are a suit of armor. I am a coward."

Caught off guard by her soft confession, Ian frowned. "What do you fear?"

"Discovering that all marriages are like my parents'. As I am certain you have noticed, they do not have a particularly amicable relationship. Indeed, they have been squabbling and generally making one another, and everyone who crosses their paths, miserable since I can recall. My life at the cottage may be dull and isolated, but it is not a slow, ghastly torture."

She felt the muscles of his arm bunch beneath her fingertips.

"And that is what you fear I will offer you? A slow, ghastly torture?"

"No. No, of course not." She stepped closer, breathing deeply of his delicious male scent. It was like a balm to her frayed nerves, soothing her fear and stirring her blood with a warmth that helped ward off the gathering chill. "For the first time in my life, I understand how a woman could find happiness as a wife."

"Then—"

"But I still do not intend to rush into a hasty marriage because you are upset at learning the truth of your mother, nor will I abandon my parents until I am certain they are being properly tended."

Shaking off her hand, Ian regarded her with a hard gaze, his features set in stark lines.

"Then we are at an impasse, my love, because I will not remain beneath this roof another moment."

With long strides he was headed out the door, not even pausing when she called out for him to wait.

Left alone in the center of the room, Mercy pressed a hand to her quivering stomach, too dazed by his abrupt departure to give in to her instincts that screamed in need to follow his retreating form.

Ian's lodgings in Duke Street were admirably situated with a large drawing room furnished with leather-upholstered wing chairs, a low sofa, and several pier tables scattered over the floral carpet. There was a separate bedchamber with a small private parlor attached and a connecting door that led to a room for Reaver.

Under normal circumstances, the rooms were comfortable, if not particularly luxurious, and perfectly suited to a gentleman who rarely spent his time at home.

These were not normal circumstances, however, and after nearly three weeks of being closeted in his lodgings without the benefit of Reaver and only grudging visits by his wary housekeeper, the place was frankly a mess.

Empty whiskey bottles lined the scrolled chestnut sideboard, trays of food that had gone uneaten were precariously piled near the door, and discarded racing forms that had been impatiently crumpled littered the floor.

All in all, it was the sort of place that could have been a great deal improved by a match and some kindling.

Ian, however, was indifferent to the chaos as he lounged in one of the chairs and absently stirred the coals of the fire with the tip of his scuffed boot. In truth, the shadowed disorder suited his mood to perfection.

Or at least it did until the infernal pounding echoed through the silent chambers. At first he tried to ignore the damnable noise. The last thing he desired was a caller. Not when his heart was mangled and his thoughts as bleak as the pits of hell.

Unfortunately, the pounding refused to end, echoing painfully in his head, still tender from an overabundance of whiskey.

Struggling to his feet, Ian weaved a path to yank open the door and glare at the intruder.

His mood went from dismal to foul as he caught sight of Raoul Charlebois standing on the cramped landing. Not only had the devil intruded into his private hell, but he was impeccably attired in a mulberry jacket and silver waistcoat with a perfectly starched cravat that reminded Ian that he had nothing more on than a wrinkled linen shirt that hung open at the neck and a pair of equally wrinkled breeches. Even worse, he could not recall the last occasion his hair had been brushed or his cheeks shaven.

The brilliant blue gaze ran a slow path over Ian's disreputable appearance, pausing at his unpolished boots before lifting to linger on the unmistakable shadows beneath Ian's eyes and the pallor of his face.

"I thought I might find you here," the older man

drawled. "Although I underestimated in just how bad a condition I would find you."

"Charlebois. What a stunningly unpleasant surprise. Should you not be dazzling the world with your—what did the critics say?—stunning, evocative, breathtakingly powerful portrayal of Macbeth?"

The golden brows arched. "The play's run ended last eve, as you well know. You were in the audience, after all."

"Was I?" Ian offered a negligent shrug. "No doubt I was foxed to the gills and one of my enemies hauled my inebriated carcass to the theatre as a lark."

"No doubt." Raoul's smile revealed he was well aware that his friend never missed one of his performances when he was in London, no matter how wretched his existence. "May I enter?"

Ian barred the opening with his arm. "Perhaps I am not alone, *mon ami*."

"Nothing would please me more than to discover you have brought an end to your morbid bout of self-pity and have decided to rejoin the world. Unfortunately, it is obvious you are still sulking alone in your gloomy chambers."

Ian stiffened. Christ, Raoul made him sound like a petulant five-year-old.

The fact that he had a niggling suspicion that was precisely how he had been behaving did nothing to ease his flare of temper.

"How can you be so certain?" he growled.

The brows inched higher. "No woman, no matter how many shillings you shoved into her purse, would consent to join you in your current state of . . . *dishabille*. Where the hell is Reaver?"

"The whereabouts of my personal servant are hardly your concern."

"They are when he has disappeared and allowed his master to wallow in the depths of the netherworld without so much as a decent cravat." The blue eyes narrowed. "Where is he?"

Despite his best efforts, Ian could not halt the heat from crawling beneath his skin.

"Go away, Charlebois, I am in no mood for company."

Raoul easily shoved his way past Ian's unsteady form, muttering a curse as he bent to pluck the racing forms from the floor and toss them into the fire. The scattered newspapers were offered the same treatment while the bottles were ruthlessly swept into the bin.

Only then did he turn to regard Ian with a basilisk gaze. "If you want to be rid of me, then tell me what you've done with Reaver."

Ian slammed the door shut and leaned against the wooden panes. His head was throbbing and his knees so weak he could barely remain upright.

"I sliced open his throat and dumped him in the Thames for pestering me," he growled. "You are quite likely to join him if you do not leave me in peace."

Raoul snorted, folding his arms across his chest. "In your condition I dare say I will be able to beat the truth from you before you could find a razor among the rubbish. Shall we lay odds?"

"Damn you, you interfering prig."

"Tell me."

Ian rubbed the aching muscles of his neck. It might have been amusing to watch the fastidious Raoul cleaning his rooms like a common charwoman if he hadn't been so wretchedly sober.

"I sent Reaver to Surrey."

"To spy upon Miss Simpson?"

The heat returned to Ian's face. The last thing he desired was to admit that he had sent his valet to keep watch on Mercy because he was worried sick that something might befall her while he was not near to protect her.

It would make him appear like nothing more than a lovesick nodcock, which, of course, was precisely what he was.

"Not to spy, merely to ensure that her journey home is without incident," he said, his voice stiff. "He will keep watch from afar and only interfere if necessary."

A slow, mocking smile curved Raoul's lips. "I see."

Ian frowned, his hands curling into fists. If he could stand straight, he would have slugged his friend's perfect nose.

"The roads are not entirely without danger, and she will be distracted by her loathsome parents," he snapped. "She will be a pigeon ripe for the plucking for any highwayman, footpad, or swindler who might catch sight of her."

Indifferent to the danger in the air, Raoul shrugged. "If you were so concerned for your delicate blossom, why did you not return to Surrey yourself?"

"Because . . ."

"Yes?"

Ian closed his eyes, realizing that he would have to confess all if he were ever to be rid of his annoying companion.

"I asked her to be my wife."

For once, he actually managed to startle the unflappable Raoul.

"*Mon Dieu.*"

"Of course, she was far too wise to accept."

Raoul blinked, then blinked again. "She refused your offer?"

Ian's smile held a trace of bitterness. "She did not precisely say no, but then again she did not say yes."

"Then what, pray tell, *did* she say?"

"A lot of nonsense about needing time for us to become better acquainted and settling her parents with a suitable companion before she could consider such an offer."

There was a long silence before Raoul gave a shake of his head.

"That does not sound like nonsense, Ian. Quite the opposite, in fact," he said, his tone considering. "I would say Miss Simpson possesses a great deal of good sense and loyalty for those she loves. The exact qualities any gentleman would desire in his wife."

Ian's heart tightened with a brutal pain. Since he had fled Rosehill, he had deliberately avoided the memory of Mercy's stark refusal to accompany him. Just as he had avoided all thoughts of his treacherous mother.

Instead, he had closeted himself in these rooms and clouded his mind with whiskey.

Not a particularly beneficial means of spending his time, but better than sorting through emotions too raw to be disturbed.

"They were merely excuses," he groused. "The truth of the matter is she does not trust me. No more than my beloved mother trusted me."

"Ah."

"What?"

Raoul stepped forward, his public façade stripped away to reveal the genuine man beneath. A man who made no effort to disguise his concern.

"It is obvious even to a gentleman of the meanest

intelligence that you have managed to tarnish poor Miss Simpson with your anger and disappointment toward your mother," he said softly.

Ian pushed himself away from the door, pacing toward the sideboard in a futile search for whiskey. Damn Raoul to the netherworld. Did the bastard have to charge into his privacy, stirring up feelings that he had worked so hard to bury?

And did that niggling voice have to whisper in the back of his mind that his friend was not entirely wrong?

"How the devil am I supposed to have tarnished the aggravating woman?" he forced himself to mutter. "I asked her to come away with me and she refused. End of story."

"I presume that you must feel something for the woman or you would never have asked her to be your wife."

His fist hit the wall with enough force to knock the pictures off the paneling.

"Of course I bloody well feel something. She is—"

"Worth fighting for?"

Spinning about, he pinned his companion with a lethal glare. "And how would you suggest I fight? Her parents have not only raised her with the belief it is her duty to be at their constant beck and call, but they have soured her on the mere notion of marriage. Hell, who could blame her for being skittish after witnessing the two of them wage war the past twenty-odd years?"

"And yet, she did not say no to your proposal," Raoul relentlessly pointed out. "If she were truly averse to the notion, she would not have offered you hope."

Ian absently pressed his fist to his chest, unaware of

the blood staining his knuckles as he rubbed the aching hole in the center of his heart.

Hope.

No, it was the one thing that he refused to allow himself.

Hope was what had led him to stupidly leap at Norrington's offer of forming a business alliance, believing that he had at long last earned his *father's* respect. Hope was what had led him to presume he could put his painful past behind him and seek to become a proper gentleman worthy of a wife and children.

And what had come of it?

Betrayal, that was what.

"Who can say what is in a woman's mind?" That annoying voice was still niggling in the back of his mind as he forced the words past his stiff lips. "She claims to love you and then refuses to offer more than a small part of herself."

Raoul clicked his tongue. "If you desire your future bride to trust you, *mon ami,* then you must earn it."

"And how the devil am I to do that?"

"Consider the matter from her point of view. You have asked her to become your wife, but while it might be an earth-shattering notion for you to commit to one woman, she is the one expected to leave her family and home and the only security she has ever known to place herself in your care. No woman would take such a step lightly."

Despite his best attempts, Ian could not entirely shut out his friend's sage words.

In his cloud of fury, he hadn't allowed himself to consider how he had thrust Mercy into an untenable position. In his mind he had decided that they should wed immediately, and even the least hesitation on her part had simply confirmed his belief that every woman was set out to betray him.

Now he grimaced at the unpleasant suspicion that he had behaved no better than Mercy's peevish parents, making impossible demands and then sulking when she did not fall in with them without complaint.

Christ, what had he done?

"Ian?"

Wrenched from his mortified thoughts, Ian shoved his fingers through his tangled hair.

"What would you have me do?"

"Prove to her that you are capable of understanding her fears and are willing to give her the time she needs to accept the fact that you are prepared to place her happiness above your own." Raoul stepped forward to clap a hand on his shoulder. "Is that so much to ask?"

"No." Feeling as if he were emerging from the fog, Ian gave a sharp shake of his head. Raoul was perfectly right. He had been wallowing in his own self-pity, nursing his injuries and making himself miserable while allowing the woman he loved to slip from his grasp. He should be horsewhipped. "No, of course it is not."

"Then why are you sitting in these dark rooms drinking yourself into oblivion?"

"Because I am an idiot," Ian muttered, striding across the room to enter his bedchamber. Pouring water into the basin, he washed and shaved before he tugged his valise from beneath the armoire. Tossing it onto the bed, he began shoving his clothes in without care to Reaver's outrage when he would discover they were creased beyond all hope.

"I will agree that you are an idiot," Raoul said from the door. "Where the devil are you going?"

"If I leave for Surrey within the hour—" Ian's words

were cut off as there was yet another knock on his door. He turned to stab his friend with a suspicious glare. "Who the blazes can that be?"

Raoul held up his hands in a gesture of innocence. "I haven't the least notion."

For a moment, Ian considered ignoring the faint taps. He had wasted so damnable much time in his stupidity, even another second's delay was intolerable. It was only the knowledge that Mrs. Elliot, his infernal landlady, was bound to come snooping if he did not answer the knock that made him curse beneath his breath and return to the front chamber.

Expecting one of his endless parade of drunken friends, Ian pulled open the door with a scathing demand to quit the place at once, only to freeze in profound shock.

Standing on the dimly lit landing was a sweet, delicate wood sprite with golden curls covered by a black bonnet, her slender body nearly hidden beneath a heavy black cloak.

Ian's breath was squeezed from his lungs, his heart forgetting to beat. The first time he had ever seen Mercy Simpson in that field of daisies, he had been mesmerized by her beauty, but in this moment he understood it was more than just her lovely features and expressive dark eyes.

It was . . . her very essence. The innocence of her soul. The kindness in her heart.

What sinner could possibly resist such temptation?

"Mercy," he husked, hesitating to reach out and touch her in fear she might be nothing more than a figment of his imagination.

She nervously wetted her lips, shifting beneath

his fierce gaze. "I know it is not proper for me to be here, but—"

"To hell with propriety," he growled, tossing aside his fears to wrap her tightly in his arms. Tears filled his eyes as her warmth thawed the chill that had held him captive for the past three weeks. "God, tell me this is not just another dream."

Tilting back her head, she regarded him with a searching gaze. "Did you dream of me, Ian?"

He gently cupped her face, his hands trembling. "I have been haunted by you night and day, sweet Mercy. I could find no peace, no matter how I tried."

Raoul loudly cleared his throat, a wicked smile curling his lips as Ian tugged Mercy into his chambers, his arms still firmly wrapped about her.

"Being an actor with an exquisite sense of timing, I am capable of knowing my cue when I hear it," Raoul murmured, sweeping them both a deep bow. "*Adieu, mon ami.* Miss Simpson."

Ian made no attempt to halt his friend as he exited the room and closed the door behind his retreating form. Instead, he tugged Mercy toward the dying fire and impatiently removed her bonnet to reveal the gleaming gold of her curls.

"How did you get here?" he demanded, taking her hands to warm them with his own.

"Ella was kind enough to bring me to London in her carriage."

Ian instinctively stiffened. "She is with you?"

"She is at the Norrington townhouse and has begged me to assure you that she will not attempt to see you without your leave," Mercy said hastily.

"I see." He gave a shake of his head, not yet willing

to sort through the churning brew of emotions attached to his mother.

She stepped closer, her expression worried. "I am sorry if it troubles you to have her in town, but I had no other means of coming to you. I could not take my parents' only carriage, and I did not precisely know how to go about hiring a vehicle to take me to the nearest coaching inn."

Any thought of his mother was dashed by the mere notion of Mercy traveling in a public vehicle, surrounded by any sort of low-life scoundrel. The image was enough to turn his hair gray.

"You considered taking the stagecoach? Alone?" He glared into her wide eyes. "Do you wish to give me heart failure?"

Far from appearing repentant, the minx offered a serene smile. "I would have been perfectly safe as long as my guardian angel continued to haunt my every step. Few would dare to cross paths with such a formidable protector."

Ian's eyes widened before he gave a startled bark of laughter. "Reaver allowed himself to be caught?"

"He is rather difficult to overlook."

"Where is the devil? He was not supposed to let you out of his sight."

"Do not blame your servant. I pleaded with him to remain below stairs so I could surprise you."

"Perhaps I should remind him who pays his wage," Ian muttered, his words without heat. It was impossible to feel anything but bewildered joy at having Mercy so near. "Then again, perhaps I shall give him a rise in salary."

"Actually, he is in part the reason I am here."

"Then definitely a rise in salary," he husked. "But how did he convince you to come to me?"

A hint of uncertainty entered the midnight eyes. "When I caught sight of him during my return to my parents' cottage, I began to hope that you had not completely washed your hands of me."

Ian sucked in breath at the wrenching regret that he had ever allowed this woman a moment of doubt.

"Not bloody likely." He leaned his forehead against hers, remorse trembling through his body. "You will never be rid of me, Miss Mercy Simpson."

"I feared . . ." Her words briefly faltered. "When you left Rosehill, I did not believe I would ever see you again."

Stroking his lips over her temple, Ian wrapped an unyielding arm about her waist.

"Forgive me, my sweet. I should never have pressed you to wed me and then charged off like a sulky child. My only excuse is that I was not thinking clearly." He pulled back, allowing his love to be written across his features. "If I am so fortunate as to earn your trust, my sweet, I will devote my life to ensuring you never know another moment of unhappiness. That I swear to you."

The shadows fled from her eyes. "You still wish me as your wife?"

"More than I have ever wished for anything in my life."

"You are certain?"

"If you would step into my bedchamber, you would discover that I was in the process of packing my bags to come in search of you." He brushed a stray curl from her cheek. Then, lowering his hand, he swiftly dealt with the hooks and buttons of her heavy cloak. There was far too much wool, and muslin, and God knew what else between them. "Although I am without doubt the world's greatest idiot, I still possess the heart of a gambler, and I know better than to toss away the finest hand I have ever been dealt." He tugged off the cloak to allow it to pool on the floor, revealing the pretty rose and ivory gown beneath. "Tell me that I have not made a total muck of this, Mercy. Tell me that you'll be my wife."

With an enchantress smile, Mercy wrapped her arms about his neck. "Well, I most certainly did not travel all this distance to become your mistress."

His chuckle was strained as his body responded to the feel of her curves pressed so intimately against him. It had been three weeks since he'd felt the least stirrings of desire. Now his body seemed determined to punish him for the absence.

"Do you ever intend to forgive me for that wretched offer?"

"Utterly and completely," she said without hesitation. "Just as I will always forgive you."

He blinked at her fierce tone. "Always?"

"Is that so astonishing?"

"As astonishing as me swearing that I shall never do anything that needs to be forgiven."

"Do not tease, Ian." Her fingers toyed with the curls at his nape, not seeming to realize that a randy, besotted gentleman needed very little to set his blood on fire. "I have at last realized that there is nothing to compel me to follow in my parents' footsteps. Not unless I choose to do so."

"Which I sincerely hope you will not."

"No." She wrinkled her perfect nose. "Actually, now that I have accepted that fate is in my own hands, it should be quite easy to go on. We at least comprehend what *not* to do in a proper marriage."

"A proper marriage." He crushed her to his body, not even a bit surprised by the rush of pure happiness. "Do you know, my love, I like the sound of that."

She snuggled her head into the hollow of his shoulder, just as if it had been made for that purpose.

"I rather like it myself."

Ian's entire body hardened with an explosion of searing need, his mind barely capable of functioning. With an effort, he squashed the urge to toss her over his shoulder and head for the bed. There was still one unpleasant detail that had to be settled.

"What of your parents? I may be the most selfish beast ever born, but I will not have you plagued with guilt." He swallowed the bile that threatened to rise in his throat. "If you wish, I will purchase a home that is close enough for you to regularly visit, although I will not tolerate having you tend to them night and day. As your husband, I demand that any tending be exclusively devoted to me."

She tilted back her head, her lips twitching. "Do you take a great deal of tending?"

He groaned, his hand slipping down to the curve of her back to press her against his aching erection.

"God, yes."

Her breathless laugh feathered over his skin. "Actually, I hired a housekeeper from the village who has agreed to move in to the cottage, and while my parents are bound to grumble and grouse, I am confident that Mrs. Norville is perfectly capable of seeing to their needs." She grimaced. "Of course, I will need to visit them quite often. For all their faults, they are my family."

"Faults and family do seem to go hand in hand."

Her eyes darkened at his unwittingly bitter words. "Ian—"

"Not tonight, my love," he swiftly interrupted. "Tonight there is only you and me."

"The two of us all alone." Her teasing fingers brushed down his nape, slipping beneath the open collar of his shirt with devastating ease. "Whatever shall we do?"

Ian might be an idiot, but he was never one to miss an opportunity. No doubt if life were fair he would never have been allowed to win the love of this extraordinary woman, let alone have a second chance to have her as his wife, but now that he had been offered paradise, he was not about to waste a single moment.

With one smooth motion, Ian swept Mercy off her feet and headed for the bedchamber.

"Well, you did mention something about a proper marriage. Perhaps it would be best if we have a bit of practice."

She met his smoldering gaze with a smile that held nothing but undiluted confidence in their future life together.

"Yes, indeed. All the best marriages must have practice."

His chest swelled with a happiness that seemed too large to fit into his unworthy heart.

"And love," he whispered.

"And love. . . ."

The Norrington townhouse was a splendid Palladian palace on Great Ormond Street. The façade was built of red brick with fluted columns that supported a balcony on the third story and towering windows that reflected the golden glow of the early morning sunlight.

Crossing the narrow courtyard behind a high wrought-iron fence, Ian mounted the shallow steps, his lips twisting as a uniformed footman swept open one of the heavy oak doors and stepped back to allow him entry.

In silence, the servant led him through the arched arcade of Corinthian columns, bypassing the split marble staircase to head toward the back of the massive house.

Ian ignored the click of his heels that echoed eerily about the lofted ceilings that were molded with a great deal of gilt and the elegant furnishings that were still hidden beneath Holland covers. During the handful of occasions he had visited the house during his childhood, he had been overawed by the majestic beauty and constantly in fear of breaking one of the priceless heirlooms that were scattered throughout. It was as oppressive and formal as Rosehill.

On this morning, he was too filled with joy to have it dimmed by ancient memories. Indeed, he was astonishingly pleased at the thought of Mercy being surrounded by such graceful beauty. This was precisely the sort of setting she deserved.

The past was gone, and in its place was a glorious future filled with endless possibilities.

The footman opened the doors to the second drawing room and Ian entered to discover Ella seated upon a crimson velvet *chaise*, sipping her morning chocolate as she shifted through an enormous pile of invitations that had clearly just arrived. Although Ella rarely entered into London society, her arrival at the townhouse was enough to stir the society hostesses to fight over her elusive presence.

She lifted her head at his entrance, her brown eyes widening in shock as the envelopes dropped from her shaking hands.

"Ian." With an obvious effort, the older woman rose to her feet, her gaze sweeping desperately over his carefully guarded expression as if it had been years not weeks since she had last caught sight of him. "I fear that Mercy has not yet risen."

Ian hid his smug smile. He had made love to Mercy for hours, savoring each and every caress. Only when the dawn was threatening to crest had he forced himself to escort her back to Norrington House.

"I did not expect her to be down yet. She had a rather late evening," hc murmured.

A knowing amusement briefly flickered over Ella's pale face. "So she did." The older woman paused, seeming oddly uncertain as she clutched her hands together. "Did you wish to leave a message for her?"

"Actually, I came to speak with you."

"Oh." Ella took a hesitant step forward. "I suppose you are angry that I came to London, but I assure you that I have no intention of pushing myself—"

"I came to thank you," he firmly interrupted.

"Thank me?"

"For bringing Mercy safely to London."

The round face colored with pleasure. "Oh, well, she was quite set on coming, and I could not possibly allow her to travel on her own."

Thank God his mother at least understood the dangers. Which was more than he could say for his soon-to-be wife.

He smiled wryly. "Although my fiancée may possess a great deal of common sense, she is still adorably innocent in most worldly matters. She would no doubt have given half her coins to the local spongers and lost the other half to pickpockets before she ever reached the first coaching inn."

"Fiancée?" Genuine happiness lightened Ella's expression. "Then you are to wed?"

"I intend to seek a special license this afternoon."

"But that is wonderful." Ella abruptly frowned. "Oh, but surely Mercy will desire to be wed in her father's church? He was the vicar there, after all."

Ian snorted at the mere notion. "And have the surly old goat scowling through the entire ceremony while her mother wails and wrings her hands in the background? No, I would never allow Mercy's wedding day to be ruined by such ridiculous theatrics. Thankfully, she is quite set on a quiet London ceremony with only a few witnesses."

Ella's smile returned. "That is no doubt for the best. May I inquire where will you hold the ceremony?"

Ian paused, briefly wrestling with his inner demons. Then, recalling Mercy's soft demand as she lay in his arms, he squared his shoulders.

"Mercy would like the ceremony to be held here, at Norrington House, if you and the viscount will allow it."

"Here? Oh . . ." Hastily retrieving a handkerchief from the sleeve of her French gray morning gown, Ella dabbed the tears from her cheeks. "Ian. Oh."

Ian shifted uneasily, his lingering bitterness no proof against the fragile hope that bloomed in the damp brown eyes.

"As I said, it is to be a quiet affair, a fortnight from Tuesday if that is convenient."

"Perfectly convenient. I shall see to a wedding breakfast, of course, and Mercy's trousseau, although it will be a close thing to have more than a few gowns actually finished by . . . by . . ."

Her words trailed to an end as she sank onto the edge of the *chaise*, her body shaking with deep sobs of relief.

With long strides, Ian was seated beside her, his arms encircling her heaving shoulders.

It was yet too soon to have entirely forgiven his sense of betrayal, but neither could he dismiss nine and twenty years of unconditional love.

Perhaps his childhood would have been easier had he known Norrington was not a cold, indifferent father and that Ella was more than an aunt. But in the end, did it truly matter?

"Enough, Ella. You will make yourself ill," he soothed.

It was several moments before the older woman managed to gather her composure and glance into Ian's softened expression.

"Ian, does this mean you have forgiven me?"

"It is not so much a matter of forgiveness, but rather one of understanding." His lips twisted. "I do not deny it will take time to adjust to the thought of you being my mother, but I do comprehend just how difficult it must have been for you. You did what you thought was for the best."

A watery smile broke through the tears as Ella lifted a hand to lightly touch his cheek.

"Do you know, Ian, if I could change the past I would, but I would never, ever change the man you have become."

"Nor would I." A soft female voice spoke from the doorway, causing Ian's heart to leap with pleasure. "He might be a hellion, a scoundrel, and an infamous rake, but he is mine."

Drawn like a magnet, Ian was on his feet and crossing the room to take the hands of the woman who had utterly and completely captured his heart.

Gazing into Mercy's wide, beautiful eyes, he lifted her fingers to his lips.

"For all eternity, my sweet. For all eternity."

Epilogue

Standing distant from the small clutch of guests that were busily tossing rose petals at the carriage that was pulling away from Norrington House, Raoul Charlebois leaned against the wrought-iron fence with a quiet sense of contentment.

There could be no doubting Ian's shimmering happiness as he had stood at the side of Miss Mercy Simpson and proclaimed his vows. It had been obvious in his every lingering touch and the manner in which his gaze had never wavered from his new bride. *Mon Dieu*, the lovesick man had even been charming to the viscount and his mother to please his bride.

Raoul could have hoped for no better for his friend.

There was the sound of footsteps, and, turning his head, Raoul watched Fredrick Colstone, the heir to Lord Graystone, approaching with two glasses of champagne in his hands. The slender gentleman with honey curls and silver eyes had arrived in London last eve along with his beautiful wife, Portia.

Raoul hid a smile as he caught sight of the smudge of grease on one ear and notepad that ruined the line

of Fredrick's Bottle Green jacket. He would lay odds
that the younger gentleman had spent the morning
in one of his damnable workshops and was forcibly
hauled to the ceremony by his efficient wife. Fredrick
was utterly devoted to Ian, but few things beyond Portia
could actually distract him once he was working on his
inventions.

Halting at Raoul's side, Fredrick shoved the champagne into his hand and lifted his own glass in a toast.

"To the demise of the renowned Casanova."

Raoul obligingly lifted his glass, a smile playing
about his lips.

"A title I believe Ian has happily retired, although it
is said that women all over England are wearing black
to mourn his nuptials and that more than one gentleman found himself in utter ruin after betting that the
Casanova would never wed."

Fredrick rolled his eyes. "Somehow I am not at all
surprised. He would not be Ian Breckford if his marriage did not cause a stir. I will give him this, he possesses excellent taste in women."

"Have you mentioned this to your wife?"

Fredrick shrugged with the confidence of a gentleman secure in the love of his wife.

"Actually, she was the one to inform me just how fortunate Ian has been. She and Mercy are already fast
friends."

"And Portia is wise enough to realize that you are
utterly besotted with her?"

"There is that." Fredrick sipped his champagne, turning his head to watch the carriage disappear among the
traffic. "Do you think that Ian will entirely forgive his
mother for her deception?"

"I believe he already has, although it may be some

time before his wounds are fully healed," Raoul assured his companion. "He has even gone into business with the viscount. Some sort of investing scheme. Once they return from their honeymoon in Paris, I believe that he intends to open an office here in London, although he mentioned something of buying a house in Surrey so Mercy may be near her parents."

"No doubt he will make a fortune. He always did possess the luck of the devil."

Raoul drained his champagne, uncomfortably aware of a sensation that was perilously close to envy piercing his heart. Not for Ian's impending fortune. Raoul had more than enough wealth to suit his needs.

No, this was . . . *Mon Dieu.* He did not know what it was. Only that it had been plaguing him since he had caught sight of Ian gazing with mindless devotion at his sweet Mercy.

"So all's well that ends well," he forced himself to mutter.

"Not quite." Fredrick leaned against the iron fence, sliding a sly glance in Raoul's direction. "There is still one of us who has yet to seek the truth of his legacy."

Raoul laughed with sharp disbelief. "You cannot expect me to follow in your footsteps?"

"Why ever not? You desire to know the truth, do you not?"

"Really, Fredrick, I thought you a great deal more intelligent. Obviously marriage has rattled your wits."

"That is a distinct possibility, since I haven't the least notion what you mean."

Raoul straightened, impatiently tossing the empty glass in a nearby hedge. He wanted to be away from Norrington House and the gathering crowd of gawkers across the street that had recognized him. Soon he would be surrounded, and he would be obliged to drive through London with a ridiculous parade of admirers trailing behind him.

With an impatient hand, he gestured toward his waiting carriage.

"Both you and Ian began your search as perfectly content bachelors and ended leg-shackled within a few weeks. You do not believe that I intend to follow in your footsteps?"

Fredrick chuckled, following in Raoul's wake as he stepped toward the curb.

"There are worse things than discovering a woman who can offer you happiness beyond all dreams."

"Perhaps, but I cannot think of one at the moment."

"Fate is a strange thing, old friend. It tends to find you no matter how you might attempt to hide behind greasepaint and ridiculous costumes," Fredrick warned. "Surely it is better to meet it face-to-face."

It was a relief when his groom pulled the black carriage to a halt before him. As much as he loved Fredrick, his mood was oddly volatile. He would not risk punishing one of his few friends with his ill humor.

"We are no longer ten years old, *mon ami*," he pointed out, pulling open the door to the carriage. "You cannot taunt and dare me into some ridiculous deed that I am bound to regret."

Fredrick made a rude noise. "If you will recall, it was always Ian who was daring us into some devilish stunt, while *I* was the voice of reason. You, on the other hand, were the one to ride to the rescue when we managed to tumble into a scrape."

"An endless and tedious duty, I assure you," he said dryly, disguising the wistful pang that tugged at his heart.

Ridiculously, he missed those simpler days when both Ian and Fredrick had depended upon him. He had grown accustomed to protecting them, to tending to their needs, even bullying them when necessary. Though he would never admit it, there was an emptiness to his life that he hadn't managed to fill since Fredrick and Ian had struck out on their own.

Perhaps sensing more than Raoul desired, Fredrick placed a hand on his shoulder.

"It is a duty that has now been taken from your hands. Perhaps it is time that you consider your own future."

A strange chill of premonition inched down Raoul's spine, and he hastily stepped in the carriage, as if he could outrun the unnerving sensation.

"By rushing off to my father's estate to meet my destiny?" he mocked with a shake of his head. "No, I thank you, Fredrick. Return to your bride and your inventions. You have no talent for soothsaying."

Closing the door, Raoul leaned back in the leather squabs and felt the carriage jerk into motion. Unfortunately, it was not before Fredrick managed to have the last word.

"Run if you will, Charlebois, but destiny is waiting for you."

And for a taste of something different,
please turn the page for a sneak peek of
Alexandra Ivy's
DARKNESS REVEALED.

Now on sale at bookstores everywhere!

Prologue

London 1814

The ballroom was a startling blaze of color. In the flicker-ing candlelight, the satin-and-silk-draped maidens twirled in the arms of dashing gentlemen, the brilliant flare of their jewels making a rainbow of shimmering fireworks that was reflected in the mirrors that were set in the walls.

The elegant pageantry was near breathtaking, but it was not the passing spectacle that caught and held the attention of the numerous guests.

That honor belonged solely to Conde Cezar.

With the amused arrogance that belonged solely to the aristocracy, he moved through the crowd, needing only a lift of his slender hand to have them parting like the Red Sea to clear him a path or a glance from his smoldering black eyes to send the ladies (and a few gentlemen) into a flutter-ing frenzy of excitement.

Much to her annoyance, Miss Anna Randal did her own share of fluttering as she caught sight of that faintly golden, exquisitely chiseled profile. Stupid really when gentlemen such as the Conde would never lower themselves to take notice of a poor, insignificant maiden who spent her evenings in one dark corner or another.

Such gentlemen did, however, take notice of beautiful, enticing young maidens who would boldly encourage the most hardened reprobate.

Which was the only reason that Anna forced herself to follow in the wake of his lean, elegant form as he left the ballroom and made his way up the sweeping staircase. Being a poor relation meant that she was forced to take on whatever unpleasant task happened to crop up, and on this evening, her unpleasant task included keeping a close eye upon her cousin Morgana, who was clearly fascinated by gentlemen such as the dangerous Conde Cezar.

A fascination that might very well end in scandal for the entire family.

Hurrying to keep the slender male form in sight, Anna impatiently hiked up the cheap muslin of her gown. As she had expected, he turned at the top of the stairs and made his way down the corridor that led to the private chambers. Such a rake would never attend something as tedious as a ball without having a nefarious assignation arranged beforehand.

All she need do was ensure that Morgana was not the beneficiary of that nefarious part and Anna could return to her dark corner in the ballroom and watch the other maidens enjoy their evening.

Grimacing at the thought, Anna paused as her quarry slipped through a door and disappeared.

Damnation. Now what? She had seen nothing of Morgana, but there was no assurance that she was not already hidden in the room awaiting the Conde's arrival.

Cursing her vain, self-centered cousin, who considered nothing beyond her own pleasures, Anna moved forward and carefully pushed open the heavy door. She would just take a quick peek and then . . .

A scream was wrenched from her throat as slender fingers grasped her wrist in a cold, brutal grip, jerking her into the dark room and slamming the door behind her.

Chapter 1

The reception room of the hotel on Michigan Avenue was a blaze of color. In the light of the chandelier, Chicago's movers and shakers strutted about like peacocks, occasionally glancing toward the massive fountain in the center of the room, where a handful of Hollywood B stars were posing for photographs with the guests for an obscene fee that supposedly went to some charity or another.

The similarity to another evening was not lost on Anna as she once again hovered in a dark corner watching Conde Cezar move arrogantly through a room.

Of course, that other evening had been near two hundred years ago. And while she hadn't physically aged a day (which she couldn't deny saved a butt-load on plastic surgery and gym memberships), she wasn't that shy, spineless maiden who had to beg for a few crumbs from her aunt's table. That girl had died the night Conde Cezar had taken her hand and hauled her into a dark bedchamber.

And good riddance to her.

Her life might be all kinds of weird, but Anna had

discovered she could take care of herself. In fact, she did a damn fine job of it. She would never go back to that timid girl in shabby muslin gowns (not to mention the corset from hell).

That didn't, however, mean she had forgotten that fateful night.

Or Conde Cezar.

He had some explaining to do. Explaining on an epic scale.

Which was the only reason she had traveled to Chicago from her current home in Los Angeles.

Absently sipping the champagne that had been forced into her hand by one of the bare-chested waiters, Anna studied the man who had haunted her dreams.

When she had read in the paper that the Conde would be traveling from Spain to attend this charity event, she had known that there was always the possibility the man would be a relative of the Conde she had known in London. The aristocracy was obsessed with sticking their offspring with their own name. As if it weren't enough they had to share DNA.

One glance was enough to guarantee it was no relative.

Mother Nature was too fickle to make such an exact duplicate of those lean, golden features, the dark, smoldering eyes, the to-die-for body . . .

And that hair.

As black as sin, it fell in a smooth river to his shoulders. Tonight he had pulled back the top layer in a gold clasp, leaving the bottom to brush the expensive fabric of his tux.

If there was a woman in the room who wasn't imagining running her fingers through that glossy mane, then Anna would eat her silver-beaded bag. Conde

Cezar had only to step into a room for the estrogen to charge into hyperdrive.

A fact that was earning him more than a few I-wish-looks-could-kill glares from the Hollywood pretty boys by the fountains.

Anna muttered a curse beneath her breath. She was allowing herself to be distracted.

Okay, the man looked like some conquering conquistador. And those dark eyes held a sultry heat that could melt at a hundred paces. But she had already paid the price for being blinded by the luscious dark beauty.

It wasn't happening again.

Busily convincing herself that the tingles in the pit of her stomach were nothing more than expensive champagne bubbles, Anna stiffened as the unmistakable scent of apples filled the air.

Before she turned, she knew who it would be. The only question was . . . why?

"Well, well. If it isn't Anna the Good Samaritan," Sybil Taylor drawled, her sweet smile edged with spite. "And at one of those charity events you claim are nothing more than an opportunity for the A-listers to preen for the paparazzi. I knew all that holier-than-thou attitude was nothing more than a sham."

Anna didn't gag, but it was a near thing.

Despite the fact that both women lived in L.A. and they were both lawyers, they couldn't have been more opposite.

Sybil was a tall, curvaceous brunette with pale skin and large brown eyes, while Anna had brown hair and hazel eyes and barely skimmed the five-foot mark. Sybil was a corporate lawyer who possessed the morals of a . . . well, actually she didn't possess the morals of anything. She had no morals. Anna, on the other hand, worked at a free law clinic that battled corporate greed on a daily basis.

"Obviously I should have studied the guest list a bit more carefully," Anna retorted, caught off guard but not entirely surprised by the sight of the woman. Sybil Taylor possessed a talent for rubbing elbows with the rich and famous, wherever they might be.

"Oh, I would say that you studied the guest list as closely as every other woman in the room." Sybil deliberately glanced across the room to where the Conde Cezar toyed with a heavy gold signet ring on his little finger. "Who is he?"

For a heartbeat, Anna battled the urge to slap that pale, perfect face. Almost as if she resented the woman's interest in the Conde.

Stupid, Anna.

Stupid and dangerous.

"Conde Cezar," she muttered.

Sybil licked her lips that were too full to be real. Of course, there wasn't much about Sybil Taylor that was real.

"Eurotrash or the real deal?" the woman demanded.

Anna shrugged. "As far as I know, the title is real enough."

"He is . . . edible." Sybil ran her hands down the little black dress that made a valiant effort to cover her considerable curves. "Married?"

"I haven't a clue."

"Hmm. Gucci tux, Rolex watch, Italian leather shoes." She tapped a manicured nail against teeth too perfect to be real. "Gay?"

Anna had to remind her heart to beat. "Most definitely not."

"Ah . . . I smell a history between the two of you. Do tell."

Against her will, Anna's gaze strayed toward the tall, dark thorn in her side.

"You couldn't begin to imagine the history we share, Sybil."

"Maybe not, but I can imagine all that dark, yummy goodness handcuffed to my bed while I have my way with him."

"Handcuffs?" Anna swallowed a nervous laugh, instinctively tightening her grip on her bag. "I always wondered how you managed to keep a man in your bed."

The dark eyes narrowed. "There hasn't been a man born who isn't desperate to have a taste of this body."

"Desperate for a taste of that overused, silicone-implanted, Botox-injected body? A man could buy an inflatable doll with less plastic than you."

"Why you . . ." The woman gave a hiss. An honest-to-God hiss. "Stay out of my way, Anna Randal, or you will be nothing more than an oily spot on the bottom of my Pradas."

Anna knew if she were a better person she would warn Sybil that Conde Cezar was something other than a wealthy, gorgeous aristocrat. That he was powerful and dangerous and something that wasn't even human.

Thankfully, even after two centuries, she was still capable of being as petty as the next woman. A smile touched her lips as she watched Sybil sashay across the room.

Cezar had felt her presence long before he'd entered the reception room. He'd known the moment she had landed at O'Hare. The awareness of her tingled and shimmered within every inch of him.

It would have been annoying as hell if it didn't feel so damn good.

Growling low in his throat at the sensations that were directly connected to Miss Anna Randal, Cezar turned his head to glare at the approaching brunette. Not surprisingly, the woman turned on her heel and headed in the opposite direction.

Tonight his attention was focused entirely on the woman standing in the corner. The way the light played over the satin honey of her hair, the flecks of gold in her hazel eyes, the silver gown that displayed way too much of the slender body.

Besides, he didn't like fairies.

There was a faint movement from behind him and Cezar turned to find a tall, raven-haired vampire appearing from the shadows. A neat trick considering he was a six-foot-five Aztec warrior who was draped in a cloak and leather boots. Being the Anasso (the leader of all vampires) did have its benefits.

"Styx." Cezar gave a dip of his head, not at all surprised to find that the vampire had followed him to the hotel.

Since Cezar had arrived in Chicago along with the Commission, Styx had been hovering about him like a mother hen. It was obvious the ancient leader didn't like one of his vampires being in the control of the Oracles. He liked it even less that Cezar had refused to confess the sins that had landed him near two centuries of penance at the hands of the Commission.

"Tell me again why I am not at home in the arms of my beautiful mate?" Styx groused, completely disregarding the fact that Cezar hadn't invited him along.

"It was your decision to call for the Oracles to travel to Chicago," he instead reminded the older man.

"Yes, to make a ruling upon Salvatore's intrusion into Viper's territory, not to mention kidnapping my bride. A ruling that has been postponed indefinitely. I did not realize that they intended to take command of my lair and go into hibernation once they arrived." The fierce features hardened. Styx was still brooding on the Oracles' insistence that he leave his dark and damp caves so they could use them for their own secretive purposes. His mate, Darcy, however, seemed resigned to the large, sweeping mansion they had moved into on the edge of Chicago. "And I most certainly did not realize they would be treating one of my brothers as their minion."

"You do realize that while you may be lord and master of all vampires, the Oracles answer to no one?"

Styx muttered something beneath his breath. Something about Oracles and the pits of hell.

"You have never told me precisely how you ended up in their clutches."

"It's not a story I share with anyone."

"Not even the vampire who once rescued you from a nest of harpies?"

Cezar gave a short laugh. "I never requested to be rescued, my lord. Indeed, I was quite happy to remain in their evil clutches. At least as long as mating season lasted."

Styx rolled his eyes. "We are straying from the point."

"And what is the point?"

"Tell me why we are here." Styx glanced around the glittering throng with a hint of distaste. "As far as I can determine, the guests are no more than simple humans with a few lesser demons and fey among the rabble."

"Yes." Cesar considered the guests with a narrowed gaze. "A surprising number of fey, wouldn't you say?"

"They always tend to gather when there's the scent of money in the air."

"Perhaps."

Without warning, Cezar felt a hand land on his shoulder, bringing his attention back to the growingly frustrated vampire at his side. Obviously Styx was coming to the end of his patience with Cezar's evasions.

"Cezar, I have dared the wrath of the Oracles before. I will have you strung from the rafters unless you tell me why you are here wading through this miserable collection of lust and greed."

Cezar grimaced. For the moment, Styx was merely irritated. The moment he became truly mad, all sorts of bad things would happen.

The last thing he needed was a rampaging vampire scaring off his prey.

"I am charged with keeping an eye upon a potential Commission member," he grudgingly confessed.

"Potential . . ." Styx stiffened. "By the gods, a new Oracle has been discovered?"

The elder vampire's shock was understandable. Less than a dozen Oracles had been discovered in the past ten millenniums. They were the rarest, most priceless creature to walk the earth.

"She was revealed in the prophecies near two hundred years ago, but the information has been kept secret among the Commission."

"Why?"

"She is very young and has yet to come into her powers. It was decided by the Commission that they would wait to approach her until she had matured and accepted her abilities."

"Ah, that I understand. A young lady coming into her powers is a painful business at times." Styx rubbed his side as if he was recalling a recent wound. "A wise man learns to be on guard at all times."

Cezar gave a lift of his brows. "I thought Darcy had been bred not to shift?"

"Shifting is only a small measure of a werewolf's powers."

"Only the Anasso would choose a werewolf as his mate."

The fierce features softened. "Actually, it was not so much a choice as fate. As you will eventually discover."

"Not as long as I am in the rule of the Commission," Cezar retorted, his cold tone warning that he wouldn't be pressed.

Styx eyed him a long moment before giving a small nod of his head. "So if this potential Commission member is not yet prepared to become an Oracle, why are you here?"

Instinctively, Cezar glanced back at Anna. Unnecessary, of course. He was aware of her every movement, her every breath, her every heartbeat.

"Over the past few years, there have been a number of spells that we believe were aimed in her direction."

"What sort of spells?"

"The magic was fey, but the Oracles were unable to determine more than that."

"Strange. Fey creatures rarely concern themselves in demon politics. What is their interest?"

"Who can say? For now the Commission is only concerned with keeping the woman from harm." Cezar gave a faint shrug. "When you requested their presence in Chicago, they charged me with the task of luring her here so I can offer protection."

Styx scowled, making one human waiter faint and another bolt toward the nearest exit. "Fine, the girl is special. Why should you be the one forced to protect her?"

A shudder swept through Cezar. One he was careful to hide from the heightened senses of his companion.

"You doubt my abilities, my lord?"

"Don't be an ass, Cezar. There is no one who has seen you in a fight that would doubt your abilities." With the ease of two friends who had known each other for centuries, Styx glanced at the perfect line of Cezar's tux jacket. They both knew that beneath the elegance a half a dozen daggers were concealed. "I have seen you slice your way through a pack of Ipar demons without losing a step. But there are those on the Commission who possess powers that none would dare to oppose."

"Mine is not to question why, mine is but to do and die. . . ."

"You will not be dying." Styx sliced through Cezar's mocking words.

Cezar shrugged. "Not even the Anasso can make such a claim."

"Actually, I just did."

"You always were too noble for your own good, Styx."

"True."

Awareness feathered over Cezar's skin. Anna was headed toward a side door of the reception room.

"Go home, *amigo*. Be with your beautiful werewolf."

"A tempting offer, but I will not leave you here alone."

"I appreciate your concern, Styx." Cezar sent his master a warning glance. "But my duty now is to the Commission, and they have given me orders I cannot ignore."

A cold anger burned in Styx's dark eyes before he gave a grudging nod of his head.

"You will contact me if you have need?"

"Of course."

Anna didn't have to look at Conde Cezar to know that he was aware of her every movement. He might be speaking to the gorgeous man who looked remarkably like an Aztec chief, but her entire body shivered with the sense of his unwavering attention.

It was time to put her plan into motion.

Her hastily thrown–together, fly-by-the-seat-of-her-pants, stupidest-plan-ever plan.

Anna swallowed a hysterical laugh.

So, it wasn't the best plan. It was more a click-your-heel-twice-and-pray-things-didn't-go-to-hell sort of deal, but it was all that she had for the moment. And the alternative was allowing Conde Cezar to disappear for another two centuries, leaving her plagued with questions.

She couldn't stand it.

Nearly reaching the alcove that led to a bank of elevators, Anna was halted by an arm suddenly encircling her waist and hauling her back against a steely male body.

"You haven't changed a bit, *querida*. Still as beautiful as the night I first caught sight of you." His fingers trailed a path of destruction along the bare line of her shoulder. "Although there is a great deal more on display."

An explosion of sensations rocked through Anna's body at his touch. Sensations that she hadn't felt in a long, long time.

"You obviously haven't changed either, Conde. You still don't know how to keep your hands to yourself."

"Life is barely worth living when I'm keeping my

hands to myself." The cool skin of his cheek brushed hers as he whispered in her ear. "Trust me, I know."

Anna rolled her eyes. "Yeah, right."

The long, slender fingers briefly tightened on her waist before the man was slowly turning her to meet his dark, disturbing gaze.

"It's been a long time, Anna Randal."

"One hundred and ninety-five years." Her hand absently lifted to rub the skin that still tingled from his touch. "Not that I'm counting."

The full, sensuous lips twitched. "No, of course not."

Her chin tilted. Jackass.

"Where have you been?"

"Did you miss me?"

"Don't flatter yourself."

"Still a little liar," he taunted. With a deliberate motion, his gaze skimmed over her stiff body, lingering on the silver gauze draped over the swell of her breasts. "Would it make it easier if I confess that I've missed you? Even after one hundred and ninety-five years, I remember the precise scent of your skin, the feel of your slender body, the taste of your—"

"Blood?" she hissed, refusing to acknowledge the heat that stirred low in her stomach.

No, no, no. Not this time.

"But of course." There wasn't a hint of remorse on his beautiful face. "I remember that most of all. So sweet, so deliciously innocent."

"Keep your voice down," she commanded.

"Don't worry." He stepped even closer. So close that the fabric of his slacks brushed her bare legs. "The mortals can't hear me, and the fey know better than to interfere with a vampire on the hunt."

Anna gasped, her eyes wide. "Vampire. I knew it. I . . ."

She pressed her hands to her heaving stomach as she glanced around the crowded room. She couldn't forget her plan. "I want to talk to you, but not here. I have a room in the hotel."

"Why, Miss Randal, are you inviting me to your room?" The dark eyes held mocking amusement. "What sort of demon do you think I am?"

"I want to talk, nothing else."

"Of course." He smiled. The kind of smile that made a woman's toes curl in her spike heels.

"I mean it. I—" She cut off her words and gave a shake of her head. "Never mind. Will you come with me?"

The dark eyes narrowed. Almost as if he sensed she was attempting to lead him from the crowd.

"I haven't decided. You haven't given me much incentive to leave a room filled with beautiful women who are interested in sharing a lot more than conversation."

Her brows lifted. She wasn't the easy mark he remembered. She was a woman—hear her roar.

Especially if he had even a random thought of ditching her for someone else.

"I doubt they'd be so interested if they knew you are hiding a monster beneath all that handsome elegance. Push me far enough, and I'll tell them."

His fingers lightly skimmed up the length of her arms. "Half the guests are monsters themselves, and the other half would never believe you."

A shiver shook her entire body. How could a touch so cold send such heat through her blood?

"There are other vampires here?"

"One or two. The others are fey."

She briefly recalled his mention of fey before. "Fey?"

"Fairies, imps, a few sprites."

"This is insanity," she breathed, shaking her head as she was forced to accept one more crazy thing in her crazy existence. "And it's all your fault."

"My fault?" He lifted a brow. "I didn't create the fey, and I certainly didn't invite them to this party. For all their beauty, they're treacherous and cunning, with a nasty sense of humor. Of course, their blood does have a certain sparkle to it. Like champagne."

She pointed a finger directly at his nose. "It's your fault that you bit me."

"I suppose I can't deny that."

"Which means you're the one responsible for screwing up my life."

"I did nothing more than take a few sips of blood and your—"

She slapped her hand across his mouth. "Don't you dare," she hissed, glaring at an approaching waiter. "Dammit, I'm not going to discuss this here."

He gave a soft chuckle as his fingers stroked over her shoulders. "You'll do anything to get me to your rooms, won't you, *querida?*"

Her breath lodged in her throat as she took a hasty step back. Damn him and his heart-stopping touches.

"You really are a total ass."

"It runs in the family."

Family? Anna turned her head to regard the large, flat-out spectacular man who scowled at them from across the room.

"Is he a part of your family?"

An unreadable emotion rippled over the chiseled, faintly golden features. "You could say he's something of a father figure."

"He doesn't look like a father." Anna deliberately

flashed a smile toward the stranger. "In fact, he's gorgeous. Maybe you should introduce us."

The dark eyes flashed, his fingers grasping her arm in a firm grip.

"Actually, we were just headed to your room, don't you remember?" he growled close to her ear.

A faint smile touched Anna's mouth. Ha. He didn't like having her interested in another man. Served him right.

Her smile faded as the scent of apples filled the air.

"Anna . . . Oh, Anna," a saccharin voice cooed.

"Crap," she muttered, watching Sybil bear down upon them with the force of a locomotive.

Cezar wrapped an arm around her shoulder. "A friend of yours?"

"Hardly. Sybil Taylor has been a pain in the freaking neck for the past five years. I can't turn around without stumbling over her."

Cezar stiffened, studying her with a strange curiosity. "Really? What sort of business do you have with a fairy?"

"A . . . what? No." Anna shook her head. "Sybil's a lawyer. A bottom-feeder, I'll grant you, but—" Her words were cut off as the Conde hauled her through the alcove and, with a wave of his hand, opened the elevator doors. Anna might have marveled at having an elevator when she needed one if she hadn't been struggling to stay on her feet as she was pulled into the cubical (that was as large as her L.A. apartment) and the doors were smoothly sliding shut. "Freaking hell. There's no need to drag me around like a sack of potatoes, Conde."

"I think we're past formality, *querida*. You can call me Cezar."

"Cezar." She frowned, pushing the button to her floor. "Don't you have a first name?"

"No."

"That's weird."

"Not for my people." The elevator opened, and Cezar pulled her into the circular hallway that had doors to the private rooms on one side and an open view to the lobby twelve stories below on the other. "Your room?"

"This way."

Anna moved down the hall and stopped in front of her door. She already had her cardkey in the slot when she stilled, abruptly struck by the memory of another night she had attempted to best Conde Cezar.

The night her entire life had changed. . . .